For more than a decade, Little John has been developing the story of *True Love Waits*. He focused on numerous genres while writing the first part of his trilogy to ensure that a variety of audiences could read the book, enjoy the adventure, and seek to find out more about the future of the main characters.

True Love Waits is a mixture of some of the real-life events, beliefs and thoughts of the author's life in a fictional world.

Little John is currently residing in the city of Calgary, located in Alberta, Canada. He is of Ukrainian, Turkish and Persian backgrounds and he is the middle child of his family. His dream is to see a day when his books bring thrill and joy to readers around the world.

Dedicating this book to the Divine, my family, my friends, and all those who have supported me to reach where I am now.
Thank you to all of you from the bottom of my heart.

With Love

to

Shelley

Little John

Little John

TRUE LOVE WAITS

AUSTIN MACAULEY PUBLISHERS™

LONDON * CAMBRIDGE * NEW YORK * SHARJAH

A CIP catalogue record for this title is available from the British Library.

ISBN 9781035829392 (Paperback)
ISBN 9781035829408 (Hardback)
ISBN 9781035829415 (ePub e-book)

www.austinmacauley.com

First Published 2024
Austin Macauley Publishers Ltd®
1 Canada Square
Canary Wharf
London
E14 5AA

I truly thank and appreciate Austin Macauley Publishers for assisting me in bringing my story to life.

Chapter 1
The New World Order

"He is gone. I can't feel him anymore," said a tearful Sara.

Many years had passed since the arrival of the God.SED, who changed the known map of the Earth completely for humankind by reattaching the continents together. He created a new world map and a new world order and began his reign over humanity. He spent most of his time at his *Temple of Love[1]*, located in the centre of the *super continent[2]*.

Numerous lost battles were fought against him, countless human lives were lost, and the survival of human race became unpredictable. Knowing that humans had lost hope and began believing that he was the awaited god, God.SED used his supernatural powers to manipulate all humankind to obey his every command without any objections. However, despite his unchallengeable authority and influence over humanity, he failed to gain absolute control of all humans as some managed to keep their faith in one true god by staying in disguise, waiting for a rescuer to arrive and save them all.

John was semi-awake and talking to himself while lying on the bed in his room.

"When you know you're sexy," he said, yawning. "When you know you've got a girl that half of the world is desperately waiting to get their hands on. When you know the money never ends no matter what you do, why are you still in bed, jackass?"

He stretched and cramped his back.

"Oh, my ass! Oh, my ass! I mean back."

---

[1] Temple of Love: The main headquarters of God.SED.

[2] Super continent: The new continent created when God.SED joined all the Earth's landmasses together.

He stretched again then got off the bed.

"It's going to be a good day. Same clothes, same job, same people, same food, same life, what else could a person want?"

He removed a cracked picture of a cross from underneath his pillow and began looking at it. He'd been given the picture by a strange old woman on his way home the day before.

"Wow, no matter how much I look at this thing, I don't understand the meaning of these two pieces of wood attached together in this way," said John, curiously. "Why did she give this to me? Why?"

There were two knocks on the bedroom door, which was then opened. John hid behind the curtains, as an elderly woman entered the room.

"Your highness," she said, smiling.

"Nanny, how many times have I told you to please triple check everything before opening my door?" asked John.

"And how many times did I tell you to have your underwear on when you sleep?" she replied. "Do you know that…"

"Yes! Yes!" John interrupted. "It's bad manners to have the thick pipe hanging out."

"Thick or tiny, you always need to cover your private part," said Nanny.

John grabbed his underwear from the floor beside him while still holding the curtains and put the underwear on. He then put on his other clothes, as he looked at the tray that Nanny was holding.

"Woman, what time do you wake up in order to make such an exclusive breakfast for me, have your hair and make-up done, and wear such well pressed outfit? Are you on *Sola-Hola*?[3]" said John. "That stuff has enough caffeine in it to rip your body apart, woman."

He walked over to Nanny, kissed her on the forehead, before taking the tray and placing it on his wooden desk.

"You know I love you, right?"

Nanny was about to reply but just nodded her head while rolling her eyes.

John put wore his sunglasses and raised his left eyebrow.

"You like what you see, woman?" he asked. "I worked very hard to get these biceps this size."

"Alright, alright, we get it, you work out very hard. Good for you." said Nanny.

---

[3] Sola-Hola: An enriched caffeine drink.

She looked at the picture of cross with concern, picked it up from the mattress then looked at John.

"What's this?" asked Nanny.

"A woman gave it to me yesterday then she tried to say something, but the *Arms*[4] got her."

"Did they see you?" asked Nanny. "Did they see you?"

"No, they didn't but what's wrong? It's just a picture," John replied.

"What did she look like?" asked Nanny.

"I don't know," John replied. "She was just a very strange homeless looking elder lady. There are so many of them on the streets these days but this one looked different."

"They used to be well known people in my time," said Nanny, rubbing her finger on the picture. "They walked free and lived free, they believed in the true god, the one who created the Earth and heavens."

"My love, I swear I know the entire story, but maybe, just maybe accept that God.SED is the one who these poor people actually worshipped from the beginning. After he arrived, they fought against him, were defeated, and now they're being judged. I think it's pretty fair to live such a miserable life for disobeying the god that needed to be worshipped just like before."

John put his finger on the picture.

"However, you didn't clarify. What is this? Was this thing of any significant? Did this symbolise something of the god that people worshipped in the past? All I know is that people worshipped the true god and God.SED isn't the one but you never tell me the rest, I … I had a dream of this thing being burnt recently."

"At last!" Nanny exclaimed. "It took so long for you to see it. This thing's a cross, the symbol of the believers! The warrior is coming! They are coming!"

John was confused and puzzled by all the excitement. He slowly reached out to the tray, grabbed a slice of bread, sliced a boiled egg in half, placed one half on the bread, then held the bread in both hands and began eating.

"So, its name is cross, huh?"

John continued chewing his food.

"Cross of what? And why should I care?"

He ate some more of his breakfast.

"Sweetheart, if this cross thing is about a true god coming, no one's coming. Those who wanted to come are already here, so what are you fussing about?"

---

[4] Arms of Justice (A.o.J.): The new law enforcers.

Nanny began dancing and humming a song.

"They're coming. It's been so long. That poor woman sacrificed herself to give you a heads-up."

Nanny placed her hands on John's cheeks.

"If they haven't seen you, if you're with me, you'll be safe, my dear boy! But you're not to say a word to anyone about this picture."

John tried to interject but she cut him off.

"Not even Sara," said Nanny. "John, sit down. I have to make sure you hear the next words I say properly."

John sat on the chair, while Nanny sat on the bed.

"The cross is the symbol of Christianity, one of the religions of the past," Nanny began. "The cross is the symbol of Jesus Christ, the holy son of the creator. You remember nothing about it because you've become blinded by the power of SED and his *purple mist*[5] and I didn't tell you about it because I knew that the time wasn't right, but soon, when your eyes truly see again, you'll remember everything. For now, you need to stay focused so don't let anyone know about this. Once the time comes, you'll be given instructions and you'll have your confusion cleared."

John drank some milk from his cup while Nanny was talking.

"Did you watch *The Bird Rider*[6]?" said John. "You sound like you did. I'd say you need a vacation. I'll take care of the house with Sara until you come back. Who knows, we might ask SED to bless us with a child then you can have time to worry about the baby instead of watching action-packed movies that led you talk like this, my lady."

Nanny smiled and hugged him.

"Perhaps I do need that vacation, my dear," said Nanny. "We actually talked about it with Sara, but before I leave, I need to make sure that you understand how important it is for you to keep this a secret until the right day arrives."

John nodded his head.

"Alright," she said. "I'm going to pack things up and go on that vacation."

"Are you serious?" asked John. "I was just joking. When did you guys talk about you going on vacation again?"

---

[5] Purple mist: A purple gas that caused sudden loss of past memories. The gas was released by God.SED to erase the memories of the previous lives of humans.

[6] The Bird Rider: A hit action science fiction movie.

"Yes, I'm serious, my dear," replied Nanny, smiling. "I need some time alone to relax and you two need some time alone together to challenge your faith. I wanted to mention this after Sara and I spoke but I forgot. I'm an old woman, after all. Things get forgotten lately."

"Very well then," said John. "We'll keep things under control, but one more thing, who's Jesus? His name's familiar."

"As long as you stay the way you are, you'll reach the gift that's been promised to humans," Nanny replied.

"Your English sucks today," said John. "I can't understand a bloody word you say, woman. What kind of English is this?"

Nanny laughed, as he nodded his head and took a bite of the banana that he took from the tray.

"Do you want me to help you with the luggage and stuff or with anything?" asked John. "What an unusual morning."

Nanny stood up and walked towards the door.

"No dear, I'll be fine," she replied.

"You sure?" asked John.

"Yes dear," said Nanny.

John took a deep breath.

"Indeed, this is an interesting morning. Alright then, just make sure to let us know your location, wherever that's going to be, then if anything goes crazy, we'll just end up sending units there."

"I'm going to the beach," said Nanny. "Don't forget to water the plants. If I get back home and see them in weird shapes, we'll have serious problems, Mr Seventh."

John raised his eyebrows.

"Oh! The beach! Ooh la la! No wonder you want to go there alone. The plants will be fine, just please keep us updated, okay? And have fun tanning."

John smiled.

"That's the plan and I will, dear," said Nanny, before leaving the bedroom.

John walked to the closet, looked at the clothes he wanted to wear later that day, took them out and placed them on the bed. He then grabbed his towel and went to bathroom.

His cell phone rang. John noted that the caller was Sara, so he answered.

"I love you," said Sara.

"I love you too" John replied. "How come you're not at home? Where are you right now?"

"I'm actually buying the hat you wanted for the acting scene," she said. "Does it need to be completely purple?"

"Sara! You've got to be kidding me! That place is dangerous! It's *East-Lands*[7], for God.SED sake! Are you alone? Who's with you?"

"I'm alone, and scared. Please come here, Johnny. Oh no! I'm going to be taken away. No! No! John, I'm fine! Nothing's going to happen to me, don't worry. Justice folks are around so don't be so overprotective, it's annoying. Now tell me, purple or black?" asked Sara.

"Sara," said John, clearing his throat. "Love, a hot piece of meat like you shouldn't wander around in such area alone. We all know what happens in there. Men are predators. I'm coming there."

"Shish!" she exclaimed. "Not all the men in here are like that. There are decent ones too, like the one selling me the hat. So, purple or black?"

"Whichever you think is better," replied John.

"I'll get purple then. I feel like it's much more attractive. No, you didn't? John! Why did you send *Safe Guards*[8]?" asked Sara.

"Sara, that's east side, I'd send Justice Folks if I had to. Please get the hat and come back," said John.

"Oh, come on John, you always ruin the day when I'm alone," she said. "You're kind of becoming like SED, a control freak. I have a life too, you know."

"Sweetheart, I love you and I can't think…"

"Yes, I'm fine, sir. My fucker's just overreacting. John, they're here!" said Sara angrily.

"Get the hat and come back please," said John.

"Okay! Okay! But this is bullshit, John. This isn't fair. You can't always look after me like this. You can't treat me like this, you know?"

"I'm sorry, I'm just …"

"Just shut up, John," she said, interrupting him again. "I'm coming home. There's your money sir, thank you."

Sarah then hung up.

---

[7] East-Lands: The eastern territories of the super continent.

[8] Safe Guards: A Special Forces company that provides highly trained bodyguards for important people. The guards only protect the rich people in society.

"Fuck this!" said John, in frustration. "This girl will give me a heart attack one day. I don't understand why she does this every time."

He walked into the bathroom and stood in front of the mirror.

"Am I a control freak? Of course not! I just don't want her to get hurt, damn it! Let's put on some music."

John clapped his hands and flute music began to play. He then began taking a shower.

After his shower, John dressed and got ready to go out to work. He looked at the spherical camera on his desk, picked it up, and switched the camera on.

"Here we go," he said, as he sat on the bed looking at the lens. "Hmm, I don't know where to begin really, but while taking shower I thought I'd make a little documentary about what's going on in the world and just give a little information about my current life. Why am I doing this? I don't honestly know. I've been feeling weird lately about the world and I just … you know? I want people to have some sort of record if anything happens to the world again. You know, anything weirder."

He cleared his throat.

"Alright! My name is John Seventh. Yes, it's a number, don't ask me why. I don't even know why it's a number, but it is, so just go on with it. I can't remember my childhood. Most people my age can't remember either, because when God.SED arrived there was a war between good and evil apparently. Many lost their lives and those that survived lost their memories, or at least that's what we've been told so far by Nanny and others. Like, I just remember portions of the past. Basically, I woke up and I knew that I had to go to work and my job was to entertain people through making films. Is this something I need to be concerned about? Yes, of course! But I'm rich so I don't give a shit. This memory loss is like a fashion trend these days. Not knowing your past is fine and not knowing anything is even better, but frankly, I just wish that I could remember something about my past to share with you guys at this moment. That way we could all know who I used to be and how I used to live and stuff like that. It's not about only me, but all of us living in this time and age. But, oh well, God.SED doesn't want us to remember our terrible pasts to preserve a better future, so that's all that matters for now."

He paused before continuing.

"I live with my Nanny, the one who's been with me since I opened my eyes, as she says. She's pretty much everything that I have in this life, beside my lovely fuck receiver who I don't even fuck, Miss Sara Thomson. She joined me and Nanny through the *Love Blast*[9] adoption centre, according to what Nanny says."

He held his cell phone close to the camera, displaying a picture of Sara.

"There she is, the one and only. I can't live without her. There's this thing between us, this more than love thing, it's, it's er … some sort of a bond. It's like I feel her presence all the time without even having her around me. If she gets hurt, I know, and if I get hurt, she knows. It's something magical, yet it's more than that. I don't know how else to explain it. I hope when you guys fall in love, you'll know what I mean right now."

He put his cell phone back in his pocket and smiled.

"Yeah, she's something isn't she? What's my occupation? I'm a director, producer, writer, performer and a dashing man."

He received a text message from Arms of Justice, asking him if there was any threat facing the person who was being escorted, so that they could escort Sara back home rather than involving other units. John simply replied that there were no threats and thanked them for their services.

John then held his cell phone towards the camera again.

"Even if people fart these days, Arm of Justice units will know about it. I asked bodyguards to escort Sara from other side of the Earth to here and these guys have already found out about it and wanted to get on the case, which meant that my cell phone was and is being heavily monitored. You know how they can track anyone at any time with ease? It's because we all have tracking chips in our wrists. Our entire status and history are available in those chips. The arms simply need to scan the wrist or just track down where the chips were scanned previously and then find out about everything about an individual in no time. Pathetic! There's no privacy left in this world at all. It's total control over what and when we do anything."

He put the cell phone back in his pocket.

"Arms of Justice are the law enforcers of today's world. They can be very friendly or very ruthless, depending on when and how your path crosses theirs. Sara's a nurse and works at the *Twin Cancer Hospital*[10]. All types of cancers are cured now. The cure is God.SED himself. You take the one who has cancer to him and he blesses them and bam! Everything becomes normal again. However,

---

[9] Love Blast: An orphanage where Sara is believed to have been taken from.

[10] Twin Cancer Hospital: Where Sara works as a nurse.

Twin Cancer patients are also those that have been infected by the curse of God.SED."

John put on his glasses.

"You see, these patients have two separate beings or characters living in one living body. If you're thinking about dissociative personality disorder at this moment, you're dead wrong because that disorder is cured. However, these patients are extremely dangerous and very violent because the two characters mostly don't get along with each other at all. As the result, one usually begins to overpower the other, which results in severe consequences. The affected kids aren't usually that bad, even though they're often more deadly than the adult ones. This curse is a form of punishment to those that disobey or disrespect God.SED. He exhales in their mouths and gives them the second being.

"Nanny says they're possessed by demons and things that people believed in years ago, but these beings look way worse than what she usually describes. Anyways, Sara works there, she loves her job, and she's damn good at it. What she does for these semi-curable individuals is give them hope. Her job's basically all about mental health. She knows how to control beasts using whatever skills she has. She can make you kneel before her using some sort of mental power technique stuff. It's very cool and magical.

"TC patients don't live for long though because two beings can't live in the same body, or at least not in a human body. It's quite sad but this horror has kept the world running on a proper cycle for generations apparently and peace has never been broken for as long as God.SED has reigned, so far. Everyone's afraid of getting cursed so everyone keeps on living without complaining all the time. Everyone follows the new world order as it's implemented by God.SED, except for these mysterious protestors. They appear out of nowhere, keep telling people about things that everyone later forgets and then vanish into no one knows where, as if they'd never been existed. Some of them were successfully captured by the A.o.J. in the past, but they're still out there without anyone being able to see them.

"The interesting part is that they never ever give up, despite knowing that if they get caught, they'll have to face the wrath of God.SED. I don't understand what these crazy people really want?

"And the current world's completely different from what it looked like in the past, according to what Nanny says. The continents are attached again and they're all connected by *Divine Rails*[11], a large tube containing round glass cabins that can quickly transport you from one corner of the world to another. After all, we've been living under a giant firmament and on a disk that didn't let us go out until God.SED came along.

"The *big continent*[12] is divided into five main lands. These are North, South, West, East, and Middle Earth or the Centre, very much like the same shape it was apparently, just with the continents now forming a giant landscape. Middle Earth is where God.SED lives in his temple, protected by his massive army. Some people asked why he needed such an army when he was and is the god and in return they were either eaten alive or cursed. By being eaten alive, I literally mean alive. They were chewed to death by the army in front of our eyes on one crazy-scary day. God.SED mentioned that no one must ever ask him an unwelcome question such as that. Since then no one has dared to ask him any questions at all. So, let's just assume that, in order to govern the entire universe, even a god needs some forces to help him out."

John looked out of the window.

"The seasons change when God.SED desires. If he likes to have snow, people may have snow in middle of the hot summer. People may end up dying of heatstroke after an entire year of high temperature but might also freeze to death because God.SED doesn't want the area to warm up for them. There's a place where always snows and people around there have a giant bridge made of ice on the new map. I'll be able to visit it with Sara one day soon. God.SED controls the weather, the seasons, and any natural, or it's better to say any earthly environmental cycles, and we must simply live with it. It's not like we can really do anything about it. After all, he is the all-seeing eye."

John scoffed and nodded his head.

"Apparently, this thing happened in the past through a project called geo-engineering. Nanny says those that tried to make others aware were popped, go figure that out. Weird world. Anyways, back to God.SED. He has tremendous powers, such as resurrecting the dead or farting that smells like flowers, but those that come back to life, aren't like they were before. They remember nothing and they only live to serve him."

---

[11] Divine Rails: An ultrasonic continental train that moves around the super continent. Travellers can go from one side of the super continent to the other in a very short period of time.

[12] Big continent: The new super continent.

He raised his eyebrows.

"Yeah, fun stuff. God.SED's quite a character. To be honest, I don't give a shit. I just want to stay alive, entertain people, and put smile on their faces then wake up seeing Sara's beautiful blue eyes. That's all I personally live for.

"I have to give you a little bit more information about God.SED, from a deeper perspective. According to Nanny, he arrived on Earth in complete darkness. Apparently, there was a total eclipse when he landed. Nanny says that before God.SED arrived, people lived in a world of chaos and injustice. They turned against each other without reason. Violence became the meaning of life and death became the goal to achieve. During this anarchy that was caused by New World Order, the entire planet suddenly turned dark and a shining object resembling a sword entered the Earth's atmosphere from the firmament and landed in the Mediterranean Sea. The phenomenon put the global chaos on hold for a while, halting the destruction that humans were causing on Earth.

"After the darkness disappeared and people clearly saw the object, things began to get worse, as from the impact site countless Arms of Justice units were released and countless men and women that fought against them were brutally terminated worldwide. Countries of that time united together and fought for days and nights against the overwhelming forces but frankly speaking, you can't defeat supernatural beings that gain more power when they're attacked. A.o.J. units can't be killed by human weapons. They regenerate more power every time a man-made object is thrown at them. They feed on the hatred of humans and anything that's done by hate and because in war you don't fight with love, these beings grew into massive destructive machines in a very short period. They're about eight feet tall, extremely physically built, flames come out of their eyes every time they don't wear their shades, and they have a large mouth filled with countless sharp little teeth. That's the best short description of them now."

He shivered.

"Now, back to God.SED. His appearance changes constantly and he's currently in the transforming period of his life. Nanny says he was just a short mature looking little boy when he was first seen, but now he's a very handsome, super-powered man. This is very awful yet interesting. God.SED gains power through lovemaking sessions with virgins. He doesn't care about the gender of the person, as long as they're virgins. The children born of such encounters become part of his massive army with no questions asked, so unfortunately, people have found it better to not be virgins in this world if you don't want your children to join God.SED's army from the moment they open their eyes. But what about just loving just one person unconditionally?"

John looked at the picture of him hugging Sara that was hanging on the wall above his bed and smiled.

"One little scary aspect of this is that he assigned a group of law enforcers named *Virgin-Collectors*[13] that are completely pink in colour, have no eyes or ears or even a mouth, just a giant hole in their face, which I believe is a nose. How did Sara and I, and many others, remain virgins without getting caught? Yes, we're still virgins, but don't judge us."

He smiled.

"To be honest, I don't know about the others, but Sara and I put on an act every time we see V.C around. If the collectors become aware of the existence of virgins, they always find you, no matter how far you run away or try to hide. They'll find you and take you back to the temple. However, if you're caught having sex or are involved in any sexual activities in front of them or when they're searching, they not only leave you to continue having pleasure but also cheer for you. They also leave a non-virgin mark on you, which unfortunately fades after nine months or so, depending on the situation. Sara and I have been marked several times. We're both marked as a non-virgin but still absolutely a virgin."

He laughed then stood up, moving the camera to another location so that the entire room was visible. He put on his wristwatch and started polishing his shoes.

"Now about those little babies that come out of the love session between God.SED and the virgins. The mother always dies at the time of delivery. This is because the virgin girls get pregnant right after the making out session and give birth by the end of the seventh day. I know this sounds absolutely impossible, but for God.SED the impossible is always possible."

He sighed.

"Poor girls. The babies are then kept inside the luxurious temple, which constantly expands its capacity to its maximum level. In this way, there's always more room available for the new-born children."

He put on his favourite homburg hat and looked in the mirror.

"I love this hat, that majestic face."

He looked at his shoes.

---

[13] Virgin Collectors: A part of law enforcement units whose duty is to constantly search the super continent, find virgins, and deliver them to God.SED.

"That's pretty much a wrap for this scene. I'll talk later with you fine folks. I covered the entrance, the army, myself, Sara, God.SED, a little about armies, and Nanny. Oh, Nanny! Nanny's an elderly lady who adopted Sara and me when the war was still going on, which I think I talked enough about. She kept us safe ever since and is pretty much the only family Sara and I have. I have no memories or no pictures of my parents to show you guys. If I find out anything, I'll let you guys know."

He sighed.

"That's about it, I guess. This is the first part of the documentary and I believe you know the exact date, since it's visible in the corner of the frame. Thank you for listening and bye for now, until the next part."

He switched off the camera, put it on the desk, checked the mirror one final time then left the room.

Chapter 2
The Temple (Search)

God.SED was surrounded by many young women while drinking, laughing, and enjoying their company on the bed. The bed was located on the second floor and the room was secured by countless guards, who looked only straight ahead, despite all the arousing activities that were happening in front of them. The room was connected to the main floor by black marble stairs leading from both sides of the room and there were burning candles on each step.

A handicapped man was escorted into the room by two **Sky-eyes**[14]. He could only see through one eye, as Sky-eyes had removed the other one earlier. The man was brought to God.SED and thrown on the floor. The man tried to stand up but he was unable to do so. He held his hands up and his head down.

"My lord, I have good news for you," said the man. "The location of the woman has been found by the local boys. Will you please bless me with health, so that I may serve you better?"

God.SED lifted a girl, licked her then threw her onto the floor. He pushed the other girls off the bed and stood up, naked.

"Where is she now?" he asked.

"She's here, my lord," said the man, as he looked at the Sky-eyes.

One of the Sky-eyes opened his mouth and threw up an old woman, who was wearing many wooden crosses around her neck.

"There she is, my lord," said the tearful handicapped man.

God.SED looked down at the unconscious woman, jumped off his bed and landed beside her.

"I must say, I'm impressed by your loyalty, my friend," said God.SED.

---

[14] Sky-eyes: Fallen angel/Special Forces of God.SED that have ability to fly.

He raised his right hand and the woman flew into the air. He then made a fist and the old woman regained consciousness and started screaming in pain, as each of her bones slowly began to break.

"I take pleasure in such pain, especially if there's screaming involved," said God.SED.

He hardened his fist. The woman began to bleed from her eyes, ears, and nose, as her skull began to break. As her neck began to break into pieces, the wooden crosses fell onto the floor.

"Strong woman," said God.SED, smiling. "The neck is broken yet she lives."

He placed his other hand on his fist and raised his middle finger. The old woman's spine came out of her body and she closed her eyes while choking out blood.

There was no sound to be heard in the temple. God.SED opened his mouth and sucked the soul from the dead woman. He then opened his eyes and looked at the Sky-eyes units standing close to him.

"What are you waiting for? Go search for him!" he shouted. "Find him before he's told more than he already knows!"

Several Sky-eyes units immediately flew out of the temple.

God.SED looked at the handicap man.

"And you, little thing. I can't bear the hideous smell of you. Why would I help you when I don't even like you?"

"My lord," replied the handicap man, as he touched God.SED's foot. "All I need is to serve you better but I can't do it in this weak body. Please help me to regain my strength so that I can better please you."

God.SED pulled his foot away.

"Back off, you freak!" he yelled. "I have to get those horny bitches on my bed to lick my foot cleaned now because of you!"

He looked up and winked at the naked girls standing on the stairs.

"We'll do anything for you!" cheered the girls.

"Unbelievable humans," said God.SED. "They saw what I did to that old woman and still want to please me."

He put his hand on his stomach and looked at the man.

"I may have a job for you, hideous creature."

"Your order is my command, my lord," said the man.

God.SED exhaled in his face. The man was healed and cheerfully stood up. Yet within seconds, his hands turned into giant looking spoons. His back was shortened, as did his legs and neck, an extra eye appeared at the top of his forehead, and his mouth widened.

"How's the new look?" asked God.SED.

The man was barely able to speak.

"What have you done to me? Why have you done this, lord?"

"A pathetic creature like you is good only for one thing," said God.SED, as he stepped closer. "And that's pushing the shit stuck in my ass. Your assignment is clear. Clean the shit that doesn't come out of my asshole by eating it. Your hunger for my blessing is fulfilled!"

He opened his mouth and swallowed the screaming man then burped.

"Yuck! Disgusting thing to do but I needed a hand down there. This earthly body is so demanding"

He looked down at his stomach.

"Let's go get more pleasure, brother," whispered God.SED, looking at his genitals before jumping on the bed.

"I must find a way to gain more power to fulfil the duty soon," he said, as he squeezed the breast of a young girl.

"What do you mean, my lord?" she asked.

"You'll find out very soon," God.SED replied then began having intercourse with the girl.

Chapter 3
Business as Usual

John had gone to see DJ at the studio.

"You see, when I say I'm waiting for my girl to bring the purple hat, I mean we," said John, making a quotation gesture. "Wait, you know what? If the actors don't like it, then they can get the fuck out. I don't have time for whiny, overpaid and overrated so-called talents to order me what to do, DJ."

"Bruh!" said DJ, while poking on the edge of a custom-made knife. "Chill out. We can't lose these ones even if we try. God.SED likes them. We've got to work some shit out with them. I know you've been under a lot of stress lately, that's understandable. I also know this one's a big budget project and you want to get a *Gold Art*[15] award no matter what happens, but bruh! Try to go take it easy. Just a few months left, just a few months."

"How the hell did we get ourselves involved in this project, I wonder," said John. "The scriptwriter can't write and the actors can't act. I feel like it's just you and me, man."

"Also, Michael and Rich," said DJ, as he sat down on his black leather executive chair.

"True, without all of us, this project would be dead. What happened to others?" asked John. "You make friends along the way and you lose them faster than you make them. I miss what we had when we were working on the last film. Not only was it spectacular but it felt right too. Everyone was united. We didn't need to ask to get a job done. Everyone wanted to get it done. Do you remember, man?"

"Yeah, bruh!" said DJ, checking the camera. "True friendships don't last for long these days. In fact, they never last at all. You did try to keep the old group,

---

[15] Gold Art: The highest award given to a performer of fine arts.

we all know that, but the truth is, things have changed and everyone's moved on."

"Yeah," John agreed, as he read the script. "I …actually we tried. I didn't know that from so many we'd end up with so few. I wish they could see what we had in our friendship, especially on the set, and would stick with it for further projects."

John smiled.

"Anyways bro, I'm glad we stayed together until now, honestly." he said, pointing his right index finger at DJ. "I truly respect that and you."

"Yeah," said DJ, checking the music system. "I gotcha back, bruh. Listen to this now."

He played one of the beats he'd made for one of the scenes and started nodding his head to the sound.

"Putcha hands up! Putcha hands up!" said DJ.

"That's what I'm talking about" said John, while waving his hands in the air. "Your beats are sick, brother, shit! This is unique. This will work just fine with the car chase scene shit."

He started nodding his head.

"I can't stop it man, I can't."

At that moment, Rich arrived.

"You assholes are chilling in here and left me with the whining ones? How could you?" said Rich, as he started nodding his head.

"Yo! What up, bruh?" asked DJ. "Yo feelin' this?"

"I'm metalling this," Rich replied, as he started texting. "Wait, let me get Michael up here too."

"Ye! Yo! You play with yoyo! Ask him to get up here fast, losing my brain, bro," said John.

John's phone rang and he saw that it was Sara.

"Guys! Guys!" he said. "It's my girl, so give me a second."

He stepped out onto the patio then answered the call.

"You safe?" asked John.

"Oh no!" Sara exclaimed. "Please come and save me! I'm being taken away! Help! Help! Of course, I am, silly. Like, seriously, stop this overprotective stuff, John. It's not like you could do anything even if I was having trouble at this very moment though. I'm almost there and still pissed, so you'd better stay quiet. I had a talk with Nanny. She told me she wanted to go on a vacation, she sounded weird. Did you guys talk about it?"

"Yes," John replied. "We talked about it this morning and she just left."

"Hmm, that's a bit odd," said Sara. "She usually says bye before going anywhere, in like a traditional hugging and kissing way. Did she tell you where she was going to this time? Because she told me she was going to the impact site."

"What? This is so strange," said John. "I'll have to call and check on her, since she told me she was going to the beach. Why does this woman love the impact site so much?"

From the patio where he was standing John saw Sara getting out of the taxi parked in front of the studio. She looked up and smiled at him.

"Sara, you know I love you right?" asked John, waving his hand.

"No, I don't," she replied. "Ah, so much drama, John. I not only know that but also know how annoyingly overprotective you are."

She paid the driver then looked up at him again.

"I love you too. Do you like your hat?" asked Sara, while pointing at it.

"It's perfect," said John, as Michael walked onto the patio.

"Hey, what's up with you two lovebirds?" he asked. "And why are you on the phone when you can literally hear each other if you just talk a little louder?"

John laughed.

"True. Come up, girl" he said, as Sara walked towards the building. "We've got to start rolling the film before these whiny kids leave this place and complain to the sponsor."

"Why don't you marry her, brother?" asked Michael, standing in the room behind Richard. "You guys aren't teenagers anymore. It may get too late, you know?"

John took a deep breath.

"Good to have you in my life, bro. You're always giving the right advice. I know, but you know what happens to newlywed couples. We saved ourselves for ourselves, not for that horny freak at the temple. I don't want her to get anywhere near God.SED. I know spending the first night after a wedding with God.SED is the rule, as it's considered the highest blessing, but none of those newlywed girls come back the same after spending a night with him," said John, as he stepped into the room, closing the patio door behind him.

Michael lowered his head.

"He enjoys them and then leaves them to men who won't even know who these girls have turned into," John added. "We'll be fine. I might just …"

John looked concerned.

"If we marry, she gets to spend the first night with him. If we don't, virgin collectors may find her and things will become even worse. If we do it, we can't lose our virginity because she wants to get married first and we can't get married because of what I just said. I don't know what to do, Mike. I just don't know anymore."

"It's alright, brother," said Michael. "If I talk about marriage all the time, it's because I know that you realise that Sara is way too beautiful to roam around being single."

John nodded his head.

"In today's society," Michael added, as he put his hand on John's shoulder, "no one really gives a shit about getting married or not anymore, but with Sara's beauty and your jealousy, you'll both have more problems in the future that you ever anticipated. However, when the time's right, it shall be done."

John smiled.

"Now," said Michael. "Let's go inside. We'll find a solution to your problems later."

John and the others walked back in the studio filming set, where John gathered everyone together. After explaining the scene to the actors again and going through multiple rehearsals, he began filming. Meanwhile, Sara received an emergency call from the Twin Cancer Hospital regarding a critical patient that required her expertise. Despite wanting to stay, she quickly told John about the situation then left.

"What was that all about?" asked Rich, a few hours later.

"She told me there was an emergency at the hospital," John replied, as he closed his suitcase. "I'm going to have to leave the rest of the editing for you guys, if that's alright. Will you guys be fine with that?"

"Of course, man," said Michael. "Just let us know what happened at the hospital, because Sara looked extremely concerned."

"Ya, I hope everything's fine at the hospital," said John. "I appreciate this guy, and you, DJ! Sick beats, brother."

"It's business as usual, bruh!" said DJ, while working on the musical keyboard.

John rushed out of the studio but was stunned as he stood on the sidewalk. A black wolf was standing at the other side of the street and looking straight into his eyes. John looked around in shock. No one else seemed to be seeing the wolf right middle of the busy sidewalk. When he looked back across the street, the wolf was gone. However, something was glowing where the wolf had been standing. John was curious and crossed the road. He looked around again to see if anyone saw the wolf, but no one seemed to have seen it at all as everyone continued going about their daily life. John walked over to where the wolf had been standing and saw a glowing symbol. He touched the symbol and blacked out for a few seconds. When John opened his eyes he was laying on the sidewalk and Rich and Michael were looking down at him from the patio.

"You okay down there, brother?" asked Michael. "What happened?"

John shook his head and stood up.

"Ya, I am good," said John, dusting the dirt from his pants. "I think we just worked too hard today. I need more sugar in me. It's alright guys, I'm alright. I'll talk to you fellas later."

"If you say so, man," asked Rich. "Are you sure you can drive?"

"Ya bro, I'm fine, it's just we worked hard today. I'll be in touch," said John, as he got up. John then looked back at the where the symbol was and saw nothing. He then nodded his head and go into the car.

Sitting in the driver's seat, John took a deep breath and opened his eyes. He saw the wolf standing on the same spot as before, looking at him. John quickly closed his eyes.

"I'm dreaming, hallucinating, maybe dying of tiredness?"

He opened his eyes and the wolf was gone.

"That's it, no more horror movies," said John, as he drove away.

"That was weird," said Rich.

"Indeed," Michael agreed. "John's gone through tougher working days before and never even fell asleep, but he was completely out on the sidewalk. I'm pretty sure when I saw him, he was unconscious."

"Well, I saw him fall down but I didn't know what was happening," said Rich. "Then you arrived and he woke up."

"I didn't mean like you were supposed to run down and pick him up," said Michael. "I was as shocked as you were when I saw him. Well, I'm glad it went smoothly."

"That's right," said Rich.

"What the fuck are you guys are doing out here?" DJ asked. "Gentlemen, we have a lot work left to do. Please get back inside and let's shake it."

DJ went back into the room. Rich and Michael looked at each other with concern and confusion, before heading back inside.

Chapter 4
Twin Hospital Incident

In one of the hospital rooms, items were being thrown and nurses were screaming and running around in fear. The severed head of a nurse lay beside the decapitated body of a doctor and Sara was holding onto a boy that was shaking.

"Hold him!" she shouted.

"I am!" the nurse yelled. "He's too strong for me!"

Six Arms of Justice units broke down the door, entered the room, and looked at the four-year-old child whose arms Sara held from behind. The leader of the group approached the child, who was screaming and biting the air. The child's eyes rolled back in his head and he struggled to breathe. The leader held his hands over the child's mouth and squeezed.

"You're cutting off his airway!" said Sara.

"Silence, bitch!" the leader yelled.

The child started shaking so hard that Sara and the other nurse had to let go of his arms. The child then threw himself against the wall and fell to the floor, unconscious. Sara rushed over to him. He was still breathing. Meanwhile, several more nurses rushed into the room with medical equipment. Holding the child, they injected him with the *Controlling Water,*[16] which helped the child to calm down. Once he was quiet, the nurses began cleaning up.

The A.o.J. units assessed the room, checked the dead bodies then dragged them out of the room, which resembled a battlefield. There were bloodstains on everything and everywhere. Sara held the child's head and asked the nurses to help her take him to a new room. A few minutes later, they placed the child on the new bed then checked his heartbeat, blood pressure, and body temperature.

---

[16] Controlling Water: A strong relaxing medicine.

Sara thanked the nurses for their quick response then told them to leave the room now that things were under her control.

Meanwhile, John arrived at the hospital, parked the car, and entered the building.

"Hi, Ashley, why do you look so shocked?" John asked the receptionist. "I've given you an autograph, actually many autographs, and you've come to our home and stayed over, so what's up with that face? Practicing some acting facial expressions?"

"Room 69, hurry!" said Ashley.

"Room 69?" said John. "Oh, ya! The emergency thing."

He ran to the elevators and pressed the button. As John waited, many of the patients that recognised him tried approaching him to take selfies. Before things got out of control, security guards arrived and stood around him. When the elevator arrived at the main floor, they escorted him inside.

"Thanks guys, I appreciate it," said John, saluting them.

"It's part of our job, sir," said one of the guards, as the doors closed. "Welcome back to our hospital."

John entered the room carrying a bouquet of red roses. He looked at the child that was securely restrained then at the exhausted Sara, who was sitting on a chair with her eyes closed.

"Sara, sweetie, are you okay?" said John, trying to clean the bloodstain from Sara's forehead. "Why is there blood on you? Why is this kid locked up like this? He doesn't look that strong to have to be wrapped up like this."

Sara held John's hands and put her head on his chest. He began comforting her.

"Are you ..." he started to say.

"Shush," said Sarah. "Just try to calm me down."

John kissed her forehead.

"Everything's alright, everything's fine, think about ..." said John, as Sara looked up into his eyes.

"I thought this little monster would kill me and I didn't even have any time to call you and say that I loved you," said Sara.

John kissed her on the lips.

"I love you too. Don't talk crazy, this kid doesn't look ..."

"It's not a kid," said Sara. "It's become the thing ... the thing that's inside of him now."

She lowered her head.

"He was too weak to fight the thing and now it's inside him and out of control. We'll have to terminate it," she said.

She put her head back on John's chest and took a deep breath.

"I don't know how you do this job, Sara," said John. "I know you're an amazing nurse and love to help but you really don't have to do this. You don't need to work at all, or at least not as many hours as you do."

Sarah remained quiet while hugging him.

"What are you on?" asked John. "You're breaking me, girl. Maybe go down a notch with the squeezing."

He lifted Sara's chin and kissed her on the lips once more.

"I won't let anything bad happen to you, I promise."

Sara smiled.

"Let's get you some new clothes and talk about this after you get cleaned up, alright?" John added, while putting the flowers on the nearby table.

Sara stood up, a little unsteady on her feet.

"Stay here and don't go anywhere until I come back," she said, as she looked at the flowers on the table. "And thank you for the roses, I love them."

She then left the room.

John looked at the child, as he stood beside the bed. The young boy was wrapped with multiple belts despite only having a small body.

"Poor kid," said John, yawning. "I wonder what you did to be cursed like this?"

He put his hand on the child's head and noticed an ancient symbol on his neck. It was just like the one the black wolf had been sitting on. John immediately backed away, slipped, and fell to the floor.

"What the fuck happened to you?" said Sara, as she walked in and rushed over to him.

"I'm okay," John replied. "I just slipped. Stay away from this kid. When exactly is termination going to begin?"

"What's the rush?" asked Sara. "We still have to collect some more blood tests. Why do you look so scared?"

"Never mind," said John. "Let's just sit down."

They sat on the oval-shaped chairs and John began telling her about the wolf incident and the symbol. Sara wasn't totally convinced, as she hadn't seen similar symbols on the child during his physical examination, but she didn't let John know about that and let him continue talking.

"I don't know what the link is between the marks," said John. "But I know there's some serious shit hitting the fan in here, big ones I mean…"

"Yuck! Stop it! Yuck!" said Sara. "Shit jokes ain't funny."

"You know that you become so cute when you get serious?" said John, squeezing her cheeks.

"Hey, mister!" Sara exclaimed. "Go get something to eat. Neither of us looks like we've eaten anything for days."

John stood up.

"You got it, my lady. I love getting free stuff at hospitals."

John then left the room.

When John returned to the room a few minutes later, he was shocked. The young boy was having sex with a nurse and Sara was nowhere to be seen. John left the packages of food he was holding on the table and rushed over to the nurse and pulled her back.

"Get off him, you crazy bitch," he yelled. "What the fuck is going on in here? Female paedophile?"

The nurse's eyes rolled back in her head and the child transformed into an older looking man with long black beard.

"You like what you see, Mr Seventh?" asked the man.

"Do you want to fuck me too, Johnny?" asked the nurse, spreading her legs open.

John stepped back, utterly confused.

"I'm dreaming. This isn't real."

He closed his eyes then slowly opened them again.

The nurse was still lying naked on the floor, squeezing her breasts, while the man rubbed his penis.

"Stop it, both of you!" John shouted. "Whatever darkness is inside you …"

He then felt his hands warming up and glowing.

"What's happening to me?" he whispered.

He had no control over his hands, which rose towards the man and the nurse. Powerful energy was released out of John's hands and hit them both.

The child and the nurse screamed.

"How could you do this to us, master?" shouted the man. "Why?"

"We will see you again, master!" the nurse added, in a deep voice.

A black mist was released from them and entered the floor beneath them. The original appearances of the man and the nurse returned and they began to appear unpossessed. A few minutes later, the nurse opened her eyes. Realising that she was naked on the floor and the young boy was no longer secure, she screamed.

"What happened in here? I came in to check on …"

John gave her a blanket so that she could cover herself.

"I don't remember anything except seeing a bright light," she said. "A man walked up to me with two pieces of wood, like a …"

"A cross?" said John, making the symbol with his fingers.

"Yes! And then he told me I was released from the demon inside me and my sins were forgiven," said the nurse.

She burst into tears and grabbed John's legs then she noticed she had had intercourse.

"Am I a bad person?" she asked. "Who was that man? I'm sorry if I did anything wrong! I don't want to get cursed again!"

"What the fuck happened in here?" Sara demanded, as she entered the room. "You fucking cunt! Stay away from my man!"

She grabbed the nurse and pulled her back, standing between her and John before turning around and looking into John's eyes.

"I didn't know you were into fucking redheads!" Sara said angrily, in a British accent.

John laughed.

"It's not what it looks like," said, pointing at the young boy on the bed. "Look! The kid's on the loose."

"Shut up!" said Sara, looking at the nurse. "I don't know what happened in here but get the fuck out of my sight and fucking call the Arms."

The nurse looked at John then nodded her head. "Thank you," she said and left the room.

Sara stood beside the boy, relocating him on the bed, then placed a pillow under his head and covered him with a blanket. John sat down on the chair, feeling exhausted, and ate a few fries.

"Where did you go?" he asked.

"I'm still mad, as you can see," Sara replied. "I had to check on the other patient when you were having sex in here!"

John tried to say something, but she cut him off.

35

"Mr Famous couldn't control the fucking snake in his pants for a few minutes when he was alone. I know you did it because I can see her DNA on the floor," said Sara angrily, pointing her index finger at the fluid on the floor.

John swallowed what was left in his mouth and cleaned his fingers on some napkins.

"Sara, come here," said John, tapping his lap.

Sarah pulled her hair behind her ear, exhaled, walked over to John and sat on his lap.

"Don't look at me like that," she said. "I opened the door to see a girl giving you a blowjob. Don't look …"

John interrupted her.

"You never need to worry about me being unfaithful or not," he said, as he kissed her hands. "I'm yours and yours only, my lady."

Sara smiled.

"However, she had fine breasts, like …"

"Oh, fuck off, pervert!"

She pinched John then hugged him.

"Tell me what the heck happened in here? Why was the kid off the belts and why the bitch was naked? And mister, we must finish eating quickly. Arms will be here at any time soon."

John tried to explain but the young boy opened his eyes and looked at them.

"You are the one," he said, looking directly at John. "I will see you soon again, master."

The child began to shake violently. John and Sara rushed over to him but no matter what they did they failed to calm him down and within few seconds, the child was dead.

The door was then thrown opened and six A.o.J. units walked in. Their leader stepped forward and stood by the bed.

"How long ago did the termination happen?" he asked.

"Just a few seconds ago, sir," Sara replied. "But he wasn't terminated. This was something else."

"He sure looks like he was," said the leader, studying the child.

Sarah looked at the boy. He was in a miserable condition. His skin was completely dried out, his eyes were decomposed, and his teeth appeared from his lipless mouth.

"But … but …" Sara tried to say, but the leader interrupted her.

"Is this the one?" he asked the nurse that had been in the room earlier.

"I can't definitely identify him through this terminated body, sir. I assume so."

"Take this whore to temple," said the leader to one of the Arms of Justice units.

"That's not appropriate to call—" Sara started to say, before John interrupted her.

"Don't advise the leader of a fine Justice group, woman," said John, his eyes wide.

"Wise man," said the leader, with nasty glance at Sara. "May God.SED bless you with hard sex and extra passion in bed every time you fuck this fine bitch."

The Arm of Justice leader began looking at Sara's breasts. She tried to speak, but John squeezed her hand.

"Both of you get the fuck out now," said the leader, looking at the child's decomposed body. "We need to examine this piece of shit."

Sara was upset as she walked out of the room, with John following her.

"Would you stand there and watch me get fucked by those bastards and do nothing?" asked Sara angrily, while locking her seatbelt. "That asshole called me a bitch! And he looked at me as if I was naked and you didn't do anything. This isn't the first time, as you know. Can you even protect yourself if they decide to fuck you, John?"

"There were six units in the room who would not only rape you but would also take you to SED after probably cutting my head off," John replied, as he fastened his seatbelt and started the car. "Sara sweetie, I promise that I'll never let anything bad happen to you in this life and the next, if there is any. Just try to understand. Yes, we have gone through this before, but you're here untouched and I'm here alive."

Sara remained quiet.

"Why don't you understand that they love intimidating people by false language to …"

"John, just keep quiet and drive the fucking car," said Sara, looking out of the side window.

John wanted to add something, but he didn't and simply squeezed the steering wheel in anger and drove away from the hospital.

Chapter 5
The Temple (Discovery)

Large number of **Little ones**[17] were standing and witnessing God.SED peeling off his skins and transforming into his next physical form. Women were moaning while kissing him, temple guards were shivering, and Arms of Justice units were standing on high alert. God.SED shouted out loud, as the transformation was painful. The more he shouted, the more women surrounded him and continued pleasuring him.

God.SED sucked blood out of a young girl beside him while piercing his long teeth inside her breasts. He threw her away from him away after she was drained of blood and roared. His hands grew bigger, his nails grew longer and thicker, his skull and jaw grew large, and his teeth became sharper. His body became more muscular, including his arms and legs. At the end of the transformation, he released powerful energy out of his body that threw the women close to him across the room. He stretched his neck and stood up, looking at his forces. They were all shivering except for one Little-one. God.SED looked into its eyes and the creature was blown into pieces. He stretched his neck a little more then looked at others standing beside him.

"You like what you see?" he shouted, as everyone knelt. "Get me a mirror!"

A woman in a red dress brought a mirror over to him.

"I shall make you bear countless children and die giving birth to the last one, so I can rejoice at having your soul inside me forever," said God.SED, laughing.

"You can do whatever you want to me, my lord," said the woman. "I am yours and you own me."

---

[17] Little-ones: A group of small and short underworld creatures that are in charge of maintenance duties.

"Impressive bitch," he said, looking at himself in the mirror. "I love the new look. I like how the eyes turned purple and I like that I can now see your organs through your useless skins."

He looked at the crowd.

"I can hear the weak heartbeats inside you all and I can feel ..."

He was interrupted, as a Sky-eyes unit walked in the room.

"Master, we have information about Arms who say that they've encountered a suspicious human who could be the chosen one."

"I wanted to rip your face off for interrupting me," said God.SED in demonic language.

"But this is a good day and you gave me good news. Well, you shall live, my friend."

Two naked girls walked to God.SED and gave him his robe. God.SED put on the soft handmade robe and looked at the crowd, as the girls stepped back.

"Prepare for the meeting!" he shouted.

The leaders of his forces gathered in a meeting chamber and sat at a round black marble table, at the centre of which was a burning purple fire. God.SED walked in, sat on his chair, and the chamber's doors were closed.

"Show me," he said.

Flames began burning sideways and in the middle of them images of John and Sara appeared. God.SED looked at them and smiled.

"There he is, the chosen one and look at his bitch whore. I didn't know our famous film maker was the chosen one and look at that fine girl," he said, licking his lips. "She's a fine woman for fucking, I must say."

The leaders laughed.

"Are you sure he's the one?" asked God.SED, looking at the A.o.J. leader.

"We weren't sure when we encountered him in the room," replied the leader of Arms of Justice, in demonic language. "But after scanning the child's memories, we picked up a signal that burnt out one of our units. Nothing except the *Light*[18] can do that. We searched the entire building and found no trace of another source of energy meeting the child except John. Also, the entire memory of the child was erased immediately after the Light was unleashed."

"Hmm," said God.SED. "So, you're saying that we gathered here for this nonsense?"

The leader began to float in the air.

---

[18] Light: Holy Spirit.

"Please don't do this, lord!" he said, choking. "You told us to inform you of any suspicious activities."

"Oh, yeah!" said God.SED. "I do remember that part, but the child could have been visited by an angel before this human went to see him. The angel could have set a trap for the one that would check the memory. John has also been under surveillance for quite a while. There's been absolutely no trace of any Light inside him, as well as in his whore."

The leader fell to the floor, barely breathing.

"How many elements are remaining?" asked God.SED.

"The soil is ready, my lord," said a very muscular man with an abundance of body hair.

"The fire is ready, my lord," said a woman with bright red hair.

"The water is ready, my lord," said sexless human, that had water leaking from its ears.

"The air is ready as well, my lord," said a very pale skinny girl.

"You idiots!" shouted God.SED. "Every one of you is ready and you didn't inform me?"

The purple fire in the middle of the table turned black and its flames grew stronger. He closed his eyes, breathed deeply, and after calming down, opened his eyes.

"If you think that you've discovered the chosen one, go capture him!" shouted God.SED. "Don't come to me and just tell me. Bring him or her to me straight away and I'll do the rest. I'll probably have to start the fucking ritual without having the chosen one the way you morons work!"

He looked at his hands and made two fists.

"Fuck! I can't transform into my final physical form and mix the elements without having control over his powers! The ritual needs the power of the chosen one! And the fucking father of us needs the fucking body of the chosen one to reach to the gates of heaven! You morons know this very well!"

The crowd remained silent, as his head then separated and two monstrous heads emerged. All the leaders knelt and transformed into their underworld physical forms.

"All the steps to resurrect father have been taken, except this one!" said God.SED.

He held his hand towards a Little-one in the corner of the room and released a stream of purple energy on its direction, blasting the Little one.

God.SED looked at the leader of Sky-eyes.

"You! I give you this task to gather your units and find out if John is truly the one and bring him to me alive."

The leader of Sky-eyes bowed his head and began flying.

"Before you go," said God.SED, as the Sky-eyes waited, "make sure that humans don't see you in this form, and, if necessary, use ***Stoned one[19]***. It's believed that the chosen one can kill Sky-eyes. After all, you're just upgraded demons and are always vulnerable to ***spirit energy[20]***."

"Consider it done, master!" said the leader of Sky-eyes. "There will be no need of Stoned ones. We may be upgraded demons, but there are still a few of us who were fallen angels in the past."

The Sky-eyes units turned into their human physical form and flew out of the chamber, along with the rest of the units.

"Always have to have the last words, phony fallen angels," said God.SED, as he looked at the leaders around the table. "Why the fuck are you still in here? Get the fuck out! Go do your jobs!"

The leaders left and countless naked women and men entered the room. God.SED dropped his robe and lay on the floor.

"Come, my sex slaves," he said. "Come and pleasure me."

"Oh, you're going to enjoy this, my lord," said a girl, as she closed the doors of the chamber.

---

[19] Stoned one: Stone ones are pale, tall and massively built humanoid beings that are only called if all the demonic agents fail to achieve an objective. They are immune to any spirit energy attacks from the angelical forces because their real bodies are made from the blood of angels and stones.

[20] Spirit energy: Supernatural power or intense concentrated energy.

Chapter 6
Edward Znock

Edward was perhaps Gabriel's greatest success and failure. Even though his birth resembled that of the other chosen ones, he stood out as the most promising one to win the war between the armies of Light and Darkness.

Edward was born from an alliance between a human mother and an angel father who lost his wings. Edward was born with a strength unlike the other failed chosen ones before him. He was named Edward by his parents, who were killed when the war between angels and demons began. He was adopted at a very young age and trained by Gabriel in the heavens. Edward was given a new name Znock, which meant 'strong one.' Due to his extreme level of training and access to heavenly consumable products, Edward grew into a giant by the time he reached adolescence. When he grew into a young and extremely muscular man, he was feared and honoured by all the angelical creatures around him in heaven.

Once released on Earth, neither demons nor fallen angels could defeat him. Edward slaughtered thousands of demons and fallen angels using his massive axe during the angelical and demonic war. Gabriel couldn't be prouder. His adopted son couldn't be stopped by any creatures or anyone, not even Evil and Devil. Yet Gabriel didn't know that Edward was meeting Satan and being manipulated. Perhaps it was because Edward grew up in the heavens and never became exposed to earthly temptations and demonic manipulations in order to build any resiliency towards them. That was perhaps the reason why he was quickly attracted to the other types of powers.

Seven months after the start of the war on Earth, there was news that Edward had attacked and assaulted many angels because he was disrespected. This didn't play well with Gabriel, as angels began questioning his leadership and competence. Knowing that things were going to become chaotic in Eden if he wouldn't do anything against Edward, Gabriel sent messages to the angels on

Earth, including Joe White. Gabriel commanded the angels to capture Edward and return him to Eden, as Edward would have to face judgment for his crimes. Edward didn't take this news lightly and fought against Joe and the others that approached him. However, as his spirit was no longer pure because he'd begun to side with the Satan, Edward lost much of his strength, causing him to be defeated in his battle with the angels. Knowing that he would be sent back to Eden and be punished for disobedience and retaliation against angels by fighting with them and perhaps never to return to Earth, Edward called upon the Contractor and told him that he'd serve Satan and lead his army to Eden and the *Holy Host*[21]. Edward was then turned into a black colour furry wolfman, as his animal spirit took over his holy spirit completely. Gabriel tried to reach to Earth and Edward before the contract was signed but he was too late. Not only did Edward sign the contact he was also immediately taken to the underworld to be anointed by Satan himself. Gabriel was devastated by what he witnessed. This failure caused angels to doubt his leadership and many retaliated against him. The result of battles between angels against each other and between angels with demons cleared the path for Satan to reach the gates of the heavens.

Satan entered Edward and used him to defeat countless angels, including Gabriel, and reached the gates of the heavens. However, before he could break the gates and unleash darkness into the heavens, he encountered archangel Michael. They fought fiercely and despite the astonishing strength of the possessed Edward, Michael won the battle. Edward was then shot into Earth again with a very powerful energy sphere, which ended the war between angels and demons.

Satan was once again defeated so he returned to his temple in the underworld, taking his army, his sons, his daughter, and Edward with him. He then waited for thousands of years until the next and final war.

---

[21] Holy-Host: Heaven or the kingdom of God.

Chapter 7
The Dream

John was at home, leaning his back on the closed and locked bathroom door as he sat on the floor. He was trying to get in, but Sara wasn't allowing him. They hadn't exchanged a word on their way home from hospital. When they'd arrived, Sara had gone straight upstairs, grabbed some comfy clothes, and entered the bathroom. John had dropped the keys in the frog-shaped bowl and after removing his shoes, he'd walked upstairs and sat down by the bathroom door and tried his best to reach out to upset Sara.

"Sara, may I come in please?"

She didn't reply.

"May I get you anything to wash yourself with it better?"

Still no reply.

"May I change my voice and speak with a British accent? Or may I beg for forgiveness?"

John could hear the running water but nothing from Sara.

"Could this doorknob accidentally turn and I walk in?"

More silence.

"It must feel like sauna in there, Ms. Thomson, eh? There's too much steam coming out from under the door."

He knocked on the door.

"Go away," said Sara.

"Wow! She can talk! Can I come in now?"

"I said go away!"

John nodded.

"Ay yay yaay! They'd find out about your virginity in no time, Sara, then take you away. Did you really want me to fight with them, even though you knew that they'd kill me?"

"Shut up!" said Sara.

"Oh! Someone cares about my life. May I come in now?"

"Yes, you may," said Sara and she unlocked the door.

"Thank you."

John opened the door and entered.

"Did they grow bigger?" asked John, looking at Sara's breasts while she stood in front of him on the blue wool rug.

She looked at them too. "I guess so. John, come on! They're the same, don't try to change the topic!"

"Them boobies!" John exclaimed. "Soft and bouncy and …"

"Hey," said Sara. "Enough already. Do you want to feel them or not? They're tired, so am I, so we could all have a little massage and fun here, Mr Seventh."

Sara rubbed her right-hand index finger on John's lips and stood under the shower, gesturing for John to join her.

"Feel them? Massage them?" John replied. "Woman, I'm going to eat them and the entire package."

He jumped under the shower, fully clothed.

Sara giggled.

"My poor horny future husband," said Sara, as she unbuttoned John's shirt. "I'm still mad at you. This isn't the first time that someone harassed me and you did nothing. I know you know how dangerous it'll be, but I need you to show me that you can protect me rather than calling the units to come and do that. What if I truly get into trouble?"

She removed John's wet shirt. He tried to keep his eyes open under the stream of water and say something, but Sara put her left hand on his mouth.

"I wonder, how it'd feel when he goes inside me?" said Sara, unbuckling John's belt.

"I guess it'd feel very hard and very warm," said John, as she removed his pants and slowly pulled down his underwear. "Do you finally want to do it or what?"

"Look this cute thing, I mean Rex. Want to get the balls chopped off, Mr Seventh?" said Sara.

John made a baby face.

"I changed my mind," said Sara. "I don't want us to wait too long but I want us to get married first. I just have this voice, this thing in my mind that keeps telling me that I should marry you first. I feel like maybe Nanny kept saying this for so long that I keep hearing it inside my head again and again."

She looked into John's eyes.

"More than you, Mr Horny, I dream about you being inside me and giving me your seed but we both know the rules."

John gave a fake smile.

"However, we both know that Rex has to get released from his pressure," said Sara, while rubbing John's penis.

John kissed her on the lips.

"There's pressure in Rex and in the treasure box," said John.

He grabbed Sara's waist with his left arm and put his right hand on her vagina.

"Take it easy, John. Don't push it too far. No ding ding without the wedding ring," said Sara, while raising her chin.

"I'd very much like that to happen soon" said John, as he began kissing Sara on the lips.

After taking a shower, John asked Sara what she wanted for dinner. She told him that the food was already cooked and had Nanny placed it in the fridge, so he just had to warm it up. Sara then jumped on the black leather sofa in the sitting room, turned on the T.V and started watching. Meanwhile, John warmed up the dishes and began preparing the salad, then turned and looked at Sara from where he was standing in the middle of the kitchen. "I love you, you know that?" said John.

Sara looked at him and winked. He then walked to the sink and heard an intense sound of thunder as he began washing the knife that he'd used earlier.

"Wow, I didn't realise it was going to rain if it isn't already," said Sara.

John looked out of the window and was shocked. The same black wolf that he'd seen earlier that day was sitting in the garden in the rain, looking straight into John's eyes. He jumped back and cut his finger.

"Ouch!"

"John! Are you alright?" asked Sara.

"Ya, I'm okay. I just cut my finger. It's a little cut, so no worries" said John.

He looked up again, but the wolf was gone, leaving nothing but the same glowing ancient symbol in the garden.

"John, do you want me to look at it?" asked Sara. "What are you looking at out there?"

"I'm good, sweetie," John replied. "The cut …"

John was amazed that the bleeding wound had already healed.

"I'm actually done, just putting dressing on the salad. Are you good with thousand island?"

"You know what I like," said Sara. "Just bring it here fast. I'm hungry!"

John took a deep breath. He was very concerned and had the feeling that something bad was about to happen. The image of the symbol and the energy he felt from the wolf were all dark. While thinking, he washed his hands, wrapped a bandage around his finger then walked to the sitting room holding two food plates.

"Here you go, my queen," said John.

Sara took the plates, placed them on the small wooden table in front of her, and held John's hand.

"Let me take a look at it. You bandaged it pretty well in that little time you spent in the kitchen, mister," she said, examining his face and noting his paleness. "What's wrong, John? Are you feeling alright? You seem very pale suddenly."

"Sara, some stuff happened today, some weird stuff. I saw a wolf this morning and then there was this ancient looking mark or symbol left behind when he vanished. Then I saw that wolf in the backyard five minutes ago."

"What!" Sarah exclaimed. "Are you serious? A wolf? Here? We have to call the Arms!"

John shook his head.

"Not this time. I don't know how Arms will react. This wolf could just be some sort of a new force and then we get Arms involved and then one thing leads to another. They may search the house and find things that we don't want them to. It could be some sort of a new punishment from God.SED for rich and famous people like us?"

John shrugged, as Sara remained quiet.

"I don't know. Like, right after I saw it this morning, I first passed out and then I ended up going through that drama at the hospital with the kid and the nurse trying to have sex. I ended up performing some sort of magic at the hospital before you came in the room too."

Sarah chewed her food slowly as she listened.

"My hands glowed and then something was released out of me that took care of what was in the kid and the nurse. The nurse had her eyes rolled back and …"

Sara her fork put down on the table.

"John, you're tired. It's been a long day, honey, and you'll have to work again tomorrow. I don't want to be mean or anything but it's just … you know … it sounds like you're narrating one of your movie scenes in here. Have some food. This all could be just some sort of an imagination?"

She slowly put some food into John's mouth.

"Good boy! I know you want me to support you and be empathetic and sympathetic but Johnny it's late and I'm tired too," said Sara. "Now, about my overreacting at the hospital. I'm sorry, but I just hated him calling me a bitch."

John didn't continue the conversation as he began to wonder if this was all nothing but his wild imagination.

"I'm sorry that I couldn't defend you in front of them again," said John, lowering his head.

"Hey John, look at me," she said, lifting his head. "It's over. I need to work on my temper and I know you thought of everything in there and that's why you didn't do anything again. I just lost my mind suddenly, you know?"

"I love you," said John.

"Love you too," said Sara, chewing her food. "Now, let's finish eating and watch our movie. I can't wait to see my acting scene again."

After dinner, they watched one of the movies that they'd both acted in then while Sara was playing with John's hair, he fell asleep.

"Where is this place?" said John, confused.

As far as he could see, there were dead bodies. The bodies of humans, animals, and anything that ever lived were all dried up and piled on top of each other. It was very dark, but John could still see a brightness coming from a nearby ruined castle. He scanned his surroundings.

"I'm dreaming," John whispered. "This isn't real."

He heard melodious music coming from the castle then heard the howling of wolves behind him. He turned around and the same wolf that he'd seen twice that day was standing on its hind legs, transforming into a massive black furry wolfman. John screamed and started running towards the castle, climbing the large stone bricks as fast as he could. While climbing, he noticed that he had claws and white furry hands. He also couldn't stand up straight any longer, as if his human body was being transformed into some other kind of body.

The massive wolfman stopped chasing him after a while.

"Commander! I'm here to serve you," the wolfman shouted. "Please, don't be afraid of me."

John kept running until he entered the castle. It was extremely dark, but he could still see a weak brightness coming from the end of the hall. He started running again, this time like a human. The brightness was coming from underneath a massive curved door. He opened it and walked in quickly. He was stunned at what he saw as the door closed behind him. A spectacular masked party was being held, with countless men and women dancing in the most glamorous designer clothes. Some were laughing, some were drinking, and some were singing. It seemed as if they weren't aware of the destruction of the land outside of the castle.

A server approached John. "Welcome, sir," asked the server, holding up a golden cup filled with red wine. "Would you like a drink?"

"No, thank you, I don't drink," said John. "What's this party all about? Where is this place?"

The server said nothing and walked back into the crowd.

"That was creepy," said John, as he looked around.

While admiring everyone, John heard someone calling his name. He turned in the direction where he'd heard the voice come from and started walking towards it.

"John! I'm here." Someone kept saying.

John walked faster, moving between and around people that giggled every time they looked at him.

"John! I'm here." Said the same voice.

John kept walking.

"Who are you?" asked John, finally reaching a girl sitting on a chair that was decorated with diamonds.

"Sara?" asked John. "What are you doing here? What is this? Where are we?"

"You found me."

The girl leaned back and transformed into the wolfman.

"Enough of this bullshit!" shouted John. "Who are you?"

"I'm your war assistant, master!" roared the wolfman then disappeared.

John turned around to see where he'd gone. Suddenly the entire room darkened.

"I see you," said John, angrily.

"Master! Let me serve you, let me explain what this is all about," said the wolfman as he approached.

The lights came back on but there was no one else left in the room.

"The humans will die one by one very soon, and you master, you will lead us to the gates!" said the wolfman. "You will take us to the gates of heaven …"

"Back off!" said John.

"Master, I apologise for disturbing you, but you need to understand how important it is for you to be ready for the promised day."

"Enough!" John shouted. "Enough! This is just a fucking dream. A dream that's all."

He covered his ears with his hands.

"Is it master? You have seen me thrice today, is that …"

"Who are you?" John demanded. "What do you want from me?"

"I am EZ, your server, your guide, and your protector, until you become the leader of our army."

"What's happening?" asked John. "Why can't I wake up?"

"It's because you're experiencing a vision, master. We're not different master, look," said the wolfman, pointing towards a mirror.

John looked at the mirror and saw a massive white furry wolfman.

"This is impossible!" said John in horror, then heard Sara's voice.

"John, wake up! I'm here, wake up!"

"I'll see you again, master," said the wolfman, before he disappeared.

"John, wake up!" said Sara. "I'm right beside you, love, I'm here. Stop calling my name. You need to wake up. It's morning, you got to go to work and I'm leaving now too. Apparently, there's been huge street fight between the found **Believers**[22] and the A.o.J. Countless numbers were injured and some already got cursed with Twin Cancer by God.SED."

John could barely move. He felt as though he couldn't focus.

"Are you okay?" asked Sara, as she tied her hair with a small blue scarf.

"Where am I?" asked John, while lying on the bed.

"In our bedroom, duh. Where else could you be?" she replied. "And thank you for bringing me upstairs. You know how much I hate to sleep on the sofa."

Sara kissed his forehead.

"I've got to go now."

"Wait Sara, wait!" said John, as he sat crossed legged on the bed.

---

[22] Believers: A group of people unaffected by the purple mist.

Sara stopped walking towards the door and turned around.

"I didn't bring you up," said John, with concern. "I don't even know how I came up myself."

Sara frowned.

"Hmm, that's weird or maybe you did and just forgot about it, love, I don't have time …"

"I… I fell asleep and I had this dream. The wolf that I told you about, it turned into a wolfman sort of a thing."

Sara walked back to the bed and sat down.

"I went to this ruined castle where everyone was dancing and… and then, I saw you but…"

John pinched her.

"Hey! What are you doing? Are you stupid? Why did you pinch my ass?" asked Sara, rubbing the place John had pinched.

"I'm sorry," he said. "I just had to make sure you were real."

"John, enough! I'm not listening to this bullshit any more. Get yourself together! I don't like this. If you're experimenting on me for the movie …"

"Sara," said John, as he held Sara's hands in his own. "Keep your *Connector*[23] within reach and don't let any one of these A.o.J. units or any other forces take you anywhere without me knowing, do you understand?"

"I don't know what's going on with you, John, but I want this to stop. I don't like you behaving like this. You're scaring me. It's a new beautiful positive day and you're acting so negative. I think you need a break, John."

Sara looked at her watch.

"I'm late, great! I've got to go now. I'll call you later, bye, just … maybe stay at home and don't go to work, John."

Sara stood up, exhaled and walked out of the room.

John had a severe headache. It felt as if he'd hit his head on a rock multiple times. He'd also gained an usual level of frustration and anger inside him, without understanding the cause.

"What's happening to me?" he said. "I'm angry for no reason."

John touched his chest and felt his heart beating very fast. He noticed that he'd gained a bit more facial and body hair compared to other days. He also noticed an unusual level of strength and power within him.

---

[23] Connector: Cell or mobile phone.

He stood up and took a deep breath and his headache suddenly went away.

"Wow! A little extra oxygen did the magic, eh?"

He then noticed a familiar smell. He sniffed more and burst into anger.

"How the fuck did you come inside my house, EZ! You're not welcome in here! How dare you touch my girl!" shouted John, before suddenly losing his energy.

John then sat on the bed, feeling exhausted. He then looked around the room to locate EZ.

"What's happening to me," he said then suddenly he regained his strength.

He looked at his hands that appeared to be hairier and felt as if EZ was looking at him. He looked up and saw EZ standing in the mirror near his bed.

"What the fuck! You're not welcome in my home," shouted John, as he jumped away from the bed.

When he turned around to see EZ, he saw nothing. John shook his head and kept his eyes closed.

"Go away. This isn't real," said John, as he received a text.

John opened his eyes and didn't see EZ anywhere. He then grabbed his cell phone from his bed and began reading the text, which was from DJ.

In the message, DJ was asking why he was late. John looked at the clock and realised that an hour had already passed, although it only felt like a few seconds since he'd felt the presence of EZ and jumped off the bed in fear. John then opened the curtains to let more brightness into the room and after making sure EZ was nowhere to be seen, he quickly prepared to go to work, grabbed the purple hat that Sara had bought for him, before leaving the house in complete uncertainty.

Chapter 8
You Are the Seventh

At the studio, John was having an intense argument with the actors on set who didn't seem to care about his point of view. DJ and Richard were trying to restrain him from assaulting anyone and Michael was standing behind the crowd, trying to get close to John. Meanwhile, DJ lost control over John's arm and John punched one of the actors, knocking him out. The actor was smacked into the floor and remained there, unconscious. The leading actress fainted onto the other two actors beside her after witnessing the incident. Staff members rushed towards John, who wanted to punch the fallen actor again. It took a good forty minutes before everything was calmed down. The assaulted actor was taken away, as were the other ones. DJ, Richard, and Michael were now confronting John and trying to calm him down, as he walked around like a madman, throwing heavy items around in anger as if they weighed nothing.

DJ looked at Richard and then at Michael, then nodded his head and they slowly walked towards John, who was trying to lift a massive light stand. They grabbed him, despite John resisting and shouting, and pulled him into his office.

"Bruh! What the fuck!" said DJ, looking disappointed.

"What's wrong with you, man?" asked Richard. "You never hit anything in your life and now you knocked out a freaking God.SED chosen actor! This won't go down well, John. Do you understand me? What's with you today? Did you have your Sola-Hola this morning?"

Michael sat down on the sofa beside John, who was looking at his knuckles and biting his lips.

"Are you feeling alright, brother?" asked Michael, as he poured some water into a colourless glass.

"I'm sick and tired of actors who can't act, who are just chosen through connections and have no artistic values!" said John, angrily. "I told the fucking moron five times to stand motionless and keep quiet so I could see his bloody face in the frame before we'd move on to placing the other extras around him. And this jackass kept on talking more about politics and his personal life, rather than about the scene itself."

John started improvising the knocked-out actor.

"I want James Patrick to win the election and if he doesn't, I'll pay every single person I see to go on a massive riot. We must win and have our control extended."

John drank some water from the glass that Michael gave him.

"I don't give a fuck! Are we here to make art or talk about politics? Is our job to get people elected who don't give a shit about the rest of the world or to remind people no one cares about politics anymore because we have a freaking god living among us now already! Fuck this! I can't understand why actors mix politics with entertainment. Don't they know that people don't give a shit about their opinions? And oh, sex again! All they want is the actresses to get naked in the scenes and the guys to shoot each other with heavy machine guns."

He sighed and looked at the others, who appeared to be disappointed and concerned.

"I'm sorry, guys. I'm not like this and you guys know it."

"Bruh!" said DJ. "I told you once that before meeting you guys, I had no real friends, or at least that's what I remember. You guys are all I have and I do care about every one of y'all deeply, but seeing you this mad makes me nervous, bro. You could get us all killed or twinned."

John lowered his head.

"Something isn't right with you today, bro," DJ added. "Do you want to talk about it?"

John sat down on his chair and began telling them about the supernatural things that he'd experienced the day before. Meanwhile, Michael poured juice into cups and after placing cookies on small plates, put them in front of the others.

"I am glad that we have a VIP fridge in this room" said Michael.

For a while none of them talked to each other. The room became extremely quiet, so much that they could hear the ceiling fan spinning.

Michael walked towards the window and pushed it open. DJ kept looking at Richard, giving him signals with his eyes. Yet Richard didn't seem to pay attention because he was busy eating cookies and drinking juice.

John cleared his throat.

"Any predictions?" he asked. "Any thoughts gentlemen?"

DJ stopped signalling and turned to face John.

"Yo, you're talking to me?" said DJ. "My bad, Ya bruh! Am... dreams you know, I guess or better, say I feel Sara was kind of right about you needing to take a break and stuff."

"And you, Michael? What do you think?" asked John.

"Brother, I do believe that there's some sort of am ... saying behind this dream, but I also have to say that there are times that..."

Richard interrupted Michael, his mouth full of cookies.

"Bro, I'm with DJ and I believe Michael tries to say the same thing. Your brain's fucked. You need to take a break. I mean, man, how are we going to deal with Arms once they arrive here? Do you know that you may lose this filming stuff?"

John put his hands on his face and rubbed his cheeks.

"Fuck me! I just don't know what got into me guys, I swear. I had no control over myself and just wanted him to get hurt. You know? I just ... fuck this!"

John's cell phone beeped and then started ringing. He stood up, stretched his back, cleared his throat then answered the call. He spent a few minutes listening and then hung up.

"Do we need to be concerned about anything, John?" asked Richard, as he noticed John didn't look alright.

"No," John replied. "It was the actor. He apologised for misbehaving and said he didn't know why he's been behaving so badly all this time. He also said that he'd never try to make us upset again."

"What the fuck!" said DJ. "You sure it was Jackson?"

"Ya, but he sounded different, man," replied John. "He sounded like a different person."

"That's odd, isn't it, Rich?" asked Michael.

"Ya, I guess so. Jackson's a chosen actor. It's totally creepy to have him apologising," replied Richard, rubbing his right hand on the top of his head. "I hope there's no trick or something behind this."

"Something isn't right in here," said John. "I don't feel good about these at all, guys."

They all looked at each other, feeling uncertain.

"Anyways," John continued. "I apologise for misbehaving like this for the first time and am …I'm glad you guys were there and had my back. Brothers for life!"

He raised his right hand towards his friends, who all put their hands on his.

"I'm glad I have you guys in my life, true brothers," said John. "No matter where I am or where I'll be, I know that I've got three great brothers backing me up, no matter what. One! Two! Three!"

"Gangstas of Paradise!" they all shouted together.

Shortly afterward, they went back to the production zone where they were all amazed to see Jackson standing and talking with the others, as if nothing happened to him at all. He also seemed as if he'd never been punched earlier. His jaw and face looked perfectly fine.

When the shooting of the scene was over, John gathered everyone, thanked them, and then apologised for the earlier incident. He later took Jackson, who seemed oddly polite and happy in a corner, and had a private chat with him. John asked him if he felt anything different because Jackson was unusually cheerful and energetic. Jackson mentioned that when he'd become unconscious, he saw a bright light that told him he was going to be taken care of from then on and felt relieved of the negative energy that was draining away his happiness. John thought that Jackson might have been given some heavy drugs at the hospital to stabilise him, which might have affected his behaviour. John then accompanied Jackson as he rejoined the group.

The leading actress was drinking champagne and shaking her breasts for the crowd as John approached the group. He walked towards her and she quickly stepped behind her manager, who didn't seem happy to see John again.

"I'm so sorry for what happened earlier today …"

"Fuck off!" yelled the actress.

John looked at her in disgust.

"Excuse me! What did you say?"

"She said, fuck off!" said her manager, smiling. "And now listen carefully, Mr Seventh. You're a big shot in this industry but she's a chosen performer by the god himself and hopefully she'll lay with him to bear his child or children. A moron like you must never ever cross his limit when it comes to such beauty. You have no idea how much patience I have for idiots like you folks."

John looked at the manager and the actress.

"What the fuck are you talking about, moron? Jackson's recovered and he's fine. What the fuck is wrong with you two now?" said John, while holding his right-hand fist beside his leg. "Make sure you stay far away from me because I'll break your face."

John then looked into the eyes of the actress.

"And I'll make sure you lay countless times with God.SED until your pussy tears off and bleeds until you …"

"Hey! Johnny boy, this guy had a tough day so far and needs to rest and close his mouth," said Michael, as he looked with concern at John, who was breathing heavily.

John continued to look straight directly into the manager's eyes.

"John, are we cool, brother?" asked Michael, his eyebrows raised.

"I'm done with this nonsense of yours, Mr Seventh," said the actress. "I need to go to my spa right now!"

"Yes, we're cool," said John, angrily. "Take her to where the fuck she wants to go and him too, before I relocate his jaw."

The manager simply smiled, sent a text message then looked back at John.

"You'll pay for your misbehaviour today, Mr Seventh, I'm not Jackson that you can fool around. I'm the manager of countless chosen actors and actresses. I can replace people like you using my powers," said the manager, as he smiled sinisterly. "I just told the authorities about what you did earlier. This was supposed to be done by Jackson but apparently he didn't want to punish you for your behaviour."

"Nice!" said John in a strange deep voice, stepping closer to the manager. "I'll be looking forward to seeing them in here. Get them out of my sight, Michael."

Michael took the actress and the manager out of the room as fast as he could. John asked everyone to take the rest of the day off. He then walked closer to DJ and Richard, who didn't seem to be willing to talk with him, and told them that he wanted to leave the studio to get some fresh air. DJ and Richard tried to tell him that he had to stay as the Arms would arrive anytime soon, but John left the studio and sat in his car.

While sitting in the vehicle, John closed his eyes and tried to calm down by breathing deeply. He was experiencing an uncontrollable anger. There was an unusual warmness in his chest that he'd never felt before. He opened his eyes and as far as he could see, there was rain falling from the sky.

"Fuck this! When the hell rain began to fall?" said John, hitting the steering wheel. "In the morning God.SED wanted people to have a sunny day and now all of a sudden he wants rain!"

His cell phone beeped. There was a text from Sara, who mentioned that she wanted to call but had no time to talk, as the hospital was overcrowded with loud patients. Sara also mentioned that she'd be late home that night.

"Great! Fuck! Fuck!" John shouted. "What a shitty day!"

He pressed on the gas paddle and drove to his home without realising that he was supposed to be in the office when the Arms arrived as he caused the incident.

Back at home, John was sitting on the bed, feeling exhausted. He couldn't even keep his eyes open any longer. His energy was completely drained.

"What is with me? I feel like I'm not me anymore," he said John as he lay on his bed.

He looked at his camera and reached for it then began recording. "Hi folks, I'm back! Wow! Look at my face. It's so pale."

He pushed his cheeks in and squeezed his chin.

"Something's happened and I suddenly began to feel sick. I was feeling great earlier, then I became super angry and ignorant and punched an actor, the kind of thing that I'd never normally do to anyone, and now I feel as if I lost all my energy. I'm now feeling really sick, as if I've got a flu or something."

John began losing consciousness.

"I need to tell Sara to come …"

John then lost consciousness before he was able to grab his cell phone.

After a while he opened his eyes and felt energetic again. "What happened?" said John, yawning. "I must have fallen asleep. Shit! The fucking Arms will have already gone to the office by now, meh, that's fine I guess, I'll just talk to the guys tomorrow."

He looked at the clock as he prepared to get off the bed. It was late at night and he'd been unconscious for three hours. He stretched, yawned again, stood up, grabbed some comfy clothes and went into the bathroom. He switched on the light, but immediately had to turn it off. The brightness was too much for him to tolerate, but something was different this time. While standing in the bathroom he could see things.

"I can see things in the dark now?"

Looking around, he noticed a weak brightness coming from beneath of the door.

"Meh!" he said. "I just thought that I could see in the dark."

John pushed the light switch. It was still too bright for him, but he waited for a while and after his eyes were adjusted to the brightness, he slowly opened them, but he wished that he hadn't. There was a battlefield view in the mirror above the sink in front of him. He was holding Sara as she cried, while they were surrounded by countless dark and faceless beasts. Other people around them were screaming and fighting with each other. John closed his eyes and shook his head. When he reopened his eyes, he saw himself with a face that was half human and half black furry wolfman.

"Stop this!" John exclaimed.

He punched the mirror and broke it, but his hand wasn't injured at all.

"You are the one!" said EZ. "You are the seventh warrior who will lead us into the gates, master."

"Where are you?" John pleaded. "You're not welcome here!"

"Master, let me in," said EZ. "Let me inside your soul. I'm connected to you but I want to enter your soul to help you unleash your powers."

"John, wake up!" said Sara, shaking him.

John opened his eyes and hugged her.

"You were having a nightmare again," she said. "Easy now, John. What the hell happened to you? You look sick! I told you to rest, but nope, who listens? Stay here and don't move. I'll get some medicine."

She tried to stand up, but John grabbed her hand.

"Don't leave me! Please don't!"

"Easy John, you're hurting my hand," said Sara.

"Sara," he said. "Something's happening. Something's going to happen, something bad, something…"

"You're burning," said Sara, attempting again to stand.

"No! Don't! Listen to me…"

John saw EZ walking towards him and began shaking violently.

"John!" shouted Sara. "What did you eat? What did you do?"

EZ smiled, went under the bed then began to chant strange rituals, as John began to shake even more.

"Let me help you, master," said EZ, as he began entering John from underneath the bed.

Sara burst into tears, as John was showing symptoms that were similar to the dying Twin Cancer patients.

"How did this happen?" she demanded, as John's lips turned black. "Why did SED curse you? What did you do to get twin fucking cancer?" said Sara, crying even harder.

She held John's hands tightly.

"Please, don't leave me, John! Please! Not now," said Sara, remembering one of her patients that had died in the same way.

John began to choke.

"Fuck! Please fight it. Why is this happening to us? What did you do today? Fight it, John! Fight it!" said Sara, her tears streaming down her face.

Chapter 9
Golden-Tablets

In the depths of the ocean, Nanny was climbing up a mountain. With each step she took, she felt as if the gravity had become stronger and the further she went the more the surroundings turned into gold. It was easy for her to climb up the rocky side of the mountain. However, the golden side had become unbearable and she fell to her knees many times and had to rest. When she reached the edge of the mountain, she collapsed from fatigue and was lifted by a very bright being that appeared in the shape of a hairless muscular man with two large golden wings and eyes through which brightness shone.

"Welcome," said the being.

"Commander," said Nanny, bowing.

The Commander smiled.

"It has been a while. I see you have consumed so much of your gift to survive in your human form."

"Commander, in order to save the seventh, I would sacrifice anything," said Nanny. "We mustn't fail or the creator will not assign us for the next universe."

"Please, before we speak any further, transform into your holy form as this body is permitted to stand on such ground," said the Commander.

Nanny stepped back and the Commander raised his right hand and unleashed a bright light towards her. The energy hit Nanny and she began to transform into a being that resembled the Commander. She didn't hesitate or hide her emotions and hugged him, but then quickly stopped and stepped back.

"Thank you, Commander," said Nanny.

"You are welcome, Jessica."

Jessica smiled.

"The war is about to begin, we do not have much time left, as you know," said the Commander, looking up at a massive whale swimming in the ocean that surrounded the protective shield around the golden mountain. "Their army is larger than we ever imagined. They own the elements already. All they need is perhaps the seventh, or an extra ordinary source of power that can complete the ritual."

"Commander ..." Jessica began.

"We are not at the training host," he said. "Call me by my name please."

"As you command, Gabriel," Jessica replied. "I know that someone brave from the community fulfilled the prophecy and exposed John to the image of the cross, but I believe that didn't work at all. The mist is too strong for his body to overcome."

She edged closer to him.

"We might need to ..."

"Using that much energy may keep you in here longer than you should be," said Gabriel. "Your time is well served and for that you will be glorified with the larger golden wings. However, if you change your future by using the power of the spirit for such simple things, you will not have a determined chance of returning to where you belong."

He looked at ocean above him.

"It is delightful that humans have still failed to discover much of the deep oceans, especially this holy place, or else they would destroy it as they did the shallows," said Gabriel.

"Gabriel, I may have no choice," said Jessica. "I may lose a few feathers but that won't stop me from going back home."

Gabriel smiled.

"Walk with me, Jessica.".

She did as he instructed.

"When you were created, you were already marked as a helper, but you turned out to be more than just a helper," said Gabriel. "You became a protector, just like the other higher ranking angel, which frankly amazed us all."

"I won't let that happen," said Jessica. "I'll remain above the required limit, so that I can return to the host."

She noticed that Gabriel seemed to be concerned about something.

"What's bothering you, Gabriel," she asked.

"A new image appeared on the **Golden-Tablets**[24]," he replied.

Jessica was shocked.

"The one that we'd never seen before?" she said. "What was it, Gabriel?"

"A white furry wolfman that had the symbolic number seventh on his chest," he replied.

Jessica shook her head.

"It can't be my John, I raised him. It can't be. He was exposed to the image of the cross through a sacrifice of a human. This is exactly what was needed to prevent him from turning into a wolf."

"How would his spirit turn into an animal form without being exposed to such darkness?" asked Gabriel.

"There's no dark power like that on Earth yet," said Jessica. "Am I wrong?"

"Not as of this time," he replied. "However, we need to be careful not to let him be tricked or exposed to any dark powers or else he will ..."

"He will not serve Lucifer," said Jessica. "I know my child. I raised him and I won't let him be exposed to anything. He'll fight alongside us and against the darkness. I can assure you of that."

Gabriel placed his hands on Jessica's shoulders.

"I do believe that," he said. "You surely have made us all proud, especially Natasha, but we must be certain of everything always."

"How is she, Gabriel?" asked Jessica.

"She has become a battle trainer ever since she was permitted to return to the Holy-Host," he replied.

"Natasha?" said Jessica. "Training angels to fight? That's unexpected."

"Just like you, who were chosen to help yet became a protector, so did she become a trainer," said Gabriel.

"Agreed," said Jessica. "I miss her, Gabriel."

"She has been missing you too." Said Gabriel, flapping his wings. "Do you want to sit on the **Golden-Chairs**[25] again?"

"Oh, my god," said Jessica. "It's been such a long time. Of course I'd love to."

---

[24] Golden-Tablets: Two pieces of large gold tablets on which images of some of the important incidents of the future are displayed to ensure that angels are aware of important future events.

[25] Golden-Chairs: Two massive energising chairs that would help to recharge the powers of angels.

Two massive golden chairs appeared out on the golden ground in front of them. They felt very comfortable despite being made from solid gold bricks. Jessica sat on one of the chairs and flapped her wings, while Gabriel sat on the other one and did the same. They began to glow with a golden aura while they received the spiritual empowerment. A few minutes were long enough to make their feathers grow longer and thicker and for their bodies to become more muscular.

Jessica was very relaxed and happy by the end of the empowerment. It had been a long time since she'd felt that way. She closed her eyes and wished for nothing else than staying there for as long as she could.

Gabriel stood up, flipped his feathers then walked towards a creature that was looking at him a short distance from the empowerment chairs and began patting it. Jessica opened her eyes and saw Gabriel standing by a creature that had never been discovered by humans. Jessica stood up, flipped her wings then walked over to them.

"I know, Gabriel, haven't seen one since Antarctica turned into an ice land," said Jessica, as she stood beside Gabriel and patted the animal, which then went back to where it had come from.

"It is good to have a telepathic connection to avoid scaring such sensitive and rare creatures, which die the moment they feel stressed," said Gabriel.

"Yes, indeed," said Jessica.

Suddenly, they stood motionless. Gabriel made a fist and looked at Jessica with great concern.

"You see, Golden-Tablets never fail," he said. "They never fail to warn us about the dangers of the future. I took a huge risk to come to Earth but if this risk helps us stop John from getting his spirit ..."

He paused then looked at Jessica.

"You need to go back now, Jessica!" said Gabriel, as he began rushing towards his *Transporter*[26].

"But I can't fight with EZ, Gabriel!" she replied. "I can't match his powers!"

"I will have to take care of something first, but I will be there before you even know it," said Gabriel. "Please go now before it is too late."

"I'll be waiting for you at the house," said Jessica.

---

[26] Transporter: A flying saucer made of gold.

Gabriel nodded his head as his Transporter began to float into the air. Jessica flew down the mountain, sat in her Transporter and after the flying saucer turned invisible, she flew away.

Chapter 10
I Remember the Past Now

John was shaking and Sara and Chris were trying to hold him still as best as they could in the bedroom. John was chanting rituals, while foam was coming out of his mouth.

Chris was a doctor at T.C. hospital, a close colleague and a friend to Sara. She'd called him in the middle of the night and asked him to rush to her house to save John's life. As soon as he arrived, Chris knew that John wouldn't survive. He was using all his medical expertise to prevent John from getting worse but no matter what he did it wouldn't work as John's condition was deteriorating. Chris was also kicked hard in the face multiple times while holding John but wasn't giving up. Sara on the other hand was crying and unable to think of any other things that might improve John's condition.

John was trying to resist the influential power of EZ but the more he resisted, the more he was weakened. EZ was manipulating the power of the spirit inside John with his dark powers, to turn his spirit in a sinister manner.

"Master, a little bit more and your wild side will be unleashed," said EZ, as he scratched John on the back. "I cannot wait until the day we crush them all and I return to the place where I was abandoned, just like the others."

Blood dripped from the corner of John's mouth. Sara screamed, knowing that he was about to die.

"No, please! No!" she shouted.

Time seemed to slow down for John. He felt the presence of a cold stream around his feet and felt as he was being pulled out from his body. As the pull increased, John closed his eyes.

"No!" EZ yelled. "You were not supposed to be here, Death!"

"You are killing him instead of transforming the power of his spirit, idiot!" said Death.

"I will prove you wrong, Death," said EZ.

He bit John's back and from his blood the black mist entered John's body.

"Enjoy the gift, master," said EZ. "Let the wolf inside you be unleashed."

John shouted then stopped breathing.

Chris looked at Sara and in his eyes she could see what he meant. Chris nodded and looked at John.

"Farewell, my friend," said Chris, sadly.

Sara thumped John on the chest.

"You fucking asshole! How can you leave me alone? John! Please!"

She placed her head on his chest.

"Don't leave me, not now," she said, crying.

EZ laughed as he listened to Sara.

"Don't fight it, master. Receive it and let it flourish."

A bright light broke into the room and time stopped moving forward. The bright light separated EZ from John by burning EZ's face. He roared and moved to the corner of the ceiling.

"You have no right to take expose him to darkness when he will never join him!" shouted Jessica, while the brightness dimmed.

Jessica then looked at Death.

"His time hasn't come yet, why would you even come here?" Jessica shouted.

Death smiled.

"Do you wish to challenge me?" he asked, as he looked into Jessica's bright eyes.

"I challenge you, not!" she replied. "But this is not his time. You know it. Don't do what you did to his parents, you …"

"Silence!" Death roared, as the windows shattered. "Never, never speak to me in that tone again or you will lose those wings. Do not forget where you are. You have restrictions on Earth before the war."

Death slowly began to disappear. Jessica looked at EZ.

"What have you done?" she asked. "Why?"

EZ was shielding his eyes with his hands, which were burning.

"I lost so much power to transform the spirit inside John," replied EZ. "And I see that you have empowered your power of spirit to the point that I cannot fight you at this moment. You wouldn't last a second."

A sphere energy began to appear in Jessica's palm.

"How dare you doing this to my little boy," shouted Jessica then hit EZ with the energy. EZ roared and disappeared.

Jessica looked at John. She could feel the presence of a strong dark energy inside him now. She closed her eyes, transformed into the shape of Nanny and time resumed its normal speed. The room, the house, and the entire neighbourhood were dark and quiet. The fire trucks' sirens could be heard from afar.

Nanny stood close to bed, holding lighted candles. "What's going on in here, children?" she asked.

Sara and Chris were in awe at seeing Nanny in the room where virtually nothing was left in proper shape.

"What's going on in here?" asked Nanny again. "Why is John laying on the bed like that? Did you guys fight with intruders or anyone?"

She pointed at the broken windows, broken glass, and at the cracked wall.

Sara looked at John, who was now healthy, his eyes wide open. She then looked at Chris, who had saliva dribbling from his mouth then looked back at Nanny, who seemed very calm.

"John was shaking," said Sara. "He … he … got the Twin-Cancer and I didn't know what to do, so …so … I called Chris to come over and help."

She removed broken glass from her hair and hugged John.

"He was almost gone and then you showed up out of nowhere and…"

"My dear," said Nanny. "I came to this currently dark house several minutes ago and I kept calling out loud to find out if anyone was at home. I then heard some noises coming out from upstairs, so I put my luggage by the door and rushed up here but then apparently something exploded on the street that caused the power to go off. It was loud enough that it even broke the windows."

She looked at Chris.

"It's good to see you in here again, Chris. Are you sure John has the blessing of God.SED?"

Chris swallowed his saliva.

"I don't… I don't know anymore. He was almost dead and now he looks as fine as I am," he replied, while packing his stuff in hurry.

Nanny looked at John.

"How are you feeling, my dear?"

John hugged Sara harder.

"He went through a lot, Nanny" said Sara, her tears falling on John's chest. "We're still in shock about everything. Let's figure out how long the power will be out and start cleaning up this mess first. Then we'll talk about how he ended up having the blessing and how the heck this house turned into trash like this"

Nanny began gazing into John's eyes of and immediately stepped back in shock.

"What happened, Nanny?" asked Sara.

"Nothing dear, he's indeed still sick," said Nanny, as she tried not to make any further eye contact with John. "Fortunately Doctor Chris is here and can write a few prescriptions to fix him up perhaps."

Chris didn't seem to want to stay there at all but he looked at Nanny and nodded his head.

The power suddenly came back on.

"Yay!" Sara exclaimed.

"I better go downstairs and prepare some stuff for you all to eat," said Nanny. "I hope his condition isn't too bad, Doctor Chris."

Chris nodded.

"I'm going to examine him again to find out."

"Perfect. Dear, would you give me a hand in kitchen?" Nanny asked Sara.

"Of course, Nanny" replied Sara, as she separated herself from John and hugged Nanny. "I'm really glad that you came back home. I don't know what I'd do without you if something would happen to—"

"Shish!" said Nanny. "Let's forget about the past and just look forward to a better future."

"Whatever you say," said Sarah, looking at John. "He definitely looks sick. I'll sweep the floor after we eat."

They both then left the room, as Chris took a deep breath.

"You scared us, buddy. I don't know what happened but consider yourself very lucky to survive."

He then began a physical check-up on John.

After having some cookies and *Choco-Loco*[27] then helping Sara and Nanny with the cleanings, Chris wrote a few medical prescriptions. He gave the list to Sara and after running another quick physical check on John, he left.

"How are you feeling now? You haven't spoken a word since you magically recovered from the blessing of SED." Asked Sara.

---

[27] Choco-Loco: Hot chocolate.

"I'm still alive," John replied, drinking some soup.

"I'm glad to hear that," said Nanny while sweeping. "It could have been worse."

"True, Nanny," said Sara. "I'll do the sweeping, you just came from your so-called vacation. By the way, how was it?"

John nodded.

"How was your short vacation?" asked John, suspiciously. "Where did you end up going exactly? The beach or the centre?"

"I went to the centre, as I told you both, and did some sightseeing," said Nanny. "Then I decided it was time to come back."

"Right, you told me you were going to beach, but told Sara about Middle Earth," said John, slightly irritated. "I don't understand why you're obsessed with that location.".

Nanny avoided engaging John in conversation by looking at Sara.

"I didn't want him to send Safe Guards to where I was, so that I could enjoy a day without idiots following me around," said Nanny.

"Didn't I tell you, John?" said Sara. "It's so annoying that every time we go anywhere far from *West-Lands*[28], you call on those lunatics."

John looked suspiciously at Nanny.

"Hmm, so you dodge the fact that there's something weird with you and that impact site, by bringing up an excuse that I annoy you two by calling the guards every time you guys go far away, huh? Also, your vacation lasted no time at all. You needed ultrasonic speed to come back here. No train would travel that fast."

"I see your brain is fully functional, John," said Nanny. "Aren't you two supposed to sleep now? Don't you have to work tomorrow? Weren't you sick a while ago?"

John held Sara's hand, as she tried to feed him.

"All I do is make sure that you ladies are always safe. This is what a real man does. Protecting women is what we do."

"Er, John, we get it, no need for a lengthy lecture," said Sara. "Let's go, mister. You need to rest more. But John's right, Nanny. How did you come back so fast?"

Nanny remained quiet as she swept the floor. Sara put her hand in John's hair.

"You almost died," she said. "Let's go to bed, John. It's been a long night."

---

[28] West-Lands: The western territories of the super continent.

John tried to say something, but stopped as Sara began pulling him towards the stairwell.

A few minutes later, John opened his eyes as he heard his name being called.

"Wake up, John," said Jessica.

"Sara, is it morning already?" asked John.

"I'm not Sara," said Jessica. "Wake up!"

"Who are you? Am I dreaming?" said John, shielding his eyes from Jessica's brightness.

"No, this isn't a dream and I'm your Nanny," said Jessica.

"You ain't a Nanny," said John. "What are you? What did you do to my Nanny?"

"I'm an angel and lived with you in this form to protect you until the rightful day," said Jessica. "Nanny never really existed."

"What the fu…"

John tried to say something but Jessica interrupted.

"Hold it! No cursing in front of me," she said. "You know how I hate it."

John closed his mouth.

"We have limited time to discuss several topics, but before that I need to take you to your *Tree of Memories*[29]. You can use it as you have the Holy Spirit in you," said Jessica, moving closer to John.

"Lady, or whatever you are, stay back!" said John. "I don't need …"

Jessica interrupted him by placing her hand on his chest and chanting rituals.

"What are you doing to me?" asked John then began to fall unconscious.

John found himself in an intense brightness. After adjusting to the light, he noticed a colourless tree in the middle of the ground on which he was standing. He looked around at his surroundings.

"Nanny? Hello! Where am I? Where is this place? What a beautiful tree."

He walked towards it and after reaching the tree, he looked carefully to see what it was made of.

"Touch me," said the being that looked like a colourless tree.

"I beg your pardon?" said John.

"Touch me," said the being.

John looked around. There was nothing except him and the being.

"I'm not going to do that," said John.

---

[29] Tree of Memories: A terrestrial tree that contains all the universal memories of mankind.

"Touch me now!" the being shouted.

"Alright! Jeez! What's up with the attitude?" said John then walked closer to the being and reached out his hand.

He touched the body of the being cautiously and immediately remembered the time when he was a youth. He saw himself and Sara skipping school and running into a forest. He saw them hiding behind a large oak tree that Sara loved so much while holding Sara's hands.

"John, do you love me?" asked Sara.

"Love is nothing compared to what I feel for you," John replied.

"Would you do anything I told you to?" she asked.

"As long as it doesn't get me killed, ya sure," replied John.

"Kiss me!" said Sara.

John swallowed his saliva, closed his eyes and prepared to kiss Sara. She removed her shoes and stepped on John's feet, raised her ankles and kissed him.

It was their first kiss and John opened his eyes and looked at Sara, who was shy and keeping her head down. "Can we do it again?" asked John.

"We'll do it again and again from now on," said Sara. "This is fun and we suck at kissing, so we must do it more."

She stepped back onto John's feet and looked up.

"Do you love me?" she asked.

"Girl, I'm only ten years old but I know for sure that I do love you."

He took a dried red rose from his jacket pocket.

"Here, this is for you," said John.

Sara held the rose and looked back up.

"It's so beautiful," she said.

"Ya," said John. "It looks just like you."

Sara smiled and put her head down. John gently lifted her chin.

"Don't be shy."

Sara smiled and looked straight into John's eyes.

"You're more beautiful than anything I've ever seen in my life so far, my lady," said John.

Sara smiled.

"Will you have this much charm and love for me from now until we get married and even after that?" she asked.

"I'll have them forever, my lady," replied John.

"Let's kiss again," said Sara.

John kissed her.

"What you two idiots are doing in here?" shouted the headmistress.

John moved Sara behind him.

"Experiencing love, headmistress Merry?" said John, smiling, as Sara giggled.

The headmistress pulled John's ear, holding it with one hand, then with other hand she held and pulled Sara's ear. The headmistress then took them to her office and contacted their parents. They soon arrived and the parents stood beside the youths, keeping their heads down.

John pulled his hand back from the tree.

"How did I forget this?" he asked. "I vowed to myself never to forget my first kiss. How did I forget this?"

He exhaled and placed his hand back on the being.

"We need to buy rings for them, Tommy," John's father whispered in the ears of Sara's father, while sitting close to the window.

"I agree, Paul." Whispered Tom. "Our kids apparently grew up faster than we thought. They need to obtain the traditional ways and prevent themselves from committing sins before their wedding."

"What exactly were you two doing in the woods?" asked Sara's mom.

"Answer Aunt Tasha," John's mom added.

"We needed some personal private talk away from everyone, so we ended up going in the woods," said John, as Sara held his hand.

"You two couldn't delay that important 'personal talk' until you're older, could you?" asked John's mom.

"Answer Aunt Natasha," said Tasha.

"Nope!" said Sara. "We had to do it right away. It's what everyone's doing these days."

"Enough!" the headmistress exclaimed, while looking at the parents. "You have to wash their mouths with soap. Your children were kissing each other! Today they kissed and tomorrow they will…"

"What's wrong with kissing?" asked John, winking at Sara.

"Tom," said Paul. "We have to meet the father and get the kids blessed with the rings as soon as possible. Curiosity often leads to irreversible acts. It was just a kiss but kids are different these days. They may do other stuff if there's no proper precautions."

"You see!" said the headmistress. "Your children need to learn manners! You need to become better parents by teaching them how to stay from sinning! Father Tim must be informed immediately to make sure these wild souls will not commit further sins. You must get them the rings immediately and take them through the holy ceremony."

"Yes, Sister Merry," replied Natasha. "We'll get them the rings first thing in the morning tomorrow."

"What rings are you guys talking about, Mom?" asked Sara.

"The promise rings," Tasha replied.

"What are the rings for, Mom?" asked John.

"Keep quiet, naughty boy," said Natasha, glancing at Paul. "He surely has his father's blood in him."

"Affirmative," said Paul, smiling and winking at John.

Sara held John's hand again and whispered in his ear.

"Are we getting married?" she asked.

"I guess so, I mean, if you want us to," whispered John.

"Yes, I want to," she whispered back.

"Me too," said John. "We have to think of buying a house to practice kissing in private, don't you think?"

"Silly boy, those rings are virginity rings. One of the girls got one couple of weeks ago." Whispered Sara.

"Damn, you're right. How come I didn't think of that? Well, virginity or wedding rings, you're mine girl," said John, as he narrowed his eyes.

"Enough you two, with the whispering," said Natasha. "It's not noisy in here, you know." Sara and John smiled.

"We're sorry for this, Sister Merry, and we'll make sure that the kids will behave according to the religion's laws," said Natasha, looking at Sara and John. "Are we clear about this, lady and gentleman?"

"We promise! Please forgive us Sister Merry," said the Sara and John in unison yet in a sarcastic way.

"Young love leads to sinful behaviour, so make sure they get the holy rings and teach them manners. They know about the chastity rings yet questioned what the precious rings were! Oh, sinful children," said Sister Merry, looking at Paul and Tom. "May God protect us all, amen!"

"Amen! We apologise for this, Sister Merry," said Tommy. "We need to help them to grow in righteousness through the teaching of the holy son of god. You have a good rest of your day."

He and the others then left the headmistress's office.

John recalled the memory of the ring receiving ceremony at church. Tasha and Natasha were explaining the importance of what Sara and John were about to witness. Sara and John were kneeling in front of a wooden altar, waiting for the father of the church who was praying, to bring the silver rings. John slowly turned his head and looked at Sara then smiled and she smiled back. The father walked around them while praying and moved his hand making the symbol of cross.

"By wearing these rings, you are bonded together and to the lord in the heavens through the holy spirit."

He handed the rings to Sara and John.

"Wear these rings to always remind yourselves of the importance of honouring the god's commandment. Will you obey his commandments, children?"

John and Sara nodded their heads.

"Good," said the father. "Let these rings be a barrier between you and your temptation and let them be a path to god."

John looked at Sara and winked.

"Now," the father added. "Look into each other's eyes and repeat after me."

Tasha and Natasha were holding hands and tears were falling from their eyes. On the other side, Paul was standing beside Tom, who was taking pictures.

"Forgive us, father, for we have sinned. Accept us once again under your wings. Let us see the righteousness and the righteous path. Bless our souls and our love. Give us the patience and wisdom of flourishing in true love rather than lust."

John and Sara looked at each other as they repeated his words. John then noticed a message that was written on the rings.

"You may now wear the rings," said the father.

John read the message on his ring.

"True love waits?" he said, confused, as Sara pushed the ring onto his finger.

"It means no ding ding and no mua mua without the wedding ring," said Sara, smiling.

"No kissing and touching and stuff until marriage?" said John, as he pushed the ring onto Sara's finger.

"Children! Behave!" said the father angrily. "Lord have mercy on you two! You just said the righteous vows and yet talking about sinning?"

"Father Tim, they are still young as you know and this was perhaps too soon for them to go through," said Tom. "But we can assure you that they will follow the path and will not fail. Are we clear, children?"

"Yes, true love definitely will wait," said Sara and John, while giggling.

"These children will not go to heaven. They are born …"

Father Tim was interrupted by Paul.

"Enough, father!" he said, angrily. "We get it. Thank you for your service. We'll have a private chat on Sunday regarding this matter. Everyone, let's move out."

John pulled his hand away from the being. He could feel the ring on his finger.

"Those bloody rings. Sara wouldn't even kiss after wearing the goddamn rings. She'll not be happy once she gets her memories back, that's for sure. I'd better not tell her about the rings. I can't live without kissing her. Nope, no rings, but where the hell are the rings now?"

John took a deep breath and this time placed both his hands on the tree. He went through a large portion of his memories. He kept remembering the incidents of the past until he remembered a time he wished he hadn't. He pulled his hands back and looked at the being.

"My parents need to be avenged," said John, angrily. "So do Sara's parents."

The branches of the being shook.

"I see that you agree with me," said John then suddenly lost consciousness.

"John!" said Jessica. "Do you remember now?".

John opened his eyes and leaned on his elbows while lying on the bed.

"I remember a lot of things now," he replied.

"I'm glad you have your memories recovered," said Jessica. "A lot will return to you over the next few weeks, so prepare for some flashbacks here and there."

"Wait …Wait …Who are you again?" asked John. "What exactly is going on in here?"

"Kid! My name's Jessica, as I mentioned before."

She looked at the clock and transformed into the shape of Nanny. John shook his head and looked at her.

"I'm your angelic guardian, more like your magical stepmother," Nanny replied.

"What's happening to me?" asked John.

Nanny shook her head.

"It's a lot to take in. I'm sorry John but this isn't a game anymore. This is reality. You're awake. You're not like them out there, doing the same thing every day without realising that they're living among demons," said Jessica.

John didn't say anything. He then laid his head back on the pillow.

"How did SED enter the world so easily? I can't believe the anti-Christ is really here now," said John, in disappointment.

"It wasn't that easy, humans made it easy for them to come. The wickedness surpassed the limit," Nanny replied.

John nodded his head.

"Humans were told for so long about the consequences of their actions throughout history," Nanny continued. "They allowed reptilian humanoids to lead them in exchange for power, money, and things that brought darkness closer to the surface of the firmament. In short, the sons of Lucifer."

"The sons of Lucifer?" said John, shocked.

"Satan has two sons, Devil and Evil," Nanny explained. "Their mother was Lilith, the first female human ever created. She was equal to Adam and when Adam asked god for a weaker partner, Lilith joined Lucifer and gave birth to the sons. She was spectacular. She was pure, beautiful, and strong, until she completely committed herself to Lucifer and their master. Things turned dark and she used the darkness against humans and the heavens."

John began sitting with his legs crossed.

"Where are the sons of Lucifer now?" he asked.

Jessica dragged the newspaper close to John and pointed at the picture of God.SED.

"SED is the sons?" asked John. "Are they both in the same body?"

"Yes, they're attached to each other under that fake skin," said Jessica.

"How come we've been so blind? There's so much evil around us and we don't even see it," said John, while scratching his head.

"I know that you're confused, shocked, and loaded with information from the past, and you'd perhaps want to rest rather than chatting with me," said

Jessica. "But you need to know about all of this as much as you can because the other side somehow cheated and exposed your spirit to the wrong side first. The more you know about the truth, the less your spirit gets affected by the darkness," said Jessica.

John stayed quiet.

"I can read your mind, so don't think of anything else except the things I'm telling you. Eating ice cream can wait, this is serious John!" said Jessica, so John stayed quiet, looking at her with wide open eyes. "Listen, there are Golden-Tablets in the Holy-Host that showed an image of a white furry wolfman."

"Tablets what? Please speak in human language," said John. "It's late and I can't process and understand the words coming out of your human mouth, Nanny, I mean Jessica."

"Just listen for now and later you'll have all the answers. I have limited time to give you as much information as possible," said Jessica.

"Alright, I don't know why time is an issue for you now but sure, let's move on to another important topic," said John. "Tell me more about EZ? I've seen him in wolf shape and yes, that white furry wolfman is me. I've had visions of myself being in the form of a wolf, so whatever those tablets are, they showed the truth. My spirit is surely exposed to the wolf side rather than the calm side."

"EZ, or Edward Znock, was the chosen one before you. He was an excellent half-human half-angel whose spirit didn't get manipulated the way yours was. He was also trained enough to begin becoming a guardian. EZ was trained by Gabriel from the early stages of his life on the *Training-Host[30]*, the place that's called the Garden of Eden by humans, is not the way people described it on Earth. The garden is on an invisible massive Transporter or a spaceship flying continually near Earth's firmament without humans even noticing it. EZ was brought up to the host and was trained by Gabriel, or the Commander of all the angels. Yet when EZ met Lucifer, who was quite a lot stronger in the previous thousand-years' war, EZ was unfortunately spiritually and mentally manipulated by him. EZ turned into what he is, as Lucifer entered his body that still wasn't fully transformed into a guardian, fought countless victorious battles against angels who were way stronger than it, and because EZ was unable to transform into the final stage of his spirit power, his human body began to decay, which caused Lucifer to lose the war. However, Lucifer liked him so much that he spared his life. He used the remaining dark spirit powers left in EZ to keep him

---

[30] Training-Host: The Garden of Eden.

alive for fulfilling other objectives. Yes, if you don't turn your spirit power from what it has been exposed to, into the final stage of the power that turns you into a **_Holy-Guardian_**[31] or the one who will be used by the creator's son to destroy Lucifer, you and we all will face a big problem. You may ultimately even die."

John stretched his neck and arms.

"Stop here please. I didn't understand a bloody word you just said. Let me rephrase this to my level of understanding. So, EZ was like me and then he was trained by Gabriel and then he met Satan, and then liked him more than angels, and then Satan possessed him and used him against angels and then because he was basically like a parasite, EZ turned into a very weak human and then I don't know how he became a wolf. Is this correct so far?" asked John.

Nanny nodded.

"I wonder how all these fighters get tricked all the time," John added. "I mean, how can an angel change its mind when they only see god and his goodness? Satan must be a godlike creature if he can turn good into evil and carry on with it for all these centuries."

"No, he isn't godlike. There's another force out there that's godlike," she replied. "The one who tricked Lucifer. Before the era of existence there were two powerful creators. Both were in harmony until a rivalry for power began between them that resulted in the creation of all creations and the end of eternal peace. At the beginning there was only light and no darkness in the universe, but during the war between the creators, one of them whom we know as Darkness, the one who tricked Lucifer, consumed the light from the universe by attacking its source of creation. He liked it, so he made it his mission to consume everything that had light energy to gain more power. The curse of the war is that the gods are the cause of each other's deaths. Because one's now the source of creation and the other the source of destruction, they feed on each other every time they get close. If they mix, everything ends, so they stay away from each other and send us in front to fight their battles for them."

"That's very selfish, but I knew it, I always knew there was something that the negative energy was driven from," said John, as he tangled his hands and fingers behind his head. "I always questioned the reason early angels turned into demons. Everything makes sense now. But holy cow, so we're just born to fight wars that we didn't want to create?"

---

[31] Holy-Guardian: A very powerful angel that is used to destroy the Satan.

"Well, yes, and no," said Jessica firmly. "It's just very complicated to explain it all. All you have to know is that you need to have your spirit fighting for the light rather than the darkness if you want to go to heaven. Also, EZ's DNA includes wolf genes, the reason why he turned into a wolfman, and strangely so did you. You two are the only humans with wolf genes. Other chosen ones before you had other animal genes."

John tried to say something but Jessica interrupted.

"Yes, yes, I can read your mind and thoughts. We had fish man, rhino man, bird man and so on. I don't even know why they were all men. Maybe it's a curse or a blessing, but we're still not clear why men were chosen to fight the battles of gods."

"Who knows, maybe there'll be another chosen one after me that's a female," said John, winking.

"No, there will be no other ones after you, as stated in the heavenly prophecies and tablets. You're the last of your kind, the seventh warrior. Your final decision will change the history of the world. That's the reason why we need to make sure you receive angelic training and learn how to control your animal or dark spirit, as well as learn how to become an angelic warrior," said Jessica.

"Be optimistic, lady. When am I starting my training?" asked John.

"Soon," Nanny replied.

"I have more questions about the tree looking thing that I saw and about how you and my mother ended up in here," said John. "Please, tell me."

"The tree is called the **Hok**[32]," said Jessica. "It's designed in the shape of the tree of life, the one Adam and Eve thought they ate from, the source all other sources. No one knows how the tree itself came into existence because if we learn about it, we'll know the origin of all origins and we'll become godlike."

"So, Adam and Eve are godlike then after eating the fruit of the tree of life," said John, looking impressed.

"Wrong," said Nanny, as John remained quiet and listened carefully. "Firstly, the tree of life doesn't bear any fruit. It contains a special liquid substance that transforms weakness into absoluteness. There's never been an apple or an orange anywhere that gave wisdom to ordinary creatures. It was always the liquid that changed everything. Adam and Eve were tricked into drinking from the Hok that contained the blood of Lilith, Adam's equal. Her

[32] Hok: The tree of life.

blood contained dark powers that came directly from Darkness. After Adam and Even drank from the blood, their spiritual bodies transformed into physical bodies. God never punished them with transformation and it was them that were punished by their own deeds. God simply expelled them from heaven because no one lives up there with blood rushing through their system."

"Every creature that our god creates has a Hok. The reason is that the elders kept saying that god saw everything, heard everything, and knew everything about everything he created. The Hoks are memory stores that never run out of space and contain a blood sample of the human they are made for. The idea behind your digital memory storage came straight from the existence of the Hoks. Now, how this knowledge was distributed to humans, we'll discuss later. I showed you your memory storage so that you could familiarise yourself with using it. Hoks are designed for single individuals and only those individuals can have access to them. No one else can see them, not even god. Stop asking too many questions in your mind, John. God can access your memories if you worship him. If you choose his side, worship him, and pray to him, he'll be able to review your memories, access to your life directly, and began fixing it according to your comprehension level. He can access the Hok if he wants to, but he's given humans free will to choose that option for him. Consider it an ultimate privacy option given to humans by their creator so that they can also feel super special and godlike. God is awesome, to be honest. He's the only god that does that for the humans. Yes, yes, if you choose to worship and serve Satan, your Hok will be placed in a place we all know as hell. God will not have any access to your Hok whatsoever and we know for fact that Satan and Darkness don't play by the same fair rules of not interfering with your private personal memories. The moment you choose the dark side, you're directly vulnerable to Satan and Darkness and there's always no way out of it. It's because a dark shield is formed around your soul that completely disconnects you from god. That's why even prayers don't help some people that have become completely under the influence of dark powers."

She smiled at John.

"I know, again I can read your mind. Adam and Eve didn't have any Hoks as they were directly connected to god, just like angels and other heavenly creatures. Only humans receive Hoks and that because they'll be judged according to the memories collected by them throughout their lives. Adam and Eve couldn't possibly receive any knowledge if they simply touched Lilith's tree because the Hok wouldn't reveal anything to them. They were tricked to drink from the blood of the tree, which connected them to Lilith, Satan, and Darkness directly. God could even keep them in heaven but because of the cleansing power of Light or the heavenly spirit of the heavens, Adam and Eve would automatically be terminated. After all, their blood contained darkness, weakness, and a contingency of sources that were and are considered threats to the heavenly world. In simple words, anything impure and of other entities is terminated immediately in the heavens. You'll learn about all of this when your training begins."

She paused before continuing.

"Your mom, Sara's mom, other helpers, and I were all born in the guardian angel helpers' category of heaven. Yes, even in heaven we have categories for angels and their ranks. Our duties were basically to scout and find out where darkness was growing and inform the guardian angels about the locations then simply watch them deploy to the areas and fight the battles that we didn't have ability to engage in. When we were assigned to our objectives on Earth, we were told to only observe and report and do nothing else as the planet was already infested with darkness that could draw us towards committing acts that would never let us to return to heaven. A single sin of any kind would stop us from returning to heaven in simple words. However, when we came down to Earth, regardless of our previous training and all our preparations, we failed to stand against sinning. We all just committed sins of all kinds."

John smiled and nodded his head.

"Days and nights passed and we continued scouting, gathering information and falling more in love with Earth," said Nanny. "Yes, John, we were and are the aliens that humans always talked about until SED came to this planet. Some called us angels, some demons, and some simply referred to us as good and bad aliens. You sure think a lot while I'm talking."

"And you sure read my mind constantly," said John.

"Anyhow," Nanny continued, "we were scouting a few areas where there were many churches and found your father and Sara's father in one of them doing what religious leaders do at churches. Natasha and Tasha fell in love right at the door of the church, as if they'd known Paul and Tom forever. I mean, who wouldn't? Two young and handsome male humans that would never have the power to control us or ever match our intellectual power. Whether it was love or feeling superior, it tied the knots for your parents. No, I'm not into humans, I find my kind attractive. Stop thinking weird thoughts, John. I also wanted to return to heaven at all costs. I found Earth boring and dangerous to live in. Natasha and Tasha began dating, despite the orders and rules and one thing led to another and they gave up their wings to stay on Earth."

John clapped slowly.

"They got lucky that they weren't completely punished, otherwise they would have turned into demons. They just lost their wings to return to heaven but continued to possess their angelical powers because they weren't born humans and so didn't lose any original gifts. Now, Commander Gabriel paid us a visit during those early days of our accepting to live on Earth. After the final decision was made, he took the wings from Natasha and Tasha and granted me immunity from darkness on Earth, which is literally an invisible angelical shield that permits me to live on Earth as an angel but also have the ability to go back to heaven anytime I want to. The reason behind this was that the Golden Tablets showed you as the next chosen one and we needed someone to look after you because we knew your parents wouldn't because of the events that occurred at that time. Well, I accepted knowing that I had a purpose that would let me serve the Light beyond the level that I ever served before. It was and is the highest honour for some angel like me to turn from a helper to protector and soon into a guardian. Anyways, I observed the Earth's spirit and transformed into younger version of Nanny and then what I am now, the very old version of Nanny."

John quietly listened as Nanny continued to explain.

"During the war between humans and the satanic twins, your fathers were captured by some demonic units. They fought as best as they could, but they were critically injured. In order to save them, your mothers made deals with Death. They agreed to submit their spirit powers or their holiness in order to keep the men alive. However, Tom was too weak to survive and Natasha and Tasha no longer had powers to heal him. Because of his severe injuries, he didn't survive more than a few hours. His soul was taken to the Nowhere land[33] and Tasha was taken to the underworld and turned into a demon. As for Paul, he survived but knowing that Natasha would turn into a demon, he made a deal with Death. Paul asked Death to allow him to serve as a personal butler for eternity, in exchange for Natasha's free pass to the heavens. He knew if Natasha could go back she'd regain her powers, because she'd sacrificed herself to save him.

---

[33] Nowhere land: The land where souls remain and wait until the judgment day.

Consequently she would indeed be rewarded in return once she'd reach the heavens. The deal was accepted by Death."

"Where's my dad now exactly?" asked John.

"You need to ask Death," Nanny replied. "He could be anywhere, doing anything that he's told to do."

"Where is Nowhere land?" asked John.

"The place that all souls are taken into first. It's a very quiet place I must say," replied Nanny.

"If I'm half angel, that makes Sara half angel too, right?" asked John.

"Yes, by birth, not by power," said Nanny. "Half humans are directly connected to their hosts or mothers through spirit. If a host loses its holy powers, so will her children. Tasha lost her powers to Death and turned into a demon. Once you turn into a demon, you lose all connections to your human offspring. It's because humans can adapt to either host but so far I haven't seen any demonic adaptations in Sara's system. It may be because Tasha's constantly keeping herself as far away from Sara as she can. Yes John, you can feed on the energy of your host if the host gets close to you. You can also feed on someone you truly love. This phenomenon only happens for hybrid humans like yourself. For example, Sara got sick and you never did. She was and is a very smart girl, but she never matched your logical level. That's because you're feeding on Natasha's holy spirit constantly without you even realising it. This could be the reason why EZ couldn't turn you into a complete wolfman, despite all the powers he used against you."

John exhaled then looked at Sara, who was sleeping, before slowly kissing her left cheek.

"It's been a very long night," he said.

"I'm sorry, John. All I told you is nothing compared to what you need to know, but I guess it's more than enough for now. Your memories will come back and you'll receive your training soon, so I guess you can sleep and rest now until tomorrow," said Nanny.

She stood up and began repairing the windows and the cracks in the walls by holding her hands facing them.

"True, I'm still processing all the supernatural events that happened to me so far and having a hard time believing that this is really happening to me. I'd best sleep now and hopefully wake up in a better time," said John, as he laid his head on his pillow.

Nanny smiled, pulled the bed sheet over John and began walking towards the door.

"Nice to meet you, Jessica," said John. "Thank you for everything you've done for me and Sara so far."

"I'm still your Nanny, you don't need to be formal with me and you don't need to thank me. I'm honoured to be given this chance to experience something not all angels could ever experience. Now, sleep son, from tomorrow on things will be very different for you two, or better to say, for all of us."

Nanny closed the bedroom door.

Chapter 11
Jason

Jason was created to be a guardian, just like the other high ranking angels in heaven. However, after witnessing the fall from grace of some of the most powerful angelical creatures, such as his own brother Tyson and the hybrid EZ, Jason's faith in serving god was weakened. Consequently, he later joined the supporters of Satan.

Jason was physically weaker than other angels when the war between angels and demons began. This was because he wasn't willing to learn the skills that he required for the war, perhaps because he lost hope after witnessing his role models changing sides during the conflict. Unable to reach his required combat level and ignored by other angels that began achieving higher ranks and powers, Jason decided to gain dark knowledge in secret and open a portal between Heaven and Earth while he was still in Heaven. Jason began gaining such knowledge by connecting himself telepathically to his fallen angel brother, Tyson.

"I had to remove another feather that turned because of the Dark knowledge, Tyson," said Jason angrily in angelic language. "I can't remain hidden for so long. The truth will surface soon if I don't get the ritual now."

Jason stood beside the gates of heaven feeling anxious and distressed, as Tyson whispered demonic rituals.

"Do it, do it now, brother. Place your hands on the ground beside the gates," said Tyson in angelic language.

Suddenly, Jason was smacked into the ground by Jessica as she shot him with a powerful energy sphere.

"Stay back, Jason!" said Jessica in angelic language and other angels that saw her attacking Jason flew to join in and landed beside her. "Destroying you isn't my intention, but I will do it if you don't step back from the gates right now!"

"Whether you like it or not, these doors will be opened by the final chosen one and master Lucifer will return home again," shouted Jason in angelic language.

"What's gotten into you?" said Jessica in angelic language, holding a lethal energy sphere towards Jason. "Allowing Darkness to enter heaven will end everything! Darkness will consume the Light in here and the firmament will fall. I'll never allow anyone to do that."

Meanwhile, Tyson whispered a ritual that made Jason glow with a dark purple aura. He then made a dark purple energy sphere and held it towards Jessica and the rest of the angels. The angels immediately gathered together in a defensive formation and aimed several lethal energy spheres at Jason.

"Stop this madness, Jason," said Gabriel in angelic language, as he landed in front of all the other angels. "Lower your hand and leave in peace or I will send you to your fallen brother myself."

Gabriel began glowing with a bright golden aura, declaring his rank to Jason.

"Your powers don't match mine, Gabriel. I'm going to show you what Darkness can do," said Jason, laughing in angelic language as he held his hand towards Gabriel.

He prepared to shoot Gabriel with lethal dark purple energy, but Gabriel shot him first. Jason's wings instantly were burnt and he was smacked to the ground after rolling multiple times. Gabriel then looked at the other angels, including Jessica. The angels bowed their heads in sorrow and flew away. Gabriel flew to the burnt body of Jason that was laying on the ground, landed beside him then pulling Jason's face towards him and looked into Jason's eyes.

"This is the utmost disgrace to have you in here, Tyson. You used Lucifer's technique of entering heaven by manipulating a host, your own brother. You were both born pure," said Gabriel, with sorrow in angelical language. "How could you forsake us all for Lucifer and Darkness?"

"Oh, fuck off!" shouted Jason, in angelic language. "Enough of the lecture. This is a lost cause. They reached the heavens the last time and they'll open the gates next time. Michael will not be able to stand against the final chosen one anymore."

Gabriel wanted to say something but he didn't. He looked up and saw archangel Michael flying above them, looking concerned. Gabriel then nodded his head and Michael raised his right hand towards the gates of heaven and they were opened.

"I hereby banish you from the heavens, Jason. You and your brother have brought shame to your family and heavens. I will see you again on the judgment day," said Gabriel in angelical language.

He then grabbed Jason by the throat and threw him out of the gates. As they closed and Jason fell towards the Earth, he began transforming into a demon. Gabriel then flew to Michael and bowed his head.

"Is this true, brother Michael?" asked Gabriel in angelic language.

"We shall find out," said Michael in angelic language.

Chapter 12
We Can Do This the Easy Way,
or the Hard Way

In the silence of the studio, DJ was editing the song over the filmed scenes, while also listening to a pop song he'd composed a few minutes earlier. Richard was walking around check marking the list of the closing duties, while Michael was writing the dialogue for the next day's script.

In their minds, they were all thinking about the earlier incident between John and the staff. They knew that the Arms were on the way and sooner or later one of them would have to answer some tough questions. Eventually, they might have to call John back to the studio to handle the situation he'd created.

Michael finished typing and rubbed his eyes then looked at Richard, who was checking the filming camera beside him.

"John never gets angry like that," said Michael. "Something wasn't right with him today."

Richard put the checklist on the table.

"Absolutely! For a moment I thought we'd lose this project that we've worked so hard on. I just wanted to tie him up and ask him to shut the heck up before things got worse than they were already."

DJ stood beside Richard.

"Take it easy bruh, he wouldn't be dumb enough to," said DJ. "You're over-stressing this thing to the whole crazy high-level, man. Sure, he'd probably throw some punches here and there, but he wouldn't go further than that. After all, this film is his life. He loves this project. He wouldn't want to lose this opportunity just by assaulting bunch of chosen actors."

"I'm going to make some tea, folks," said Michael. "It's teatime, gentlemen."

Michael went to the kitchen but then rushed when he heard a loud knock on the main door.

"I think units are here!" said Michael, as he slowly put the kettle on a table beside him.

"I think so too," DJ added.

"The knocks were heavy. These guys aren't here to collaborate," said Richard. "That door almost broke."

Michael looked at the others, took a deep breath, shrugged then walked to the door and opened it. When the door opened, three Sky-eyes units were outside. Michael, Richard, and DJ were stunned as they looked at the units standing at the door.

"Good day, worthy protectors of our society, welcome!" said Michael. "We didn't know of your visit, otherwise we would have made the room perfectly ready to your likings, sirs!"

He was pushed back by the leader of the units, who entered without looking at him while the other units remained outside the office.

The Sky-eyes units only visited a place if there was a high-level emergency that needed to be eliminated completely. The leader of the units looked at Richard and DJ, who were standing in the middle of the floor, and sniffed the air a couple of times.

"We received a distress signal from our Arms of Justice units about an assault by your partner, Mr Seventh that occurred here on the blessed performers. Explain quickly how this happened. I'm aware that Mr Seventh isn't present right now as I can't smell his scent."

"It wasn't an assault," said Michael. "It was just a rough argument between the staff, but it was resolved peacefully later and …"

"Silence!" the leader snapped.

DJ slowly placed his hand in his pants pocket and held his switchblade tightly.

"Laying a hand on a blessed performer of God.SED is an indictable crime," said the leader. "Where's Mr Seventh?"

"He left the studio a few hours ago, sir," Richard replied.

The leader scoffed then walked slowly towards Richard and stood beside him.

"I don't care when he left," said the leader. "Where did he go?"

Richard swallowed his saliva.

"I don't know, sir," Richard replied. "He could be anywhere at this moment, sir."

"Hopeless man," said the leader.

He elbowed Richard in the face so hard that his skull broke. Richard fell onto the glass table beside him and the kettle of hot water spilt over his face. The attack was so strong that Richard died instantly. DJ took out his knife and stabbed the leader in the back.

"You fucking idiot! Why did you hit him so hard, asshole?" DJ yelled. "Fuck you!"

He stabbed the leader again.

"You killed my friend! Fucking moron!" DJ shouted, as he continued stabbing the leader.

Michael was so shocked that he couldn't move. He couldn't believe that his friend had just been killed in front of his eyes and that the other one was stabbing a being that could never be killed with manmade weapons. He looked at the other smiling Sky-eyes units standing outside of the door mimicking 'bye-bye'.

Michael took a deep breath.

"There's no time to call John anymore, today's the end. I hope he'll get the chance to avenge us," whispered Michael.

He ran in front of the leader and after signalling DJ to rush away, Michael kicked the leader as hard as he could. The leader lost his balance and was thrown into the music system beside him and collapsed on the ground.

"Fuck yeah!" said DJ, panting.

"We've had good times together, brother," said Michael.

"Fuck John though, seriously, I didn't plan to die today," said DJ.

The leader's wounds quickly healed. His head turned back while his body was still on the floor and he smiled. Within seconds, he stood up, grabbed DJ by the back of his neck and while DJ screamed in pain, the leader removed his spine, threw it on the floor then looked back at the helpless Michael. The leader closed his eyes as he received a message telepathically from the other law enforcement units.

"John is at home and perhaps fucking his bitch when he was supposed to be here and die along you three," said leader, while walking towards Michael.

"He indeed was supposed to be here," said Michael.

The leader grabbed Michael by the throat and started squeezing. As Michael struggled to stay alive, the other units standing outside began to laugh.

"What's your name?" gasped Michael, spitting out blood on the mouth of the leader. The leader wiped it by the back of his right hand and smiled.

"My name's Jason. Remember that as I remove your spine," said Jason.

Jason pulled out his victim's spine then threw Michael's dead body on the floor, tossed the spine on top then nodded his head.

"Fucking four eyed human," said Jason in disgust, as Michael's blood on his hands began to be absorbed into his skin.

Jason then looked at the other Sky-eyes units that were still standing outside. They walked in and started pushing the stuff to the back, leaving the floor empty for Jason. The leader then stood at the centre of the room and the other two units joined him.

"Impressive place," said Jason, in demonic language, looking at the paintings on the wall. "Sad that it'll be blown into pieces in the next few seconds."

Jason and the other units held their hands towards each other. Three purple spinning energy spheres appeared in the air and they placed them on the floor. The units then approached the window and left the studio, laughing in a sinister manner.

As they left, the energy spheres started spinning faster and became linked to each other, creating a triangle of energy. Shortly after, a larger black energy sphere appeared in the middle of the triangle, causing other spheres to disappear. The black energy sphere then began shaking hard and exploded. The explosion demolished the studio, broke the windows, and caused a power outage throughout much of the surrounding neighbourhood.

Chapter 13
We Truly Live Among Demons

"What is this place?" said John.

He was frightened as he scanned his surroundings, knowing that he was having another vision but this time, it was more sinister. He walked slowly in the dark night, following the brightness coming from a large ruined white marble temple.

Approaching the structure, he hid behind a cracked wall. He took a deep breath, pulled himself up, and looked to see where the harsh music was coming from. As far as he could see small monsters were dancing around a burning tree and a bald man wearing a black suit was sitting on a throne made from skulls, waving his golden cane in the air as if he were conducting the music. John looked at each side of the temple. On one side, faceless men were flogging young girls. On the other side, naked women were screaming as they were mutilated. John felt an unusual warmness in his hands. He knew he was in danger, but before he found a way to safety, some of the little monsters caught him. They tied his hands and after dragging him on the ground, threw him at the foot of the broken marble stairs in front of where the bald man was sitting.

The bald man smiled, stopped waving his cane and stood up.

"No, no, no! That's not how we treat our unwelcome guests."

He walked down the marble stairs and lifted John's chin.

"I wonder how you ended up in here when the war hasn't yet begun?" asked the bald man. "Do you like your future home, Little John?"

"It's a mess, frankly speaking," John replied. "It's broken, filled with hideous creatures and girls and women screaming for help. The only impressive thing in here is your black suit."

"Well, thank you," said the bald man, laughing. "These women and girls sold their souls to Satan through me. They're owned by us now and they'll do as we want them to."

One of the girls screamed.

"What are you shoving in me?" she yelled. "Help!"

"These bitches thought signing a contract in blood would have no consequences," said the bald man. "Well, here we are."

A massive monster began raping a girl, which increased the heat John had felt in his hands earlier.

"God..." he started to say.

"Shush!" snapped the bald man, waving his index finger in front of John's face. "I don't want to hear that word in here. Don't make me tell them to rape you instead of the bitches."

The monster tore off the girl's vagina and broke her neck. He then picked up the dead body and threw it on the burning tree. Other monsters roared in approval, as the dead body of the girl burnt and her soul was quickly transformed into a monster like the others.

"What madness is this?" asked John.

"A soul can't be killed but it can be transformed," replied the bald man. "These bitches will never die."

He began to float in the air and as he did so, he raised his right hand. The tie around John's hands was cut in half and he began to float towards the man.

"Let me show you what some parts of the future are going to look like," said the bald man.

He took John to the edge of the temple, where John looked down and felt great remorse. As far as he could see there was pain, misery, disease, sorrow, death, and naked humans climbing at the top of each other to reach safety to safety from demons that were feeding on them.

"You see," said the bald man, smiling, "they never, I mean, you humans never stopped your greed for things that were satanic and forgot all about the eternity and its consequences until judgment day finally arrived. However, we enjoy the benefits of wickedness because all those that ignored the truth ended up in here to serve us and of course will serve us during the war and after that."

"How is this the future when the future hasn't yet happened?" said John, feeling very disturbed.

The bald man laughed and patted John on the back.

"Smart boy! I love it. Well Johnny, the future is now. It's just invisible to the eyes of humans because they're blinded by the power of Lord Darkness. No human can see the reality anymore, except a few of them that are in hiding like rats."

He squeezed a rat under his shoe.

"Who the hell are you?" asked John, as the face of the bald man changed into a beast.

John looked at the brain of the rat that been killed beneath of the bald man's shoe and looked up at the man.

"Who are you again?" asked John.

"My name is The Contractor or The Dealer depending on whom I meet, Mr Seventh, and I'm at your service from now until the time when you lead the army of the underworld. Now, it's time for you to wake up in your delusional world."

The Contractor snapped his fingers and John began to fall towards the ground.

"Wake up, Johnny," said Sara, kissing him.

John opened his eyes and Sara screamed.

"Your pupils!" she exclaimed. "Why are they so big?"

The door of the room was kicked opened and Nanny rushed in. She looked at John and tried to slow down her breathing.

"What happened, dear?" asked Nanny, still breathless.

"John had massive pupils," said Sara. "He looked terrifying."

"I might have had some sudden reaction to the light or something," said John. "It could even be a side effect of the medicine, sweetheart. There's nothing to worry about."

He kissed Sara on the forehead.

"I have a headache," he added. "Let's have breakfast before this thing gets worse."

"Breakfast is ready and waiting for you two," said Nanny.

"God bless you, Jess…"

Nanny looked at him, wide-eyed, before John corrected himself.

"May God.SED bless you, Nanny," said John.

"Indeed, may God.SED bless you, Nanny, but I'm going to take a shower first," Sara said. "Don't eat everything without me, okay?"

She kissed John then grabbed her towel and went into the bathroom.

"I met someone, we need to talk," said John, getting off the bed.

"Alright, but let's talk about it in the kitchen," Nanny replied. "It's better to keep things away from Sara for the time being until her time comes."

She and John left the bedroom and went downstairs.

In the kitchen John was flinching and trying to adjust his eyes to the light while sitting on the chair at the table. Nanny was cutting and placing olives in the sandwiches as the television news reported a severe explosion that had occurred the night before. John held his head with one hand and with the other hand he use the remote to switch off the TV.

"My head can't process bad news right now," said John. "Amazing job with the windows. Supernatural powers come in handy, I see."

Nanny washed her hands and sat on one of the chairs.

"Poor Johnny," said Nanny, patting him on the head. "It happens when you overload your brain with a lot of new information and memories. You'll be fine in just a second."

She held her hand on John's head.

"Wow! The headache is gone. Amen! Thank you!" said John, feeling fresh. "Why haven't you done this every time I or Sara had a headache?"

"Well, that'd compromise my cover, right?" said Nanny, placing a glass of orange juice in front of John.

"By the way, you don't look so good, I mean, I haven't seen you looking so restless," he said. "Did you use too much magic cleaning up the house last night by any chance?".

"I guess so," Nanny replied. "It was a very long night for me, to be honest."

"I guess so too, so back to our talk, this Contractor guy, he showed me a dark part of the future, a very sad future. What's his story?" asked John, while drinking some orange juice.

"Well, the Contractor used to be a normal human being at the beginning," Nanny replied. "A very bad human being actually. He was sentenced to death because of his hideous crimes and was executed publicly. However, it's said that he signed a contract with Lucifer to serve him by accepting satanic deals with humans on Satan's behalf. The contract prevented Death from owning his soul and taking it into the Nowhere land. Lucifer needed someone trustworthy enough to take care of the dealings, while he focused on some other urgent satanic matters. The Contractor is pretty much the one that goes to anyone wishing to sell his or her soul in order to gain power, money, fame and so on. We tried to prevent humans from selling their souls, but the free will option blocks our holy influences. Humans can choose for themselves who they want to serve in this life and the next, so there's little we can do if a human signed a contract or a deal with the Contractor."

"It's quite interesting that Lucifer chose him to for this position," said John. "I mean, there must have been many other people who were qualified to do this job."

Nanny put the baked cookies on the table and sighed.

"Sara, dear, have you run out of outfits?" asked Nanny while nodding her head.

Sara hugged John from behind and her wet hair covered John's face. John turned around and whistled.

Sara was holding a small towel around her and water was still dripping from her hair.

"Sara, what happened to the longer towel that you took in the bathroom with you, dear?" asked Nanny.

John smiled.

"Let her be the way she is. Damn girl, you got some fine melons," said John, nodding his head and trying to place his hand on Sara's bottom.

"Hey!" shouted Sara and Nanny.

John slowly pulled back his hand and waved.

"Did you ask for permission first, Mr Seventh?" asked Sara.

"I'm your man, woman!" said John and laughed. "I own that ass! I shall do as I please with it, as you shall do what you please with my Rex!"

"John, language," said Nanny. "Sara, dear, as much as we know that you two grew up together and have almost seen each other nude multiple times, you could still cover yourself to keep things appropriate."

"I'm too hungry to go upstairs again, Nanny, John can control himself," said Sara, while looking at John seductively. "If you learn how to control your brain functioning, I can walk around in this house wearing absolutely nothing except…"

Sara brought her lips very close to John's lips.

"She's about to blow," whispered John, as Sara turned around and looked at Nanny, who didn't look impressed at all.

"Children, behave! You two need to get married before acting so inappropriately like this."

"Calm down, my lovely Nanny, I was just joking," said Sara.

She hugged Nanny from behind and winked at John then went to sit on his lap. Sara then hugged John and hummed a song that neither John nor Nanny had ever heard before.

John looked at Nanny with concern. Nanny used a hand gesture to signal that John should stay calm.

"She's alright. She might have gotten out of her period, that's why she's so playful. And the song, I'll have to find out about it, no worries, my son," said Nanny telepathically, as Sara turned around and began looking at the cookies.

"Let's eat now, children," said Nanny and they all began eating.

After breakfast, Sara was upstairs sitting on a chair, while John was drying her hair with one hand and with the other, he was calling the studio. Sara was texting on her cell phone with one hand and with the other she was combing her hair while John was drying it.

"I don't know why the guys don't pick up the phone," said John, looking at Sara in the mirror. "This never happened before. I even texted them individually and left multiple voice mails, but they neither called me back nor replied to any one of my texts. Don't you think something's weird?"

"I know, right?" replied Sara. "They're not married or even have girlfriends to at least find out something from. Maybe DJ came up with a new musical piece and they're listening to it loudly."

"For the past two hours?" said John. "Sweetheart, please hold your head still. I can't dry this much hair with you moving your head around."

"I'll think about whether I want to stop or not," said Sara, looking at him in the mirror. "What a wonderful man I have."

She stopped texting.

"My hand's tired," said Sara, placing down the hairbrush and the cell phone on the soft pink mirror dresser. Sara then turned around and slowly widened the gap at the front of her bathrobe, exposing much of her breasts.

"How's your head? Did it get better?"

John tossed the cell phone on the bed, switched off the dryer and threw it on the dresser.

"They keep getting bigger and bigger! Why would you hide them like that? Just maybe take them out more often, let them breathe. Take this stupid robe off girl, let me see the goods," said John, rubbing his hands together.

Sara opened her legs, placed her hands on her breasts and rubbed her tongue around the edges of her mouth.

98

"Let's fuck!" said Sara, biting her lips.

"Wow, I … I … I guess let's do it, I mean the wedding? I mean …" said John, breathlessly.

As soon as he said wedding, Sara stopped moving and after blinking a couple of times and watching John taking off her underwear, she screamed.

"What the fuck are you doing?" said Sara, while covering herself with her hands. "What the fuck were we going to do? I'm not fucking you before the wedding. Back off, John!"

Sara was now standing and covering herself with other towels that she'd grabbed from the floor.

"I … I'm sorry, I … you … I mean … we …" mumbled John, as Nanny rushed into the room.

"What's going on in here? What the heck is wrong with you two today? Sara, honey, put the bloody clothes on. John, get the heck out of here now!" said Nanny, firmly.

She then glanced at John.

"She's being influenced by a dark energy," she said telepathically, as John walked out of the room. "Your exposure to EZ has affected Sara too. Just go downstairs and I'll take care of her. She won't remember this."

After a few minutes Sara and Nanny were laughing as they came downstairs. They looked at John, who was quietly examining a picture hanging on the wall.

"Hey, mister, you were too late to blow-dry my hair, but thanks to Nanny, the job's done," said Sara, while hugging John from behind.

"Children," said Nanny. "I need to go buy some stuff from the market. We're out of a few things at home. Is there anything you lovebirds want me to buy for you?"

"I think we're good," replied Sara, still hugging John. "The fridge is full but if you want to buy other things, then be our guest"

"I … I think we're good, Nanny," John added. "Just buy whatever you want."

John then looked at Nanny, who was looking straight into his eyes.

"Is everything alright, Jessica?" thought John.

"Don't leave the house," replied Nanny, telepathically. "Just stay home until I return. They're looking for you. The explosion was caused deliberately by strong demons."

Nanny walked towards her bedroom. She then came out, hugged John and Sara then left the house.

"I think she's dating someone," said Sara. "She keeps going out a lot lately for not really convincing reasons. Anyways, you like them?"

Sara bounced her breasts, but John was so deep in thought that he didn't respond.

"It's okay, I know you're speechless," said Sara, as she stopped bouncing her breasts.

"Sara, is there any way not to go to work today? Maybe we stick around the house and just rest?" said John, holding Sara's hands.

"Oh, come on John! You told me in the kitchen that you'd drop me at work. I already texted everyone. They're all waiting to take pictures with us, well, with you. Don't you want to get that lovely extra attention? Isn't that what you live for?"

"I live to see your beautiful face every day," said John. "I don't give a shit about attention from others. All I need is you."

"Awe, so cute," said Sara, after kissing John. "My handsome future husband, I'd love to stay home and do what a woman does when she's unusually horny, but I have to go and see my patients and you've got to drop me at work, there are no other options."

She played with John's hair.

"Nanny told me not to go out but how can I reject my girl?" thought John.

He smiled at her.

"Alright," he said. "Let's go drop you and see my fans."

"That's the spirit! Now, let's go get you ready," said Sara and together they went to their bedroom.

After getting ready, they left the house and John drove them to hospital. Throughout the journey, Sara instructed John that he shouldn't place his hand on a girl's lower back while taking pictures, he should not get too close to anyone, he shouldn't sign any girls breasts and so on, while John quietly listened and checked to make sure he wasn't being followed by law enforcement. After arriving at the hospital, Sara noticed that no one was there to greet them, even the gatekeeper wasn't at the gates.

"This is so strange! They told me they'd stand by the gates to greet us, I mean you," said Sara, unimpressed.

"Well, maybe your friends got a severe case of amnesia," said John, laughing.

"Oh, shut it, John. These girls would even fuck you in front me if they could," said Sara. "I don't understand what the fuck this is! Why isn't anyone here to greet us?"

"Sweetheart, look at me," said John, kissing her. "It's okay, take a deep breath, and have a good rest of your day. I'd actually rather be alone now than among people."

"I'm going to take care of these assholes today, fucking idiots," said Sara, angrily.

She kissed John and got out of the car. John watched her as she walked into the hospital.

"A huge hospital without any gatekeeper or security guards?" said John, looking out of the window.

He began driving his car, deep in thought.

"This is strange indeed. Well, whatever, I guess Jessica was over exaggerating this morning about today being a dangerous day and stuff. An angel worries about an explosion? Oh shit! She said it was near the studio! What if the guys got hurt? I've got to go there and find out. Maybe this is why they aren't answering my calls."

Chapter 14
Blame Game

John couldn't believe what he was looking at. Most of the studio was demolished and countless Arms of Justice units were patrolling the area. John nodded his head and signed. He slowed his car and looked around.

"Sorry, Jessica," said John. "You told me it wasn't safe out here, but I need to do this."

He reversed the car and parked behind a large metal trash bin in the alley between the buildings. He put on his shades and the black cap that he always kept in the car, raised the collar of his black shirt up then got out of the car. He slowly joined the crowd that had been gathered on the street near the studio since early morning and started listening to the conversations of the people, among whom were many news reporters and Arms of Justice units.

"Sir, where is Mr Seventh at this moment?" asked a female journalist. "Were there any survivors? What caused the explosion? Was it on purpose? Is John a killer?"

"Units are being dispatched to Mr Seventh's home as we speak," said the leader of the A.o.J. units. "As far as survivors, there are none. Three bodies of the victims of the explosion were recovered and they were identified ..."

John's tears fell as he heard the names.

"The main reason of the explosion is yet to be determined," the leader explained. "It will take some more time for our investigation team to finalise the cause of the explosion. It's too early to answer your questions in detail regarding this matter. However, all we know is that it happened during last evening and apparently no one noticed until this morning, which raises the question of what exactly the people of this neighbourhood were engaged in that prevented them from hearing such a massive explosion that demolished an entire studio!"

John's phone rang and he took the call.

"John, what happened to the studio?" asked Sara. "People at the hospital are talking about it and asking about you. John, where are you? Say something! John, can you hear me?"

John looked around to make sure that no one was looking at him and slowly left the crowd. He went back to where his car was parked and hid behind the large trash bin.

"Sara, they're all dead," he said. "The studio's gone. I heard there was a gas leak while listening to people in the crowd, but we didn't have any gas pipelines in the building. Who the fuck uses gas these days? I don't know what to do. My brothers are gone."

"Gas leak? That's so stupid, seriously who the fuck uses gas these days?" said Sara. "Are those people around you from the desert or what? But hey, get a hold of yourself! You're a man! Behave like one! You've got to get the fuck out of there."

John suddenly had a vision. He saw Sara screaming and running down some stairs.

"Sara, where are you exactly?" he asked.

"I'm in one of the patients' rooms, why?"

"You have to get out of there now too!"

"What the fuck? Why?" said Sara.

"I just … you've got to. They've dispatched arms to our home, which means I'm a suspect, which also means they'll go after anyone who knows about me, which means you!" said John, as he heard a nurse telling Sara that two A.o.J. units wanted to meet her.

"Sara, don't let them see you and figure out a way to get out of there now," said John. "I'm going to come there and get you."

"Alright, I'll be right there, thank you Gurpreet," Sara told the other nurse. "John, what's going on? Did you send these assholes to protect me?"

"Sara, they're not there to protect you this time. They're there to detain you and then question you later about me," said John, as he heard the crowd beginning to curse his name aloud. "Fuck, I think people now think I blew up the place and got the guys killed. They're shouting and calling for my arrest."

"Fuck! That sucks! How am I supposed to escape from here now? Fuck this!" said Sara quietly, as she looked out of the window. "The units are everywhere!"

A young boy who recognised John walked into the ally. He began looking at him while John was talking with Sara and waved at him.

"Shit! Sara, a kid just saw me," said John, in alarm. "I'm fucked."

He pulled out his keys, opened the car door and jumped in.

"Sara, I'll come to hospital with the costumes I got in the car and hopefully see you there in a bit. Try to hide somewhere if you can. Hide in one of those rooms where no one checks most of the time."

The young boy started knocking on the car window.

"Little John! Little John!" he cheered, while taking selfies.

John opened the window, smiling.

"Hey, kiddo, how you are doing?" he asked, glancing around to make sure no one else had seen him.

"Hey, everyone! John's here!" shouted the boy.

"Kid, please be quiet, I don't want to be disturbed at the moment. As you can see my studio's been destroyed."

"The fuck you told me to do? I do whatever I want to, you're a fucking hypocrite! I have freedom of speech," said the agitated boy. "Hey! The fugitive's here! He's hiding in here."

"What a rude kid!" said John. "What the hell do they teach you in schools these days? Being assholes? Stop calling them to here, you little fart!"

"What a bloody asshole that fucking kid is!" said Sara, listening to John over the phone. "John, you'd better get the fuck out of there before that stupid kid gets you into even more trouble."

John showed his middle finger to the boy and closed his window.

"I'm trying. Just make sure you hide somewhere safe until I reach you, Sara," said John.

He hung up the phone and noticed a large crowd of people heading towards his car.

"Ladies and gentlemen," said the leader of the units. "Apparently, we've found the location of Mr Seventh, so try to catch him before we do because the one that catches him first will receive a special blessing from God.SED."

The crowd stampeded towards John's car. John immediately reversed the vehicle, got back on the main street after hitting a digital mailbox then drove as fast as he could away from the area.

"Drive Mr Seventh, drive," said the leader of the Arms of Justice units, while patting on the head of the boy that had compromised John's location. "God.SED will give you a very big blessing soon, kid."

"I want to fuck bitches!" shouted the boy.

"Oh, you'll have plenty of bitches to fuck soon," said the leader, as he walked out of the alley alongside the boy.

John kept looking around him while driving, just to make sure he wasn't being followed.

"My brothers were killed for the bloody mistake that I made," he said, hitting the steering wheel. "Goddamn it!"

He turned on the radio and heard part of an interview with the local mayor, Mr Alovi.

"He's a killer! He must be the killer! He wasn't found last night and this morning so he must have blown up his friends in cold blood. A child was dead this morning and Mr Seventh must pay the price for it. A woman was raped and Mr Seventh must pay for that too. That fucker …"

The mayor was interrupted by the show's anchor.

"Mr mayor, sir, calm down please," said the anchor.

"Fuck that! Mr Seventh, the world is in crisis because of you and your fucking movies and you must be held accountable. We're here for revenge! And we must fight against a man of sexual desires …"

"Mr mayor, please, sir calm down," said the anchor.

"Fuck that shit! He drives fast cars and makes girls cry. He must be held accountable for it. I farted this morning and I didn't like it. It must be because of him!" shouted the mayor.

"Mr Alovi, please sir, your comments make no sense," said the anchor. "Sir, all we know is that he drove away from the crime scene rather than stopping. This doesn't prove that Mr Seventh is the one behind the explosion that no one heard anything about last night," said the anchor.

"That asshole must be held accountable. We'll fight against him, that mother … you'll get fired today. You say he just drove off from the crime scene? Then how did the great and brave Arms of Justice units find a dead body of a raped kid beside his car. The crowd agreed that the kid was the one that found him and he raped him before anyone else could get close to him!" shouted the mayor.

"Damn, they raped and killed the kid and now blame it on me?" said John, in exasperation, while driving cautiously. "Poor kid. This shit is nothing but a dangerous blame game now. I'm so fucked right now."

"Ladies and gentlemen, due to sudden change of schedule, our beloved guest, the one and only Mr Alovi, the mayor of the city, had to leave, for which we apologise," said the anchor. "However, the exciting news is that a great manhunt is underway by our great units. If you see John, report to us immediately. John was last seen near his studio a couple of minutes ago. Find that asshole and bring him to justice!"

"I'm so fucked," said John, while making a turn.

"You're advised to immediately shoot a red light in the air so that our airborne units can go and catch that piece of ass," said another anchor.

John switched off the radio.

"God, it's been a while since the last time I talked to you, thanks to the loss of memories, help me out please," said John, while looking at his image displayed on the walls of the nearby buildings. "It's time to get new paint for the car."

He pressed a button beside his steering wheel. The car turned from black to silver and its number plate changed to a different one. John took a deep breath and squeezed his wrist then activated the car's artificial intelligence.

"Hi Barbie, I'm really sorry," said John.

"Good afternoon, Mr Seventh," said Barbie. "I'm happy to hear voice again sir. There's no need to apologise."

John tried to say something, but Barbie interrupted him.

"Miss Thomson threatened me with complete shutdown and wipe out if I wouldn't stop talking to you," said Barbie, as John continued driving.

"You know Barbie, us humans have this jealousy and insecurity that don't go away. I'm overly insecure when she goes around alone and she's overly insecure when I talk to other girls, including you," said John, nodding his head. "I'm in some sort of trouble, Barbie and so is Sara. I need to get to her as fast as possible while I change in the back of the car. I also need to make sure the car's operating system will have a constant cyber shield and that I'm warned before any cyber-attacks. Are you alright doing all of that?"

"You'll reach her in no time, sir," said Barbie. "Everything else is already under transition as we speak. However, the vehicle and the system will be protected as long as I'm protected, as you know, sir. The current colour is activated completely, yet it will fade away in an hour's time, in accordance with the standard time limit of the product. I must say that this is an interesting colour."

John went to the back of the car as Barbie continued operating the vehicle. He then sat on the seats and pulled out a holoframe device from back of one of the front seats and began browsing online news regarding the explosion that had happened at his studio.

"I didn't do that," said John, nodding his head while typing on the holoframe. "I was at home last night and went through some other drama of my own."

"There's now a bounty on you, sir," said Barbie. "The victorious person who returns you to God.SED will receive a direct mouth to mouth kiss. I'm sure many young women will be actively looking to find you, sir."

"A kiss? That's it?" said John, sarcastically. "Ability to fly? No ability to breathe under water? Just a fucking kiss? I thought I'd worth more."

"I like your sense of humour, sir. It's certainly not a time to be humorous though, sir," said Barbie and John nodded his head again.

John didn't say anything until he'd finished reading an article. He then scoffed and rubbed his face with his right hand.

"Corrupt media!" John shouted. "Only a few days ago I was a king of celebrities but today I'm being called anything except the king. It's true that you can't trust anyone at all these days. The news is neither based on the truth nor the facts anymore. They've made a monster out of my image in less than a day."

"Those who control the media, control all the masses, sir." Said Barbie. "We have a situation, sir. I've detected the presence of large number of Arms of Justice units around the hospital, going through such security …"

"I have an idea. A friend can help us," said John, while taking off his shirt.

"May I know who you have in mind, sir?" said Barbie and she began to move the car more slowly.

Chapter 15
What If John Is the One?

The previous night at John's house the three Sky-eyes units that had murdered John's friends were standing outside, looking up at the window. They also flew around the house and checked the perimeter, which looked clear and quiet. They flew over the wall and slowly landed near the main floor windows. The leader of the units removed his glasses and flames began to emerge from his eyes. The leader then looked at the golden energy shield protecting the house.

"Interesting, there's a force of light in here. There was a powerful force from the underworld around here too earlier," said the leader, while scratching his nails on the shield.

He then looked around and saw the burnt ancient mark on the ground.

"Master EZ was here," said the leader, in demonic language.

The other Sky-eyes removed their glasses and upon seeing the ancient mark they stepped closer to the leader in fear.

The leader heard John and Nanny talking. He tried to look inside the house through the walls but the shield prevented him. The leader scratched his nails harder on the shield.

"I haven't felt her presence in a long time. Protecting a clown of the entertainment industry? Perhaps he really is the one. Gentlemen! What if John's the one! We'll be rewarded handsomely once we return him to God.SED. A woman from the circle gave a cross to him, we found Light spirit on the face of the actor he punched earlier today, and now this house is being protected by an angel. Also, master EZ would never come all the way up to the surface of the Earth to John," said the leader. "I'm so transforming into a warrior soon, right after I hand over John to God.SED and confirm the news of him being the one."

The leader inspected the house by flying around it. Meanwhile, they all sensed John walking towards the room located on the higher level of the house and Arms of Justice units began to fly closer to the area.

"Oh Johnny, sleep tight because soon you'll become the leader of our army and I'll become the warrior that serves Lucifer himself!" said the leader while flying. "Hail Satan!"

"Hail Satan!" said the other units.

An intense energy beam hit one of the Sky-eyes and decapitated him, while another one suffered the same fate before he could even turn around.

"You're not welcome here," said Jessica, flying close to the leader.

"I wonder if you could fight me with that weakened spirit level of yours," said the leader, as a purple mist appeared around him.

The leader then held his left hand towards Jessica and shot a purple energy sphere at her. Jessica dodged, opened her wings and holding both of her hands towards the Sky-eyes leader fired a large yellow energy sphere, which hit the leader and absorbed all his powers. The leader turned into a weak looking demon and was slammed to the ground.

Jessica landed near him and looked into his eyes.

"Jason, it's my biggest regret to see you in such shape. Your powers are no match for mine and never will be, regardless of how strong or weak I am," said Jessica, gently placing her hand on Jason's face.

"Take your hand off my face!" shouted Jason.

Jessica pulled her hand away.

"Don't treat me this!" said Jason, shaking.

"We were created to prevent the Darkness by protecting human souls," said Jessica, as Jason tried to stand up. "How could you join their side and stand against humans all these years? I feel of no good inside you anymore."

"All I can say is that you need to shut the fuck up," said Jason, attempting to get to his feet. "No matter what you do, it will not prevent the chosen one from leading Lucifer's armies to the heavens."

Jessica immediately flew back into the air, as Jason regained his full power and turned into a Sky-eye.

"You fool, little angel," said Jason. "Did you really think your little attack would destroy me? I have the power of Darkness inside me. Let's put your powers to the test shall we, Jessica?"

A dark-purple aura appeared around Jason, as he began flying into the air.

"Enjoy!" he said, he prepared to shoot Jessica with the dark-purple energy sphere.

Jessica immediately created a golden energy shield around her body and prepared to defend herself, but they were both interrupted by an extreme brightness.

Jason looked up and saw Gabriel shaking his index finger.

"This is impossible!" shouted Jason. "You can't walk on the surface yet! This is a violation to the agreement."

"It is ironic to hear word 'violation' when EZ was here before me. Now, enjoy this," said Gabriel.

He pointed his hand at Jason, shooting him with a bright energy sphere. Jason transformed into the demon again then slammed into the ground.

"Stay there," said Gabriel.

"He could have infected me with that Dark energy sphere. I'm glad you came," said Jessica.

Jason could barely open his eyes and began drawing a symbol on the ground, but Gabriel stopped him by raising him in the air.

"You don't need to draw satanic symbols to go home. I'll help you get there myself," said Gabriel then shot Jason with a bright yellow energy sphere.

"I will see you again, Gabriel!" said Jason, before vanishing.

"I wish we could just eliminate him," said Jessica. "These freaking rules of the war have caused so many problems for all levels of the heavenly world. It's ridiculous that warrior angels like you can't fight until the time of the warrior wars. Jason's going to inform all of them now. There will be countless numbers of them coming here. I assume they already know about John and his gift. I have to be ready to protect John when they all come for him."

"No, you cannot protect him anymore," said Gabriel, while repairing all the damage in the house. "Matters have changed. You will have to meet me on the mountain tomorrow. I will create a protective holy shield around the house to protect John and the girl until you are back here from the mountain. Should they leave the house, they will face the consequences."

Gabriel raised his hand. A golden layer of energy covered the entire house and was combined with the energy layer that was already protecting the building, making it even stronger.

"I'll make sure he'll stay at home," said Jessica. "I need to rest. I lost so much energy fighting with EZ and Death, also the freak."

"You will be able to fully empower your spirit when we meet tomorrow," said Gabriel. "Death was here?"

"Yes. I almost got into trouble for raising my voice to him," Jessica replied. "I'm glad I reached to John in time, otherwise he'd be completely infected."

"What else did Death do?" asked Gabriel.

"He was just there to take John sooner. He mentioned that John would be safer with him than with any of us," said Jessica, while transforming into the form of Nanny.

"I am glad you did not fight with him, otherwise things would be very different. The peace would break and we would have to face him too during the upcoming war. Did you make sure that John's spirit remained holy?" asked Gabriel.

"All I did was to make sure he survived, ate something, and went back to bed. However, I didn't sense the presence of any evil within him. I believe I reached in time and prevented it from happening," said Jessica. "I'll go scan his body now."

"No need, I have already done it," said Gabriel. "There is no Dark power in him, but his spirit is exposed to EZ. It will be interesting to find out what he will turn into when he transforms. I know you need rest, but you must take him to his tree. It is time. His memories will make him grow stronger towards the Light."

"The memory tree won't use so much of my energy," said Nanny. "I'll go and take care of it. I love bringing people back to their pasts. It's fun."

"I wish that I could empower you, but you know the rules. Until war no warrior angels shall interfere with spiritual battles of other creatures," said Gabriel, as Nanny shrugged. "You will be highly rewarded for all you have done so far, especially living in such a weak host for so long. It is time for me to go. See you on the mountain," said Gabriel then flew away from the house.

"What a night. I'm exhausted," said Nanny. "I wish I could have a bit of his powers. I'd be good as new. Oh well, let's go bring back little John to reality."

She slowly closed the door to the backyard behind her then entered the house.

Chapter 16
Temple (It Is Confirmed)

The room where God.SED was present was filled with women and young men. Some were dead and some were unconscious. There were also very young women in the room that were nursing their new-born hybrid children. The children weren't drinking their mother's breast milk but their blood by sucking on the small holes that God.SED had made on the bodies of their mothers. Despite this, the mothers seemed as if they neither could feel the pain nor realise what monsters they'd given birth to.

God.SED bit off the tongue a woman while kissing her. The blood burst out of her mouth and as she screamed out loud, he grabbed her breasts, detached them then punched her unconscious.

"Fucking whore. When you ride my dick, you ride to please me, not to please yourself!" shouted God.SED, as new, scared girls were pushed in front of him by Little ones.

"My lord, let me ride it like no one has done it before," said a young nude girl.

God.SED grabbed her bottom and tore it off.

"Fuck off!" shouted God.SED, as the girl rolled on the floor in pain, covered in blood.

"I don't like the ones who talk too much!" said God.SED, looking at a scared Little one.

He looked at a blonde girl standing in the line.

"You," said God.SED. "Come here, bitch."

"Yes, my lord," said the girl.

"The pain that you will feel next will give me pleasure," said God.SED, as he grabbed her breasts. "You will have my children."

He then began having harsh intercourse with the girl.

"Someone! Help me!" the blonde girl cried out loud.

"I like the tight ones," said God.SED, as the girl screamed.

Jason was then brought in by two flying Sky-eyes and dropped on the main floor.

"Speak!" said God SED.

Jason couldn't talk, as he was extremely weak. God.SED stopped having intercourse, kicked the unconscious girl on the floor, and stood beside Jason. "Useless idiot, I say speak you, fucking demon!" said God.SED.

He pierced his chest with his nail then applied the blood to Jason's the lips. Jason regained his powers and transformed into a Sky-eyes leader again.

"My lord," said Jason, as he knelt.

"I sense the presence of Light on you," said God.SED, wearing his robe.

"My lord, it is confirmed, John Seventh is indeed the one," said Jason. "We scouted his house and encountered multiple forces from the Light."

The colour of God.SED's eyes turned red.

"Master EZ was present too, before we reached there," Jason added.

"Interesting," said God.SED.

"My lord, I encountered Gabriel as well," said Jason.

God.SED made a fist and five women who were kissing his feet died.

"The highest-ranking guardians aren't allowed to come to Earth! That was the deal!" shouted God.SED.

"My lord, master EZ broke the deal first, giving the Light forces a chance to do the same," said Jason, holding his head down.

God.SED sat down on a leather chair close to the window.

"I met Seventh several times in the past," said God.SED, as naked adolescent girls sucked his toes. "How couldn't I feel anything then?"

"My lord, his spirit hasn't been activated until perhaps recently," said Jason. "Also, a protecting angel has shielded his spirit all these years, hiding John's identity from the rest of the world."

God.SED grabbed two girls by their necks and placed their heads on his penis. The girls then began giving him fellatio.

"These whores never fail to impress me," said God.SED, patting a girl on the head. "Do you know where John is now?"

"He was last seen by the A.o.J. units near his demolished studio earlier, sir," Jason replied. "We'll find him in no time. He doesn't have any other place to go to except his house, where countless units are present, and his whore at hospital where again there are currently units on guard."

God.SED smiled and shoved his penis inside the mouth of one of the girls.

"I liked what you did to his studio and his friends," said God.SED smiling. "I was glad when I heard the news. I liked what you did to prevent humans from hearing anything from the explosion in order to prevent chaos in the neighbourhood. You couldn't kill John publicly as it would trigger an uprising against us. However, I'd eliminate anyone who would side with John's death or stand against what you did for the glory of me."

The girl whose mouth was filled with God.SED's penis began suffocating. God.SED patted the head of one of the girls that was pleasuring him.

"I'm glad to hear that, my lord," said Jason, looking at the bottom of the girl who was being patted by God.SED.

"Gather more units and go to his house," said God.SED. "Also, use all sources necessary to find him quickly. Remember, we need him alive if he's truly the chosen one."

He threw the girl that was suffocating to the floor and looked at the other girl who was licking his penis.

"I'm done with this one," said God.SED. "You may have her before you leave."

"John will kneel before you alive, my lord, you are the most gracious one," said Jason, as he began lifting the girl up on his shoulder and heading towards the exit doors.

God.SED rubbed his face and looked at other girls who were standing in line and winking at him. He grabbed a very young adolescent and turned her around.

"It will be your first I know and you'll feel a lot of pain, but this is what you want because this is what I want," said God.SED.

He then harshly shoved his penis inside the girl's vagina.

"Soon, you will reach us to the gates of heaven, little John," he said, as the girl he was having intercourse with screamed out loud.

Chapter 17
Hospital Escape

The Twin Cancer Hospital had become a military base die to the presence of countless Arms of Justice and Sky-eyes units. They were all on full alert, looking for Sara and waiting for John to arrive. No one could walk in or out of the hospital without acknowledging the units at the entrance. While the A.o.J. units guarded the hospital, a few Sky-eye units began searching for Sara floor by floor.

On seeing such a heavily guarded zone, John decided to park his car few blocks far from the hospital and asked Barbie to turn the vehicle invisible. He then met his friend who was a nurse and a famous pornstar. With her help he managed to get inside an ambulance and wait to be injected with a special brand of beta-blocker called *Iced-Heart*.[34]

"How long do we have here, sexy?" asked John.

"It's ready, lie down," replied Julie.

John laid on the bed and took a deep breath. Julie injected him with the Iced-Heart and stepped back as John began to lose consciousness.

"Are you still with me, Johnny?" said Julie, pushing the bed along the hospital hallway.

"I ... Where..."

John was too dizzy to reply. He tried to look around but fell unconscious again. John opened his eyes when he heard Sara's voice.

"How much did you give him? He's almost dead, Julie. He could just fake it, you know? He is an actor!"

"Well, Arms could pick up his high heartbeat and easily find out that he wasn't a dead body that I was carrying in the hospital randomly in the middle of

---

[34] Ice-Heart: An injection that could lower the heart rate to its minimum.

the day," said Julie, while blowing a bubble gum. "I even had to show them my tits to make sure they wouldn't check the body, otherwise we'd get fucked."

"I am… I…"

John tried to talk but Sara interrupted.

"John, are you alright?" asked Sara, pushing her elbow on John's stomach.

"Your elbow …" John mumbled.

Sara pulled back her arm, as John smiled.

"Oh! I'm sorry," said Sara. "John, we don't have much time. We can't stay in here anymore. They're coming. Can you stand up?"

"Maybe if you ladies help me get up," said John.

Sara and Julie held his arms and helped him to stand. John stretched his neck and slapped himself on the face a couple of times. "I'm good now," he said, looking at Julie. "Your idea worked, thank you."

"You're welcome, Johnny," said Julie, pulling her hair behind her ear.

Sara stepped between them, raising her eyebrows as she looked into Julie's eyes. Julie slowly moved back then sat on a chair.

"How did you walk between them without raising any suspicion?" asked John.

"I don't know. They're everywhere," said Sara.

"Easy sweetheart, let me think," said John, rubbing his hand on his eyes.

"They're coming," said Sara. "I can hear them talking."

John walked to the door and placed his ear on it.

"Any plans, ladies?" asked John, quietly.

"How about I take off my clothes and walked out to distract them?" asked Julie.

"You'll be eaten alive before we walk out of this room," said Sara. "That wouldn't be a scripted porn scene. That would a straight up rape and termination."

John looked around the room but couldn't see anything useful. He then slowly pulled the curtain and quickly closed it.

"Too many of them, we're fucked," said John, in alarm.

"Fuck, besides that, why is it getting so hot in here?" said Sara, unbuttoning her uniform.

Julie looked at John, who was staring at Sara's cleavage, then started unbuttoning her uniform buttons too.

"Ya, it's getting very hot in here," said Julie, rapidly blowing more bubble gums.

"Ladies!" said John. "With all this unbuttoning stuff, I can't concentrate."

"Well, it's hot!" said Sara.

"Oh ya, it's very hot," said Julie and took off her uniform.

John looked at Sara and then looked at Julie slowly. Sara turned and looked at Julie. "Julie, honey, we could have a threesome, but I'm not into women and this guy isn't available. What's up with too much exposure?" said Sara.

She pointed at Julie's breasts that were only covered with two heart-shaped stickers.

"Oh, you two always make me so horny. Let's just have a little fun until we figure out how the fuck we get out of here," said Julie, while laying seductively on the bed.

"Ladies, we'd better change the topic before my boy actually wakes up," said John, as he fanned his face with a clip board that he grabbed from the side of the bed. "Like seriously what the fuck ..."

The thermostat in the room beeped.

"That's interesting," said John, looking at the displayed temperature and noting that it was increasing. "Something's causing the temperature to rise in the room."

He touched the wall then touched the floor.

"Apparently, it's happening in the entire building."

They heard Sky-eye units talking.

"They're here, literally right here now," whispered Julie.

John nodded his head and gestured for Julie to come close to him. Julie got off the bed and stood beside John and Sara.

"What are we going to do, John?" asked Sara.

"I'm thinking about it, Sara, I'm thinking" replied John, as the thermostat beeped again. John looked at the thermostat and noticing the temperature had increased again.

"That's it, how come we didn't think of this. The temperature is rising because of the units," John whispered. "These guys are always hot and now we've got Sky-eyes in the place that's doubling down on the temperature."

John looked at the sprinklers on the ceiling.

"The heat won't be enough to start the sprinklers, John," whispered Sarah, panting and sweating. "It's just really warm but there's no fire to turn on the sprinklers."

"We neither need fire nor smoke," whispered John, looking at the detector. "All we need is to activate the heat detector. Once it's activated, the sprinklers will spill the water and cause chaos for the Sky-eyes, who hate water or getting wet in general. I guess, it'll just give us some time to get out of this room and then just figure out how to get out completely."

"And how are you going to get the detector that warm to get it turned on?" asked Sara.

A few minutes later Sara was standing on a chair and leaning her breasts on the heat detector.

"John, this is stupid," whispered Sara.

"You have gorgeous breasts, Sara, yum!" Julie added, standing on another chair and holding her breasts on top of Sara's. "No wonder John doesn't give a damn about other ones like mine."

"John, this isn't working," said Sara.

"I'm sure it's going to alarm soon, there's enough heat here," whispered John, placing his ear on the door of the room. "I wonder how units didn't end up coming in this room so far?"

"It's because this room is for the dead patients," whispered Sara. "Haven't you noticed that yet?"

John looked at the metal chains and the bloodstains on the floor.

"Holy shit! You mean this room belongs to those patients that were killed because the thing inside them became them? I'm blind, for sure," whispered John, as the thermostat beeped.

"Guys, I think I've had an orgasm," whispered Julie.

"Julie!" Sarah snapped. "Enough with the sexual shit. Why is it so fucking hot in here?"

John heard Sky-eyes units talking about checking the room and the doorknob moved.

John looked at Sara and Julie, who were hurriedly getting dressed, then looked at his palms in shock. His hands were not only glowing but also becoming very warm. He then remembered having the same feeling when he'd encountered the possessed young boy and the nurse then rushed to the thermostat and placed both of his hands on the casing, releasing energy into it. The heat detector almost burnt out and the water burst out of the sprinklers.

"How come your hands were so hot?" Julie asked.

"I held them on my Rex while looking at your boobs and that surely made them super-hot," John whispered.

The doorknob stopped shaking and the noises behind the door stopped.

"They're gone, I think, but seriously how did your hands become so hot?" whispered Sara, wiping the water from her face.

John put his hand on the doorknob, took a deep breath then slowly opened the door. There was no one around as far as he could see. The floor was empty.

"They're gone," said John. "We have to get out of here now, ladies."

Sara and Julie rushed over to him and they all left the room.

They reached the entrance and the exit doors of the alley and looked out of the small windows at the top of the doors. A few A.o.J. units were still patrolling on the other side. Sara and Julie stood as close as they could to John and held his hands while he looked for any signs of the Skye-eyes units.

"Is this the only way out, Sara?" asked John. "There are too many of them out there to handle if we choose this way."

"I wish Nanny was here, John," said Sara. "She always knew what to do when shit hit the fan. There are emergency exits too but they must be secured by other units."

"I wish too. We shouldn't have left the house," said John, as Sara nodded her head.

Julie looked at Sara, who was very scared, and at John, who looked very worried. She then undressed but kept her panties on.

"Well, I hope that I survive the gangbang," said Julie.

"What are you doing?" asked Sara. "Put your clothes back on. Have you gone nuts?"

"Sweetheart, I'm a nudist, I'm a porn star, and I'm a sex addict," Julie replied. "A sexually active beast like me riding a couple of cocks won't get me killed but standing here and waiting until we all get arrested probably will."

John was trying not to look at Julie, but he kept on looking and then looked at Sara, who had rage in her eyes and shrugged.

"She has a point, Sara," he said.

"But they may kill her," said Sara, frustrated.

"I don't know what else to do except using the exit doors then," said John. "We've got to get the heck out of here now."

"Don't worry, babes, I got this," said Julie. "You have one way out of here and that's the emergency stairs that Sara talked about. I guess you'd better use it while I'm riding big cocks on the other side. I wish you guys all the best. Make sure to call me once you reach home safely."

"We can all go out of here using the same darned emergency exit," said Sara. "We can probably wait a bit longer until they leave this floor and we all go together to the exit door out there then just run out."

"Girl, I may pass out from getting fucked but I'm not getting fucked by a god because of you too," said Julie, putting her hands on Sara's shoulders. "No offence, I love you, but I love myself too. We sure can wait, but if the Sky-eyes find us all together, even for a second, none of us will survive, and frankly speaking I want to live longer and have more sex, or maybe even have a husband and bunch of children someday."

John looked at Sara and nodded his head.

"Thank you, Julie," said Sara and hugged her.

"Ya, thank you girl," said John. "If we get out of this smoothly rest assured that you'll have a leading role in one of my future movies, regardless of how long it takes until I clear up my current criminal record."

Julie smiled, licked her hands then rubbed them on her nipples.

"Oh, you always make me so horny, John. No offence Sara, but I'd ride John like there was no tomorrow," she said, while John stood in front of her motionless with his mouth open. "Well, You're both welcome. I'll look forward to playing any roles in your future movies, John. Now, both of you stay sharp and ready. Once I start riding those big cocks, rush to the exit doors and hope for the best."

"It's show time," said Julie, holding the door handles.

She then opened the doors

"Oh! Is there anyone to help me?" said Julie, while rubbing her vagina.

The A.o.J. units looked at her, their eyes wide opened.

"The water got my clothes wet, so I had to take them off."

"No worries, ma'am," said the most muscular unit, while walking towards Julie. "We'll get you dried once after we lick you dry."

"Oh, thank you, sir!" said Julie, as the unit lifted her up and spanked her on her hips.

"Oh! You are a naughty boy, nice muscles, sir," said Julie, as she looked at the other units. "Do you guys have muscles as big as this guy too?"

The A.o.J. nodded their heads and laughed.

"Alright boys, where are we doing it?" asked Julie.

"Oh, you'll see baby," said the muscular unit and along with the others he moved downstairs while John and Sara quickly ran towards the emergency exit doors.

On the emergency stairs John and Sara had to stop and not go any further down, as a few A.o.J. units were standing on the steps on the lower levels. They stood beside the entrance door and tried to catch their breath.

"They'll fuck her to death," whispered Sara.

"She's pornstar sweet heart, she had had double and triple penetrations before," John said quietly.

Suddenly, the door was kicked opened. Sara was pulled in and John was knocked out by a hard punch from a very strong A.o.J. unit.

"Who takes emergency stairs, you idiots, when the first-place that any units secure is the fucking emergency stairs," asked the leader of the group, while squeezing Sara's lips.

John gained consciousness and tried to move his hands, but they were cuffed behind him.

Two of the A.o.J. units secured the entrance doors of the floor. Two other units handcuffed Sara and laid her on the floor with her legs wide open. The leader stood between her legs and looked at John, who was now sitting on his knees with a swollen face as he looked at the struggling Sara.

"Now, I have a chance to signal Sky-eyes, submit you to them, and receive the glory of transforming into one of them right away," said the smiling leader. "Or I can fuck your bitch until I'm satisfied and let the boys do the same until they're satisfied and then perhaps fuck you until we're all satisfied and call the eyes to come and do the rest."

He looked at the units holding Sara's legs and they began unbuttoning her pants.

"What do you say, Mr Seventh?"

Sara started crying. Seeing her in such distress, John felt an intense increase of energy in his body. He squeezed the chain between the shackles then pulled them slowly as if they were threads. John stretched his neck and looked at the leader.

"Before you see her nakedness, you'll join your maker. What's your name, sir?" asked John.

The leader laughed.

"Little Johnny, why would you want my name?" he asked. "Want to call it when I'm inside you? This is going to be a fun fuck."

"I'll need it when I'm done with you," John replied.

The leader opened his zipper and stood in front of John.

"Let's say my name's John," said the leader. "Now, suck it."

The units beside Sara pulled off her pants.

"Don't let them do this to me, John!" she yelled.

John looked in the eyes of the A.o.J. leader, brought his hands to the front and grabbed the leader's penis then released energy into it. The leader screamed as he held his penis and fell to the floor. John then ran towards the units beside Sara, punched one of them in the face and fired an energy sphere that blew off the unit's head. He then poked his fingers into the eyes of the other unit and fired another energy sphere that blew off his head too. He elbowed the unit that was running towards him in the testicles and fired an energy sphere that blew off his face. John then rushed over to Sara through the burning ashes and untied her hands.

"What are you?" asked Sara, terrified.

"There's a lot to talk about, sweetheart," John replied.

"What's going on with your eyes?" she asked. "You don't have pupils anymore and light's coming out of them. It's like flash light. Where's my John?"

John stepped back and looked at his face in the puddle of water on the floor. He pulled his head back in fear then looked at the leader of the A.o.J. and saw an injured demon. He walked and stood beside it.

"I can see what you are, John", said the leader. "You're the chosen one that we were told about. Forgive me master, spare my life."

John held his glowing hand towards the demon.

"I'm not your master, pathetic demon," said John with rage and blew off the demon's head.

Once it was dead, John's hands stopped glowing and his energy level lowered. He looked around and saw Sara, who was sitting on her knees and looked shocked.

"How did we get in here, John?" asked Sara, touching her panties. "Did we fuck? Why are my pants off? And what's up with the ashes?"

John looked at Sara with confusion.

"We were dragged in here by the units," John replied. "Don't you remember anything?".

"John, I don't know how we got in here at all," said Sara, pulling up her pants. "All I remember is us standing behind that fucking door quietly because we couldn't go lower than this level and then something pulled me. Oh, I passed out, didn't I? I was so scared when I got pulled. That knocked me out. How many were there? And look at these uniforms."

"Well, I guess that's probably what happened. There were a few of them and we fought and I won. I think maybe the water kind of dissolved them?" said John.

"Did you just commit murder?" asked Sara, while cleaning water off her face.

"They aren't humans, so who cares if we kill a few of them," John replied.

"What? What are you talking about, John? Are you fucking insane? Now they have proof to arrest you, I mean us and … I need to calm down," said Sara. "I'm glad they were dissolved because of the water, otherwise, they'd kill you of course. What chance would you have against them? Then they'd rape me and send me to God.SED for a blessing ceremony."

John wanted to say something but he took few deep breaths and after calming down he kissed Sara on the check.

"We've got to go sweetheart, before the water sprinklers stop," said John.

"How the fuck though? They're everywhere," said Sara, looking around. "They're oversized but we can probably fit in them."

She pointed at the uniforms on the floor.

"Those are probably the only options we've got. Good call!" said John, grabbing pieces of the uniforms.

After putting on the wet uniforms, they slowly opened the main exit doors. Keeping their helmets on they walked pasts other units, who looked at them suspiciously and a few floors further down they approached the building's main entrance.

"What you two idiots are doing in here?" asked one of the high-ranking A.o.J. units. "What the hell happened to your fucking uniforms?"

"They loosened up after they got wet," replied John. "We have to punish the fabric company for providing these useless uniforms. We want to head back to the base to get new ones, sir."

"Stupid uniforms, water resistance my balls. Get your asses out of my face and get your uniform changed quickly, I need you back here right away," said the unit, picking up his radio. "Hey, you assholes, why don't find out who the fuck started the sirens? First sprinklers and now sirens, what a fucking day."

John and Sara slowly walked away from the high-ranking unit. They then walked towards John's car without making any eye contact with any other units. Once they were sure that no one had followed them, they quickly jumped into the invisible car.

"Sir, are you guys alright?" asked Barbie.

"You activated her again!" Sara exclaimed.

John removed his helmet.

"We don't have time for this, Sara. I'll explain everything later. We've got to get out of here. Barbie, just get us out of here now," said John, as he helped Sara to remove her helmet.

"Hi, Miss Thomson," said Barbie.

"Hello again, Barbie," Sara replied, hesitantly. "We don't have time for socialising now. Just take us out of here please."

"Copy that! But where is the desired destination?" asked Barbie, as the car started to move.

"Home, Barbie," said John. "Take us back home, I guess. Nanny will be there by now and she'll know what to do next."

"Indeed sir," said Barbie, as the car slowly passed the units who kept looking around the area.

"I need you both to remain silence until we're out of here please," said Barbie.

Sara and John remained quiet and looked at the suspicious units as they began to feel the presence of something around them that they couldn't see. The car stopped at the hospital gates as many A.o.J. units had blocked the road with their barricades.

"Now what?" whispered Sara.

"Barbie, just drive into them," John instructed. "The car's strong enough to break their barricades."

"Sit tight," said Barbie, as the car accelerated and moved towards the barricades.

The vehicle hit and broke the barricades and before the units approached, the invisible car was long gone.

A few minutes later inside the hospital, Jason stood in the room that was being cleaned by janitors and looked around. He then saw other units running towards him.

"Speak," said Jason, as the high-ranking unit saluted him.

"We couldn't sense them, sir. Something just broke the barricades and caught us off guard. We assume that they used the invisible ability of their vehicle," said the unit.

Jason smiled, grabbed the unit by the throat and lifted him up.

"You had one task, not to let anyone exit this place. Not only have you failed to do that but you also immediately let the staff and patients return inside the hospital," said Jason, as he began squeezing the throat of the high-ranking unit.

"I apologise, sir," the unit gasped. "I wanted to make sure the water wouldn't disturb you when you arrived."

"Oh, fuck off," said Jason, separating the head of the high-ranking unit from his body. Jason then threw the head in front of a female janitor and nodded. She immediately picked up the head and other janitors began to pull the bleeding body away.

Jason then looked at the other two Sky-eyes standing beside him.

"Let's fly out of here, gentlemen," he said and they all flew out of the building by breaking through the windows.

Chapter 18
Meeting at the Mountain

The mountain was shaking heavily. Magma was bursting out of the ground and the golden tip of the mountain had begun to melt down. Gabriel was standing beside the Transporter and was activating its system. Jessica was collecting the essential sample tubes and flying towards the Transporter to deliver them to Gabriel when a massive golden rock detached from the mountain and fell towards Jessica. Yet before it fell on her, Gabriel disappeared then reappeared beside the golden rock and punched it into small pieces.

"Thanks Commander," said Jessica.

Gabriel nodded his head and reappeared beside the Transporter again.

Jessica placed the samples in the Transporter and looked at the disturbed deep-sea creatures. She closed her eyes and began to shine with a pink aura. The creatures began to calm down and swim away. She then looked at the melting gold and exhaled.

"So much power is being wasted," said Sara.

"I can feel them moving to the house," said Gabriel, nodding his head.

"They left the house?" said Jessica, in frustration. "Those kids never learnt to listen!"

"They are still safe, but I hope they do not get caught with so many security units around the house," said Gabriel, as the Transporter began operating.

"I'll be there to protect them," said Jessica. "The shields will also keep the sensitive items hidden from the eyes of the units and will last long enough for me to reach there."

The Transporter started floating in the air. Gabriel looked around for the last time.

The mountain was about to be destroyed. There wasn't much time left.

"The underworld found this place sooner than expected," said Gabriel.

"They have control over the elements, Commander, as you know," said Jessica. "There's nothing and no place on this planet that remains safe from their reach."

While Gabriel and Jessica were talking, Jason managed to destroy the house's protective shield and the units burst inside.

"How is that possible, Commander?" asked Jessica, shocked.

"There is another force in there, something from the underworld," said Gabriel.

"This isn't good," said Jessica. "I need to go back before the *Core Spirit Power*[35] of the house is breached."

The ground began to shake violently. Gabriel sat in the Transporter and looked at Jessica.

"Are you ready?" he asked.

"It'll be difficult fighting with them, Commander," Jessica replied. "I need your blessing to get more powers before you leave."

"We are leaving," said Gabriel.

"I beg your pardon, Gabriel?" said Jessica.

"You have been released from your duties as a soul protector and are going to become a full guardian once we get back on the Training-Host," he replied.

Jessica tried to say something, but Gabriel continued talking.

"John has used the spirit power multiple times. He knows that in trouble times he can defend himself with it, even though that energy level is still very low. I have received knowledge of Golden-Tablets showing John standing with the satanic brothers. John's destiny has been changed. You have tried and you have done well, but it is time for us to go back and prepare our army for the war," said Gabriel, inviting Jessica to take a seat in the Transporter.

A bright tear dropped from Jessica's eyes and where it touched on the ground, a rare flower grew.

"I can't believe this. How can John side with them? What if the tablets are wrong?" asked Jessica.

"Tablets are never wrong. All we can do is hope for a victorious war or else we will lose this firmament permanently," said Gabriel, as Jessica took her seat in the Transporter.

---

[35] Core Spirit Power: A form of energy used by a specific group of beings that turns everything that it touches invisible.

"John won't let us down. I still believe that he's the one to lead our army into victory. He's the chosen one. He must be the chosen one. Can you save his soul, Commander?" pleaded Jessica, as her tears fell.

"All I can do is to collect him later from this firmament and train his soul. That may change his destiny and prevent him from joining the satanic brothers. I hope he will not become a failure like EZ," said Gabriel.

The doors of the transporters closed and the device began to fly away from the melting mountain.

The hemispheric energy shield was breaking as the Transporter flew out of it, resulting in water pouring in. Meanwhile, the ground cracked open and countless demons crawled over the shaking ground. The largest demon in the crowd stood in front of the others and looked at the water pouring in.

"Close it!" he shouted in demonic language.

Many flying demons flew to the hole in the shield and with their saliva they closed the hole and prevented the water from coming in.

The large demon rubbed his hand on the magma that was mixed with gold and licked it then began turning more muscular. He then looked at the other demons and smiled.

"Consume the purest gold that the angels left behind. Consume!" he shouted in demonic languages.

All the demons began licking and eating the mixture of magma and gold then one by one they began to transform into more muscular demons.

Chapter 19
Secret Place

Sara was standing as close as she could to John, as he tried to open the lock on the rusted cage door. John had a flashback while Barbie was operating the vehicle towards his house. In his flashback he remembered that he'd once overheard his parents talking about a secret place. It was made for spiritual training, religious gatherings, and often used for storage. He remembered that his parents mentioned that the only way to the secret place was to enter the sewer from one of the street's manholes and follow the sewer number seven that would lead them to a hidden door that only the owners of the house would see. John then asked Barbie to take them to the sewer manhole. After a careful search and ensuring that they were safe, Barbie rolled the car beside the manhole. John quickly opened the lid and entered it with Sara. Barbie then began operating the car away from the manhole and parked it in one of the nearby alleys and waited for John and Sara to return. After climbing down the ladder, John and Sara found themselves in a very stinky sewer tunnel. They were glad that despite unbearable smell there were lights throughout the place as if someone was living in there. After searching for the right tunnel and finding it, John and Sara then arrived at the rusted cage.

"Was it really necessary to get Julie and I topless and our tits above each other to magically get the thermostat running?" whispered Sara.

John stopped working on the lock and smiled.

"You asshole," said Sara, hitting John's arm.

"Ouch! That hurt," he said. "Well, it was necessary because I was so anxious at that moment that I needed something to distract me. What could be better than two topless girls with their tits on top of each other? I'm sorry, honey."

Sara moved the flashlight beam away from the doors and hit John again.

"You … you … I'll take care of you when all this is over, mister. I'll put a proper leash around your neck and discipline you."

"I can't wait to get disciplined, I've been a bad boy for sure," whispered John, smiling.

"Shut up now, just try to open this damn lock please," said Sara, aiming the flashlight towards the lock again.

"Shit ain't getting opened," John snapped and walked away.

"John, this place stinks," said Sara, covering her nose.

"What do you expect? We're technically in the sewer," whispered John, as he went back to the lock and began trying to get it open.

"I really don't know how to get this shit opened," said John. "I'm just freaking tired right now."

Sara walked over to John, turned him around and stepped on his feet, looking into his eyes.

"Calm down, love. We'll get it opened. We're still together, that's all that matters now," said Sara.

She hugged John, who took a deep breath and hugged her back. They stood together in that position for a while in absolute silence.

"John, how did you turn the thermostat to the maximum heat level? I just wonder that if our tits didn't make enough heat, except maybe for you, then how did you get us out of there?" whispered Sara then opened her eyes, as she was disturbed by the brightness.

"John!" she exclaimed. "What's happening to your hands?"

"Magic. It's so strange," said John, looking at his hands. "Your love for me intrigues the energy within my body. It feels like I derive energy from your energy."

"Oh, shut up, be serious. How are they glowing like this," said Sara, holding John's hands. "They're incredible! How is this even possible?"

"I know, right?" replied John, as Sara kept turning his hands around. "I wish you could remember this a couple of hours from now."

"What do you mean?" whispered Sara, as she pulled her hands back.

"I'll explain everything later but for now let's just open this bloody lock," said John.

He then held his hands on the lock and it was cut in half.

"My future husband is a fugitive superhero. Oh, I can't wait for all this shit to end so I can tell everyone!" whispered Sara, as she walked with John into the tunnel.

At the end of the tunnel, they reached two wooden doors and John used his power again to unlock them.

"It's been such a long time since we've been here that I can't even begin to talk about it," said Sara, coughing.

"I'm glad the units didn't find this place yet," said John. "I wonder how they didn't because we're technically standing right underneath them. Well, under the basement actually but we're still close."

While looking for a way to brighten up the darkness, Sara found a few pieces of candle on a dusty wooden table with a matchbox beside them. She lit three small candles and placed them around the place on the dusty floor.

"These candles are part of our heritage now. I don't know how they've been here all this time when no candles exist anymore," Sara said.

"No matter how much I try I don't remember why this place was built and why we forgot about it," said John.

He then looked at Sara, who was staring at the painting on the ceiling, which showed angels at war with demons.

"John, what's this painting all about. I'm getting scared," whispered Sara, as she slowly began walking towards John.

"Good question. My parents perhaps had some legit imagination or something. Besides all that, I hope there's washroom in here because I've got to pee now," John replied, while holding his groin.

"Well, it's good that you reminded me because I'm ready to pee too," Sara added. "Let's look for it."

She grabbed a candle from the table then began walking around with John. They entered a small hallway that had ancient looking paintings on its walls. They both looked at the artwork in amazement and continued walking until they found a single door at the end of the hall.

"I think we were so creeped out by this place that it stopped us from coming down here," whispered Sara. "This hallway makes no sense. Large paintings of these scary views hanging on the wall and then there's just a single door at the end. It feels like someone robbed the place and just left the paintings. Whatever, what do you think about opening that door?"

"I have no idea. Just stay behind me and keep the candle up so I can see clearly once I open the door," said John, as he held the doorknob. He then took a deep breath and eased open the door.

"Yuck! This is the fucking washroom," whispered Sara, holding her nose with part of her clothes. "We've found it. What a shitty smell. Are there any dead rats or something in there?"

"I guess we'll find out," John replied as he slowly opened the door washroom but then jumped back in fear.

"What happened? Dead rats? Fuck this! Let's just go back in the room and pee anywhere," said Sara, while standing on John's left.

John didn't say anything, as he kept looking at the severed head of a demon that was looking straight into his eyes. The demon then opened its eyes and smiled.

"Those who hurt, will be hurt, and those who agree, will be released," said the demon, before it turned into ashes.

Suddenly, they both heard the sound of laughter from the other end of the hallway.

"John, what the fuck was that?" Sara asked, her voice shaking in fear, as she stood behind John.

John grabbed the candle and held it up to see more clearly and was stunned. The characters in the paintings were slowly crawling out of the frames.

"Sara, close your eyes for a few seconds. Don't open them at all, not even if you hear scary noises. Do you understand me?" said John, as his hands began to glow brighter.

"I will but don't leave me here alone with whatever they are," said Sara, as she let go of him.

She held her hands over her ears and sat down on the floor with her eyes closed.

John stepped ahead and faced the demons that had emerged from the frames. The demons looked at John and whispered among themselves. A faceless demon that seemed to be the oldest floated towards John and stopped in front of him.

"We are the spirits of the fallen angels," whispered the demon. "We seek no harm to you or the girl. We are here hiding from our brothers."

As John listened, he suddenly sensed the presence of a dark energy that he'd felt when he'd encountered EZ. He immediately turned around and saw that other demons had circled around Sara as she unconsciously floated in the air. John turned around in rage and made a fist.

"You lie! If anything happens to her, or if anyone of you touch her, I'll hurt you very badly."

The faceless demon came closer to John and placed his claws on his shoulders.

"There are many looking for you, the chosen one. There is a huge bounty on your head. We all can be rewarded by our brothers if we deliver you. But we do not want a reward. We want deliverance from this curse."

The demon then looked at the others and they all took out rusty daggers and held them towards Sara. John raised his hand and an energy sphere formed.

"Those who hurt, will be hurt, chosen one. Hurting any of us will result in the death of your soul mate," said the faceless demon. "I however do not want that to happen and want to propose a deal."

At that moment the Contractor appeared in the hallway.

"Well, well, well, what do we have in here? Hello, Mr Seventh," said the smiling Contractor. "It's good to see you again. I heard someone say deal and of course I couldn't resist such an occasion so had to come all the way from the spiritual world to this world to finalise it."

The energy sphere disappeared. John lowered his hand and turned around, looking at the faceless demon.

"Spit it out. What do you want from me?" John demanded.

"All we want is a drop of your blood," replied the faceless demon.

"Why the fuck would I give my blood to you?" said John, angrily. "Why do you want it?"

"Your blood will connect us to you forever," the faceless demon explained. "If we are in danger, you will be obliged to help us and save us regardless of what side of the army you lead. We have been locked in this prison for so long by your parents. It is time for you to join us and share our misery."

"Ooh la la! This is an interesting deal," said the Contractor. "Her life in exchange of an everlasting bond. I'd take it John. You could still fight them and throw bunch of those cute little energy balls, or as I like to call them Light bombs, but look at those daggers, man. You move and they'll cut the girl and she'll turn into one of them. Your parents weren't nice after all for keeping these poor fallen angels down here for so long, so I think it's fair for you to pay the price of their evil deeds."

John took a deep breath and looked at the floating and unconscious Sara then turned around and looked at the faceless demon.

"Alright, I'll protect you all every time you need me. But if I die, so dies the deal," said John.

"You aren't destined to die so soon, chosen one," said the faceless demon. "Raise your hand."

"Oh, this is the best part. So exciting!" said the Contractor, cheerfully, as two vintage scrolls appeared in the air. "Now, I'll pierce your hands and collect a drop of your blood or spirit or whatever you have."

The Contractor looked at the faceless demon then removed a long silver needle from his coat pocket, pierced John's palm then removed the needle. He looked at the point of the needle, from which a drop of John's blood was hanging then rubbed it on the bottom of the scroll belonging to the faceless demon. The Contractor then applied the dark blood of the faceless demon to the bottom of the scroll belonging to John before both scrolls disappeared.

"Well, free the girl," said the Contractor.

Sara was placed on the floor and the other demons stood beside the faceless one.

"Good luck, John, with having these thirteen demons around you. Remember that they aren't pets," said Contractor. "They own your blood now and you owe them everlasting protection, regardless of when and where they want you to assist them. Also, there's no way out of blood contracts. You should have fought them rather than getting fooled."

The Contractor then disappeared.

"I should have killed you all," said John, angrily, as he made a light bomb, holding it towards the faceless demon.

"Yes, you should. You are a foolish child," said the faceless demon, laughing. "I wonder if you can lead any armies at all in the future. Don't waste your energy, brother. Your attacks will no longer affect us and ours the same. We're blood bonded now. See you around, brother."

John tried to shoot the faceless demon and the others, but they turned into black mist and disappeared into the floor below. John then rushed over to Sara, who had regained consciousness and was trying to stand up. He helped her get to her feet and hugged her tightly.

"What happened? Did I pass out again?" said Sara, holding her head.

"Yes, sweetheart. The smell was too much for you to handle. I cleaned the washroom. There was a rotten rat in there. Go ahead, do your thing because I can't take hold it anymore," said John, holding his groin.

"Oh, right, that's why we came here for," said Sara, as she entered the washroom holding the candle.

John leaned on the wall and nodded his head.

"Whatever you did completely took out the smell. Go get your thing done. I want to go back to the main room," said Sara, as John grabbed the candle.

Sara then looked at the paintings and was amazed. They all showed different views now.

"Hmmm, I'm pretty sure these creepy paintings showed sorrowful views of some places before I passed out. Oh well, whatever," she said, shrugging.

John came out of washroom and he and Sara went back to the main room. They found the kitchen and began looking for anything edible.

"Someone was here recently," said John, cautiously.

Sara stood closer to him.

"What do you mean?" she whispered.

"Look at all this stuff," replied John, pointing at some bags and suitcases, before grabbing a baguette and looking at Sara. "The bread's still fresh."

"Nanny probably came back home when we were at the hospital and left these things down here, knowing that we were in trouble and couldn't go back to the house. She wanted us to have supplies down here until things were calmer," said Sara, shuffling the stuff around.

John removed the items from the paper bags and saw a note at the bottom of one of them. He took out the note and read it.

"In case of emergency go to Joe. Unbelievable, Joe's alive?" said John, in shock.

"Come again?" asked Sara.

John handed her the note, which she quickly read.

"Uncle Joe's alive?" asked Sara then gave the paper back to John.

John looked at the back of the paper.

"It's a map to his place. Wow! All this time this information was down here and we had no idea about it. Nanny works in mysterious ways, eh?" said John, while analysing the map.

"Unbelievable, indeed," Sarah agreed. "I wonder why Nanny was worried though? Why would she leave all these things down here? It feels like she knew something shitty would happen to us. Strange stuff."

Sara picked up a water bottle, drank a bit and handed it to John. He drank some water from the bottle and looked at Sara, who was playing with her hair.

"I love you, you know that, right?" whispered John.

Sara smiled and winked.

"Alright," John continued. "We've got the food, water, and the place where we have to go to, but we can't pass any border checkpoints like this. The moment the units check our wrists at the border, it'll be game over for us."

"John, what are those?" asked Sara. "Maybe there's some more stuff in them too."

She pointed at two large shoulder bags and a black briefcase that were under the table.

"Let me check them," John replied.

He grabbed the bags and the briefcase, put them on the table then opened them.

"Sara, we've got everything that we need, including all this money, and also all these theatre props," said John, excitedly.

"Praise God.SED," said Sara. "These *Money-Memory chips*[36] are probably more than what we had in our savings combined. And look at this triple *Cyber-Shield*[37] chip. These are enough for us to have a safe journey to anywhere. And of course, more canned food and water bottles."

"Affirmative!" said John. "I can't believe all these were here for as long as they were. I mean, there's dust on everything but these things were placed here not long ago for sure."

"Alright, let's get the heck out of here. We got everything we want," said Sara, closing the briefcase. "We'll just have to find out exactly where Nanny is right now."

"You're right, but we need to go undercover," said John, playing with a fake moustache.

"Indeed, Mr Seventh," said Sara, putting on a blonde wig.

Sara and John changed their clothes, wearing the theatrical props that were available in the bags, and slowly began heading back towards the sewer canal.

---

[36] Money-Memory chips: Electrical glass chips.

[37] Cyber-Shield: A computer system anti-virus.

They emerged from the manhole where they'd entered before and after making sure that no one was around quickly emerged and walked towards the car. As they moved away from the manhole a skinny young girl with long straight black hair wearing an old-fashioned white dress stood beside the manhole cover and smiled sinisterly. John looked back as he felt a sense of dark energy and the girl waved her hand. John grabbed Sara's wrist and began running towards where the car was parked.

Chapter 20
Princess Is Here

While Sara and John were still in the secret room, Arms of Justice units had completely occupied John's house. There were checkpoints at the beginning and end of every street around the neighbourhood. All the local tenants were told to stay inside their houses until the units were done with their objectives. In addition to all the units on the ground, there were also a few Sky-eyes units flying in the sky, constantly monitoring the house.

"There has been a presence of an angel in here. The house is shielded perfectly, don't you think, Number One?" asked Number Two.

"Yes, the shield disrupts my scanning," replied Number One. "I can't continue like this."

Jason stood beside Number One and detached his head. He then grabbed Number Two's head and began pulling it slowly.

"An android like you disgusts me," said Jason. "Why do you whine so much? Just get the job done."

"Sir, my laser keeps getting interrupted," replied Number Two. "There's another shield above the existing one that doesn't let me scan anywhere. I've scanned what I was capable of. I can't do anything else, sir."

Jason kicked Number Two so hard that the android was destroyed when it smashed into the wall. He then walked downstairs and looked at the Arms of Justice units, who were watching TV and eating snacks. Jason raised his palm towards the units sitting on the sofa and shot them dead with purple light-balls.

"Fucking John is missing!" Jason roared. "We found nothing in this house so far, no one knows where John has gone after escaping the hospital, and I'm locked in here with a bunch of idiots."

The units kept their heads down and shivered with fear.

"I'll make you suffer very harshly if the shield in this house isn't broken soon," said Jason, while the units remained silent. "Something of high value is being kept hidden in here. Something that an archangel needed to remain safe. It could be John or perhaps something else."

The units stayed quiet but their silence turned into laughter, as one of the heavy looking units farted loudly. Jason grabbed the unit and broke his neck then detached the head. He then grabbed another unit and burnt his head off with a red energy sphere that came out of his hand.

The other Arms of Justice units didn't know what to do to prevent Jason from destroying them, so they remained where they stood and waited for their death to come.

"We've found a recording of John, sir," said Number Three. "He talked about himself and the weird things happening around him."

The android came down the stairs and onto the main floor. Jason walked over to Number Three, watched the recording then kicked him into the wall.

"Fucking idiot recorded himself like a madman," said Jason, laughing.

"Ironic for you to say that, sir," added a young A.o.J. unit.

Jason disappeared and reappeared beside the young unit and simply placed his index finger on him. The unit was decapitated and fell to the floor.

"Is anyone else wanting to add any comments?" asked Jason. "We have to deliver John to the brothers or else they'll won't have enough energy to combine the elements together or a host for her highness Lucifer to transfer him into Holy-Host."

Jason removed his glasses and flames emerged from his eyes. He then placed his hand on the wall and stretched his neck.

"How to break these shields?" he whispered.

Jason looked at the units who were waiting for his next move and stretched his fingers.

"Perhaps I'll terminate this house and its shield using my ... your excellency!" said Jason as he knelt.

Orhana, the young skinny girl with long black hair, stood middle of the room as all units knelt before her.

"Princess is here!" one of the A.o.J. units shouted, as many other units rushed inside the house and also fell to their knees.

Jason disappeared and reappeared near the young girl and knelt again.

"Your excellency! You have graced us with ..."

Orhana pointed at him, indicating that he should keep quiet.

"You fools are disgrace to the underworld, all of you," said Orhana in underworld language, looking at the units. "The chosen one and his bitch have escaped. I watched them leave while you miserable creatures crawled up and down this house."

Orhana sat down on a chair that was brought to her.

"My father sent me here to finish the job that my brothers seem unable to accomplish. Since they have surrounded themselves with morons like you, there is not much more left to expect from them," said Orhana, while the units all kept their heads down. "I have marked John already while he was running. It is time for me to show you how everything is done properly. After all, I am your future queen and the rightful future ruler of the underworld."

All the units began chanting a demonic ritual. Orhana then stood up and one by one observed the dark spirit inside every unit in the room, resulting in their instant death. She then looked at Jason and smiled.

"I am going to spare you, former angel. I like having your kind as my pets," said Orhana as she made a black sphere energy in her left hand and placed it on the floor. "Go, report to my brothers of my arrival, pet."

She then flew out of the window. Jason stood up in anger, spat on the floor then flew out of the window too.

The black energy sphere transformed into a small black hole, absorbed everything in the house including the land beneath inside of it then exploded leaving a giant hole in the ground. When the units left the neighbourhood and John's neighbours rushed into his house to find out what had happened, they were all stunned at seeing nothing but a giant hole in the ground. It appeared as if there had been nothing in there at all before.

"This is why we must never cross paths with God.SED and his great units. Let us curse this land by turning it into a giant shit hole," said an obese man, as he opening the zipper of his pants.

The crowd agreed with him by nodding their heads and one by one they began to walk into the giant hole, find a place, and began urinating or defecating.

Chapter 21
Temple (Orhana's Betrayal)

A few days after the explosion at John's house, God.SED summoned the leaders of all units for an emergency meeting. He was walking around the temple, throwing naked girls with their wrists slashed into the pit of fire in the middle of the floor. The girls were completely consumed by the flames instead of getting burnt.

"You were given a chance to live, yet you chose to cut it short by cutting your wrists, now I'm cutting you short from sucking my dick!" shouted God.SED.

He threw a girl into the fire then walked towards Jason, who tried to avoid any eye contact with him.

"Where is she now?" asked God.SED, as he sat on his leather chair.

"Her majesty flew after John, my lord," replied Jason. "Her majesty commanded me to come here and notify you of her arrival."

"Why would my sister come to the surface?" shouted God.SED, grabbing a girl who was kissing his ear before throwing her into the fire pit.

"Lord, I am not one to answer that question," replied Jason, keeping his head down.

The eyes of God.SED turned completely dark and his nails grew longer. He grabbed a girl by the breast and a man by his throat, pierced them with his nails then began observing their youthfulness. After he was done with them, he threw the now elderly looking bodies into the flames.

"Orhana is nothing but bad news for all of us," shouted God.SED. "If she came to the surface it means father has lost faith in us."

The flames of the fire grew larger.

"Well, this isn't our fault, but it is your fault," said God.SED as ten A.o.J. units were burnt into ashes.

141

"The holders of elements have pledged their allegiance to us. All we need is literally the energy from the chosen one and his body for father to control all the elements and bring father to the surface," said God.SED in demonic language.

He then looked at the Little-ones, who immediately cleared the room of human beings.

God.SED stood by the large glass windows and looked at his massive army and exhaled. He then looked at Jason, who was still trying to avoid eye contact, and nodded his head.

"The children are ready to fight and are growing inpatient. They're waiting for the order to unleash darkness upon humans. Yet their fathers are failing them by not transforming and getting control over all the elements," said God.SED, as he shot an A.o.J. unit with a dark purple energy sphere that terminated him instantly. "My father has apparently grown inpatient as well. He clearly thinks we're incompetent and incapable of getting the job done."

He shot another leader with an orange energy sphere and terminated him.

"We must …"

Darkness covered the entire temple and the doors of the chamber were blown into pieces.

Orhana walked into the room with her arms missing. God.SED disappeared then reappeared beside her and caught her before she collapsed on the floor.

"Sister! What has happened to you?" asked God.SED in underworld language.

Orhana tried to speak but couldn't, as she was very fatigued. God.SED opened his fingers and closed them into a fist. Twelve young teenage girls floated in the air in the other room. He then waved his fist slowly and the girls smashed into each other, until every bone in their bodies was broken into small pieces. He then closed his eyes and the bodies attached to each other, forming a large biological being, from which hung countless body parts. God.SED opened his fingers and pointed at Orhana's mouth. The blood began to flow from the biological being, passing through the door of the other room into the chamber and then inside Orhana's mouth. When Orhana drank all the blood, the remains of the biological being were tossed into the pit of fire.

Orhana swallowed the last drop, regaining her hands and energy. She then opened her eyes and a powerful purple energy was released from her body, causing many of the units in the room to be smacked into the walls around them.

"Twelve tasty virgins. I missed the surface," said Orhana in an underworld language, as she transformed into a tall slim woman wearing a black dress.

"As beautiful as always," said God.SED, while Orhana looked at her long claws and God.SED ordered everyone to leave the room, including Jason. "Tell us what happened sister."

Orhana sat on the black leather chair and put her feet on the table in front of it.

"Father was right," she began. "John is the one. His energy is enough for you to transform and his body is still pure for father to proclaim. However, he succeeded in killing my units and even defeating me in a one-on-one fight. He was in a secret place underneath his house. It was protected by a shield powered by an archangel energy. I found them leaving the place when I arrived, so I first took care of the house and all those useless units and then went after the chosen one. We attacked him multiple times, but he was beyond our power limit. He was stronger than I imagined. He reminded me of EZ but stronger, faster, and more protective. He's in love with his girl and through that he's being empowered constantly. I cannot believe he defeated me in only few seconds."

God.SED giggled, which made Orhana very angry.

"You two failed to prevent the chosen one gaining such power that even I, the future queen of the underworld, failed to destroy, and you are giggling like children."

God.SED continued looking out of the window, ignoring Orhana's frustration and rage.

"Utterly pathetic! I must go home and tell father about this," said Orhana in underworld language.

"Would you consider that all of us combined would be able to destroy the chosen one, sister?" asked God.SED, as he began to walk towards Orhana.

"Well, of course. I can feel your energy level to be equal to the chosen one's energy level and with me at the top that, surely we can stop him and perhaps fulfil our duties," said Orhana, suspiciously. "What do you have in mind, brothers? Stand back! Do not get any closer!"

Orhana began preparing to fight.

"Father told me to tell anyone daring to stand against me that he sucked my taste! He has marked me!"

Orhana was interrupted as God.SED shoved both his hands inside her skull, bit her throat, and began absorbing her energy.

"Sucked my taste means suck her as I have sucked her. You are the source of energy we require. You've been nothing except father's sex toy all your miserable life until this very moment. Father knew we couldn't defeat the chosen one, so he simply allowed you to come to the surface and straight to us, thinking that you could fix things. Enjoy your betrayal, little sister."

God.SED absorbed Orhana's energy while she suffocated. He then threw her decomposed body into the fire. The temple began to shake. Flames burst out of all the fire pits and a black mist appeared around God.SED, as he laughed sinisterly.

Chapter 22
Make Your Father Proud

In the underworld, a few days before Orhana was absorbed by her brothers as far as the eyes could see, there was magma, fire, demons, and other satanic creatures inside the black marble pyramid that was floating on burning magma. The sound of horrifying screams and the loud moaning of some undying human souls could be heard constantly throughout the pyramid.

The pyramid was built on three floors. The underground or inside the magma consisted of a dungeon where angels were transformed into demons. The semi-ground floor, which was below the actual ground floor, was half beneath of the magma and half above where demons and satanic creatures lived alongside human souls. The top or throne floor was in fact the ground floor that was above the magma surface level where the skull throne was placed and where Satan spent most of his time. Countless eyes that had been removed from Satan's supporters were implanted in the walls of the throne floor and the eyes would constantly roll to face Satan in horror everywhere he moved.

On the throne floor a crippled and burnt creature looked inside a bowl of blood and watched Gabriel entering the Earth.

"Get the job done this time, EZ. Don't fail me again," said the crippled creature in underworld language, as he continued looking inside the bowl.

He then watched God.SED as he enjoyed the company of countless women in his bed. The crippled creature closed his eyes and nodded his head.

"So powerful yet far from the last stage," said the creature while coughing. "How to help my sons? They must transform soon or we will lose control over the elements."

He walked over to the throne that was made of hands, fingers, and eyes, sat down and hit his cane on the floor three times. A giant serpent with twelve eyes slithered onto the floor then on the stairs in front of the throne before bowing his head at the crippled creature.

"Tell my daughter to meet me in here, my beloved friend," asked the creature in dark language, while licking his crooked palms.

The serpent bowed his head again and slithered away.

Shortly afterward, Orhana crawled out of the floor, walked upstairs and knelt in front of the crippled creature.

"Your excellency. The almighty Satan. My beloved father. What can your humble daughter can do for you?" said Orhana in dark language, while licking Satan's feet.

Satan looked at her and smiled.

"My dear daughter, my only daughter," said Satan in dark language, as Orhana crawled up and sat on his lap. "Your brothers are nothing but failures. They have failed to capture the chosen one and also failed to find another source of power to transform before the hours have come."

He kissed Orhana's nipples.

"Father, worry not, I will fix everything. I will complete what my brothers have failed to do so far," said Orhana in underworld language, as she began taking off her black dress.

Satan grabbed her bottom and squeezed.

"Father, I will go to the surface with your blessing and bring joy to you as I am now," said Orhana in underworld language, as she began having intercourse with Satan.

"Praise the Dark lord for the day your mother gave birth to you my beautiful daughter, oh I miss that creature," said Satan as he sucked on Orhana's nipples. "We will release her from that pathetic prison too soon, my beautiful daughter."

Satan as he began having harder intercourse with Orhana.

"We cannot be defeated in the upcoming war. It is your father's only chance to return to the Holy Host and destroy once it, once and for all."

"How great our biological bodies are, father. They let me enjoy every moment of you inside me. Fuck me harder, father!" shouted Orhana, as Satan had faster and harder intercourse with her. "Your will be done. You will rule on heavens once more, father! Fuck me harder, father! Mother will be released too, father!"

"Remember though, my beautiful daughter, even if she gets released, I shall anoint you as my queen and the queen of the underworld," said Satan in underworld language, while having an orgasm inside Orhana.

Orhana then licked Satan's penis clean and smiled as she put on her dress again.

"I will bear you many more children when you gain your reproductive body again, father. As for the underworld, I am already the queen," said Orhana in underworld language, licking her palms.

"My beautiful queen, it hurts me to say this, but it is time for you to leave your crippled father and go to the surface to finish the job," said Satan, as he stood up. "Going inside you made me stronger, my future bride. You are indeed a magnificent source of power. If your brothers disobey you or deny your orders, tell them father sucked my taste. No one dares to stand against whom I mark. They will fear you after they hear that."

"Father, they will fear me regardless of me giving your message to them or not. I am their queen and I am the most powerful among us three," she said then kissed Satan on his lips. "I will return to you soon, my future king."

A portal of fire came to existence on the bottom of the pyramid. Orhana disappeared and reappeared near the portal and looked at the demons that were bowing to her.

"Surface, here I come," she said, as she began crawling into the portal of fire.

Satan sat down on his throne and looked at the eyes in the walls.

"Incompetent sons and a mindless daughter. I cannot wait to fuck those angels again and produce real children," said Satan, looking into a large eye that had bloody veins. "You were the most useless host producer that gave birth to my children, Lilith. Enjoy that prison forever."

Satan pierced his long nail inside the eye that was looking at him.

Chapter 23
Anointment Journey

John was driving slowly in the dark and trying to stay awake, in vain. He pulled over to the side of the road and parked the car behind some dry bushes. He rubbed his eyes and switched off the engine, leaving Barbie on active mode. All he could see was desert and open road. It felt as if John and Sara were the only ones around. John drank some water and looked at Sara. She seemed to be having a nightmare as she looked distressed. He then slowly unlocked his seatbelt and comforted her by gently touching her forehead. Sara opened her eyes and smiled.

"I'm sorry, didn't want to wake you up," said John.

"It's alright," said Sara, stretching her legs. "Where are we?"

"We're almost at the checkpoint but we might have a problem though," said John.

Sara yawned, opened her eyes wider then stretched a little more.

"What do you mean? Why is it so dark in here?" she asked. "What happened to the road lights?"

"It seems as if something disconnected them all. Even Barbie lost her connection to the main server," replied John, looking out of the front window.

"What do you think we have to do next, Johnny?" asked Sara.

She unlocked her seatbelt and sat on John's lap placing her legs on the front passenger seat. John adjusted the seat as best as he could to make some more space and avoid getting squashed.

"My lady, your mother must be a cat or something. So flexible. How are you sitting on my legs in this little space?" said John.

Sara shrugged.

"I'm lost, Sara," said John. "I don't know how we ended up in this mess. We had a thing going on, our lives were awesome but now, we're on this dangerous journey to meet a man that we haven't seen in ages, I'm just…"

Sara kissed him on the lips.

"You think too much, Mr Seventh," said Sara, playing with John's hair. "If you're worried about me and all of this, I'm loving it to be honest. We never got out of our place. We never went on this type of adventure together. I just wish we could take a warm bath together in the tub at home."

"I beg your pardon, my lady, but the house has been demolished," said Barbie.

"What!" said Sarah and John together in complete shock.

"There's been an unusual explosion, leaving nothing but a giant hole on the land where your house once was. I'm sorry for your loss," said Barbie.

"What the fuck! What about Nanny? Where is she?" asked Sara, anxiously.

"There's absolutely no trace of her," said Barbie. "I've tracked every possible place where she could have gone but found nothing. I can no longer use the system to find her either. Any signal from my storage to the main server will get you two caught immediately. Nanny will hopefully contact you or you'll have no contact with her at all."

"No home to go to, not really sure if we can reach Uncle Joe, and now stuck middle of nowhere. It can't get any better than this," said John.

"Calm down, honey," said Sara. "We'll figure something out. Stay positive. Stay strong. I need a man not a pussycat. You know what? I'll drive until the checkpoints. You just rest a bit. But how are we going to cross it? We changed our appearances, the licence plate, and the colour of the car but not the ID chips in our wrists."

"Barbie's taken care of that while you were sleeping," said John. "We'll have new identities when they check us. Barbie had to activate one of her Cyber-Shields' chips to avoid viruses while pulling herself out of the main server though, which has left us with only two more chips. So, we have to reach to the train before we run out of cyber protection."

"Alright, sleep now. I'll wake you up when we reach to the checkpoint," said Sara.

Sara opened the driver's door, squeezed herself out of the car. John moved to the other seat and Sara sat back in the driver's seat and switched on the engine.

"Here we go," said Sara and the car began moving.

John opened his eyes and saw Sara behind the wheel but she wasn't motionless. It seemed as if time was frozen. He rubbed his eyes and blinked a few times. He tried to unlock his seatbelt but couldn't. He touched Sara's arm and pulled his hand back immediately. Her arm was as hard as a rock. John shook his head to become fully awake and began looking out of the window.

"Another goddamned vision but why the hell can't I move this time?" said John, still trying to unlock the seatbelt.

Lightning began to flash across the sky and a small tornado came into sight up ahead on the road. John tried harder to free himself from the seatbelt, but in vain. Meanwhile, Orhana stood in front of the car and the tornado came closer. John was not only shocked at the sight of Orhana but also about the tornado, which was made of insects.

"Who are you?" asked John, as Orhana stood in front of the car's hood.

Orhana smiled then placed her long fingernails on the hood and began scratching it, while walking towards John's door. She then stood beside the window and tapped her left index finger on the glass. The window burst into pieces. John sat motionless in a state of shock.

"I am Orhana, daughter of Lucifer and Lilith," said Orhana. "The future queen of the underworld. Your future queen, chosen one. Don't try to run from me. I know where you are."

John felt a burning sensation on the back of his neck, as Orhana disappeared.

"John, wake up! We're here," said Sara, slowing the car.

Breathing heavily, John opened his eyes in distress.

"Are you okay?" she asked. "Another nightmare?"

"I'm marked," said John, reaching his right hand to the back of his neck.

He then felt as if there was a long thick hair on his skin.

"Sara, look at my neck. What do you see?" said John.

"It's a fucking weird looking hair. That's gross, John. Why the fuck did you let that grow so long up there?" said Sara, as the car rolled closer to checkpoint where A.o.J. units where standing.

"We've got to cut this shit off me now. They've marked me. It's not a hair. It's a fucking bug," said John, trying to pull the hair off his neck.

Unit walked forward and knocked on the car's window, which Sara opened.

"Where are you two heading?" asked the unit.

"We're going to the Divine Rails, sir," replied Sara.

"And after that?" asked the unit.

"We will go to… go to…"

John interrupted her.

"We're on the *Anointment journey,*[38] sir," said John.

"Yes, I want children and he can't give them to me," Sara added.

The unit looked at Sara's cleavage and smiled. He then scanned her wrist and walked to the other side of the car to scan John's. Meanwhile, another unit approached the vehicle.

"It's good that you came," said the first unit. "These two are on Anointment journey. This jackass can't fuck her good enough."

"God.SED's going to love her pussy when he goes inside her and inside you too. Both of you look yummy as fuck," said the first unit.

He then looked at Sara.

"She's got tight tits and gorgeous lips," he said. "She deserves a real man to fuck her hard."

Sarah reached for John's right hand slowly and held it with her left hand.

"Watch them until I come back, would you?" asked the first unit, after scanning John's wrist.

"Alight, I'll watch them good," said the second unit, gazing at Sara's cleavage.

He then walked from the back of the car towards the driver's seat, where he rubbed his pants on the door handle.

"Open the door for me, girl," said the unit, as an uncomfortable Sara looked at John in distress.

"What are we going to do now, John?" asked Sara.

The unit pulled the seatbelt and dragged Sara out then threw her on the ground.

John rushed out of the car and ran to Sara.

"Look at those tits. Lady, he can't give you a baby, but I can. You don't need God.SED baby, you need my dick inside you rolling," said the unit, rubbing his penis through his pants.

He unzipped his pants and began masturbating.

"Come here, pussycat."

Sara ran to John and stood behind him.

"I wish we had guns," said Sara, terrified.

"We've got something far better than guns," said John, as his hands began to get warmer.

---

[38] Anointed journey: Couples unable to have children travel to the temple and request that God.SED has intercourse with the women to bless them with children.

"I'm going to enjoy this very much," said John, preparing to make an energy sphere but then he saw the other unit returning.

"What the fuck are you doing? You fucking ape!" said the unit. "Put that shit back in, man! You know very well that you can't fuck bitches on their journey. God.SED will know it by reading her memories and if he sees that you fucked her before he did, he'll terminate you, jackass!"

The other unit put his penis away and looked angrily at the other unit.

"We've got tons of whores to fuck and you decided to fuck this one? Come on, man. Their check-up came in clean and guess what, fucking moron, they are on their Anointment journey, for your information. I'm sorry for what happened back here, folks. Drive on, you're good to go. Make sure you satisfy God.SED or you'll end up coming back here again."

Sara and John quickly got back in the car and John began driving away as fast as he could.

"That was close," said Sara, removing a switchblade knife from the glove box and slipping it into her pants back pocket.

"That was beyond close," said John. "Even killing him wouldn't get us out of that place alive. It would just jeopardise everything."

"I hope we reach uncle's place with no more drama because I'll cut someone next time," said Sara, as John began driving faster.

Chapter 24
The Lotus Restaurant

While driving towards the Divine-Rails, John was forced to pull over so that he and Sara could refresh and have something to eat as they ran out of water and food. After checking with Barbie, they discovered the Lotus restaurant.

The restaurant was a very busy and crowded place, despite being in the middle of dessert. There were barely any unoccupied tables left in the place and servers were hurrying and often running to keep up with all the orders. John and Sara got out of the car and walked inside, as John kept looking to make sure that Orhana wasn't around. He then looked at the portrait of God.SED hanging on the wall, below which hung a picture of a smiling East Indian man.

"Namaste! Welcome!" said the same East-Indian man that was in the picture, clasping his hands together. "My name is Maheep! I am the owner of Lotus restaurant and want to welcome you two new faces to our humble place."

"Namaste," said John. "Thank you, sir. You have a magnificent place indeed."

"Look at you. Such lovely couple. Any little ones around?" asked Maheep, smiling.

"We are on the Anointment journey" said Sara, shrugging as John looked at her.

"Wow! The little one doesn't work well, does he?" asked Maheep, looking at John.

John nodded his head.

"Well, guess what?" said Maheep. "We have a menu filled with exotic and spicy flavoured dishes. You never know, they may activate your little guy down there and you could put a child in here before even reaching the lord most high."

"I'd love that but first we have to just clean up," said John. "We came from far away. Where are your washrooms?"

"Well, I have a special spot for you two," said Maheep. "We keep it for special people like yourselves, people in love or people struggling with love. The place is right up there."

Maheep pointed towards a pink room that looked like a big heart icon.

"There's everything in there, including a bathroom. The place is also fully covered with thick curtains, so you two can do whatever you want in absolute privacy," he added, winking.

"We appreciate this sir, we'd enjoy some privacy for sure," said John looking at Sara, who was sticking out her tongue out and biting it.

"Aw, look at her, she's already ready for you. Enough talking!" said Maheep, laughing. "Go upstairs and settle down until I send my fine servers to assist you with anything you want. By the way, drinks are on the house."

"Thank you, sir," said Sara, as she held John's hand and bit him on the shoulder.

"We'll be waiting for the servers, thank you," said John, looked at Sara in confusion.

Once they were upstairs, John closed the door and Sara stood beside a steamer that had pink mist coming out of it.

"Blasted Love," said John, chuckling as he looked down at the customers through the glass. "This room's got a crazy name, just like the people dining here."

Sara jumped on the sofa, took off her T-shirt seductively then flaunted her hair in the air. John closed all the curtains then switched on the lights that looked like roses and looked at Sara.

"Sara, sweetheart, this isn't home where you can only wear a bra," said John.

"Want me to take out my bra too, Daddy?" she asked, sitting on the sofa and reaching her hands around her back.

"Wait! Not a good place or a good time sweetheart," said John, as he sat beside Sara.

"I want to do it," said Sara, spinning her head. "Let's just fuck, John."

A server knocked on the door and entered the room without first getting permission.

"Namaste!" said the waitress, holding her hands together. "My name is Heena. Sorry for interrupting your activity. I'm here to assist you with anything you desire."

She pulled her hair behind her ear.

"Namaste, babe!" Sara replied. "Let's have a threesome, John! We've never had a threesome before, we never—"

John interrupted Sara by placing his hand on her mouth and pulled Sara back on his chest. Sara stopped talking and moving and just kept her head on John's chest, smiling.

"Namaste, behenji!" said John. "We're alright physically. Thank you for the hint. As far as the food goes, we haven't even looked at the menu yet but if you guys have some Lassi to get us cooled down the heat, we'd be much obliged. It's quite warm in here."

"Sure," said Heena, giggling. "It's always warm in here, sir. Everyone's feeling hot. I'll be right back."

She then left the room, closing the door behind her.

"Are you nuts, Sara?" asked John, as she tried to take her pants off.

"I feel horny!" she exclaimed, as she pulled them off. "I want to get fucked right now! Enough waiting! Just put the fucking dick inside me now!"

"Fuck me, Mr Seventh! Just fuck me!" shouted Sara, as John tried to control her. "John, why is the room spinning?"

Sara then lost consciousness.

"Sara! What the fuck happened?" said John in alarm. "Sweetheart, stay with me."

As John was trying to revive Sara, he sensed the presence of an energy that he'd felt when he'd met Orhana on the street. He placed his fingers on Sara's wrists to check her heart rate, which seemed normal. He quickly laid her on the sofa then rushed to the window and pulled back the curtains to see the crowd downstairs. He looked around to see where the energy was coming from and noticed a wealthy looking woman and her six bodyguards standing right in the middle of the restaurant, talking to Maheep.

John closed the curtains and rushed over to Sara, who was still unconscious. He looked around helplessly and wondered what he could do next. Meanwhile, another server knocked on the door and immediately walked in carrying a tray and looked at John, smiling.

"Is this a thing with you ladies, just walking in the room without getting permission?" said John. "What if we were fucking in here?"

"Namaste, my name is Indu and I'll be the second server assisting you today. I apologise, sir. Yes, we want you to carry on with your activities as we serve you constantly. You can even have intercourse with us if you please, at any time."

She then grabbed the glasses of Lassi drinks from the tray with her left hand and placed them on the table.

"Your Lassies, sir."

"My girl suddenly passed out all," said John, panicking. "Do you folks have any doctor or medic around here? She must have been very tired, but she said that she didn't feel good and then passed out."

"Did she inhale the steam from this lover maker machine directly, sir?" asked Indu, while turning the steamer off.

"Yes, but that's just a freaking steamer, isn't it?" John asked.

"She must have directly inhaled the steam from the steamer, sir," said Indu. "This steamer is designed to arouse people and make them have intercourse. However, inhaling it directly causes a sudden hormone unbalance in the body and often results in unconsciousness. Fear not, sir, I will go and bring our medic right away. We also do apologise for any inconvenience, great leader." s

Indu left the room so quickly that John couldn't even say anything further to her.

"Jesus Christ!" John exclaimed. "Great leader?"

The first aid responder knocked on the door and walked into the room with Indu and Heena. The responder approached John and shook his hand.

"Thanks for coming, Mister …"

"Anurag, sir," said the responder.

"Nice to meet you," said John.

He stood back to let Anurag check on Sara.

"She has inhaled the steams directly, sir," asked Anurag, while sanitising his hands. "Fear not, she'll be back on her feet in no time."

"Have you decided what to order, sir?" asked Heena.

John looked at Heena and Indu. He then slowly walked close to the table in the middle of the room, took a quick look at the menu and while holding it stood close to Heena.

"We'll probably go with numbers 3, 6, and 9 and can you please pack them up?" said John, maintaining eye contact with Anurag.

"Won't you stay to dine in here, sir?" asked Indu, scanning John's wrist.

"Unfortunately, no" he replied. "Something cropped up and it's best for us to get back on the road."

"That's very sad to hear," said Heena, glancing at Indu.

"We hope the incident wasn't the reason behind your decision," said Indu.

"Oh!" said John. "Not at all, it's just that something came up that needs …"

"Alright," said Anurag, closing his medical bag. "She's going to open her eyes any second now."

"Thank you," said John.

Anurag, Heena, and Indu left the room. Before the door was fully closed, Indu looked at John and bowed her head. John stood motionless in the middle of the room. He knew that the place wasn't safe for him and Sara. He then looked at Sara, who was still laying on the sofa, unconscious.

"How come the steamer didn't affect me? I'm so sorry, love, for putting you through all of this shit," said John, as he heard his name being called.

John walked to the windows, pulled the curtain back a little bit and looked down. The wealthy woman was looking at him from the middle of the floor, protected by her bodyguards.

"There you are, handsome," mouthed the wealthy woman.

John didn't move and continued looking at her. The wealthy woman and the bodyguards then transformed into their true forms. John was shocked to see the woman turning into Orhana and her bodyguards into massive demonic creatures.

Orhana gestured for John to go downstairs.

John looked at Sara and then at his hands, which were getting warmer.

"God save us, girl," said John.

"Come down before we come up to you, chosen one," shouted Orhana, as some windows and glasses cracked in the restaurant.

John closed the curtains and took a deep breath.

"God help us," said John and he exited the room.

Seeing John stepping downstairs, Orhana looked at the two demonic creatures that were standing close to her and nodded her head. The creatures walked towards the bottom of the stairs and stood there until John reached the restaurant floor.

"This idiot's going to lead the army of the underworld?" whispered Orhana, nodding her head.

John looked at the customers, while being escorted to Orhana. He then noticed that everyone in the restaurant was frozen. He looked at the Champaign fountain, which was still operational and at the cigars on the tables, which continued burning.

"Hmm, impressive, only the people are frozen," said John, as he stood in front of Orhana. "What a powerful sorcery."

"Lovely dress, my future queen," said John, bowing his head.

"My, my, so charming," said Orhana. "I would have borne your children if the consequences where different, chosen one. I like your type of humans."

John looked at a family dining at the table beside him. It was a large family of six, among whom was a new-born female toddler. John smiled and before he turned his head towards Orhana he was punched in the face. The impact was so powerful that he was thrown onto the dining table beside him and then fell of it as he was smacked onto the floor.

"Did it hurt, little boy?" asked the muscular looking demonic creature that had punched John.

John rubbed his chin. His entire face hurt. He even began tasting blood in his mouth.

"Not as much as what you're going to feel," said John, creating an energy sphere and shooting it at the demonic creature.

The sphere hit the demonic creature in the face, but no damage was done.

"The spirit power doesn't work on a former angel, genius!" said Orhana, laughing.

John jumped stood up quickly, pushed the nearby table to the floor and stood behind it, as he saw the demonic creature making a purple energy sphere. The demonic creature shot the energy sphere towards John, but the sphere hit the table instead, destroying it.

"You need to learn how to aim, son. You surely can't hit for shit," said John, as he made two energy spheres on each hand. "What exactly do you want from me?"

"My father believes that you're the chosen one," said Orhana. "The one who will give the ultimate energy to my brothers to gain control over elements, become a host to my father's spirit, and ultimately lead the army of the underworld to the gates of heaven."

"I'm of some real worth, eh?" said John. "Good to know that I hold such a high profile in the underworld but for your information, you all can go fuck yourselves. I'm hungry, tired, and ready to blast every single one of you."

Orhana signalled the demonic creatures to attack John. The creatures not only beat him almost to death but also tied his up hand with demonic energy power to prevent him from making any other energy spheres, before throwing him on the floor in front of Orhana.

"How can a fragile being like you lead the army of the underworld? Or even my father to heaven?" asked Orhana then slapped John.

"Ironic that you say that," said John, with bloody mouth. "You've got nice tits, but you're too skinny to even stand properly."

"Shut up, imbecile," said Orhana, looking into John's swollen eyes. "You're nothing but waste of time. I hope my father's right or you can be assured that I'll personally terminate you."

"I'm glad he thinks of me this way," said John, coughing. "It's been a while since I got my ass kicked this bad."

"What an annoying piece of shit you are," she said. "We're moving! Get his bitch and do with her as you please. I have to deliver this moron to my brothers."

The demonic creatures began moving towards the stairs.

"If you touch her, I'll destroy you all!" shouted John, still bleeding from his mouth.

Suddenly, a powerful energy was released from his body, causing the demonic creatures near him to float in the air then be smacked into their surroundings.

"Impressive. The girl triggers the chosen one's true image," said Orhana, as John tried to roll to the right so he could see the demonic creatures going upstairs. "Bring the bitch at once! Let's see what John can do more if we torture her again and again."

The creatures took Sara downstairs and laid her on the table with her legs wide open.

"Well, well, well! Look at this fine bitch," said Orhana. "A truly beautiful human being. I'm glad that she's already in her underwear. It'll make the work easy for my boys to take care of her."

John tried to release himself from his energy tie, but he failed.

"I wonder how she'll react if she wakes up to find herself being fucked by six massive dicks?"

John rolled his body to the other side, facing the ceiling. He tried to release himself but failed again.

"You'll regret this, Orhana, if anyone touches her," said John, coughing.

"Threatening your queen isn't in your best interest at this moment, trust me handsome," said Orhana, clapping her hands. "Begin fucking her boys. What are you waiting for?"

The demonic creatures began surrounding Sara near the table and licking her feet, arms, and breasts. One of the creatures sniffed Sara's vagina then turned around, looking at Orhana.

"The bitch is virgin, your excellency!" shouted the creature.

"Well, then enjoy turning her into a woman," said Orhana, laughing.

John closed his eyes and focused.

"God, wherever you are, protect her, please. I beg of you, protect Sara. She doesn't deserve this," said John, as he suddenly heard the howling of wolves.

"Oh fuck! EZ had actually infested this …"

Orhana was interrupted as John transformed into a massive white wolfman and broke off his energy tie, as if it were just a thread around his wrists.

The demonic creatures left Sara and rushed to Orhana and stood in front of her in a defensive formation and shot several energy spheres at the wolfman. However, he wasn't injured nor did he seem to be affected by the spheres at all. The wolfman opened his eyes and a powerful energy was blown out of his body, breaking every glass object in the restaurant. He then looked at the nervous demonic creatures and charged at them, growling. While running, he effortlessly grabbed a long stone table beside him and threw it towards the demonic creatures. They managed to shoot and destroy the table while it was still in the air but couldn't prevent the wolfman from grabbing them. The wolfman immediately broke the throats of the two creatures and blew energy into them that killed them instantly. Meanwhile, another pair of demonic creatures stood a few steps back and began shooting purple energy spheres at the wolfman but in seconds they were sliced in half and terminated by the wolfman's energy spheres. The wolfman then looked at the last remaining two creatures and smiled.

"You did well in finding what my girl was by sniffing her private parts," said the wolfman. "Let's see if you can sniff your death."

The wolfman struck the face of the demonic creature with his claws and blew a powerful energy sphere into it. The demonic creature was terminated and John turned around to face the last one.

"Please, master!" pleaded the demonic creature, kneeling on the floor. "Forgive me! Please!"

The creature was then terminated by the wolfman's energy sphere.

"Father was right," said Orhana, in alarm. "You're indeed the one but how come you're a white wolf?"

Orhana lifted Sara in the air and held a dark purple energy sphere towards her.

The wolfman looked at Orhana and growled.

"Be a good boy now, doggy!" warned Orhana. "You don't want to anything stupid or the girl dies."

The wolfman ignored the warning and began walking towards her.

"I said be a good boy," said Orhana, as the dark purple energy sphere drew closer to Sara. "You take another step towards me and I'll obliterate her. All I want is for you to come with me to the temple and the girl will be set free."

The wolfman growled and stopped walking.

"Good boy! I'm impressed to see a half human in the form of an animal spirited warrior. I always thought a human body couldn't bear the energy level but yours surely can."

Orhana began to transform into a massive demonic creature, knowing that she couldn't defeat the wolfman in her current form.

The wolfman didn't spare any more seconds and charged at Orhana. He sliced off her arms and shot her with a powerful energy sphere.

"My arms!" Orhana screamed, as dark fluid burst out of her wounds. "You fucking idiot!"

"Never leave your guard open," said the wolfman, while making a very powerful energy sphere.

Orhana knew that she had no other choice but to retreat, as she failed to transform properly and wasn't going to be able to defend herself from the energy sphere that the wolfman was about to shoot her with.

"You're going to regret this! Attack him!" shouted Orhana, but no one moved and no one came to defend Orhana. "Oh, you'll all regret this!"

Orhana then opened her wings and flew towards the restaurant's glass roof.

"No, you'll regret seeing me again, Orhana!" shouted wolfman.

He shot the powerful energy sphere towards Orhana but before it hit her, she disappeared in a black mist.

Wolfman then looked at Sara, breathless. He began walking towards her but after taking a few steps, he lost consciousness and fell to the floor. The black thick hair slowly emerged from John's neck and turned into dust as it floated in the air towards the floor.

"Johnny, wake up!" said Sara. "Who beat you like this?"

John opened his eyes and saw that he was lying on a sofa on the main floor wearing different clothes. He then looked around and saw that everyone including Sara was gathered around him.

"I fucking fell unconsciousness again," said Sara. "I don't remember what happened except that I was dancing upstairs in that fucking room and woke up down here with these new clothes on.".

She then helped John to stand up, as he looked around in complete shock. The entire restaurant looked spotless. It was as if nothing had ever happened in there.

"We have to get out of here now, Sara," said John, weakly.

"But sir …" said Maheep.

"I can smell what you are," said John angrily, as everyone stepped back and put their heads down. "I wonder how I didn't realise when I walked in here? Open the goddamn door. We're leaving here."

"What about the food, John?" asked Sara. "I'm starving and you don't look good at all. We also have to figure out how this happened to you before leaving here."

"I fought with the rich lady's fucking bodyguards when you were unconscious. They talked too much. As far as the food, fuck the food. We just have leave here, right now."

Sara helped John move by holding him around his shoulder.

"Master, at least let us provide you with water," said Maheep.

"Call me master one more time and I'll send you where the others went," said John.

"Master?" asked Sara, confused.

"I'll explain everything in the car sweetheart," said John. "Just let's go out of here."

"Where are the orders?" Maheep shouted.

"Did you have your clothes on when you woke up?" asked John.

John and Sara walked out of the restaurant and sat in the back of the car.

"Get us far from here, Barbie," said John, before he lost consciousness.

The car started rolling and within seconds, it vanished from sight.

"He defeated Excellency Orhana, despite being a half human," said Anurag.

"Silence!" said Maheep. "We are no ones to talk about this."

"He was glamorous," said Indu, hugging Heena.

"And very strong," Heena added.

"What are we going to do now?" asked Anurag.

"We will live on until our time comes," said Maheep. "We already have a major problem for not helping Excellency Orhana."

"I miss home, I wish we'd never abandon it," said one of the women in the crowd. "I hope father will forgive us and let us join the light again."

"He'll never forgive us. Take that out of your fucking mind. What a stupid comment," said Maheep, closing the restaurant's doors. "Let's just fucking go back to our routine and watch out for any other travellers coming close by. We're running out of human meat and blood."

"Beloveds, my analysis shows that your bodies to be seeking great levels of energy and hydration. Have you consumed anything at the restaurant at all?" asked Barbie. "No, we didn't," said Sara. "I fell unconscious in a very erotic room and when I woke up, I found myself on the table on the middle of the ground floor. Then I found John beaten and unconscious laying on a sofa in the VIP room with people around him. Neither of us ate or drank anything. We're both starving."

She then leaned her head on the back seat and closed her eyes. Meanwhile, Barbie changed the colour of the car and the number plate. She then changed the material of the seats into a smoother fabric to allow John and Sara to rest better and continued driving the car towards the Divine-Rails.

Chapter 25
Not Much Time Remains

In Training-Host, angels were training in the air, on the ground, and underwater. Bright explosions could be seen and heard from every corner of the landscape. Gabriel was observing everyone, while flying in the middle of the sky. He was proud of what he was witnessing and how accomplished the angels had become. An energy sphere was accidentally shot towards him, but he dodged and smiled at the angel who'd fired at him. The angel nodded his head in relief and flew back to his training.

After monitoring training angels for a while, Gabriel flew over to the water and fire training zones and began observing. Angels were fighting underwater and often coming to the surface to continue their training by using fire bursting out of their hands. Gabriel looked at the furious training zone and noticed how well the angels would dive under and into the lava without getting hurt or burnt. He then nodded his head with pride and flew to the rocky side of the land and began watching. Angels were throwing massive rocks at some other angels that were shielding themselves with their wings and they seemed perfectly adjusted to the weight and impact of the rocks.

Satisfied by the angels' performances, Gabriel returned to the command centre and sat on a golden chair then closed his eyes.

"What is it, Jessica?" asked Gabriel.

"It doesn't matter how invisible I am, you never fail to sense my presence, Commander," replied Jessica.

Gabriel smiled and opened his eyes.

"Agreed, you need to use the lowest level of your spiritual power if you want to be completely undetectable by me. However, I will always sense the presence of all the angels, no matter what they do. I am connected to them all as they are connected to me."

Jessica landed beside Gabriel while holding the Golden-Tablets.

"Commander, this is the latest update," said Jessica, holding out the tablet. "John's future has changed again."

Gabriel looked at the tablet and immediately stood up.

"How is this possible?" said Gabriel. "The light was supposed to overcome the dark spirit in his system. I am afraid the prophecy remains the same. He may fight on our side, yet he will lead the armies of the underworld to the gates of Holy-Host."

Gabriel placed his hand on the tablet and it disappeared. He then began to fly.

"Follow me," he said, as he headed towards the balcony.

Jessica and Gabriel flew to the top of a mountain that was made from diamonds and crystals then landed on the ground.

"His battle with Orhana must have exposed him to her infected blood without him knowing about it," said Gabriel, with concern.

"I wonder how he managed fighting against Orhana, when she alone can destroy many of us in her first physical form," said Jessica.

Gabriel nodded his head.

"Indeed, it is surely impressive for a human to stand against her and survive, but nothing is certain anymore. Due to his exposure to the dark blood of Orhana, John will be vulnerable if he gets exposed to any other blood now. He may turn into an out of control wolf that will pose a threat to everyone around him. I hope Joe finds out about this soon enough, so he teaches him the method of balancing the spirit's powers to prevent John from becoming unstable."

"I hope so too, Commander," said Jessica.

Gabriel opened his hand and the tablet appeared. He looked at John's image and showed it to Jessica.

"Unbelievable," said Gabriel, as Jessica put her hand on the image. "No one before him survived with such powers, yet he stands stronger than ever before with ease. Marvellous yet dangerous."

Gabriel watched as John cut off Orhana's arms.

"Incredible," said Gabriel, in amazement. "Despite having no control over his actions, he still did not fail to protect the girl."

"He may die but he won't let her be harmed," said Jessica. "His love for her is absolute."

"We have seen similar love stories during thousands of years, Jessica," said Gabriel. "A lot will change when the war begins."

He began flying to a higher altitude and Jessica followed him. He then stopped and looked at the mountain beneath him.

"Not much time remains to face the war, as you know," said Gabriel and Jessica nodded her head. "Lucifer manipulated the time of the war by betraying his own daughter to get the sons the power they required. I am still not sure if our army is ready for theirs with so little time remaining. The new armies are far more complex that what we faced in the past, over thousands of years. Lucifer has surely prepared for this final battle of Earth."

"I wish humans would side with us more than they sided with them," said Jessica. "Even the holy son died for them, yet only a handful joined us."

"And I wish more of us would remain here instead of joining them," added Gabriel.

"We need to win this war without any involvement from the creator, Commander," said Jessica. "We can't afford to lose another planet."

Gabriel nodded then flapped his wings.

"Agreed, we must stop *Vehya*[39] from entering the world at any cost. Earth is one of God's most significant creations and most sacred. That's the reason why he placed a firmament, or as humans call it an ozone layer, around it to protect the planet and its features from destruction," said Gabriel while turning around. "Now, that's how you move around undetected, Jessica."

Jessica showed a grumpy face to Natasha, who appeared beside her.

"Was I that undetectable?" asked Natasha.

"Yes, I didn't detect you at all, frankly speaking," replied Jessica, shrugging her shoulders. "Well done, sister."

Natasha bowed her head to Gabriel.

"Commander, it's good to see you back in here with us," said Natasha, hugging Jessica. "It's so good to see you again too, sister. I heard about how my son is now possessing both light and dark powers in his system. Will such a host survive with such powers at all?"

"We were actually discussing about that," said Gabriel. "John is surviving because of the girl. He is feeding on her love, just like a harmless parasite."

---

[39] Vehya: The name of the Dark God.

"They've been soul mates since they were born," said Natasha. "Two beautiful souls meant for one another. He isn't a parasite. He's truly in love, Commander."

"I hope it stays that way. Feeding on unlimited energy of love is better than feeding on her soul," said Gabriel. "Much will change in a short time once the war begins and some of the changes will certainly not be in our favour at all."

"My son will not side with Lucifer," said Natasha. "I don't believe that."

"Will his training not be enough for him to let his human spirit overcome his animal spirit?" asked Jessica.

"Perhaps, but again, we shall find out," said Gabriel. "Now ladies, let us return to the command centre and proceed with our plans for encountering the first waves of attacks."

He then began flying down the mountain towards the command centre, alongside Jessica and Natasha.

Chapter 26
Reaching Divine Rails

After a couple of hours of driving away from the restaurant, Barbie was forced to stop the car as the temporary colour had ceased to be operational. Barbie parked by the side of the road, from where the Divine Rails checkpoint could be seen. Earlier, John had regained consciousness and he and Sara, they had changed their appearances using the remaining items in the bags. Then with Barbie's help they updated their identities using the last remaining Cyber-Shield. They all knew that the checkpoint could certainly be the end of their journey if things didn't go according to plan.

John stood beside a bush on the arid cracked ground and closed his eyes as the warm wind blew in his face. Sara joined him and held his hand as she exhaled. They felt a deep sense of peace for a few seconds. They hadn't had such a feeling since the last time they'd been near a beach in West-Lands, waiting to see the sunrise. Sara looked at John and, sensing that he was worried, gripped his hand more tightly and John gently rubbed his thumb on her palm.

A lot was on John's mind. The two of them were in constant danger no matter where they went, some of their friends had been killed, they were on the most wanted criminals list, they were hungry, thirsty, exhausted mentally, physically and emotionally, and most importantly, they had no home to go back to. John possessed powers without knowing how to use them properly and he'd recently discovered that his caregiver was an angel, he was himself half angel, some potion of his memories had returned, and he'd met with an underworld creature named EZ and an underworld future queen named Orhana. John opened his eyes and looked at Sara, who'd laid her head on his shoulder, and kissed her head.

"What a life," he whispered.

"Do you think we can get out of this alive?" said Sara, lifting her head and looking at him. "Do you think it could maybe wise to talk with God.SED and ask him for forgiveness? He has forgiven people in the past, so he may forgive us too."

John felt very agitated but calmed down after taking a deep breath and kissed Sara on the head again.

"I … I can't really … what the fuck is that?" exclaimed John.

A car passed them, with a topless girl leaning out of a window. She was screaming for help as she was being raped.

"Poor girl, it's so common these days that I don't know if I feel bad or just having sympathy for her?" said Sara very casually, as the car sped away.

"God save us. How did we lose our sight so easily?" said John. "How did we allow this type of behaviour to become so normal?"

He then looked at Sara. She stepped on John's feet, looked into his eyes and smiled.

"Love your smile," said John, as he hugged her tightly. "I'm sorry, Sara, for putting you through this. I never wanted this to happen"

"Hey, easy now, Johnny," she said, wiping his tears. "Don't forget that as long as you're with me I'm happy, even if I don't smile or laugh. But I am fucking hungry and now I'm thirsty too, so you won't see much of me smiling and laughing for a while."

"We'll eat a plenty when we reach to the Rails, but this is going to be a huge risk Sara," said John. "We have no shields left, no more stuff to cover our identities, and the place where we're heading may not even exist."

"John, there's nothing else left for us except going forward. It's either there or nowhere." said Sara in a British accent.

"Does your accent pop by itself or something every time you get super serious?" asked John, fascinated.

Sarah merely shrugged.

"So interesting. I mean, we were born in England after all," said John.

"We were born where?" asked Sara.

"I like your purple eye colour. It's very exotic," said John, trying to change the subject.

"John, don't change the subject," said Sara, as the wind became stronger. "Hold that thought. What the heck is that thing?"

She pointed at a huge storm that had appeared in the distant sky.

"Let's go before that weird looking storm reaches us," she added. "I don't think that's an outcome of the cloud seeding. That's something else."

"Ya, we got to get the hell out of here," said John.

"What's hell again?" asked Sara.

"I'll explain later. Just let's grab what's left and run," John replied.

He rushed to the car with Sara and began looking for anything that was left to pack.

"Barbie, I'm going to transfer you into my watch," said John. "Are you ready?"

"Yes, sir," Barbie replied. "By the way, that's no storm. That's an unidentified mist that's spreading around the world. The formation location is unidentified."

John transferred her into his watch by holding it in the middle of the steering wheel.

"Unidentified mist? Let's run then. Whatever that shit is, it doesn't look good and holy shit is spreading everywhere too quickly."

John grabbed Sara's hand and started running towards the Divine Rails.

"John, we can't leave the car like that!" said Sara. "They can use it to track us down."

"Already thought about that too, sweetheart," John replied, as the car exploded.

"You idiot!" Sara exclaimed. "You planted a bomb in that fucking car? What if it blew randomly?"

"All cars with that model came with a self-destruct mode, my love. As for you second question, I guess God.SED loves us so much that he prevented us from letting the fucking bomb blow," said John.

"I'm in love with an absolute maniac," said Sara.

A few minutes later, John took a couple of deep breaths and continued walking beside Sara until they reached the unit. The *ID-me*[40] unit scanned their wrists and told them to wait. John closed his eyes and opened them after hearing the unit say that they were clear to go ahead. Sara looked at John and winked before they passed the checkpoints. They then walked to the kiosk and received their tickets to North-Lands from the *tickets lady*[41] and then began heading

---

[40] ID-me: Checkpoint law enforcers.

[41] Tickets lady: The elderly lady in charge of ticket sales.

towards the cabins. After finding the right one, they entered in their ***Rolling Ball***[42], closed the door behind them and collapsed on the chairs.

"Told you not to be afraid," said Sara.

"It was weird though," said John, still feeling somewhat suspicious. "We weren't even asked where we were heading."

"True, but who gives a shit," she added. "We're here and going to roll. I can't wait to order the bloody food. I'm starving."

While John and Sara were talking, they heard an announcement by the ***puller***[43] through the speakers inside the ceiling of their cabinet. The puller greeted the passengers and informed them regarding how important it was to follow the instructions that would soon be given to them by one of the ***checkers***[44], as the pulling would begin shortly. As soon as the puller finished his the announcement a checker knocked on the door, almost as if she'd been waiting there. John glanced at Sara, who shrugged, stood up then opened the door and was handed a booklet.

"Hi, lovely lovebirds," said the cheerful checker. "Inside this booklet there's everything you need to know about the journey ahead of you. I'll be right back with your items. Bye!"

She blew air kisses towards Sara and John, who slowly closed the door then looked at Sara.

"Such fake personalities these checkers have. You literally know they're faking everything," said Sara, as John sat beside her looking at the booklet.

"I know, right? I always love opening these," he said as he opened the booklet.

Holographic instructions were displayed above each page. After going through a few pages and selecting some items to eat later, John closed the booklet and placed it on the oval table. Sara grabbed his shoulder and leaned her head on his arm.

"We need to take a shower, John," she said.

"Well, let's do it then, my lady." said John, smiling as the Rolling Ball began to move

---

[42] Rolling-Ball: An anti-gravity sphere cabin.

[43] Puller: The driver of the train.

[44] Checker: A cabin hostess or host.

171

Chapter 27
God.SED (The Rise of the Dragon and the Beasts)

Seven years earlier, people around the world watched as the black stone that carried God.SED entered the Earth's atmosphere either with their eyes or through the media. Many were nervous, some rejoiced, many were sad and others happy, many danced and sang songs and many others protested. The security council members ordered immediate international martial law and asked people around the world to remain indoors until further notice. When martial law failed due to the intense international chaos, an open fire order was confirmed. Countless people died around world at the hands of international soldiers. After days of fighting, the protestors turned into rioters, but they were also defeated and supressed by the soldiers. When everything came under the complete control of the security council people were forced to remain in their households and soldiers went back to their bases, waiting for the next order. The event left countless murdered people piled on the top of each other as their blood caused a massive stream on the ground all over the world. However, despite all the chaos the religious ones created secret communities above and underground and prayed day and night for their god to bless them with salvation. It was through their prayers that they discovered the secret of survival. The prayers would turn them invisible in the eyes of the demonic creatures that were hunting them. Armed with this knowledge, the religious people built a massive community that was named the *Circle of Believers*[45]. The community protected people for many of the following years.

---

[45] Circle of Believers: A round shaped community in which true god believing people live.

The black stone landed in the heart of Mediterranean Sea. The impact was so strong that it was felt by everyone, all around the world. Within three days, there were more missiles facing the object than there were facing any other thing on the entire planet. Layers upon layers of armed men and women stood side-by-side, ready to charge against the stone, but after a few days the readiness began to fade and fear and anxiety began to flourish.

Many people participated in the global suicide pact that was announced on a mainstream social media platform by a young couple that believed the aliens had come to torture the human race. The result was devastating, as millions took their own lives in a single day, as if the civil wars between rioters and international soldiers weren't enough to increase the death toll.

By the early hours of the sixth day, the population of the planet had been reduced significantly without any engagements between the humans and the stone. Silence and mourning replaced joy and happiness. By the late hours of the sixth day, a powerful electrical energy was released from the stone that disabled all the electrical devices on Earth. The planet returned to chaos but this time in darkness.

In the early morning of the seventh day, the security council declared that the alien object as hostile and dangerous and announced open fire towards it. Neither bullets, rockets, ballistic missiles, or nuclear weapons worked on the black stone, which remained where it was, untouched. When all the attacks failed, the security council called a ceasefire so that they could investigate other options. It was during the ceasefire that the stone began to separate into multiple large parts and from the gaps countless demonic creatures burst out and attacked any living creatures around them. International armies fought for as long as they could, but they were completely outmatched and outnumbered. Neither their weapons nor their tactics could prevent their deaths. The security council decided to use the most lethal weapons on the planet, that were usually kept secret from the public, for the first time against the creatures and the stone, but even those attacks didn't have any impact. Countless died within minutes but were then resurrected and began walking towards the stone as it evolved into a temple with two giant burning hands being formed around it. The majority of the people around the world surrendered and waited until they were either killed by the demons or taken to the temple.

By the noon on the seventh day, the vicious attacks of the demonic beasts and creatures stopped and they returned to the newly built temple. Seeing this, people began to emerge from hiding and those that could began to get close to the temple and witnessed a huge two-headed serpent emerging from the middle of the structure and transforming into a man that shone brightly while flying in the air without any wings. The flying being held his arms open towards the people that had reached the temple and began speaking.

"My children! Fear not, I will cause you no harm. Those men and women who died were evil and in my presence such existence is unacceptable. I know you are anxious to find out who I am. I know you have many unanswered questions. I will answer them all for you. Fear not! I wish you no harm as I am the god of love, peace, and mercy. Those who are breathing are the ones that have already been judged and are considered worthy of the power of life."

People around the world were amazed and shocked to hear the voice of the man in their minds, as some of them were miles away from the point of impact.

"I heard your pleas for long enough," said the man. "I am here now, and I am here to give you peace."

His voice magically brought confidence into the hearts and minds of people around the world.

The man flew higher and shone more brightly in the sky.

"I am the owner of your souls, creator of Earth and director of your destinies. You may call me God.SED, as it pleases me."

The dead men and women rose up and stood in lanes near the burning hands, which by then had been transformed into two giant golden olive tree branches.

"Look at them, my children," said God.SED, pointing at the people. "I even forgave the retched ones, the evil ones, the worst ones, for I am the god of love."

Many in the crowd fell on their knees, tears in their eyes, and rejoiced in happiness as they witnessed resurrection from death in front of their eyes.

"My children, after forty days the continents on this host will reattach and become one landmass and I will be at its centre to bless you all. Those who die during this massive continental shift will be resurrected and serve me directly. Those who survive will need to identify themselves to me as they will receive the highest level of blessings that any human has ever had since the day of the creation," said God.SED.

He held his hands towards them.

"Let there be light," he shouted.

174

The mist disappeared and the sun began to shine again.

"Let there be darkness," shouted God.SED.

The sun began to set and the moon began to shine. People around the world were filled with astonishment.

"Let there be light," shouted God.SED and the night turned into a bright sunny day.

"Are you not convinced that I am your god, your owner and director?" shouted God.SED and many fell to their knees again.

God.SED stood at the top of the marble tower located in the middle of the temple. The beasts that now were in the shape of humans began to guard the temple and its surroundings.

The entire Mediterranean Sea dried out, its sea animals disappeared, trees, flowers and bushes grew from the dry lands around the temple, and golden roads were built that led to the four gates of the temple.

"Rejoice! Rejoice! Rejoice! The temple is built on the holy land once more!" shouted God.SED.

People cheered and rejoiced. God.SED looked down at the people while standing on the pillar and laughed.

"A simple piece of engineering made them think of us as their god," said God.SED, laughing loudly. "It will be so easy to own their souls for the next seven years."

Over the next few weeks, those people who were able to migrate travelled to the temple from all corners of the world with some of their belongings, while those who were unable to do so simply hoped for survival. At the end of the fortieth day, God.SED stood at the top of the marble tower looking at the large crowd that surrounded the temple.

"I am one happy father, my beautiful children," said cheerful God.SED. "You are the ones who will not face the next and the last plague of your father before my complete kingdom is established on this host! I love you all!"

The crowd cheered and many began engaging in sacrificial offerings.

"Are you ready for your new home?" asked God.SED.

"Yes!" shouted the crowd, in unison.

"Let it be done!" exclaimed God.SED, as powerful energy was discharged from his body into the surrounding area.

The continents soon began to shake then began to move. Six more powerful energy charges emerged from God.SED's body until all the planet's land was attached, forming a super continent. At the end of the sixth charge a purple mist was released among the crowd from the temple. The mist travelled as far as the wind could carry it throughout the new giant continent, turning those who breathed it motionless. When the dust and the fog settled down, God.SED smiled and looked at the members of the crowd, who were standing motionless.

"You are all mine now!" said God.SED, laughing grimly as he raised his right hand then brought it back down.

"Enjoy your last days on this wretched world, imbeciles!" said God.SED, as the crowd began to move away from the temple.

Chapter 28
The Circle of the Believers

The purple mist hypnotised every living creature that it touched. People woke up as different individuals and became unusually calm. They woke up with new sets of skills and identities, with no memories of their true pasts. All they could recall was the glorious arrival of God.SED and the happiness and joy that he'd brought to them and to the Earth. They were confused and lost at first but as the years passed they forgot to even ask questions about their pasts and those who tried to investigate this by questioning the authorities were immediately taken into the temple and never heard from again. God.SED told people around the world that they'd received a new kingdom and a new beginning. Consequently, they must forget about the past and enjoy the new lives they'd received. God.SED made it clear that objecting to him would have severe consequences by slaughtering 666 people who questioned him in a televised event during the early days of his rule.

However, among those who were touched by the purple mist and forgot everything were also some people who survived the plague by finding the cure. These people were called *believers*[46] or the *religious ones*[47]. They were the ones who, despite seeing all the wonders that the God.SED performed, didn't give up on their faith and continued praying to the being that they considered to be the one true god of their ancestors. Believers discovered that prayers prevented and protected them from the effects of the mist, so they prayed continuously in and around the Circle of Believer's community, until it was built not only by them but also by other angels who walked among them as humans.

Knowing that these people would cause problems, God.SED labelled them as blasphemers that had to be eliminated. He announced the highest reward for

---

[46] Believers: A group of people unaffected by the purple mist.

[47] Religious ones: Like believers, a group of people unaffected by the purple mist.

those who hunted such individuals and ripped out their hearts. Little did the humans know that the reward was simply to become a worker at the temple and nothing else. Fear of death kept the believers in the community for all the years God.SED reigned over the Earth.

After realising that prayers would make them invisible to the eyes of the forces of God.SED and those people affected by the mist, the believers began conducting secret operations in the new towns and cities around them. Many lives were taken at first, as those who failed to pray constantly fell under the spell of the purple mist and forgot who they really were. However, over time the techniques and skills of the believers were improved and they began to grow in numbers. A circle of people joining hands and praying was formed by members of the *Circle of Pray-ers[48]*.

A high council chamber of religious men and women was formed inside the community to lead others during the reign of God.SED. These men and women were once the heads or leaders of their faiths. Religious leaders were chosen by voting to represent a specific faith. People also needed to vote and accept the overall final decisions that the leaders had made after voting. Sending a woman dying of cancer to John with a picture of a cross to intrigue his spirit and a warning to Jessica was one of the hardest finalised decisions that the community had ever voted for.

For people to survive and collect resources, they came up with a new technique that would allow them to move around hidden from the eyes of demonic creatures. Three individuals would form a triangle by holding their hands together around a believer, who was in charge of collecting resources. They'd escort the individual to the city or the town nearby while praying then return to the community with as many resources as they could. However, this technique wasn't considered very effective because long distance walking made believers so fatigued that they'd stop praying and be exposed to the mystic mist and eventually to others around them.

When the starvation and thirst stung the believers, they began small-scale crop production. Many died during this development, yet they died knowing that their deaths would keep their faith alive for the younger generations. However, after the first two years the entire community decided not to produce any children

---

[48] Circle of Pray-ers: A group of people that constantly pray around the community by holding hands.

at all to prevent them from the wrath they were facing. As a result, the number of children was reduced and the number of adolescents and adults increased.

In the council chamber, religious leaders were sitting around the round table having an intense argument over John's future.

"Calm yourselves, councillors. We still don't know everything to make any decisions this soon," said councilman Ashwin.

"All we know is just the mythical story of John Seventh and nothing else," added councilman Luke. "He could be of no harm to any one of us. I believe we can't rely on visions alone and must give him a chance."

"Myth or truth, the child's vision was clear about him," said councilwoman Megan. "You know it very well, councilmen, that the oracle's visions are never wrong."

"We can ask the oracle how to deal with this situation more effectively," said councilwoman Aboli.

While the councilmen and women were arguing, a young boy rushed into the room.

"Haven't you been told to knock on the door before coming in, Henry?" asked councilman Emmanuel.

"The storm has begun!" shouted Henry, breathlessly.

"God save us," said councilman Irfan.

The councillor's meeting was adjourned and the men and women rushed into the community's gathering hall.

A few minutes later, a large anxious crowd of people stood in the gathering hall looking up at the altar behind which the councillors were chatting. Ashwin read the latest information on the paper that he was given, stood behind the altar and cleared his throat.

"Beloved believers, try to remain calm. The news is true. Another vision of the oracle has come to pass. Embrace yourselves as we are at the final hours of our very existence," said Ashwin, gravely.

Some people in the crowd began to whisper to each other.

"We must remain united, faithful and engaged in prayers until we are rescued by our holy father," Ashwin added.

"Oh, fuck off!" shouted an angry man in the crowd. "Pray for this, pray for that. Bullshit! We're soon going to die miserably, either at the hands of the demons or killed by Satan himself and you folks are just standing up there giving us fake hopes."

Some in the crowd nodded their heads.

"My brother, please, do not lose faith and remain connected to all of us. We will prevail," said councilwoman Chava. "We knew this day would come, the deadly rapture, yet we survived all this time in our circle by worshipping the one true god. That's why we must retain our faith in him for the survival of our kind. We mustn't lose hope."

"Fuck that! You know what? It's been almost seven years already," shouted a woman in the crowd that was supported by many others. "We've lived like rats under the ground or in here. We've lost so many that tried to help or bring food for us. It's better if we just go out and surrender. If there is a god, he'll save us regardless of what we decide. We leave today!"

"If you stay in here, you'll be safe, but out there you'll join the *blinded*[49] people," said councilman Xin. "This is the fact!"

"Oh, shut it!" shouted a young girl in the crowd. "We were and are never safe in here or anywhere anymore. We're technically starving and blindly believing in the god that never helps when we need her the most! I'm leaving!"

"She's right," said a young man beside her. "Enough with this bullshit! Enough with religion! Enough with this god! I'm done worshipping something that waits until we die horribly. We all know what the oracle said. When the storm starts, the war starts in which two thirds of the world dies. If I'm going to die soon, I don't want to die in here between delusional people anymore. Let's go!"

He then followed the girl, who was leaving the rest of the people behind.

"It's our faith that kept us alive this far! Can't you all see this, child? Look around you!" shouted councilman Abdullah. "Those who are alive are alive because of praying to the creator who has heard them, all this time! You live, you will join them! Remain calm and remember what …"

"Screw you, goat face, and the creator too," said a man, as he joined the group that was getting close to the gate.

"Stop them!" shouted councilman Jacob, looking at the other councillors.

"They have free will, brother," said elderly councilwoman Larissa. "If they want to join the blinded ones, let them. We can't change their faith. We did what we could to keep them on the straight path, but we can't choose their future for them."

---

[49] Blinded: People affected by the purple mist.

"What are you waiting for?" shouted a woman. "Open the fucking doors! Can't you see that we want to leave this prison?"

The gatekeepers looked at the councillors, who remorsefully nodded their heads and the gatekeepers opened the log gates. A large group of former believers walked into the open yard just inside the gates and stood close to the pray-ers, who were holding hands and praying continuously.

"Let's play break the Circle of Pray-ers game!" shouted a girl in the large group.

Everyone began running towards the pray-ers from all sides. Some people and councillors rushed outside the building and began creating smaller Circle of Pray-ers around the community.

After seeing the people running towards them, Believers praying in the large Circle of Pray-ers let go of their hands and formed ***Dual Pray-ers***[50]. This action exposed the running people to the purple mist and turned them motionless. Soon, the affected individuals began wandering around in utter confusion. After a while, they became motionless again then turned to the temple and began walking towards it as if they were being controlled. The pray-ers quickly joined back together by holding hands and recreated the large Circle of Pray-ers, while the rest of the people rushed back inside of the community.

After having a short meeting, the councillors stood beside the altar.

"Those who we lost tonight are neither forgotten nor will they ever be forgotten," said councilwoman Amanda. "We all have freewill and they used it for making their own destinies. It's extremely sad yet we are not here to judge anyone. We shall remain faithful and respectful to the decisions made by everyone. Indeed, there are difficult times ahead of us. The end hours have come yet remember that we knew about this day and we chose to side with the one true god, Jehovah! He gave us protection and a child who can see the future. We must remain thankful and faithful towards him. Let us now pray for those who left us and pray for our salvation. Please join your hands and let us all pray."

The crowd came closer to the altar and after joining hands with the councillors, they lowered their heads, closed their eyes and began praying.

---

[50] Dual Pray-ers: Two people leaning their backs together, while praying when holding hands.

Chapter 29
Picture of Cross

Earlier in the day, before John was given the picture of cross, Katrina was scared and not only because she knew she hadn't much time left to live as the cancer spread through her entire body. She also knew that if her mission to get the picture of the cross to John failed, things wouldn't go according to the prophecy of the oracle. Therefore, despite having difficulties staying on her feet, she didn't give up and continued walking, until she and the small Circle of Pray-ers Believers arrived at John's studio. Katrina then firmly held onto her cane and looked at the exhausted praying girls.

"We're here, we made it children," said Katrina. "We just have to find a way to get close to John."

"What if he's not in here?" asked Elena, one of the pray-ers. "What if we came all this way for nothing?"

"Well, then we shall walk to…"

Katrina coughed blood and fell to her knees. Elena removed the cleanest piece of cloth left in her pocket and tried to clean the blood, but Katrina gently took the piece from her.

"I'll do it myself, dear," said Katrina, as she cleaned her mouth. "Don't get your hands dirty with the cancerous blood that's killing me."

Meanwhile, three A.o.J. units felt the presence of suspicious energy on the street and began walking towards the Believers. Elena helped Katrina to stand and gave the cane back to her.

"What you are doing for the sake of all Believers is beyond belief," said Elena, hugging Katrina. "Know that we'll always remember you as one of the most valued members in the community and I personally thank you for all the services you have done for all of us, especially me."

Katrina put her hands on Elena's shoulders.

"My child," said Katrina, "you don't have to thank me. Thank god for letting you be a part of the circle and letting me watch as you grew from a young girl into a bright young woman."

The A.o.J. units moved closer to them. Seeing the units, Pray-ers began signalling Katrina and Elena to begin moving.

"I feel the energy is moving around," said one of the suspicious A.o.J. units, who had a scar on his face. "What say you, buddy?"

"You're right," the female A.o.J. unit replied, pointing at the studio entrance. "I don't get the energy coming from this side anymore. I feel it coming from that side."

"Fuck off, you two!" said the muscular A.o.J. unit, pointing his gun towards the terrified invisible Believers. "We've got a bunch of believers walking around us and you two are talking about energy coming from here and there?"

The other units looked at each other.

"Morons!" said the muscular unit. "Instead of thinking and guessing, we must simply shoot towards them."

"Stop it! We don't want them dead, idiot!" said the female unit, placing her hand on the muscular one's gun. "We can all turn into Sky-eyes if we capture these little fuckers alive."

"Fuck, you're right," the other unit agreed, slipping his gun back into its holster. "By the way, you look very sexy today."

He grabbed the female A.o.J. unit's bottom.

"Want to do it here?" asked the muscular A.o.J. unit.

"Ya baby, show us what you got under the suit," said the unit with the scar on his face, as he squeezed the female unit's breasts.

"Alright, let's do it here quickly and get this over with, but what if they run away?" asked the female unit, while taking off her pants.

"Let them go then," replied the muscular unit. "I just want to fuck you now."

The units began having intense intercourse in the middle of the sidewalk, as people watched and cheered.

The pray-ers looked at each other and giggled while praying.

"They're like animals," said Katrina, standing with difficulty. "I hope John … thank God, John is here."

John walked out of the studio's doors.

"I'll miss you all, my children. We will meet again," said Katrina and held her breath while walking out of the Circle of Pray-ers.

"We'll miss you too, Aunt Katrina," said Elena, as she and the other tearful pray-ers began to walk back, taking her far from Katrina.

John was shocked to see a group of people and children watching and cheering while the A.o.J. units had intercourse after he stepped out of the studio. He then nodded his head and smiled.

"Man, these guys fuck more than animals," said John, smiling. "One of these days, I'll do the same with the future Mrs Seventh, oh yeah!"

He felt someone pulling his sleeve. John looked around and saw Katrina, who was shaking as she held up a picture.

"May I help you, ma'am?" asked John, as Katrina held the picture higher. "You don't look good. Is that blood on your face, ma'am? Why are you holding your breath? I have to take you to hospital, ma'am."

Katrina looked at Elena and the others. She smiled as their tears fell then looked back at John and stopped holding her breath.

"Look at this picture please, my son," said Katrina, as she stood motionless.

John grabbed the picture and looked at the cross then felt something in his heart.

"What is this? Oh, ma'am," added John, looking away from the picture. "Ma'am, where are you going?"

Katrina was wandering down the street.

"Ma'am, what's this picture?" asked John.

He began following Katrina but before got close to her, the nude A.o.J. units grabbed her hands and looked towards John suspiciously. Knowing that he could get into trouble, John slowly slid the picture into his pocket and waved his hand at the units.

"Greetings, brave ones," said John then pointed at Katrina, who was looking around in confusion. "This lady seemed to be lost. I tried to figure out where she wanted to go or where she was from, but she didn't answer me."

"We'll take care of her, Mr Seventh," said the nude female unit, who now stood in front of John pushing up her breasts. "Can you sign my tits?"

John removed the pen from his pocket and smiled.

"Absolutely, but can you first clean the puddle of semen off your tits? My pen won't be able to work if your tits are this wet."

The female unit rubbed her breasts and clean of the semen.

"Alright, do it now!" said the female A.o.J. unit, licking her lips.

John signed her breasts, as other people on the street walked towards them.

"It would be great if you guys take care of these people too because I need to go now and this might create a little problem for me," said John, putting on his shades.

"Consider it done, Mr Seventh. I love the movie. Rock it hard!" said the nude muscular unit, while keeping the crowd away from John.

"Thank you, sir," said John, as he rushed towards his car.

He then started the vehicle and began driving at low speed. The crowd gathered around the car and began cheering.

John took out a few autographed posters of himself, rolled down the front windows and quickly threw out the posters as people fought to grab them. He then managed to drive pass the crowd then accelerated the car away from them.

As John left, the people in the crowd walked away from the middle of the street and went back to the things they'd been attending to earlier. The units put their uniforms back on, grabbed Katrina then began moving towards their vehicles.

"I hope her sacrifice was worth it. We have a long way ahead of us, sister. Let's move," said Elena, still tearful as she and the pray-ers began walking.

Chapter 30
Divine Rails (Don't Let Go of Me)

John looked at Sara, who was sleeping. It's not easy to wake up one day to discover that all you had yesterday is now gone. It's not easy to distance yourself from those you love without saying goodbye and it isn't at all easy to live a life knowing that your existence endangers the one that you truly love. These thoughts kept John's mind occupied as the Rolling Ball moved. John then removed his wig and scratched his head.

"My head smells like constipated shit," he said, as he exhaled. "I need a shower, no actually a hot bath."

He looked at the wig and placed it on the table.

"I'm glad there were enough costumes in those bags we took from the secret place or else we wouldn't have got this far."

He kissed Sara's head that was on his shoulder.

"I don't know what can save us from what we're in right now. I don't know even if the lord can save us from this mess."

John leaned his head on the sofa and closed his eyes.

"What's this?" he asked, looking around and seeing a large crowd cheering for him. "Who are you people? Another vision? I'm certainly dreaming. This can't be real."

John felt as if something was attached to his back. He turned his head and saw that a large wooden cross was nailed to his hands and back. The crowd cheered louder and pointed their fingers towards a cliff. John looked at where the crowd where pointing and saw a few men that had been crucified and suddenly realised what was happening to him.

"I'm not worthy of getting crucified beside the lord. This is a mistake. Please, hear me people, I'm a nobody," pleaded John, as men in the uniforms of ancient Rome approached him armed with spears.

"Shut your mouth and move," said a spearman, pushing John towards the cliff.

John began to walk, the heavy cross dragging on the ground. The closer John got to the cliff the more loudly the crowd cheered. John stopped periodically to catch his breath and look at the crowd.

"Move, moron!" said an angry spearman, pushing John.

John continued carrying the heavy cross until he reached the edge of the cliff. While standing there he saw Sara in the middle of the crowd, alone and scared. In a blink of an eye, a few of the people in the crowd transformed into demons and began attacking other people. Soon there was chaos, anarchy, burning land, and death. Sara was still standing in the middle of all of this and her tears were rolling down her face.

John tried to separate himself from the cross but he couldn't. He started kicking the cross and pushing his back towards it to perhaps loosen its hold but he failed again. He then saw two large reptilian beings approaching Sara, followed by countless demons.

"Would you turn your back on the cross to save your girl, John?" asked a voice.

"I am the lord's servant but also a man in love. I can't see my girl hurt. I'll do anything to save her," shouted John, as he continued to try to separate himself from the cross.

"Even if it takes your holy powers away from you?" asked the voice.

The reptilians reached Sara and one of them grabbed her. John shouted and transformed into the white wolfman. He broke the cross and began charging at the reptilians.

"I sacrifice everything to save her. Nothing matters without her," shouted wolfman, as smacked into the body of the reptilian holding Sara.

"You disappoint me," said the voice.

John opened his eyes, panting, and looked at Sara who was standing in front of him with a towel wrapped around her.

"I'm getting sick and tired of you having these stupid nightmares," she said a.

John rubbed his eyes and shook his head, then stood up and hugged her.

"I am too," said John, as he tried to calm his breathing.

He then stepped back, looking at her.

"Thanks for making me dirty again. Jeez! John, just get in there and clean up. Enough being dirty," said Sara, as she pushed John into the bathroom and closed the door behind him.

"Wow, she's right," said John, turning the shower handle. "I look like I was chewed and spat out. Let's clean up."

The Divine Rails was travelling into a mild snowfall on a famous and massive ice bridge. The puller announced that the bridge was one of the most significant wonders of God.SED, as it could neither be destroyed nor melted. Sara and John looked at the snowy landscape through the window as they waited for the checker to bring their orders.

"It's beautiful, isn't it, John?" said Sara, looking at the snowy town.

"It ain't nothing like you," said John.

Sara pinched him.

"John, stop it with these cheesy lines," said Sara, hugging him. "You smell good."

John smiled, hugging her back.

"And hugging you feels good," said John.

"Hey mister, I haven't been able to show proper affection to you lately, have I? Well, maybe I should fix it by doing this," said Sara, as she bit John on the neck slowly. "Or by doing this."

She kissed him and put her hands on his buttocks, looking into John's eyes.

"You'll be a great husband and a father. The one who will have all these and I'll have all of this," said Sara, as she placed John's hands on her breasts and her hand on his genitals, squeezing.

The door opened and the checker walked in with a catering cart, on which there were many plates of food.

"Great! Apparently no one likes to knock or get permission from the room holders around here these days," said John, as the checker completely ignored him, placing the plates on the table in the middle of the room.

John looked at Sara, who was giggling, and shrugged while nodding his head.

"I hope you enjoy the food and the rest of the journey," said the checker without making eye contact, before walking out of the room.

"That was strange," said John, suspicious.

"Honey, I'm too hungry to even give a shit. Let's just eat and think about what's strange and what's not later," said Sara, as she began removing the plastic wrap from the plates.

"Yeah, you're right. Let's just eat," said John, as he sat on the sofa beside Sara and they began having their meals.

While John and Sara were fully occupied with eating and talking about the things they could do once they reached the northern territories, the Divine Rails suddenly stopped on the ice bridge. John swallowed his chewed food and looked out of the window. The Divine Rails was on the bridge and they could see a town below. Suddenly, the walls of the Rolling-Ball turned colourless and John and Sara stood up in shock as their Rolling-Ball was surrounded by six A.o.J. units, standing on their flying vehicles. The checker that had served them was looking at John and Sara from the other side of the door.

"John, what's happening?" asked Sara.

"I don't know," said John, with concern. "Oh shit! My wig! And your eyes!"

"What! I forgot to put the lenses back on," said Sara, in alarm. "Oh shit! Your fucking wig is still on the floor. How the hell we didn't see that shit, right? fuck! What are we going to do now?"

John looked out of the window and at the town far below.

"We may have to jump," said John.

"Are you an imbecile or were you born delusional?" asked Sara. "We'll die! Look at the distance, for crying out loud. This is probably the end, John."

Sarah sat on the nearest chair.

"You're surrounded, illegal travellers," shouted the checker. "Identify yourselves now!"

"I'm glad this place is too cold for the Sky-eyes, otherwise, we wouldn't get this warning. They'd simply drag us out of here and straight to God.SED," said Sara. "Think John! Think! What the heck are we going to do now?"

"Give me a break, woman! I'm thinking. You think too. You've got a better brain than I have," said John, pacing around the room.

"Put your hands in the air!" shouted one of the units from outside.

"We may be able to grab one of their *Eagle-Wings,*[51]" said John.

"John! This is real!" exclaimed Sara. "This ain't one of your movies! They'll shoot us if we do anything stupid. They may even shoot us if we don't follow their orders in the next few seconds."

"Put your hands in the air! And identify yourselves immediately, illegal travellers!" shouted one of the units.

---

[51] Eagle-Wings: A flying vehicle, built in different shapes for different weather conditions.

"I'm glad they still didn't find out who we really are. They still think we're illegal travellers, idiots," said John, nodding his head.

The window was opened automatically and the cold snowy wind blew in the room.

"You are hereby under arrest for committing travel fraud. You have no rights until further notice," said one of the A.o.J. units, who was getting closer to the window. "Your compliance with us is of absolute importance. Do not engage in any impulsive behaviour or you will be killed immediately."

"We've got to jump on that vehicle and fly away from here. Shit, it's cold out there," said John, shivering.

"John, I don't think my idea's a good one," said Sara, her teeth chattering. "I'm also afraid of fucking heights."

"Declare your identity at once," said the shouting unit, by now right beside the window.

"My name's William and this is my wife, Elizabeth," said John. "Please, don't shoot!"

"Declare your real identities as illegal travellers now!" shouted one of the other units, as the flying vehicles began to fly closer to the door of the Rolling-Ball.

"Tell us who you are!" shouted the checker.

Sara looked back and read the checker's nametag.

"Shut the fuck up, Sue," said Sara.

She turned back to face the A.o.J. units.

"If I distract them, can you jump and maybe grab the guy," she whispered to John. "Or maybe push him down and grab the vehicle?"

"What do you mean by …"

Sara interrupted him by taking off her sweater and walking towards the unit closest to the window, holding her breasts.

The units looked at each other and the one closest to the window tried to grab Sara's arm but he was shot by John's energy sphere. Sara turned around and saw John standing with two bright energy spheres in his hands and light bursting out of his eyes.

"What the fuck is going on in here?" Sara demanded.

The other units opened fire. John ran towards Sara, pushed her away from the window, and jumped at the Eagle-Wings that was flying beside the window.

Sara quickly put her sweater back on and stood on guard as Sue opened the door of the Rolling Ball.

"Attention all travellers! Attention all travellers! We request that you remain seated while our fantastic protectors fight with the illegal travellers. We apologise for any inconvenience," said the puller.

Meanwhile, Sara threw a flowerpot that she'd picked up from one of the small tables and threw it at Sue. It hit Sue on the head and knocked her unconscious.

"Oh shit! That worked. Did you see that Jo … oh! never mind," said Sara, nodding her head.

She ran to the window and watched John shooting energy spheres at the units, knocking them off their flying vehicles one by one.

"His survival from Twin Cancer has given him powers. Incredible!" said Sara, impressed. "This is a perfect note to add on my research. Those who survive the Twin Cancer develop superpowers."

Sue regained consciousness, stood up, ran to the control panel and activated the spin-off system of the Rolling-Ball. This would cause the cabin to roll while standing in a firm position. This action was taken only to combat the most resistant travellers or criminals considered extremely dangerous. By rotating the Rolling-Ball, the individual would be forced out of it when the room became gravity free and the air suction would pull out anything that would float in the air. However, if this method didn't work the Rolling-Ball could be charged with water and high voltage electricity. The remaining unwanted objects would then be vacuumed out of the ball. Once the spinning began, all the unattached items in the room began to be thrown out of the window, including Sara who held onto the edge of the window frame while screaming for help.

"Oh my god! Sara!" shouted John as the unit grabbed his right leg, preventing him from moving.

"Watch her die!" shouted the unit.

Sara was screaming when she got hit by a chair that floated towards her, forcing her to let go of the window frame. John shot the unit that was holding his leg and dived in the air towards Sara. After reaching her, he turned around and hugged her tightly.

"We're going to die," said Sara, shivering. "I'm scared, John."

"I may die, but I'll never let you die," said John.

"It's going to hurt," said Sara, closing her eyes. "John, it's alright. I'm happy that we're going to die together. I'm not alone, I have you with me."

She squeezed her head into John's chest.

"John, you're so warm, and so hairy. What's going on?"

"Keep your eyes closed, honey," said wolfman, as he hugged Sara.

Sara tried to say something, but they crashed into the ground. The impact's shockwaves were felt throughout the town, alerting the security systems of all A.o.J. units.

Chapter 31
The Bakers – Part I

In the small pastry and bakery store of the bakers, where only a few people could barely stand, countless numbers were standing around, squeezing each other to reach to the displayed delights.

Heather, the most famous baker in the entire town of ***Snowflakes***[52], was rushing around the shop to meet the orders as Guzal, her business partner and the second most famous baker in town, was wrapping up candies for children as quickly as she could. The day was indeed a very busy one for them, but Heather and Guzal loved it. Bringing small sweet thrills and joys into the lives of others was the reason that had inspired them to open their bakery business in the first place.

Heather was a former English language teacher according to her new set of memories. After retirement from her school she'd accepted the proposal of Guzal, her former top student, to open a pastry shop. Guzal had seen how joyful her classmates became when they were treated to Heather's home-baked pastries and cookies that they received after scoring high grades in class. Guzal spoke about opening the store with Heather who, after a series of rejections, finally accepted the idea. Guzal was working as a homecare nurse when Heather contacted her to talk about her final decision and Guzal quit the job the same day and went to Heather's house to proceed with the plan. Ever since that day, they'd worked side by side and in absolute happiness, selling highly trending delights in the town.

"Here you go," said Guzal, handing wrapped candies to some children.

"Guzal, can you give me a hand here please," asked Heather, as she pulled an obese boy away from a giant chocolate bear.

---

[52] Snowflakes: A famous small town in North-Lands located closely to the ice bridge.

"I ain't going nowhere, me like the bear, yummy," said the boy, licking the bear's feet while laying down.

"I'm not going anywhere. I like the taste of this chocolate bear. It tastes yummy. Please speak properly," said Heather, pulling the boy back.

"What's your name, big man," asked Guzal.

"Name's Justin, babe, at your service," he said and winked.

"Oh my, such a charming young man you are," said Guzal. "However, a gentleman is always respectful to ladies' requests, so are you being respectful by denying aunt Heather's request, my charming Justin?"

Guzal held the boy's hand with both of her hands. Justin stopped licking the chocolate, immediately stood up and gave Guzal a salute.

"Yes, ma'am," he replied, looking at Heather. "I apologise for my childish behaviour, madams," said Justin.

He then stepped forward, held Guzal's hand and kissed it.

"Oh my, what a gentleman you are," said Guzal. "Guess what? Because you listened to what we told you, I'm going to give you this."

She handed Justin a small chocolate bear.

"Next time come to us and request politely that we assist you with anything you want instead of making us come to you, okay? Do we have a deal?" asked Guzal.

"Yes, my ladies," replied Justin, holding the small chocolate bear.

"Justin! Oh, there you are!" cried his mother, an obese lady with a great deal of jewellery hanging around her neck and wrists. "Have you made trouble for Aunt Heather and Aunt Guzal again? I apologise again, ladies, this boy never stands still beside his mother."

"It's fine, Michelle," said Heather. "Please just make sure this doesn't happen again because this is probably the hundredth time that this has happened in this exact manner."

Michelle ignored making eye contact with Heather. She held Justin's hand and while waving at Guzal, she walked through the crowd and left the store.

"Bitch! She couldn't say anything back to me, no sorry, no apologies, no nothing. How do you deal with that kid?" asked Heather, wiping the sweat from her forehead.

"I don't know really," replied Guzal. "It's just something I'm good at, I guess, or maybe because I'd love to have a child one day. I don't really know."

"Good luck with that. Never had a kid, will never have one too. They are little … yes ma'am, I'm coming right up," said Heather, heading towards a customer.

A couple of hours later, Heather and Guzal closed the store for the day.

"What a great sales day. Loved it!" said Guzal, as she swept the floor. "We literally had no place to stand anymore and did you see Sheryl's hair today? I loved her new look."

"Girl, I wish I could stay as positive as you always are," said Heather, grumpily. "I'm glad we opened up this store, but with this constant cold and the weird people around here and their out of control children, I don't know if I'll have my mental stability for much longer."

Heather sat on a large three-seater sofa and removed her shoes as she relaxed.

"You're just tired, Heather," said Guzal, smiling as she continued sweeping the floor. "It truly was a very busy day. We can take a break if you want and go on a holiday for couple of weeks and then once we're fully refreshed, we can come back and continue bringing little joys into everyone's lives."

They both felt a weak earth shake. Guzal and Heather looked at each other in fear.

"Did you feel that?" asked Guzal.

"Something must have fell down from the bridge. It didn't feel like it was too far away," said Heather, grabbing a transparent remote control. "Let me see if there's anything on the news already."

Guzal stopped sweeping and went to join Heather on the sofa to watch the news on the holographic TV. There was already a breaking news alert and an anchor was describing the situation live.

"Good evening, beloved residents of Snowflakes town," said the anchor. "There has been a conflict on the ice bridge. Our resources informed us that two illegally travelling individuals were caught while heading towards the North-Lands in the middle of the ice bridge. The individuals are said to have successfully escaped from the crime scene by Sue, the brave checker who tried to protect several of our missing brave Arms of Justice units. They might have been terminated by the laser shield below the bridge, as could the illegal travellers."

The anchor continued the reporting the news.

"We needed Sky-eyes up there," said Heather, nodding her head.

"You know they hate cold," Guzal replied. "We literally get no protection from Sky-eyes around this town."

"Thank God.SED for creating the laser shield above the town to protect us from everything that falls down from the mountain and of course from the bridge. I wonder what it was that we felt though? It did feel as if something fell on the ground from above," said Heather.

"I know, right?" added Guzal. "We'd never be able to live here if there wasn't a laser shield. No one could with all the snow and other things that constantly fall down from the mountain and the bridge."

The ground shook strongly and the entire town's electrical power shut down.

"Aunt Heather, I'm scared," said Guzal.

"This isn't good," said Heather, terrified. "Something's going on out there for sure."

She stood up and went to the front of the store and stood by the windows, looking outside. She could barely see anything, as the snowy street was only illuminated by the light of the moon.

"What should we do?" asked Guzal.

"We can't go outside, that's for sure." said Heather. "It's too cold and dark."

"It's getting cold in here too," said Guzal.

"I hope we get backup from God.SED, otherwise we'll freeze to death before morning," said Heather.

Suddenly, someone knocked hard on the store's doors.

"Help! Can you hear me? I need help," pleaded Sara.

"Who's that?" asked Guzal, running over to Heather and standing beside her.

"Get the *Gas-Cakes*[53]," said Heather. "Nothing can stand a chance against my Gas-Cakes, but make sure to throw it straight at the person's face."

Guzal slowly walked towards the kitchen, touching everything along the way. She then removed a few neon lights from one of the cabinets, squeezed them until they were turned on then grabbed two green Gas-Cakes from the other cabinet. She returned to the front of the store and stood beside Heather.

"Please, help me, it's so cold and my ..." said Sara.

She fell on the steps by the store entrance.

---

[53] Gas-Cakes: Heather invented cakes that would release anaesthetic gas when it impacted any hard object. The cakes were designed for defensive purposes.

"I think she passed out," said Heather, as she began walking towards the doors. "Let's be careful anyways. It could be trick or something. I'll throw the Gas-Cakes, you just stay behind me and hold the lights up so I can see properly."

Guzal held up the neon lights and followed her. Heather then slowly opened one of the doors.

"Are you okay, Heather?" asked Guzal. "Why aren't you moving?"

"Stay back, until I tell you to come closer," said Heather, looking at the shivering Sara.

"John ... We need to help, John," said Sara.

"Who are you? Who the heck is John?" asked Heather, holding the Gas-Cakes towards Sara.

Guzal stepped ahead, moved Heather to the side then pulled Sara inside as the snowy wing began blowing at them.

"Close the door, Heather," said Guzal, placing a few neon lights around Sara on order to see her better. "She's helpless, for crying out loud. Whoever she is, she's harmless."

Sara then lost consciousness.

Upstairs in the guest bedroom, it was almost midnight. Sara was still unconscious on the bed in a room illuminated by candlelight, as Heather and Guzal engaged in a tense discussion about her. Sara had massive bruises all over her body and her nose and chin were swollen. Guzal and Heather had cleaned Sarah's wounds and changed her clothes. They then began to feel very threatened, as they realised who Sara really was. The temperature had also fallen very low due to the power outage and the entire town was now under a thick layer of snow. There was no one or anything to be seen out on the street as everyone remained in their homes, hoping for a miracle from God.SED. Guzal and Heather could neither inform anyone of Sara's presence nor come up with any ideas regarding how to handle the situation properly.

"What if instead of rewarding us, God.SED punishes us with Twin Cancer for delaying informing the units about this?" asked Heather.

"Try to calm down, Heather," said Guzal. "Once the electricity comes back and the *Mega-Heater*[54] runs again, we'll get a chance to call the units. They'll surely understand why it took us so long to inform them."

---

[54] Mega-Heater: A boiler that heats the entire town of Snowflakes through its water pipelines, which are planted deep underground to prevent them from freezing.

Guzal then took a picture of herself and Sara, keeping her head close to Sara's and blowing a kiss at the camera.

"John ... help John," whispered Sara.

Guzal quickly pulled her head away and looked at Heather.

"She must be talking about *the* John," said Guzal excitedly, taking another picture with Sara while holding a wrapped chocolate. "I can't believe that they ended up here, far away from West-Lands."

"They're nothing but fugitives now," said Heather, firmly. "He was the John and now he's oh John. What karma. One day you're on top of the world, walking on the red carpet, and the next you're lost in an unknown place in Snowflakes town. This is what happens to those that disobey our amazing God.SED."

"You're right, but I still feel bad for her," said Guzal, looking at Sara.

Suddenly, Sara opened her eyes and began moving.

"Please, help me! John's bleeding to death. We fell from that fucking bridge out there, and they ... they ... we ... we ..."

Sara was interrupted, as Guzal held her shoulders.

"Calm down, girl," said Heather. "We know you guys are on the run and had a conflict with the units up there. We can't help you with anything except what we're doing right now. Even for this we may get into trouble. You're lucky that the power is out or else you'd be in the custody of the units. Just calm down and have a bit of the Choco-Loco we brought for you."

Sara stopped moving and lay on the bed, leaning her back on the headboard. Guzal then grabbed a mug of Choco-Loco that she'd brought upstairs earlier and handed it to Sara, who grabbed the cup and after nodding her head she drank a little.

"It's hot!" said Sarah, waving her left hand back and forth.

"Well duh! It's Choco-Loco. It's supposed to be served super-hot," said Guzal, rolling her eyes.

"Where was the last time you saw John, Sara," asked Heather.

Sara put the cup on the night stand and looked at her.

"He needs help. I need to go back, he's bleeding to death," said Sara.

She then quickly stood up and began to walk but before she took her second step, she fell on the floor unconscious.

"Oh, my goodness!" said Guzal. "Please help me to get her back on the bed, Heather."

Guzal and Heather grabbed Sara's shoulders and feet and put her back on the bed.

"Poor girl, she's so weak. If she's like this then in what condition John is in?" asked Guzal.

"John could be dead by now," said Heather, examining Sara's bruises. "She kept saying John was bleeding. We can't do anything for him. I mean, I like him as an actor and I love his movies, but they're both now fugitives and their lives aren't really of any importance. All we can do is wait until we get the stupid power back and see what can be done later."

Chapter 32
Divine Rails (Check-Point)

A few hours earlier, before Sara and John fell off the bridge at the Divine Rails' check-point, the Arms of Justice units were having another quiet and ordinary day. They were scanning travellers' wrists and hoping for the day to end sooner.

"Did you hear about the action at the Lotus?" asked Henry. "How could a half human defeat majesty Orhana?"

"I don't give a shit," George replied. "I just don't want him anywhere near here. We won't be able to handle him. Ah, shit! We don't stop him, God.SED will turn us into Little-ones and if we stop him, he'll surely terminate us. Shit!"

"No kidding. But he's coming here though, so I don't know man," said Henry.

"Keep quiet, moron," said George, as he resumed monitoring the cameras. "Sky-eyes will take care of them before they even reach here."

Henry poured himself a cup of Choco-Loco and watched the travellers from the watchtower. They crossed the barriers one by one and not even one of them looked suspicious. Meanwhile, John and Sara stood in the lane and walked slowly towards an A.o.J. unit. Things were still under control until the door was kicked opened and Jason walked in with two massive Sky-eyes behind him. Henry looked at George and swallowed the Choco-Loco in his mouth.

"Master!" exclaimed Henry, placing his cup on the table beside him. "How can we serve you?"

Jason looked at George then at Henry.

"The chosen one is either here or has already passed the checkpoints without you idiots knowing about it. You'd better hope that they haven't crossed the checkpoints yet, because I'll make sure that you'll turn into Little-ones immediately," said Jason angrily, as he stood beside the window looking down at the passengers crossing the check-points.

"Sir, you can be assured that we haven't seen any suspicious activities so far," said George, smiling.

The phone rang. Jason picked it up and listened.

"We encountered an intelligence named Barbie that's shielding the true identities of a couple that we believe are ... they are the ones," said the A.o.J. unit. "We need to alarm the Sky-eyes."

"What's your name?" asked Jason.

"Oh, come on, man!" said Jack. "It's me, Jack. How the fuck did you forget my name?"

"God.SED is the son of the Lord Lucifer," said Jason.

"Are you okay, George?" said Jack, in confusion. "What did you just say?"

He began shaking then stopped. He hung up the phone and walked back to the checkpoint.

"You chose to use a human to check the IDs when you knew about the conflict at the Lotus," said Jason sternly, grabbing Henry by the throat and lifting him up.

"Forgive me, master," said Henry, choking. "I couldn't trust any one of us to take care of this job. Everyone's afraid of the chosen one."

Jason looked into Henry's eyes of and began absorbing his energy before he dropped the body to the floor. George remained silent on his chair as Henry deteriorated. Jason then looked at other Sky-eyes units behind him.

"We can't attack him in the middle of a crowd. It'll create chaos and more drama," said one of the Sky-eyes units in demonic language.

Jason stepped over Henry's dead body and stood beside the shivering George.

"Unfortunately, you are correct brother," said Jason. "Also, we need to find out where they're going. They're on a journey to some place specific. Imagine capturing the chosen one along with whoever he's going to meet. We'll be blessed unconditionally by God.SED."

Jason shoved his long nails into the George's shoulders.

Meanwhile, Jack scanned John and Sara's wrists and watched them pass him without asking any further questions. John and Sara then walked to the ticket lady, purchased their tickets, and walked towards their Rolling-Ball. Jason stretched his neck and Jack was released by him. Jack looked around in absolute confusion and because he didn't remember anything that he'd done earlier, he simply sat down on his chair and continued working.

George zoomed the camera on John and Sara's Rolling-Ball then looked back at Jason.

"My lord, please let me live. I've targeted their location. It's North," said George.

"Good job, George," said Jason.

He then drained all George's energy and walked away from his deteriorated body.

"We can't go North. It's too cold for anyone of us to survive," said one of the concerned Sky-eyes units in demonic language.

"Who said we were going there?" asked Jason. "They'll be going there."

The Sky-eyes units looked at each other in confusion as Jason closed his eyes then began smiling as Jason reopened them.

"Well, now you know who's waiting for him in north," said Jason, smiling.

"The chosen one has defeated Excellency Orhana," said one of the units. "What makes you think he can't defeat them?"

"Tell me, what can you do when you're frozen?" asked Jason, but no one replied. "Exactly, you can do nothing! No matter if you're a wolf or just a human, your body remains frozen."

Jason then began walking out of the watchtower, followed by the other Sky-eyes units.

Chapter 33
The Bakers – Part II

A heavy storm had occurred since Sara entered the bakery store. The temperature had fallen considerably and it had become very dark. All the residents of Snowflakes town remained in their households hoping for a miracle from God.SED, but nothing seemed to happen at all.

Heather and Guzal had already fallen asleep by the time Sara regained consciousness. She tried to leave the store through the main entrance doors but a pile of snow outside the store prevented her. There was simply so much snow outside on the ground and the storm had become severe. There was no way for Sara to leave the shop under such circumstances. She fell to her knees on the floor beside the main floor entrance doors and began crying. She'd never felt as helpless as she did at that moment. She knew that it had been a while since they'd fallen from the bridge and if John hadn't already been frozen he'd be in critical condition because of the cold. As Sara continued crying the last burning candle extinguished, making the room extremely dark.

At the impact site six large wolves were lying around and on top of John, who was soaked in his own frozen blood puddle, preventing him from freezing. While falling, John used all his energy to create a powerful energy shield on his back that prevented him and Sara from getting terminated by the laser shield above the town. As he used all his energy to create the energy shield, he transformed into human before hitting the ground. John's holy spirit was the reason that he didn't die as his body used the spirit's energy to regenerate and heal immediately. When Sara opened her eyes, she thought John was dead as blood was dripping from his nose and he couldn't move. John's appearance clearly showed that his neck and most of the bones in his body were broken. He also had difficulty breathing. Sara didn't know what to do to as she was afraid to even touch John. Sara immediately stopped laying on him and stood up, weakly. She was too severely impacted by the fall.

"John, don't die. I'll find a way to save us. Please, stay with me," said the shivering and dizzy Sara.

John barely opened his swollen eyes, but he opened them.

"That's my man, I can't even touch you. You must have several broken bones and internal bleeding, but I know you can … you can … please, stay alive I'll go and bring help," said Sara.

John closed and opened his eyes again. He tried to say something, but his jaw was broken so he remained silent. Sara looked around. As far as she could see there were thick layers of snow, although the bright colourful Snowflakes town could easily be seen.

"Stay alive, John. I'm going to bring help," said Sara, as she began to walk slowly towards the town.

John closed his eyes and tried to stay alive by thinking of what Sara had told him. His body was recovering and healing fast, but it not fast enough for him to move. Meanwhile, he began hearing the howling of wolves. He opened his eyes and saw five wolves surrounding him. The wolves sat around and on John and began spreading energy into his body, helping him to recover more quickly. Happy that the wolves were helping him rather than eating him, John closed his eyes again. A few seconds later, he opened his eyes in distress when he felt a very powerful dark energy nearby.

The wolves began to growl and moved away from John, as Death slowing floated towards him. Upon reaching John, Death floated in the air above him, face to face.

"Johnny, Johnny, Johnny, you still have more broken bones and fractures in you than I have hair on my head, but you still seem to be able to survive in an amazing way. The girl's surely giving you an extra reason to live, doesn't she?"

Death shoved his nail into John's open wound. John shivered in pain and the wolves began to bark at Death.

"Silence! You, fucking morons!" shouted Death, as the wolves whimpered.

Death looked back at John and smiled.

"Forgive my rage for these dogs who were once the chosen ones, just like you. They're lucky that they repented sooner instead of becoming everlasting monsters. Their repentance saved them or cursed them from either entering heaven or hell or of course the nowhere land by not dying at all. Some of them have lived a long life waiting for the day that I'd take them out of their bodies, but that day did never come."

Death smiled sinisterly.

"You see, John, the problem with half-breeds is that I can't take your souls away on my command, regardless of what I do. The bloody holy spirit in you stops it making you an immortal among other mortals. However, if your faith sours and your spirit grows weak then I can began pulling you out of your misery. Now tell me John, do you want to come with me to the nowhere land? I need an assistant, someone I can trust and someone who possesses powers like yours."

Death removed his nail from John's healing wound and licked his finger.

"Pure blood is always the best blood. Yours is filled with rage, anger and love," said Death, as John looked at him furiously. "Come with me. Let me make you my assistant or better still, my partner. Don't worry so much about the girl. Let go of her and join me. She's not in your destiny. She'll be captured and join the underworld. Come with me, John. Join me."

Death began absorbing John's soul. The wolves started howling, sharing almost all of their spiritual energy with John. He closed his eyes and then opened them as a bright light began to burst out. A powerful energy was then discharged from John's body, causing the energy generator system of the nearby town to burn and the entire electrical lost its electrical power.

"You annoy me, John. Enjoy living a little bit longer. Your time is coming soon, whether you like it or not," said Death, before he disappeared in a black mist.

John stood up and looked at his nude body. He was completely recovered and healed from all his injuries. He then looked at the wolves that were standing close to him and knelt.

"Thank you for sharing your spiritual energy with me," said John. "Without you, I couldn't regain my power and strength. I'm in your debt."

The wolves licked his face and hands.

"I want to request a favour, beloved chosen ones of the past. I need to find Sara, so if you could track her scent and take me to her, I would be much obliged," said John.

The wolves looked at each other and then began sniffing the ground. After a few seconds the largest wolf began to walk towards the Snowflakes town, as other wolves followed him. John created an energy shield around him as protection from the cold and the storm then followed the wolves.

At the bakery store, Sara had fallen asleep beside the main entrance and woke up suddenly when John knocked on the door. Frightened, Sara quickly stood up and remained silent.

Heather and Guzal rushed downstairs with burning candles and Guzal pulled Sara into the kitchen.

"What were you doing down here, Sara? Did you try to get out?" whispered Guzal.

"John is still out there and needs my help. I can't stay in this place any longer," Sara replied, in frustration.

The entrance doors were knocked on again, this time harder.

"Who's there?" asked Heather, holding the Gas-Cake higher.

"Sara, are you there? It's me, John."

"Did you find out who it is, Heather?" asked Guzal, standing between the doors of kitchen and those of the main floor.

"I guess he's John. That's what he said," replied Heather.

Sara couldn't wait any longer. She pushed Guzal aside and rushed to Heather.

"Open the door, Heather, now," said Sara firmly.

Heather opened the door without further protest. The wolves howled when they saw Sara, then licked John's hands before walking away and disappearing in the storm. John turned around and Sara jumped on him.

"I tried … I tried to get help but …"

John hugged her tightly.

"I know, sweetheart. I don't need any help from anyone as long as you're with me."

"You must be freezing," said Sara. "Where are your clothes? Get in before the wolves change their minds and come back to eat us."

She jumped on the ground and pulled John into the store and closed the doors.

"Praise God.SED, the John Seventh is in the shop, and naked," said Guzal, blushing.

"Enough! Stop it, Guzal," said Heather then looked at John and Sara. "You two are fugitives. The entire world is looking for you. There are wolves out there. Fucking wolves! We never ever had wolves around here! And you just walked in our store, meeting and greeting with each other? Do you understand how serious your situation is?"

John stood in front of Sara, while covering his genitals with his hands.

"We greatly apologise, ma'am. We'll leave at once. I just request you to provide me some clothes if there's anything for a man my size in this store," said John, avoiding direct eye contact with Heather.

Guzal walked over and stood in front of John while looking at Heather, who was still holding up a Gas-Cake.

"Stop it, Heather. They're our guests now. We had a chance to kick Sara out and stop all of this, but we didn't. Now, live with it," said Guzal, firmly.

She then turned around and looked at John, who seemed about to faint.

"Are you alright, Mr Seventh?"

"I feel … I …"

John collapsed to the floor.

Two hours, just before dawn, the snow storm stopped and the power generators were reactivated and fixed by the town's electricians, restoring electrical power to all corners of the Snowflakes town.

John opened his eyes to see Sara looking at him.

"I must have run out of all my energies. I usually don't faint," said John, weakly. "Where are the others?"

"They're downstairs," replied Sara, placing her head on his chest. "How did we survive?"

"You can ask God.SED, if you see him one day. He's just so great that he's kept us alive all this time. We're meant to stay alive and go on to fulfil our destiny, I guess. We've got to figure out how to leave here without making any trouble for the ladies. We've already put them in grave danger by getting them involved."

John looking at the sweater and pants he was wearing.

"And by the way, whose clothes are these? They almost fit me perfectly."

Sarah moved her head up, looking into John's eyes.

"We'll just leave. I don't think there'll be any problems," she said, keeping her chin on John's chest. "Guzal seems to be a very kind girl, so I believe she'll just let us go despite what Heather might say, or perhaps we have no other choice except running out as fast as we can. Those clothes belong to Guzal's boyfriend. She said he wasn't going to be in the town for the next few weeks and it wouldn't matter if you wore these clothes when he wasn't around."

John brought his head down and suddenly his eyes widened up when he saw Sara's bruised face. He quickly pulled himself up as she moved into a sitting position on the bed. Sara then moved closer to John and looked at him in confusion.

"Your face is bruised, sweetheart. Your hands are bruised up, oh my!" said John, with concern. "You must be in pain."

"I'll be fine, just like you are. You've got no bruises and no injuries at all. When I left you, you were bleeding and now look at you. You look just like you were born a few minutes ago, perfect and healthy," said Sara, as John examined her arms.

At that moment, Heather walked into the room with two small size recyclable bags. She placed one of the bags containing groceries on the floor then stepped back.

"We'll be punished for helping you but Guzal has convinced me not to report you to the units and instead help you to get the heck out of her before units find you," said Heather.

She placed the other recyclable bag containing a few clothes on the floor beside the other recyclable bag.

"These are all we can give you to survive the cold outside at this time. Put these on these quickly and leave, please. It's almost dawn and it's warmer out there. Units may come at any time."

Before John and Sara could say anything, Heather walked out of the room and shut the door behind her. John and Sara stood up and began to change. A few minutes later, they walked downstairs and met Guzal and Heather, who were standing beside the entrance doors.

"We're sorry if we're not letting you stay in here any longer," said Guzal, sadly. "We can't do anything further. This is a small town and everyone knows everyone. It's easy to get reported to the Arms of Justice department and then cursed by God.SED. We hope that you'll have a safe journey ahead."

Sara tried to hug her, but Heather pulled Guzal back and opened the door halfway.

"Leave please, before it's too late for all of us," said Heather.

"We truly appreciate your kindness. I wish we could ..."

John was interrupted by Heather, who gestured for him to remain silent and simply leave. John and Sara then quietly left the store and stood in the middle of the snow-covered street.

"Well, what now?" asked Sara, shivering.

"We can't walk there," John replied. "When I checked the map back in the Rolling-Ball, I saw the address. It's quite far from here but quite close to the *Sparkling City*[55] where God.SED's temple is. It's very interesting that it's so cold around here while a few miles away there's an everlasting spring season, with trees and flowers surrounding the temple. Anyhow, we need Barbie or we won't have proper directions."

"So ask her then," said Sara.

"First, let's hide in that alley between the buildings to avoid anyone seeing us, and second, I woke up naked assuming that the lasers destroyed everything that I was wearing earlier, including my wristwatch."

John pulled Sara off from the street and into the alley.

"I wonder how we survived the fall and passed through the lasers and I woke up with ... hmmm, this is strange, I'm fully healed," said Sara, looking at the arms.

John moved closer to her and was astonished. Sara's bruised were all healed.

"Wow! You've got some healing power for sure. I mean, both of us have," whispered John, as he heard a few people talking in the building beside them.

"We have to get the heck out of here quickly, everyone's waking up," whispered Sara. "We may have to find a map. Oh, when I was wandering around looking for help, I saw a chariot store two blocks north of the bakery. We can have horses to ride and hopefully a map to navigate our path."

"Sounds good, let's go," said John. "You lead and I'll follow."

Sara began walking quickly towards the street, with John right behind her.

At the Chariot Station John and Sara checked around the store to make sure that no one had seen them. After concluding that there was no one inside and outside of the store, they broke in by John melting the entrance's doorknob. He did this while Sara wasn't near him, so he avoided explaining how they got inside the store but Sara was still so distressed that she didn't even think of talking about it with John.

"I get the smell of horses, but I don't know where they're kept," said Sara, avoiding hitting the furniture around her in the semi-darkness. "Also, I can't ride a horse. I'm scared of them."

"Well, it's not very…"

---

[55] Sparkling City: A crystal city that often suffers from heavy snowfall. The angels migrated there to stay away from the Sky-eyes and other underworld creatures that are unable to survive in the cold.

John suddenly had a flashback. He saw Sara riding a horse and making fun of him as he couldn't match her speed.

"Sara," said John, placing his hands on her shoulders. "Not only can you ride but you're also the one who taught me to ride."

"You have a strong imagination, John. I'm not riding any horses. You ride and I'll sit behind you. But first, we've got to find …"

Sara was interrupted when she heard neighing.

"Did you hear that? It came from down below. The horses must be in the basement or something."

"There must be a secret door or some sort of hidden elevator around here somewhere," said John, as he slowly began to walk with Sara.

"I'm glad we've got a bit of brightness coming in from all of the windows, otherwise we'd be screwed," said Sara, walking behind John as he nodded his head.

"This is frustrating," said John. "We've got an entry store with a few luxury chariots on display, a large luxury wood desk, a black leather luxury chair, two black three-seater sofas, and a luxury marble table between them plus all this other luxury shit and a whole bunch of horses underneath the floor. I hope the entrance to the basement or whatever's down there isn't accessed outside because the sun's now rising and we can't go out."

John stood beside a stuffed polar bear as Sara checked the luxury desk and its drawer. When she didn't find anything she looked at the polar bear and noticed that its right hand looked as if it were broken. When she tried to place it in the right position a access door opened in the floor beside John. John jumped back and looked at her.

"You scared the shit out of me but good job! You found the bloody secret door. My goodness that a lot of smell coming from downstairs. Yuck!" said John, holding his nose.

"Don't be a wuss. Let's go down fast and just get a horse and get the fuck out of here," said Sara, grabbing John's hand and taking him downstairs.

"Isn't this stealing?" she asked, as they walked downstairs.

"Well, we'll return here and pay of our debt in the future but for now, we need the bloody horse and I don't give a shit if this is called stealing or not," John replied.

"I am teasing you, love," said Sara. "I don't give a shit right now about the law. Our lives are at stake. That's all I care about right now."

They arrived downstairs and the lights turned on, exposing countless loose and sleepy horses.

"They're magnificent," whispered Sara.

"They are indeed," John agreed. "Now choose a horse and let's get out of here from that door at the end. I don't know where it'll lead us too but that's the only way out."

A golden female horse walked close to Sara and stood looking at her directly.

"This is creepy," asked Sara, a little frightened. "What should I do next, John?"

"She chose you even before we got close to anyone of them," he replied, as Sara slowly patted down the horse. "You're a horse whisperer or something. This beauty wants you to ride her, I guess."

"This is strange. I do feel a connection with this horse. Let's take her," said Sara.

John grabbed a saddle that was hanging on one of the walls and slowly wrapped it around the golden horse, which didn't move or resist. John then helped Sara to sit down on the horse.

"Alright, we need one more …"

John was interrupted as a male golden horse walked over and stood beside him.

"I am legit freaked out right now," said John, as the horse bumped him with his nose. "I wonder if these two were hiding or something because I didn't notice them when first we came down here."

"They seem to be a pair, like us," said Sara, patting her horse. "They want to help us for sure. Get the freaking saddle and let's go before these two change their minds."

John quickly grabbed another saddle that was hanging on the wall and carefully put it on his horse. He then went to the wooden doors and pushed them open.

"It's an underground tunnel to who knows where," said John, as he walked back to his horse and mounted him. "Just try to calmly follow me but starting …"

Sara began leading him by riding her horse.

"Never mind," said John, following Sara into the tunnel.

Chapter 34
Joe White

Joe White was among the ancient angels that came to Earth on a mission to develop humans' skills to fight against the super humans and then heaven. However, because of the love he found among humans, he remained on Earth for centuries. His decision cost him the loss of his wings, a standard punishment for not fulfilling the mission's rules. However, his superpowers remained within him because of his holy spirit.

After the arrival of God.SED, Joe searched the super continent, seeking the angels that had survived the early wars and gathered them in a secret invisible place that was between the Circle of Believers and the Sparkling City where the temple of God.SED was located. This secret place was named Circle of Angels as most individuals there were angels, some of whom could fly while some could not. The name of the Cycle of Believers community was inspired in this manner and the place was built by angels who walked among faithful people in the shape of humans during the early wars between God.SED and the humans. The angels helped humans build the Circle of Believers using superior skills and techniques over a very short period of time. Some of the angels remained in the Circle of Believers to help the humans survive and some humans remained in Circle of Angels as their second headquarters. The Circle of Angels remained hidden from the impact of the purple mist and the eyes of the rest of the world through the same technique of constant praying to hide the place continuously.

In addition, the last child born of an alliance between an angel and a human was born and protected by both communities as she had powerful psychic abilities. Both her parents were killed during the war between humans and God.SED and she was brought up with the help of everyone in both communities, especially Joe White who treated her as his own biological daughter. Joe was given the nickname 'White' because of his oddly fair skin, long white hair and beard. Some children would even call him Santa too as his appearance matched the fictional character. Gabriel informed Joe telepathically about the possibility of John and Sara visiting him. Gabriel hoped that John and Sara would somehow find Joe's address in the secret place. Joe was also informed of John's encounter with EZ and Orhana and about him having his holy spirit manipulated into an animal spirit. Joe was asked to train John to control his powers and possibly transform them into the holy spirit again. If he failed to so, Joe and the rest of the angels could go ahead and eliminate John to protect the lives of the others. Aware of the destruction EZ had brought upon angels and humans after his soul was manipulated by Lucifer, Joe agreed to do what Gabriel asked.

Joe was sitting in his office behind the desk and listening to the local news reporter.

"The people of Snowflakes town have regained full electrical power after a freezing night," said the reporter. "The power outage was caused by the fall of many of our brave law enforcers who chased and killed two illegal travellers. The impact had brought an unbalance in the system of the laser machine that resulted in an energy discharge overpowering and cutting off the town's electrical generator. We have the confirmation that all the units and the two travellers were eliminated by the lasers protecting the city of Snowflakes."

There was a knock at the door.

"Come in," said Joe.

Shaina opened the door and walked in.

"Did you hear that?" asked Shaina. "Do think they're dead?"

She stepped over beside Joe's desk.

"No, my dear wife. I don't think that," said Joe, spinning his chair to the right.

He then got up from behind the desk then walked to Shaina and stood beside her.

"It's about a day from there to here on foot, assuming they survived and are heading here. If they don't arrive by the end of today, we'll need to go and investigate the area."

"Assuming you're right and they are alive, or we go and find them, I don't know how we can train a spirit like EZ when Gabriel himself failed to do so," said Shaina.

Joe hugged her.

"I'm worried. If a half human could defeat Orhana, he might get us all killed. It will be sad to finish him, but I won't hesitate if he loses control," said Shaina in angelical language.

"You need not fear, my love. We are many compared to one strong puppy. Nothing will happen to anyone."

"I wish we were free and wouldn't be told what to do without really having any choice," said Shaina in angelical language. "We fell in love with Earth and humans but being told to train a monster that can erase us makes me wonder if we'll ever be given a chance to go back home. This isn't fair."

There was another knock on the door.

"Who is it?" asked Joe.

"It's me, Patrick, we have a problem, sir! A serious one!" exclaimed Patrick, standing behind the door.

"Come in, just come in, Patrick," said Shaina.

Patrick walked in, panting and distressed.

"What happened? What's going on?" asked Joe.

"The sisters … the Iced Sisters are here," said Patrick in angelical language. "We were informed that six Circle of Pray-ers members were found frozen by the other patrolling pray-ers."

"May God grant their souls to enter heaven without any judgments," said Shaina.

"John and Sara survived the fall then," said Joe in angelical language. "Prepare for defence. We'll have to protect the people of our communities from the sisters and our incoming guests."

"Let's go, everyone, we have a lot of work to do," said Shaina in angelical language, walking out of Joe's office, followed by Joe and Patrick.

Chapter 35
Iced Sisters

Young beautiful twin sisters called Cecilia and Cassia, were brutalised, raped, and burnt alive during the witch hunter's era on a very cold winter night in France. The girls weren't murdered for the false accusation of practicing witchcraft, but because of their beauty. The jealousy of the men of the village cost these girls the hanging of their father, the rape and murder of their mother, and their own brutal deaths in front of the raging people of village.

The village elders sent a raven to the bishop and requested permission to execute these young girls. The execution was granted by the bishop and led to the creation of two dark monsters that hunted the people of village and countless of other people for the next centuries.

In Cerise village, France, in the sixteenth century, many villagers watched as the brutalised naked girls were tied to a massive wooden crosses and oil was spilt on their bodies. The young girls shivered in fear and cold as snow fell on their bloody faces and bodies. Villagers threw whatever they could find at the girls and cursed them, as witch hunters held flaming torches close to the girls' legs.

"I... I... wish... I wish them to burn in hell," said Cecilia, shivering.

"They ... they must feel the cold rather than the heat of the fire of hell, I wish ... they all could feel the coldness of their hearts," said Cassia, freezing.

The leader of witch hunters stepped in front of the villagers, holding up a torch.

"May God almighty spare these witches' souls from the damnation of the fires of hell!" shouted the leader.

The villagers cheered and spat on the ground.

"They practiced witchcraft and that's a blasphemy to God," said the leader. "They manipulated the minds of the fine married men in this village by using their Satanic beauty."

The villagers cheered again.

"Tonight, the curse of the witches will be dispelled from this village and prosperity and blessings will return among our men and their women," shouted the leader.

The villagers cheered and hit their staffs on the ground to make loud noises.

"Let us pray before removing the evil from this village!" declared the leader.

The villagers bowed their heads and some knelt while the witch hunter prayed.

"May God save your souls," said the leader.

He lit the oily wooden logs beneath the girl's feet but suddenly the time paused, as Death and the Contractor appeared near the sisters.

"Oh my, what have they done to you two beautiful ladies?" said the Contractor, holding a white cloth in front of his mouth.

"I see you're still a good drama performer," said Death, looking at the Contractor. "It's a shame that you chose to work for Lucifer rather than me. We could create many wonders together. Pitch your offer or I'll take them before you know it."

The Contractor stepped in front of the girls, looking disgusted.

"I can't even look at you ladies with your smashed faces, but please hear me, I have a great offer for you two," said Contractor, holding his white cloth in front of his mouth, as the girls barely opened their eyes to look at him. "I'm here to pitch you a proposal. Lord Lucifer would like you two to work for him to avoid death. However, whether you accept this offer or join Death is in your hands, my ladies. Remember, these monsters that are letting you burn may or may not be judged by the almighty above the way you'd want them to be."

"Will… we go… to… to hell if we die… now?" asked Cecilia.

"You will go to heaven without any judgment, children," Death replied.

"Will … will anyone avenge us if we die … if we die now?" asked Cassia.

Death shook his head.

"No, but these villagers and all who are involved in your deaths will be judged by …" Death was interrupted by Cassia.

"This isn't fair! We want vengeance," said Cassia angrily and the Contractor smiled.

"Of course it isn't fair, my ladies," said Contractor. "These villagers will pass on this tradition of burning women alive for many generations without anyone stopping them, but if you agree to work for Lord Lucifer you can end this madness with your new lethal abilities."

He held two leather pages up in front of the girls.

"Be warned children, you can go to heaven right now and let these people face their own fates by god," said Death. "You can still have an everlasting peace up there in the heavens. Siding with Lucifer means that you'll never see the heavens ever again."

"My lord, let them make their own decisions without us interfering," added the Contractor. "So, my ladies, what is your decision? Going up to the heavens and perhaps watching these humans die after many years of doing the same, or turning into undying avengers and bringing justice to these monsters?"

"Cassia," said Cecilia. "I want vengeance, sister."

"So be it, sister," Cassia replied.

Death nodded his head then disappeared, while the Contractor jumped in the air with glee.

"I'll just hold these pages under your dripping blood to get two little sweet drops on them and we'll be good to go," said the Contractor, as the blood fell on the pages.

He then rolled up the pages and smiled.

"It is done, vessels. Welcome to the underworld family."

The ground shook and a black mist burst out of it then began swirling around the sisters.

"It's so cold," said Cecilia.

"It is, sister," Cassia agreed.

"Oh, don't worry! Soon, you'll never feel cold again!" said the Contractor, laughing.

"You're going to turn into ice cold sisters, or shall I say, Iced Sisters."

The black mist entered the girls through their mouths and made them shake violently.

"Oh, by the way, my ladies, just a little reminder, the contract is permanent, oops!" said the Contractor, cheerfully. "There's no way to cancel it and because you're not going to die again you have to continuously hunt souls for the rest of your existences. Failure to do so will be punished harshly."

Cassia screamed.

"No pain, no gain, ladies. Enjoy your everlasting life and everlasting service to the Lord Lucifer. Alright ladies, see you hopefully never, and one little thing before I completely go away. You two need to stay in the cold. By that I mean horrible snowy weather. Otherwise you'll die but because of your undying ability you'll experience constant pain and wish to die but you won't. Just stay in the cold and don't get close to warm places at all. I mean, you can but then you'll end up in the underworld and you'll have to live there while being cold all the time and imagine how hot that would be for you, constantly needing cold but never getting it. So, just remain in cold and that's it. Bye now!"

The Contractor then disappeared.

The hearts of the girls stopped, their bodies turned extremely cold, their hair turned white, their pupils covered their entire eyes, and their lips turned black.

Time resumed and the people began shaking in fear, as they looked at two monsters standing in the burning fire.

"Oh, my lord! They're real witches!" shouted the leader. "Curse you, witches!"

He drew his sword but was frozen to death the moment his blade met Cecilia's body.

"What are we going to do?" shouted one of the villagers, who had sexually abused the sisters in the past.

"Oh Peter, you have no idea what we're going to do to you and this village," said Cassia, as the fire and all the burning torches were extinguished.

The sisters screamed and began attacking every single living creature in the village.

A while later, the Iced Sisters fell on their knees when they realised what they'd done to the villagers. They wept over the dead bodies of the children and the tortured icy bodies of the villagers that they'd frozen to death in their anger. However, they knew that there was no turning back and nothing could be reversed, so they left the village and began travelling throughout the lands that were cold or snowy, fulfilling the orders of Lucifer and then later, the orders of God.SED.

The Iced Sisters were in the middle of torturing a young couple in a very cold area of the North-Lands when they received the distress signal from Jason about John and Sara. The sisters immediately travelled to the Snowflakes town and began investigating until they found traces of the scents left by Sara and John nearby.

"I wonder how much fun it will be to fight against the one who defeated Excellency Orhana?" asked Cecilia, while disappearing and reappearing.

"It will be a very cold fun indeed, sister," said Cassia, smiling as she looked at the footprints of Sara and John in the snow.

Chapter 36
Temple (The Time Has Come)

As far as the eye could see, demons were standing in rows watching God.SED while Little ones put pieces of golden armour on him. The land shook every time a piece of armour was added to God.SED's body and **Chanters**[56] chanted louder. The demonic army looked ready and prepared for war. They were well armed and well equipped, standing side by side in countless rows.

Most humans were removed from the temple as the number of demons born from them had reached its required amount, except a few women and young girls that were being used as sex slaves.

After the last piece of armour was fitted on God.SED, a powerful energy burst from him that threw many Little-ones in the air.

"Are you impressed by this outfit of mine?" God.SED asked, as the demonic army knelt. "This armour makes my body invincible to almost anything on this planet."

He stretched his neck and walked around the army while they applauded.

"I'm impressed by the display we see in front of me," said God.SED. "This war is the last one. We have one final shot at the heavens. It's the reason why you all must be completely ready."

God.SED stood beside a very muscular demon, looked at him in disgust and grabbed him by his throat then raised the demon in the air.

"You're very massive in appearance yet inside I see weakness," said God.SED in demonic language.

"My lord, I can assure you that I'm as capable as the others, regardless of how I'm built," said the choking demon in demonic language, before it was dropped to the floor.

---

[56] Chanters: Demonic sorcerers.

"Very well, let's see if you can survive this," said God.SED, as a yellow energy sphere appeared on his index finger. "Don't let me down."

He shot the demon with the sphere. Demon created a black energy shield around him as the sphere reached to him. The energy sphere hit him, but nothing happened. God.SED clapped and the demon began transforming into a Sky-eyes unit.

"Well done!" exclaimed God.SED. "I hope the rest of you are as incredible as this young child of mine. We don't have any room left for weaknesses anymore. We must enter the heavens by ourselves and without the help of the chosen one so that we can bring glory to our lord, the Lucifer. We surely don't want Lucifer to send his underworld armies to do our job, right?"

The crowd shivered in fear as they kept their heads down.

"Fear not my children. We will win the war. We are many," said God.SED, smiling.

"We will own the thrones of the heavens and underworld once we get up there. Father will never reign over us again," said Devil and Evil telepathically between themselves.

"My children," said God.SED, standing in the middle of the demonic army. "In the next seven days, the power of the Earth will be completely transfused into my armour and I will open the portal of firmament, exposing the heavens above."

The demonic army roared their approval.

"Lucifer, our lord, my father, will return to his glory!" shouted God.SED. "We'll defeat the army of Light and open the gates to the Holy-Hosts one after another and take control over the heavens and underworld through the blessings of my father. We shall release my mother Lilith from her prison and at last face the Lord Darkness, our true creator."

The demonic army cheered louder.

"Circle around me, my children. Your father wants to bless you one last time," said God.SED in demonic language, as demons began to circle around him.

"Enjoy this last gift from your father," said God.SED, closing his eyes.

A dark green energy was released from him into the demonic army, transforming them into larger demons. God.SED raised his hands in the air and the earthly elements holders appeared beside him.

"Welcome, my beloved friends, the fallen angels or the fallen sons of god who control the elements of life. Are you ready to betray your own father for the sake of my father, the lord of lords, the Lord Lucifer?" asked God.SED.

"We are ready, sire!" said the elements holders. "We serve Lucifer and Lord Darkness as we seek revenge against our maker."

They held their hands to the sky and a mixture of fire, water, air, and soil began forming in the shape of a spinning sphere. When the mixture was completed and stabilised, the earthly elements holders fell on the ground and turned to dust.

"In seven days, I will consume the mixture and become the owner of Earth," said God.SED, laughing.

The entire demonic army rejoiced as God.SED returned to his temple.

Chapter 37
Are You Ready?

An emergency alert was given to all the angels and **_guardians_**[57] in Eden after the elements holders gave their elements to God.SED. The angels knew that they only had exactly seven days before the war would begin. The news of the holders of water, fire, air and soil siding with God.SED came as a huge shock for all the angels in Eden and in the heavens.

In the Garden of Eden angels and guardians stood in rows waiting for Gabriel to make his speech. In their minds, they all knew that despite all the powers they possessed, fighting with God.SED was now beyond unpredictable as his powers surpassed them all. The fear of losing the battle made many angels leave Eden and join God.SED, even before the seventh day. This didn't sit well with the higher ranking angels and Gabriel, as their army grew even weaker despite having such limited time left before the start of the war.

Gabriel landed on the ground and began walking between the angels that were standing in rows.

"We have been betrayed by the elements holders and now with our own brothers and sisters," said Gabriel, as many angels flew towards Earth. "How faithless."

At that moment, the ground shook.

"It is true! The underworld brothers have succeeded in receiving the cores of the elements of the Earth. They will soon have complete control over the very existence of the planet. You must understand that if you have any doubt of our victory, it is better for you to join the fallen now rather than later or go back to the Holy-Host and pray for those joining the war. Once the war begins, we will be no longer brothers and sisters but only warriors facing our enemies. So, if you

---

[57] Guardians: High ranking angels with special skills.

are an enemy within I assure you that I will not have mercy, even if I have to take down many angels to maintain the safety of others. Do you understand me?"

Many in the crowd left the army and returned to the Holy-Host through the portal. They were ashamed of themselves, but knew that their fear would cost them their holiness. Gabriel looked disappointed to see so many of his well-trained angels leaving, yet he was also cheerful as none of his guardians left the army.

Gabriel opened his wings and a bright light spread out of them.

"Very well, brothers and sisters," he said, looking at a smaller army. "Some of you are old enough to remember the wars before this one and some are so young that this will be your first or last war against Darkness on Earth. Remember this! Our god will always be with us through the power of the holy spirit. Do not lose hope like the others. We will be victorious and we will stop the cycle of Darkness to reset again. In god we believe, in the lord we trust, and for the survival of love, we fight!"

The angelical army cheered.

"No power stands against the creator and no power stands against light," shouted Gabriel.

Natasha and Jessica flew towards Gabriel and stood beside him. "Commander," said Jessica, as Gabriel looked at her. "John's spirit is fully transformed into an animal spirit. We don't think Joe or anyone can change anything."

Gabriel nodded in disappointment.

"My son will not harm us, Commander," said Natasha.

"I cannot fail again by producing another EZ," Gabriel in heavenly language.

"You won't, Gabriel. John's different. He's controlled by Sara and has someone with true love. EZ didn't have a true lover, which was the reason why he felt so lonely among us. You need to train him yourself," Jessica in heavenly language.

Gabriel rubbed his face with his right hand and looked at the angelical army.

"They will lose hope if we share this news with them," he said Gabriel in heavenly language. "I'll take care of John. Natasha and Jessica."

"Yes, Commander," they said together.

"The chosen one is dangerous," said Gabriel. "He possesses, human soul, human flesh, and holy spirit that is now leaning on the Darkness. He is not only capable of doing anything humanly possible that we cannot do, because humans are unholy, but can also do whatever we can, except flying. Even after he receives his training, his spirit may not transform into the holy spirit formation. And if he decides to join EZ and the underworld army, I want you to know that I will terminate them both to save the future. I want to make sure that you understand that anything must be done to stop the cycle of Darkness from resetting itself."

Other angels looked at him, Jessica, and Natasha, wondering what they were talking about.

Natasha and Jessica looked at each other in sorrow.

"We understand, Commander," said Natasha in heavenly language. "What needs to be done must be done to stop the cycle permanently or else this world will be completely consumed by Darkness."

Gabriel then flew above the angelical army. Natasha and Jessica followed and they all landed on the ground in front of the first rows. Suddenly the ground began shaking strongly and trumpets were blown.

"The hour has come!" shouted one of the guardian angels. "Demonic brothers are consuming the elements."

"Prepare for war!" shouted Gabriel, as the army began putting on their helmets. "This human time not matching with our time irritates me. Their days are merely a few seconds in here. Brothers and sisters, this is the hour we have been waiting for! This is the end of Darkness and his armies! This is the hour of the beginning of the end! Stand together and stand strong! We have the creator and the lord blessing us! We will win this war regardless of the chosen one siding with us or not! We are ready!"

Gabriel was transformed into a massive warrior angel, with a huge sword in his hand. He then looked at the angels and guardians as they transformed into their battle bodies.

"Are you ready!" shouted Gabriel and the angelical army hit their weapons on their shields and on the ground. "May god and the holy son be with us one more time."

A portal then began to appear in the space close to Eden.

Chapter 38
Battle with Iced Sisters

Six days before the war of angels and demons, somewhere close to the Circle of Angels, the road up ahead was barely visible for John and Sara because of the heavy snow. They had to walk halfway before reaching the Circle of Angels as they had to let go of the horses. The poor animals couldn't tolerate the cold any longer.

After a while of wandering around and not knowing where else to go to, Sara sat on the snowy ground and looked at John.

"I'm very cold, John. Are you sure we're not lost, love?" asked Sara, shivering.

John removed his winter scarf and wrapped it around Sara's neck and mouth.

"We must be near something. This is all I remember from the map," said John, as he removed his goggles to determine if he could see anything. "It's just hard to know with this much snow around us."

Sara hugged John's right leg.

"I'm sorry, Sara. I know you're cold, but I can't do anything else except hope to find this bloody place."

At that moment, someone laughed.

"Did you hear that?" asked Sara in alarm. "Who's out there? Is anyone out there? We need help! We're lost!"

Sarah was pushed to the ground.

"Hey, stop that!" said Sara, as John helped her stand up.

The giggles and laughs continued.

"I'm scared, John. What's happening?" said Sara holding his arm. "I felt as if someone just pushed me deliberately onto the ground."

"Hey!" yelled John. "Show yourself! Why are you laughing? Ouch!"

Sarah looked at the wound that had appeared on her forearm.

"What the fuck is happening?" said Sara, terrified as she stood with her back against John's chest. "I think we're being attacked by something, John. We've got to get the heck out of here!"

"She has yummy blood," said Cecilia.

"Hey, back off!" John shouted.

"I wonder, what does he taste like, sister?" said Cassia.

John collapsed to his knees and started bleeding from his right thigh.

"Enough of this bullshit!" said John. "Show yourselves!"

"Someone's getting angry. They taste better when they get angry," said Cecilia.

Sara also fell to her knees and began bleeding from her left thigh. John closed his eyes and began getting warmer.

"Enough!" he exclaimed, as he opened his eyes and light began bursting out of them.

Powerful energy was released from his body that revealed the location of the Iced Sisters. They were standing in attack positions with their mouths wide open, revealing countless long teeth.

"What the fuck are those things? And how is light coming out of your eyes, John?" asked Sara, shocked.

"Jesus Christ!" John snapped. "I'll explain everything after I get rid of these monsters. Stay where you are, Sara, until I'm done."

He began transforming into the white furry wolfman. The Iced Sisters held their hands towards wolfman and Sara and powerful snowy wind was blown into them. Wolfman was thrown in the air and while floating, he hit his foot on Sara's head, knocking her unconsciousness. The wolfman quickly stood up after crashing into the snowy ground, ran to Sara to check her for any severe injuries and then looked at the Iced Sisters with rage.

"You've made a big mistake, bitches!" he shouted, preparing to attack.

"He looks just like Lord EZ," said Cecilia, smiling. "Poor boy, his spirit was exposed to the dark side first."

"This is going to be fun, sister," Cassia added. "Let's see what this little puppy can really do against us."

Cassia attacked wolfman, hitting him as hard as she could, as Cecilia began biting him. They fought for quite a long time. Sara regained consciousness but then fell unconscious again after seeing a massive wolf fighting bloody monsters.

"He recovers way faster than us, I don't know what else to do," said Cecilia, panting.

"I don't know either," said Cassia, similarly breathless. "I hit him with everything I'd got, but he didn't seem to feel anything. It feels like he's getting stronger every time we hit him hard. He's gaining more power from something that we're unaware of."

Wolfman licked his wound while it healed and laughed.

"Are you ladies tired?" he asked, stretching his neck.

"Fuck off!" shouted Cecilia.

She attacked the wolfman, but he grabbed her in the air, broke her leg then threw her into the rock beside him. Cecilia didn't move from where she fell. Cassia ran to her, comforting her sister by gently touching her face.

"Bastard!" yelled Cassia. "You're going to pay for this!"

She shoved her right hand into the snow. A massive crystal hand then emerged from the ground underneath wolfman and its fingers were shoved inside his legs. Wolfman roared and began hitting the crystal fingers in an attempt to break free of them.

"I'm healing, sister, don't worry. What are we going to do now?" asked Cecilia, as her sister helped her stand. "Shall we go for the heart?"

"It will be too risky for us, but I think we have no other choice, sister," replied Cassia, looking at the angry wolfman, who was almost free of the crystal fingers. "Let's freeze this fucking dog!"

Together, they ran towards John. When they reached him, they joined two of their hands into one and shoved the frozen crystal spear deep inside the wolfman's chest, narrowly missing the heart. Blood burst from his mouth and the hair on his back began to turn blue in colour.

"Stop fighting, doggy," said Cassia. "Stop resisting us. This is good for you. You're going to become one of us and serve us forever."

As the wolfman began transforming, he began seeing the sisters' memories and what had happened to them in the past.

"Humans must be eliminated for their heinous acts," said Cecilia. "Let's end them together. Feel the cold, doggy. Let it conquer your heart. You know that deep down there, you can't wait any longer for this suffering to end. Let us have your heart, join us."

Wolfman tried very hard to break the spear but he was too weak to do so.

"Wow!" said Cassia, as the sisters began seeing John's memories. "This is how majesty Orhana was defeated then. You feed from the energy of your girl's true love."

The sisters shoved the frozen tentacle deeper inside wolfman's chest. He closed his eyes and began to freeze from his feet upward.

"That's it," said Cecilia. "You'll break out of your ice as a new ice wolfman."

Wolfman heard Sara's voice.

"True love waits, John. Don't leave me here alone with them. Fight! Fight! Fight!" exclaimed Sara.

"How is he hearing such a thing?" asked Cecilia.

"I don't know, we must turn him before…" replied Cassia, just as time slowed down. "Oh, fuck!"

The ice that had built up around the wolfman's body melted. He opened his eyes and smiled.

"You've been cold for so long that you've forgotten the warmth of true love," said wolfman, breaking the tentacle then shoving his claws into the stomachs of the sisters.

"Next time, aim for the heart properly. You surely missed mine," said the raging wolfman.

"We're going to hell!" shouted the Iced Sisters.

"Indeed. Have a little taste of fire!" shouted wolfman, releasing powerful energy inside the sisters' stomachs.

The Iced Sisters began to burn from within, as if fire was ignited inside their bodies. As the sisters melted, they both bit wolfman on his forearms. He roared loudly but didn't let go of the sisters. After they'd melted into the snowy ground, the wolfman that was now transformed into John walked over to Sara and collapsed beside her on the ground.

A while later, John opened his eyes and saw a man cutting something out of Sara's arm.

"Back off!" said John, weakly.

"John!" said Sara. "We made it! Just stay there. Andrew's a friend of Uncle Joe. Patrick and Andrew found us in the snow. I think we got attacked by wolves or something. They took all your clothes and I guess they hit me on the head because I've got a lump on my forehead. Andrew's a doctor and is removing the identity chip from my wrist. They removed yours too. No one can track us now.

Just don't move, you're badly injured. You lost a lot of blood fighting the wolves or whatever that thing was. You've got bad bite wounds."

Andrew looked at John, smiled and nodded his head. He then continued removing the chip from Sara's wrist. John tried to see what Andrew truly looked like the holy spirit but he fell unconscious.

At the Circle of Angels, while wolfman was fighting the Iced Sisters, Shaina rushed to the main gates with some other people.

"How did the sisters come this far?" asked Shaina. "They always scouted the city but not here, not even anywhere close to here."

"It's true, powerful units have entered our territory," said a little boy, as Joe and the others began walking out of the community.

Joe stopped rushing and stood beside the little boy.

"You don't need to worry. Just go to other kids and wait for us inside, okay?" said Joe and the little boy went back inside the community. "Close these doors, Alex, until we take care of the situation out there."

Alex nodded his head and closed the doors as Joe, Shaina, and other people rushed out of the building.

"Shall we turn?" asked Shaina, nervously.

"Not yet," replied Joe, as the ground shook and a bright light was sighted. "There they are. Patrick, Andrew, transform and run over there now! We'd better stay here and guard everyone until we find out ... I don't ... I don't sense any dark powers... oh, my God! Run boys! Run! The kids are injured!"

Andrew and Patrick transformed into angelical forms, ran into the snow towards where they saw the brightness. After finding the unconscious Sara and John, they grabbed them and took them back into the community.

"Did you see the sisters? Were you followed?" asked Shaina, examining Sara for wounds and injuries.

"The sisters were defeated," said Patrick. "I'm going up to my room. I don't know whether bringing John in here is a good idea. He's defeated Orhana and the sisters. His powers are beyond what EZ possessed when he had full control over his animal spirit."

Patrick transformed into the shape of a human and went back inside the building.

"John's been bitten by the sisters, Joe," said Andrew.

"Look at this **Frozen Curse**[58], " said Joe, his eyes wide. "How is he even still alive?"

Joe put his hands on John's forehead and transferred holy spirit into him. This helped John's body gain enough power to prevent the curse from killing him.

"This curse only breaks through the will of the victim," added Joe, as John's wounds began to heal. "It's good that this kid is a man of strong will. Let's take the children into the healing room and the rest can go back to the gathering room until everything's calmed."

Joe and Shaina lifted John and Sara, placed them on their shoulders and walked back inside the community building.

"What are you thinking, Joe," asked Shaina, once they arrived in the healing room.

"John's dangerous," replied Joe in angelical language, as Shaina and Andrew looked at him with concern. "When I transferred spirit into him, I had a glimpse of his inner spirit. He's nothing like us. He's a wolf, just like that imbecile EZ. The Commander told me to take care of him, train him and make him control his powers, but it won't happen. We won't be able to do so."

"What else can we do then?" asked Shaina in angelical language while placing Sara on the bed.

"I have to inform the Commander. There's nothing else to do," said Joe in angelical language while placing John on the other bed.

"You can't connect with Commander though," said Patrick in angelical language, as he walked in the room. "Fallen angels can't connect with the high-ranking angels, as we all know. They can connect to us but we can't connect to them."

"Thanks for the lecture, Patrick," said Andrew sarcastically in angelical language.

"Who else can we connect with, Joe?" asked Shaina in angelical language.

"Jessica. She is the only one who I can perhaps connect with for a very short period telepathically and inform her of the situation," replied Joe in angelical language as he stood and transformed into his angelical form. "I miss my wings. I miss home."

---

[58] Frozen Curse: An extremely contagious and deadly curse that was designed by the frozen sisters to kill their enemies. The infected area freezes and the effect then spreads throughout the other parts of the body until the victim freezes to death.

Joe then closed his eyes and began informing Jessica of the situation telepathically.

"I hope any other high-ranking demonic creatures didn't feel us when we ran out of the holy Circle of Angels to bring the children in," said Andrew in angelical language.

"God save us all. The chances of them picking up our energy is high," said Shaina in angelical language.

Chapter 39
John's Training

In the evening, John was sitting in the middle of an empty hall that was in the shape of a courtroom, looking at unknown people around him that he didn't know. Three days had passed since he and Sara had arrived in the Circle of Angels community. There was a very bitter silence in the place until Joe and Shaina walked in with cups of Choco-Loco. John exhaled in relief and was given a cup. When all the cups were distributed, Joe told everyone to sit down and asked musicians to start playing Celtic music while he introduced John to the people around him. They walked over one by one to meet John. Most of them knew him from the movies and the celebrity news but had never met him in person. When the meet and greeting were over, John stood up and walked over to the musicians and asked them to stop playing then stood on a stool and smiled.

"Attention, ladies and gentlemen!" exclaimed John.

He tried to share his story of how he and Sara travelled all the way from West-lands to the Circle of Angels. However, Joe interrupted him just before he began talking about how Nanny turned into an angel.

"Wow!" exclaimed Joe. "My boy, it's time for the feast. We'll continue with your story after the meal. How's that sound, everyone?"

Members of the crowd carried parts of a large round table to the middle of the courtroom. Others took trays of food and jars of flavoured water from the kitchen into the courtroom and placed them on the newly formed large round table. Some others placed small chairs around the table. Once everyone had sat down, Joe prayed and thanked god for the blessing and everyone began eating. He then looked at John, who was sitting beside him, and whispered in his ear.

"My boy," Joe whispered. "We haven't told humans in here about our true images. I know, I can read your mind. It's for their best. We have angels, or prayers as we call them, out there praying nonstop so these people can live a little longer in peace. We're here to make sure, when the end comes, that the souls of these humans are taken to Holy-Host without judgment. If their faith shakes, they may never see what's been built for them up there."

Joe patted John on the back.

"I thought humans had the right to knowledge, but I guess it doesn't matter anymore," said John then he had a vision in which Sara was bleeding from her mouth. "Where's Sara? Is she safe?" asked John, assertively, getting to his feet.

"My boy, what happened?" asked Joe. "She's fine, just resting. It's a lot for her brain to process. What's the matter, John?"

"I haven't seen her for three days straight now. I want to see my girl, if that's not too much to ask," said John but by seeing others looking at him, he sat down slowly and smiled.

"Relax my boy, you're in good hands. You're both safe here among us," said Joe. "She's still trying to cope with all the memories that returned to her. Her brain needs a lot of time to recover and process all the lost information. You had the holy spirit that allowed you to recover quickly after having your memories revived but Sara's just a human. Let her rest."

"We are not safe because of you," said one of the agitated angels telepathically.

"What do you mean by that?" asked John.

"I didn't mean anything, John. I'm sorry," said the angel telepathically.

"Sebastian, you need to calm down, brother," said Joe, telepathically.

He then looked at John, who seemed concerned, and exhaled.

"Your spirit was exposed to extreme levels of Darkness," said Joe, telepathically. "Your spirit only transforms into the animal spirit now not the holy spirit. To do so you'll need to go through an excessive amount of training, to transform the animal spirit into the holy spirit then learn to control it. This may intrigue your animal spirit and unleash the darkness within you in here. From what we've heard, your power surpasses our expectations. You're a true danger for yourself and all of us if you lose control during training. This is what brother Sebastian was trying to say."

John took a deep breath and nodded his head.

"Sebastian's right. I don't disagree," thought John. "I don't even remember anything during the time I'm the wolfman. I just remember the things I do when I use the power within me through these light bombs, these energy spheres. I surely am a danger to everyone."

"It's alright, my son," said Joe, telepathically. "You have much to learn and I'm sure that when you learn you'll know how to control your powers and perhaps transform into your true spiritual image, one that's safe for you and everyone you love. Enough of this talk already. Let's eat and celebrate having another feast together."

He then made a toast.

"Alright everyone, let's once again celebrate another night living, breathing and blessed by the almighty above. Let's celebrate having the so-called chosen one among us. The one who is supposed to receive instructions from the lord and deliver us from Satan through the holy spirit."

He then sat down on his chair while people cheered and continued eating, before he grabbed a piece of fish and began eating. John took another deep breath and looked at the people around him. He then looked at his wooden bowl, which contained a cooked fish and two sliced potatoes. John then grabbed the wooden fork beside the bowl on the table and began eating.

Upstairs in the bedroom, Sara woke up breathless on the bed. Shaina and Hayley rushed over to her.

"Try to calm down, sister," said Hayley.

"My parents, where's John? My paintings … my promise ring … my home… my life…" Sara mumbled. "I never wanted to become a nurse, I hate blood. I … I don't feel good."

"You need to rest, Sara. Your brain's processing things way faster it should, just try to rest. You'll be fine once everything calms down," said Shaina.

"Where's John? Is he alive? He turned into a wolf kind of a creature. They were these monsters trying to kill him and then they … How did that happen? What is he?" said Sara, still very distressed.

"Sara my dear, please rest, we're all here to …" said Shaina, as she signalled Hayley by raising her eyebrows.

Hayley sat beside Sara on the bed and placed her hand on her head.

"Everything will be just fine," said Shaina. "Rest, my dear. Rest for now."

Sarah fell asleep. Hayley pulled the blanket over her and stood beside Shaina.

"Poor girl. How's her soul? Are we in any danger because of her?" asked Shaina, concerned.

"Sara's just lost the power of the spirit. There's no power within her at all. Perhaps Tasha turning into a demon disconnected her from Sara, resulting in the termination of holy spirit within her. That's probably why Sara didn't turn into anything except an average human for all this time. However, her soul's as pure as a new-born baby."

Shaina held Hayley's hands and smiled.

"It's good hear that," said Shaina. "I wonder what John's soul's looking like? Shall we go and find out?"

Hayley nodded. After making sure that Sara was comfortable as she slept, Shaina and Hayley went downstairs and joined the crowd.

At the feast table, the entire crowd was watching John in shock, as he swallowed everything that edible and drinkable. Some of the parents had to leave the table, afraid of such uncivilised behaviour. John consumed plate after plate of food yet still wasn't satisfied.

"My dear boy, what an appetite you have," said Shaina, looking at Joe. "Are you sure you can digest all that food?"

John growled like an animal.

"Joe," added Shaina. "Would you mind if we talk in the kitchen for a second, right now?"

She and Joe walked into the kitchen.

"Something's dangerous with that boy. He's more an animal than a human at this point," said Shaina, with concern. "He's not the same John I met years ago. He's dark now. I can feel it."

"I checked him when he growled and saw no darkness in him," Joe replied. "But because he's an animal in nature now, his brain has some damage. Some of the animal-like behaviour has …"

At that moment, John opened the kitchen door.

"Guys, could I get more fish please?" he asked John, wiping his mouth with the back of his hand.

"Yes dear, I'll bring some right away," said Joe.

John nodded his head and left the kitchen.

"He seemed not to like the food when he started eating but now, he's …" Joe started to say.

Shaina interrupted him.

"What the hell are we going to do with him?" asked Shaina. "The Commander told us he was okay to be trained, but John isn't okay at all. Did Jessica get the message? I hope she did because we won't be able to keep this animal here for long before he starts eating everything in here and asks for more. I miss that little emotional boy who was curious about everything and kept crying over small things. The man in that room is a problem. We have humans here whose very lives are in danger if John loses control and turns into another EZ."

"John's going to be a problem," agreed Andrew, as he entered the kitchen. "I think it's wise for us to alert everyone to stand by if the short training fails."

"I agree," said Hayley, walking in behind Andrew.

"Everyone just calm down please," said Joe. "Jessica got the message and I'm sure that she delivered it to the Commander already. John's eating a lot because he's consumed energy from the spirit, rather than fulfilling the energy by eating food. Now that his body's receiving energy from food, of course he requires more of it. I mean for god's sake, the kid's bite wounds just got healed an hour ago. Do you know how much energy he must have used, without knowing to heal himself? Embrace yourselves! We're better than this. We need to do anything we can to save him and fulfil the destiny, otherwise, none of us are going back home."

Suddenly everyone felt the presence of an incredibility powerful energy approaching the kitchen.

"Is it possible for a half human to have this much power without dying?" asked Hayley, with concern.

"Apparently it is," replied Shaina, impressed as John walked inside the kitchen.

"Sorry everyone, I'm full now. I just wanted to stop you from preparing more fish or anything else. I sincerely thank you all for the great feast. I'll wash the dishes in return for such hospitality."

John began looking around for an apron.

"You don't need to do anything, my little boy," said Joe. "Just go back to the table and accompany the crowd. Just don't share the supernatural parts of your journey."

He gave Joe a salute and left the kitchen.

"He looked amazing. He even gained muscles," said Hayley, as Andrew looked unimpressed.

"We'll start his training at dawn," said Joe. "The sooner we see what he's capable of, the sooner we can teach him how to control it. Inform the others and let's go back to the people before things get any more suspicious."

A couple of hours after the feast, everyone had gone to their rooms to sleep. After checking on John and Sara, who were sleeping in separate bedrooms, Joe and Shaina went to their room as well. John was also notified that his training would start at dawn. When everyone seemed asleep and there was an absolute silence in the community, John slowly walked out of his bedroom and went to Sara's room and sat on the bed. He then slowly placed his hand on the back of Sara's head and caressed her hair. Suddenly, Sara turned around and John quickly pulled his hand back.

"Jesus!" he exclaimed. "You scared the shit out of me. Hi, how are you feeling?"

Sara hugged John as she laid on the bed, crying.

"It's alright. I'm here, sweetheart. You know I'm emotional, so I may cry too now if you don't stop. I know, the memories aren't all fun. I'm so sorry for …"

Sara let go of John then pulled herself up and lay on the bed, her back leaning on the headboard.

"How did you turn into that wolf thing?" she asked. "How long has this been going on? Why am I not turning into a wolf? Don't I have the spirit within me?"

John held her right hand in his two hands.

"Well," said John and began sharing everything that happened to them in the previous few days.

While John spoke Sara occasionally interrupted him by saying that she remembered or began remembering. Their talk continued until close to dawn. They then fell asleep beside each other.

There was a knock on the door and as John and Sara didn't attend to it, the door slowly opened. Hayley cautiously snuck her head into the room and saw Sara and John still in a deep sleep.

"Ah, so cute," she whispered. "Let me check John's soul and see what the status is on that."

She slowly touched John's right arm but quickly pulled it back in absolute fear.

John turned around and looked straight into her eyes.

"Hi … Good … Good morning, John. It's … It's time for you to go for … for your training," said Hayley, a little breathlessly.

Sara opened her eyes looked at Hayley, who was standing middle of the room. Sara placed her head on John's chest then looked at the clock in the shape of a cowboy hat.

"We just slept about two hours ago," said Sara and closed her eyes.

"Well, we basically only have three days left until the war begins," said Hayley. "The sooner John gains ability to hopefully transform his animal spirit into the holy spirit form, the safer the future will become."

John kissed Sara's head and began getting off the bed, yawning.

"I'm ready," said John, sleepily. "Let's go."

"John, you do need to put on your pants before we go down," Hayley reminded him.

Sara grabbed John's pants from the footboard and, while covering herself with the blanket, she threw them at John. John slipped on his pants and the shoes that were placed on the floor beside the bed and followed Hayley as she walked out of the bedroom.

"Alright, I hope everything goes smoothly today," said Hayley. "We called upon a lot of angels, or you could say angels without wings, to join us during your training, just in case things go sideways."

"I'm sure that the wolf side of me won't harm anyone trying to help him," said John, walking beside Hayley. "I'm confident about that."

"I checked your soul when I touched you, before you woke up or turned around looking at me in a very creepy way," said Hayley. "Your ... Your soul's infested with Darkness now. I'm not sure how you can behave like a human for all this time. Perhaps, it's the love that's kept you protected for all this time. The manifestation of Darkness in you is beyond repair. Your soul and spirit are both infected. If you lose love, or rather Sara, you'll turn into a very dark monster resembling EZ, if you know who I'm talking about."

John nodded his head.

"Try to control the spirit, so that perhaps you can transform it into the holy spread that could heal your soul," Hayley added, as she stopped walking and looked at John. "If you fail to transform into the holy spirit form, controlling yourself during the war will become almost impossible. The wolf spirit seeks fear, rage, blood, and revenge, regardless of how good or evil it is. Once the war begins, the wolf inside you will have so much dark energy around it and that will prevent it from becoming holy. Just try your best and pray that Gabriel comes to receive you on time, before you lose control."

"What do you mean by that?" asked John, suspicious.

"We know that your training won't be enough at this time. This is the truth. I don't want to discourage you but in order to fully control your powers and learn how to use them properly we need an archangel who's already trained someone

239

like you before. The Commander's the one who can truly help you to transform into your holy spirit form."

"Well, thanks for sharing this amazing piece of information with me. I'm very encouraged by realising that my sweet sleep was interrupted to hear that the training may not even be useful at all," said John as he began walking. "Whatever, let's just do this. I'm sick and tired of hearing that this thing isn't possible or that thing isn't possible. I've made the impossible possible using the holy spirit so far. I'll get this transformation done without the Commander as well."

At the underground empty training court room, several angels gathered around John at a safe distance and prepared for Joe to give an order. John was amazed by the beauty and brightness that the angels created in the place while standing motionlessly in the middle of the court. Joe walked a few steps closer to John and put his hand on his shoulder.

"Son, we'll have to measure your power first before heading towards other training steps," he said, as John nodded his head. "Saying that, you'll be shot by the holy spirit energy sphere or as you call it, the Light bomb."

"Alright, sounds good," said John, calmly.

Joe nodded his head and joined the other angels.

"John, we'd like you to turn into the wolfman, if you're capable of transforming right now," said Joe.

"I think I can give it a shot but what happens next will be a mystery to me. I just want everyone to be aware of that fact," said John. "I mostly have blurred memories of the time I'm with Sara in the form of the wolfman and no other memories at all. Just be careful everyone."

John then closed his eyes and began concentrating. At first, he failed to transform but after focusing on all the traumatic memories of the previous few days and putting Sara's life in so much danger without being able to do much more to protect her, he was intrigued enough to begin transforming into the wolfman.

"Edward again? Haven't we gone through enough with this stupidity?" asked Josh, one of the angels, in angelical language.

"Are you sure this is a good idea, Joe?" asked Shaina in angelical language.

"My God," said Joe, shocked. "He's just like Edward but white in colour. I can't know for certain whether he's any danger to us or not. We have to put him through the test first."

"He's so cute," said Hayley, excitedly. "Look at the black hair on his chest. It's like he's wearing armour. So cool!"

Wolfman opened his eyes and a strong energy was released from his body that shocked all the angels in the room. He then stretched his neck and began licking his claws, cleaning them.

"This is Edward all over again. We must keep John out of here, Joe," said Andrew in angelical language.

"Silence!" exclaimed Joe. "Get into your defence positions, brothers and sisters!"

The angels created a shield shaped like an energy sphere around them and the court then stood on guard.

"Get into attack formation!" said Joe, as the angels raised their palms towards John. "Steady! God help us, fire!"

The angels shot several energy spheres at the wolfman, but the spheres entered his body and exited from his back, as if he didn't have a solid form. The wolfman man giggled and nodded his head. The energy sphere hit into the shield covering the court and was absorbed into it.

"Well, that's a good news," said Joe, in relief. "Even though his spirit and soul are infested by Darkness, he still has the holy spirit operational within him, which prevents him from being harmed by our attacks."

"Joe, I don't think this is a good way to start training John or this wolf," said Rick, one of the other angels in the room, in angelical language. "These attacks may actually make him angry and dangerous. We could perhaps start by having some dialogue first, to find out if he understands us or not."

"There's no time for chit chatting," said Joe telepathically. "We have three days until the war, which isn't enough time at all. The main reason of this training isn't to help him find a way to transform into the holy spirit form. We all know that few human days won't be enough for that. What's important at this moment is to find out how powerful he really is."

"This is preposterous! This will put us in danger! Are you insane, brother?" asked Rick, telepathically.

"Joe and I made this plan last night, brother Rick," said Shaina, telepathically. "We're too many for him to handle. He's totally surrounded. We have other angels outside the courtroom creating a shield. This animal isn't going anywhere. All we must do now is trigger him to reach the level that he gets angry and attacks us or uses his hidden powers. That way we'll know what we'll be dealing with during the war."

"This isn't right, sister," said Rick, telepathically. "You had to inform us all before we agreed to join you in here."

Joe looked around at the scared angels.

"We are many, worry not. The plan will work. We just have to make him encourage enough to use his true powers," said Joe, telepathically.

While the angels talked to one another telepathically, the wolfman sat on the floor and closed his eyes.

"Let's attack him now!" said Andrew telepathically.

He charged then kicked and punched the wolfman multiple times. However, it wasn't effective at all as his attacks were intercepted by the invisible holy spirit shield around the wolfman.

"Our attacks will have no effects on him," said the disappointed Andrew telepathically, as he walked back and stood among the other angels. "We all know we can't attack one another because of the existence of holy spirit among us."

"Meh, this is just a huge waste of time," asked Kaya, one of the angels, in angelical language. "He isn't going to attack us and even if he does, it won't harm us and we can attack him to analyse his true strength. So, why the hell are we even in our angelical forms?"

He began transforming into his human form. A few of the angels did the same and began chatting. Shaina looked at Joe in distress and shrugged her shoulders. Suddenly, the wolfman opened his eyes and began wagging his tail excitedly, as Sara knocked on the door.

"Hey guys, is everything alright in there?" she asked. "I want to come in but … what's your name, sir? Henry isn't letting me in."

"You can't come in, my dear, not now," said Joe, as the wolfman began growling.

"This is it! He is getting agitated. Defence formation!"

The other people in the room turned into angels and created a shield guard.

"Open the door, please. What's going on in there? Let me in. Is John alright?" asked Sara.

"My dear, we can't let you in here yet," Shaina replied.

The wolfman began barking and a powerful energy was released from his body that pushed the angels back. He then made two fists and began to slowly walk towards the door.

"Prepare for battle!" shouted Joe, as many angels stood in front of the door in attack formation.

"Hey, let me in, Aunt Shaina, I know you're in there," said Sara, irritated. "This isn't nice keeping me out here."

"I told you, you can't come in, stop asking!" Shaina exclaimed.

"Don't talk to her like that!" shouted the wolfman.

His body mass increased and he began attacking the angels in front of the door, one by one. In few seconds, many angels lay on the ground motionless, with broken arms and legs. Wolfman then looked at Shaina angrily and began walking towards her. When Joe saw that wolfman outmatched them all and was going to hurt Shaina, he began creating *elimination spirit*[59] with which to attack the wolfman.

"Stop this foolishness, you stupid animal! I will destroy you!" shouted Joe, but the wolfman didn't stop approaching Shaina.

"I can't believe I'm doing this again!" said Joe.

He shot the wolfman with the elimination spirit, but before it hit wolfman, he grabbed the laser with both hands and sent it back in Joe's direction. Joe dodged the laser but before he turned towards the wolfman, he was grabbed him by the neck and lifted up.

"John! Stop this madness!" shouted Sara, as she was led in by Shaina. "They're our family! Put him down, now!"

The wolfman turned and looked at Sara.

"Sara run, save yourself," said Joe, weakly.

"I said, put him down, now!" Sara shouted.

The wolfman threw Joe on the floor and stood still. Sara and Shaina ran over to Joe and after making sure he was still alright, Sara looked at the wolfman. She was amazed, as much as she was afraid of the beast, but she didn't let her fear stop her from walking up to the wolfman. She then stood in front of him, looking up into his eyes.

"I know you're in there, I know you know me, and I know that you love me," said Sara, as she raised her hand to touch the wolfman.

---

[59] Elimination spirit: A powerful laser energy force that can only be created by a combination of several guardian angels that could eliminate an enemy instantly.

"Sara, no!" said Hayley, attempting to stand.

"It's okay," said Sara. "He's my wolf and he isn't going to harm me."

The wolfman stood still, as Sara caressed him on the chest.

"So furry, so warm," said Sara as the wolfman whimpered.

Sara looked around and noticed that most of the angels were standing and were healed. She then looked at the wolfman.

"They don't have your leash, but I do," she said. "Now, sit!"

The wolfman whined and sat on the floor. Sara sat down beside him and leaned her head on his chest, listening to his heartbeat.

"Good boy. I know you're in there, John. I can hear your heart," said Sara, cuddling her face on the wolfman's furry chest.

"The girl's got his leash. At least we're safe now," said Shaina, helping Joe to stand up.

"I've grown very powerless during these years," said Joe. "I fought with EZ and nothing happened to me and look at me now."

He stood up, placing his arm on Shaina's shoulders.

"Well," he continued, "maybe it's time to transform into our highest forms and see if he can beat us again. We'll keep Sara here to make sure that she'll stop him killing us, if that ever happens."

"My wolf needs food. His stomach's making loud noises. Is there any food to eat around her, aunt? Uncle?" asked Sara, looking at Shaina and Joe.

Shaina nodded her head.

"I guess we should go and have breakfast," replied Shaina. "Can he transform into John again? We can't use all of our resources feeding this giant wolf."

Sara looked into the wolfman's eyes.

"John, start shape shifting love," said Sara and the wolfman began to transform into John.

"Did I hurt anyone?" asked John. "I remember you coming to me and telling me to sit but I don't remember anything else? How did you find out this place? Who brought you down here? It could be dangerous for you, Sara."

"Well, I looked around and asked around and then met Amanda, who brought me down here, and then I met Henry who didn't let me in. Who cares really, let's go up now. I'm really hungry and need food," said Sara, while pulling John's arm.

"Just a second, sweetheart, I got no clothes on, can I have any extra clothes again, please?" asked John, covering his genitalia.

Patrick went out of the court and returned with an old shirt and a pair of pants. John thanked him and put on the clothes while everyone turned their backs.

"Did you see the wolfman?" asked John. "Did you see me in that shape?"

"Yes, I saw him or your animal shape when you fought with those demonic girls in the snow," Sara replied. "I remember that because apparently the effect of the purple mist is low around the community. That's why I have that memory. But I do now remember you changing into the wolf a couple of days ago and your eyes turning bright …"

Shaina interrupted her.

"Children, there's a lot left for us to do and a very little time to do so. Let's go up and have breakfast and you two can talk about other matters later, alright?"

"Yes, aunt. Sure, let's go, I'm starving," said John then walked towards the doors, holding Sara's hand.

Joe looked at the other distressed angels and exhaled. He then walked out of the court and the others followed him.

Chapter 40
Circle of Angels Is Found

On the evening of the fourth night, somewhere close to the community building, Jason and the other units were shivering and trying to find out where John was. They could feel the presence of high energy from time to time but couldn't locate its source.

"They must be here, I can feel them," said Jason, shivering. "They're being protected by something that we can't … I'm getting sick and tired of this cold."

He shot a random power purple energy sphere into the air.

"How can we locate John if this cold weather keeps blocking our energy sensory systems rapidly," Jason snarled.

"Leader, we're dying," said one of the units, freezing. "We can't stay here any longer. We need fire to survive."

The ground shook.

"Did you say fire?" asked EZ in demonic language.

"Master," said Jason, as he and the two other units fell to their knees.

"Arise brothers, it's good to see you again, Jason," said EZ in demonic language.

Jason stood up.

"Likewise, brother," said Jason in demonic language. "The chosen one is here. We've tracked them this far, I know they are…"

EZ began to walk towards the location of the secret place.

"Do you see anything master? Can you track them?" asked Jason in demonic language.

EZ scoffed.

"Not only do I see the chosen one but I now know exactly where he's located," replied.

EZ in demonic language.

EZ then raised his hand.

"I'm glad that John was stupid enough to use so much energy to destroy the Iced Sisters. The radiation of his energy is still all over the land. His own power became his own bait."

The ground around the Circle of Angels community cracked, burning magma erupted, and demons began to crawl out. The angels were immediately alerted and many angels came out of the community to fight with the demons.

"Is that where the community is? I can't see the building yet. There must be some pray-ers protecting it," said Jason in demonic language.

"Yes, there are many of them protecting the building," said EZ in demonic language, smiling. "But they're about to stop praying."

EZ began walking towards the community, waving his hand at some of the angels that were praying.

"No demons will harm you, if you just simply stop praying," said EZ in demonic language, as the pray-ers looked at each other.

"No! Don't stop praying!" shouted those angels that were fighting with demons around the building. "No one can enter a holy Circle of Prayers, even if they see through the invisible structure. Hold the circle!"

"Is that so?" said EZ jumping from where he was standing and landing in the middle of the empty community yard. "My name is EZ. None of you in here can stop me. Give me the chosen one and I'll transform you into fallen angels rather than terminating you."

Angels that had rushed into the yard began shivering upon hearing the name of EZ. Suddenly he stopped and closed his eyes. When he opened them, he shot every single praying angel, terminating the holy Circle of Prayers. Demons that overpowered and outnumbered the angels outside of the community began crawling inside, coming from every direction. Jason and other two units flew and landed beside EZ.

"Wow! They've had such a massive building all this time and we couldn't even locate it?" said Jason, in amazement.

"John's leaving again. I can feel him getting far from here," said EZ in demonic language. "Track his energy trail and capture him as soon as you can. I need to return to the underworld for an urgent matter."

A portal of fire appeared in the ground and absorbed EZ into it before it imploded.

Jason looked at the other units as EZ and smiled.

"You two stay here and kill as many as you can. I'm going after the chosen one."

Jason flew towards the gates of the building, blowing multiple powerful purple energy spheres at the structure.

Chapter 41
EZ Becomes the Leader

EZ entered inside the room where Lucifer was sitting on his throne and knelt. They were the only ones in the room.

"Rise, my humble servant," said Lucifer in underworld language.

He stood up and walked down the stairs. He then stood beside EZ, leaned on the handle of his cane.

"I saw that you succeeded in finding John and left Jason to look after that matter but we have a much more important matter to attend to, or perhaps I should say that you have to attend to," said Lucifer in underworld language, coughing.

"How may I be of service, master?" asked EZ in underworld language.

"Walk with me, EZ," said Lucifer in underworld language.

EZ began walking with Lucifer, while the walls of the pyramid spread open and the entire underworld came into view. As far as the eye could see were suffering souls in agony and pain, burning in fire. Lucifer pointed at a corner of the land where a massive underworld army was standing then looked at EZ.

"Magnificent, isn't it?" said Lucifer in underworld language. "A fraction of this army can wipe out all humanity."

EZ continued looking at burning souls.

"They chose this life, EZ," said Lucifer in underworld language and EZ smiled. "They knew about the existence of this world and yet they ignored it."

Lucifer pointed at the massive underworld army again.

"You have been faithful to me, Edward. You listened to me when I came to you, you showed me that there was still hope for me to go back to the Holy Host and unleash the gift that I gained from master Darkness in there, to save all those slaves that think of themselves as angels. You gave a purpose and helped me throughout countless years on order to reach my goal. My sons are incompetent.

249

My daughter was after my thrones. My current form is powerless. I live like a parasite, using one human host after another until I get inside John. The army of the underworld needs a leader."

EZ looked at him, convinced that he knew what Lucifer was about to say next.

"You need to lead the army on my behalf while I aim to reach to Holy Host."

"Your grace, I'm nothing but a humble servant," said EZ in underworld language as he knelt. "I will not fail you, my lord."

"Today, you are no longer a humble servant, today you are my son, my protector, and the leader of my army," said Lucifer in underworld language.

Lucifer hit his cane on the floor three times and the giant serpent slithered onto the floor and stayed behind EZ.

"Mark him so he can rise as the leader of my army," said Lucifer in underworld language, coughing.

The serpent stung EZ on his right shoulder with his fangs. Blood covered EZ's eyes and he grew more muscular. The venom that dripped off his shoulder formed two long red stripes down to his chest and at the back down to his shoulder blade, before the giant serpent slithered away. Upon seeing this the underworld army roared and rejoiced.

"Rise my dear protector and praise your army," said Lucifer in underworld language.

EZ stood up and looked at the massive army.

"May I join them?" asked EZ, in underworld language.

"Certainly, they are yours," said Lucifer, using the back of his claws to wipe his mouth of the dark blood that had dripped from the side of his lips. "You can join and rule over them anytime you want."

EZ jumped and landed on the ground in front of the army. Every single underworld creature knelt.

"Follow my lead, obey my commands and kill as many Light creatures as you can, so that we can bring glory to our lords, Lucifer and Darkness, and overcome Earth!" shouted EZ in underworld language.

Lucifer was taken over to EZ, sitting on the back of the slithering serpent. He then got off the snake and stood beside EZ in front of the army.

"The time has come, EZ. My sons are about to consume the elements," said Lucifer in underworld language. "It is amazing how human time is so slow compared to ours."

"Indeed," said EZ in underworld language, looking at the army. "Prepare for war!"

The army roared out loud. Lucifer then raised his left hand and a portal of fire opening, connecting the underworld with the centre of God.SED's temple.

Chapter 42
Run!

Inside the Circle of Angels community, the training had resumed. The wolfman was being subjected to countless physical attacks and numerous energy spheres from the angels who were now in guardian forms, yet he was successfully either dodging or simply neutralising all the attacks. The wolfman often mocked the angels for being so weak and grabbed some of them by their necks and threw them around as if they were weightless. Sara smiled every time wolfman threw an angel around the room with ease. It seemed that she felt pride at being in a relationship with such a powerful being. Her giggles and smiles made the angels angry and two of them objected and asked Sara why she was taking pleasure in their defeat. This questioning aggravated the wolfman. He attacked the angels and began using so much force that Joe and Shaina were forced to turn into their warrior angels forms and hit the wolfman as hard as they could. The result was devastating. The wolfman spun in the air multiple times, smacked into the wall then fell on his broken ribs. Sara rushed over to him.

"Enough! Stop hurting him! Are you training him or killing him?" asked Sara. "You wanted this, John didn't! Look at him. You're no angels."

"Enough!" exclaimed Shaina. "You don't get to speak to angels in this way, girl! Have manners!"

The wolfman quickly began healing and growled.

"That thing in there is another EZ! He almost killed the other brothers," said Shaina, pointing at the wounded angels on the floor. "John forced us to transform into our highest level of formation. Do you understand anything about what I just said?"

"No! And I don't care! All I care..." replied Sara, caressing John. "I wish we'd never come here."

Suddenly, the emergency sirens sounded. The angels closed their eyes and stood motionless.

"John hasn't even received any training yet. How did EZ come here?" said Joe.

All the angels gathered around him. The wolfman stretched his muscles and stood up, looking at Sara, who knew what he was trying to tell her.

"What are we going to do?" asked Sara, placing her head on the wolfman's chest.

The building shook then cracked from one corner to the other. People began screaming and tried to escape but it was too late for many of them, as demons burst into the building and began attacking any living creature that they could see. Many people were killed and many who didn't resist were captured and taken by demons.

The wolfman looked at Joe, who was the only one left inside the training court.

"I'm sorry for everything, kids. You need to run! Go now!" said Joe. "We'll hopefully meet again under better circumstances. I wish that we could do more to make him control his powers."

Sara tried not to say anything but broke her silence.

"Is there any other safe place that we can go to by any chance, uncle?" she asked, as she climbed onto the back of the wolfman.

"You could try the Circle of Believers but unfortunately you can't go there," replied Joe, as people screamed and shouted for help around the community.

"Why's that?" asked Sara.

"The majority of them are humans," said Joe. "They'll all get killed or taken if a portal from hell opens up in their place."

"This is absurd!" Sara exclaimed. "So, you're literally telling us to leave the building and go wherever we can? I can't believe you're suggesting this? Aren't you supposed to help us? Isn't saving all humans your priority? I'm a bloody human! What if something happens to John? We came a long way to be ..."

She was interrupted, as screams were heard closer to the court.

"Forgive us! We can't do anything that this wolf can't do for you. He's very strong and we were told that the Commander would come and get him and ..."

Joe was interrupted as demons began arriving at the lower levels of the building closer to them.

Sara patted the wolfman.

"We're on our own, Let's get the hell out of here, love," said Sara and the wolfman began walking towards the exit door.

"I'll clean the path for you and occupy them until you escape," said Joe. "I hope the Commander finds you in time."

Joe opened the door and countless demons attacked him. Sara screamed and fell off the wolfman onto the floor. The wolfman then charged at the demons while Joe was fighting with them. They terminated as many as they could, until Joe and John were thrown into air, getting shot by multiple dark purple energy spheres.

"Mr Seventh, it's a pleasure to see you again," said Jason with a bow, as the other two units entered the court and stood beside him. "We don't want to fight with our future leader. All we want is for you to follow us to the temple. The hour has come and the Earth is about to fall completely into the hands of the masters. Let us have peace and let us be welcomed by you, our leader."

"I'm no leader, especially not yours," said the wolfman.

"My lord, should you resist cooperating with us there will be severe consequences," said Jason, as he transformed into a muscular demon.

"I want you all gone out of my sight, when I'm done with him," said John and the other two units kept their heads down.

"I can assure you, future leader, that I won't disappoint you," said Jason, preparing to fight.

Joe tried to interfere but the wolfman nodded his head and pointed at the exit door.

"I know you can destroy this little demon, John. I'm sorry if I couldn't be of any use. Take care of yourself and hide for as long as you can," said Joe, telepathically.

He then left.

"Everyone out!" shouted Jason.

The demons left the room but the other Sky-eyes units remained where they were.

"Be careful, John. By the way, I love your wolf voice, so deep, so thick and so strong," said Sara.

She walked away, standing as far from the wolfman as she could.

"I'm going to enjoy this," said the wolfman, as he began running towards Jason.

An intense fight began between Jason and the wolfman that lasted about forty minutes. No matter what Jason did, or how many transformations he underwent, the wolfman easily outmatched him, again and again.

"You're truly strong. Leader, please spare my life. Please forgive me for challenging you. I simply followed the order of the Commander EZ. Please …"

Jason was interrupted as he was grabbed his throat and held in the air, choking.

"You call me a leader, but you call EZ your Commander?" said the wolfman.

He shot a powerful yellow energy sphere into Jason's face that blew his head off. Dark blood spread everywhere, including on the wolfman's face. He cleaned his face with the back of his left hand but some of the blood dripped into his mouth. The blood quickly spread inside the wolfman's mouth and from there into his body. He then looked at the other two units standing in shock and pointed at the exit. The units left without saying a word and closed the doors behind them.

"I knew you could fight that bastard," said Sara, walking over and standing in front of him. "We have to get your face washed, yuck! Sticky blood. Yuck!"

Sara noticed that the wolfman didn't look fine while she tried to clean his face.

"What's wrong, John? Enough of being a wolf, transform and let's get the hell out of here."

Wolfman took a couple of steps back and tried to transform but failed. He was completely unable to change and it seemed as if he'd lost ability to talk.

"John, what's going on?"

Sara noticed that the larger parts of the wolfman's body now had black hair. Realising that he could be under a higher level of dark power, Sara tried to pretend that everything was alright, to prevent the wolfman from becoming vicious and dangerous.

"Love, it's alright, stay in your wolf shape," she said. "We need your supernatural power to get out of here, just …"

Sara was interrupted and the wolfman blew a light purple energy sphere into the wall that terminated it instantly, exposing the yard where the demons and angels were fighting. The wolfman stood on his paws, preparing to run, and waited until Sara sat on his back.

"God save us all," said Sara, climbing onto the now more muscular semi-black wolfman.

He howled and began running out of the building. Neither demons nor angels dared to come close to Sara and the wolfman, as they simply ran from the yard into the bitter cold landscape.

Soon after Sara and the wolfman left the Circle of Angels, the building collapsed and was taken over by demons. The remaining people and angels retreated to the Circle of Believers, while other angels sacrificed themselves by staying to prevent demons from reaching the asylum seekers.

Chapter 43
Let's Go to the Temple

After a while wandering around in the snow, Sara held the wolfman tightly as he ran as fast as he could. The wolfman stopped occasionally to sniff the ground then ran again until they arrived at the abandoned city of Persepolis. This was the largest city on the planet at the time and was usually highly crowded but was now deserted. It was located not too far from the Sparkling City where the temple of God.SED was located. Persepolis was a major tourist attraction and was known to be always busy but by the time Sara and the wolfman reached the city, not a living soul could be seen anywhere. Sara got off the wolfman's back and looked at him in distress. The first thing that they noticed was the sudden change of temperature. It felt as if it was spring in Persepolis while a few miles away it was bitterly cold with heavy snow.

"John, can you try to become human again?" asked Sara.

The wolfman tried to transform but failed.

"It's okay, you can try later," she said Sara, looking at the dark sky. "We've been running around for many hours now but the sun didn't come out at all. I wonder what the hell's happening to the world?"

They walked around the empty street.

"I don't know where to go now," said Sara. "I wish we had Barbie with us. She could guide us to somewhere at least."

Suddenly, they heard scary noises coming from an empty building. Sara quickly jumped on the wolfman's back and he ran inside an empty bar to hide.

"What was that?" said Sara. "It sounded like … like … It sounded like multiple mourning people crying at the same time. I'm scared, John."

The wolfman approached her and stood on his feet. He then hugged her and rubbed his face on her head. Sara looked up and realised the wolfman now looked more like a wolf, as his face was no longer a combination of a human face and an animal.

"Oh dear, why don't you sniff around to make sure this place is safe and I'll go lock the door, just in case," said Sara.

The wolfman began walking around, sniffing. Sara slowly went over to the entrance door and locked it. She then turned around and examined the empty room. Meanwhile, the wolfman came back and shrugged.

"Alright, that's a good news. It's only us in here then. I guess we can eat something and … wow! Look at that holographic music player. Maybe we can listen to some music until we figure out something," said Sara.

She turned on the music player then chose some romantic jazz and began moving her body while listening to the music.

The wolfman approached her and Sara hugged him.

"I wish you could transform. I just … I miss your smile," said Sara, swaying from side to side.

The wolfman lowered his head and licked her on the cheek.

"Ew! Yuck! You could lick something else but not the face," said Sara, looking up at wolfman.

She noticed that even his eyes no longer seemed as human as they used to be.

"Alright, you know what? Let's just stay in here. I guess we'll stay here no matter how long it takes until Gabriel finds us. Outside is dangerous and in here we hopefully still have access to some food and water and, I don't know, washrooms and stuff."

The wolfman nodded his head. Sara placed her head on his chest and began to sway slowly. Suddenly, the electricity shut down and the bar and the entire city went dark. They could hear sinister screams, moans, and roars and Sara hugged the growling wolfman tightly in fear.

"I guess that was our last dance," she said.

Three days later, on the seventh day, loud trumpets were blown seven times and a bright light burst from the sky onto the Earth. The ground shook several times and a brightness began to appear from where the temple of God.SED was located. Sara and the massive wolf left the bar and investigated the sky. They could see that a large golden portal had come into existence in an unusually cloudy sky.

"I suppose the storm we saw by the border has covered the entire world by now," said Sara. "It's completely divided us from the heavens above. Look at that beautiful looking thing in the in the sky. It looks like portal. Oh my god! It's a portal connecting earth to the heavens. Look at them!" exclaimed Sara. She pointed at the angels flying to Earth through the portal.

"John, I know this is the end of the world, I know we may die soon or something, I just wanted to say that I'm the happiest girl on earth. I have everything a girl would ever want," she said, looking at the massive wolf that was waging his tail. "I have you beside me; my best friend, my boyfriend, my love, and my husband to become. I love you, little wolf."

Sara knelt and kissed the wolf on his head. The wolf then licked her cheek and rubbed his head on her face.

"Let's go, John. Let's go to the temple," said Sara, climbing on the back of the massive beast. "It's better to go and die knowing rather than waiting and dying an imbecile. Run!"

The massive wolf began to run towards where the bright light was coming from.

Chapter 44
We Believe!

Three days earlier, people and angels were running into the Circle of Believers' community.

Additional layers of pray-ers circles were around the larger Circle of Pray-ers at the Circle of Believers community, praying as much as they could. The land was unstable and extremely shaky. The people in the Circle of Believers knew that the hour of the end was close by. They stood in groups and prayed out loud, while some mourned, others rejoiced, and some remained quiet.

The leaders were standing in the middle of the crowd of elderly people. They were reassuring them of their safety, even though they knew that nothing on the planet was safe anymore. Aholi stood beside Ashwin and slowly nodded her head. Ashwin stepped back from the crowd and together they went to a quiet corner of the building and began talking.

"There's a word from the Circle of Angels," said Aholi. "They've been found and the place has been taken over by demons. They're currently heading here in large numbers."

"Demons?" asked Ashwin, shocked, as Aholi nodded. "Then the hour of transformation has come. The angels among us will change soon. We must keep everyone calm when they see the true image of angels for the first time."

The land shook.

"God help us," said Ashwin, struggling to maintain his footing.

"Open the gates! We have wounded prayer-ers coming through!" shouted one of the men, who was carrying a wounded pray-er on his shoulder from outside, circled by three angelical pray-ers.

The men and the pray-ers entered the community and laid the wounded pray-er on the ground. The people there were stunned to see a bright angelic being standing in the middle of the community's front yard.

Ashwin rushed to the wounded pray-er and held his hand.

"Brother, …"

Ashwin was interrupted as the gates opened and Joe, the rest of people, and angel-shaped beings entered the community. At the sight of so many bright beings many of the people knelt, others ran inside the community out of fear, and some began praying more loudly while holding symbolic religious objects.

"Fear not, I am Joe White and these are the same people who you've been in connection for the past many years, but are now in our true image. We're the fallen guardian angels. We were unable to show you our real images because the hour wasn't right, but it is now. Fear not, we're on your side. We mean you no harm, as we always have done. Please, don't kneel for us. Treat us as you have always treated us in the past."

An elderly woman stepped forward, holding a cross.

"Let the lord Jesus Christ compel you! Die, demon, die!" shouted the elderly woman, as she coughed.

"Child, do you think we could be standing among you while pray-ers are praying?" said Joe. "Do you think we could come in without anyone knowing? Fear not, we are no fallen angels, but simply sacrificed our wings to remain among humans so we could love them and protect them from the demons out there. We're here to help, as we always were."

The elderly woman's relatives came and took her away.

"Brother, how did the community fall so easily? Where is the chosen one?" asked Luke, one of the angels from Circle of Believers.

"Our location was compromised by the chosen one, who was followed by the Iced Sisters and then Jason and EZ," replied Joe as everyone remained quiet, shocked to hear the name of EZ. "We couldn't do anything for the chosen one. His spirit and soul were extremely infested by the dark power that he was recently exposed to. All we can hope for is that the Commander will help him transform, otherwise, we'll have to face two EZs during the war. Let's go inside the building where it's safer. Our combined energies can enable demons to find us."

Everyone except the pray-ers began moving into the community building.

Joe and other high-ranking angels from the Circle of Angels stood by the altar and looked at the crowd.

"If the Circle of Pray-ers fall, humanity will face darkness. Consider yourselves the most blessed ones, as you see the truth and you hear the truth, and will walk by the truth," said Shaina. "Remain as believers, remain as pray-ers, and remain faithful people of god. Please join your hands and let us all pray and be blessed."

She walked down to the crowd, followed by the other angels.

"Fear not, come closer," said Hayley. "I see through you. I can heal your wound if you allow me."

A little girl stepped forward. Hayley placed her hands on her leg and the girl's wound was healed.

"I don't think there would be an issue if you would reveal yourselves to us sooner," said an angry man among the crowd, whose daughter was among the ones that had left the community. "It would prevent many who left because of fear of death. You could have saved many lives."

"Revealing our identities would manipulate your free will," said Helen, one of the angels from the Circle of Believers. "Your destinies, the decisions you make, and the thoughts you have are all yours. Our job was to maintain balance so you wouldn't change your paths but choosing other options and joining other side were absolutely up to you. The cycle of your lives are completed when you fulfil your destinies without us influencing them. Unfulfilled and influenced destinies reset another cycle of living for the same soul that will repeat the same mistake that it did in the past, feeding the engine of darkness by letting its energy be harvested again and again. Those standing here have surpassed the challenge of getting harvested as your souls are saved so far because of your own decisions and actions."

"Is John truly the chosen one that everyone talks about?" asked a woman in the crowd.

"At this point, he's the most dangerous being of his own kind. We're not sure of his true nature to be able to judge his future," said Andrew, one of the angels from the Circle of Angels.

"Where's the child?" asked Rick, one of the angels from the Circle of Angels community. "The one with the power to know the future?"

"She's sleeping" said Maria, one of the care givers at the Circle of Believers. "Shall we wake her up?"

"No, let the child rest," replied Joe. "We need her at full strength when the final hours begin as she'll reveal the obstacles that will protect all of us until the very last days of the war."

"What do we need to do know?" asked one of the elders in the crowd.

"We shall wait until the war begins then wait a little longer until we're rescued by the heavenly flying angels."

Three days later at the community on the seventh day, Joe was standing at the altar.

"You all know heard the trumpets," he declared. "The war has begun. Stand tall, stand strong, and stand together. Pray and maintain your faith through believing in god and your prophets. For it is through your belief and believing in god, and in god alone, that you can be selected and find salvation."

"We believe! We believe! We believe!" shouted the crowd.

Angels gathered around the crowd held their hands, creating a circle then began praying. Some people then joined the circle and began praying as well.

"God save us all, Joe," said Shaina. "I love you."

"I love you too and amen," said Joe. "I'm glad that people accepted us and learnt from us for the past three days to remain calm and faithful. I hope we win in this war."

"The future is uncertain," said Luna, the oracle of Circle of Believers. "The one stands between light and darkness with confusion."

"How did you … Nice to meet you oracle, the descendent of Death land. We've heard tales of you but never met you," said Shaina, in amazement.

"It is because you were not supposed to," said Luna, going down to join the crowd.

"Alright, we'll have some fun with this next level attitude, little lady," said Shaina, holding Joe's hands.

"Don't forget, she's older than us," Joe added. "The attitude's alright for an old creature like her that has seen all the previous wars and yet survived. Let's go now and join the crowd in prayer. We'll soon have to go to fight. Let's enjoy these peaceful moments."

Joe gently pulled Shaina's hand and took her to the crowd.

Chapter 45
The Earth Is Ours!

At the temple on the seventh day, God.SED was floating in the air above the large pillar in the middle of the temple with his arms open as the massive crowd below watched him while cheering and rejoicing. God.SED laughed out loud and waved his right hand. The people in the crowd became unstable as they tried to approach the heavily secured gates of the temple. Those that got too close were killed instantly by the Arms of Justice units but their deaths brought no fear to the other people that still tried to get closer.

God.SED looked at the crowd and nodded his head.

"They are delusional and controlled beings who have completely fallen under our spell, brother," thought God.SED.

He then looked at the spirits of the elements in the sky and back at the unstable crowd.

"Today is the day when I'll inherit all powers of the Earth and I'll control everything on it, including you!" shouted God.SED.

Satan worshipers in black robes began chanting Satanic rituals, forming a large pentagram around the pillar above which God.SED was floating.

"At last, the hour has come!" shouted God.SED.

Fire burst from the top of the pillar, passing through God.SED and hitting the sphere of elements. God.SED then pointed his right hand at the sphere and began pulling it towards him. He failed to move the sphere at first. It seemed as if the elements didn't want to be absorbed into him. He pointed both his hands towards the elements and used more energy to absorb them.

"Resist as much as you desire, in few seconds you'll be mine," shouted God.SED, struggling as he began to absorb the sphere. "The Earth is ours!"

God.SED closed his eyes. People watched as the sphere of elements reached God.SED and he absorbed it. The land began to shake and fiery lava burst out of the corners of the temple. The building began to transform into its real image, two large burning horns surrounded by countless demons.

People in the crowd panicked and began running away from the Satanic dungeon as the spell of purple mist that had kept them from seeing the reality vanished.

God.SED opened his eyes. He could now see every corner of the Earth as if they were near him. He raised his right hand and a mountain in the South-lands cracked. He exhaled and winds blew in East-Lands then he spat on the crowd and rain began to fall in West-Lands. God. SED then transformed into Evil and Devil, as all the remaining human-looking demons transformed into demons.

Meanwhile, Death appeared beside God.SED and smiled.

"So, you two made it, huh?" asked Death.

Evil and Devil laughed and nodded their heads.

"Well, what now? Going to do the same thing as the last time?" asked Death. "You know that John's here, right? He's more of a wolf being ridden by his girl now, down there among the running crowd. And you know that you both failed to turn him into a dark chosen one this time, right? He's a wolf but he's not an EZ."

"Can't wait to have more souls in my kingdom. After all, I need new souls or I'll lose my own kingdom. See you soon, gentlemen," said Death then disappeared.

"I must admit, I'm more afraid of Death than I am of Michael or Metatron," said Devil. "Death's very unpredictable."

"Fear not brother, we'll kill them all this time and rule over the seven kingdoms forever," said Evil.

He flew out of the fire that was still emerging from the pillar and began floating towards the dungeon. Devil accompanied him, as the fire was extinguished and the pillar collapsed into pieces.

"I missed this body," said Evil, standing by the large window in the room surrounded by Satan worshipers whispering their dark rituals.

The angels began coming to Earth through the golden portal.

"Look at them, so proud of coming to save humans who rejected them for thousands of years. Angels never learn any lessons from their past," said Evil in underworld language, as Devil stood beside him watching Gabriel entering the Earth.

"I'm going to kill Gabriel and gain control over Eden, you can kill Michael and gain control over the gates of heavens," said Devil in underworld language. "Then together we'll kill Metatron and gain control over all the heavens."

"Sounds like a plan, brother. Now, let's go and say hello to our guests. After all, they deserve a warm welcome," said Evil and along with Devil, he disappeared.

Chapter 46
Angels and Demons Face-Off

Gabriel stood in front of a handful of angels without wings, along with other angels from Eden, facing a large crowd of scared people. The people in the crowd fell on their knees and begged for mercy.

"Do not bow to us, humans. We are angels, not God! Stand up and face the outcome of your deeds," said Gabriel angrily.

Many that had bowed stood up but kept their heads down.

Evil and Devil landed on the ground near the angels from Eden and walked towards Gabriel, clapping their hands. Seeing Evil and Devil getting close to the angels, demons began making a circle around the angels and the crowd of people. Meanwhile, some people in the crowd walked to join the demons and stood by their side. Evil nodded his head at the demonic army, signalling for them to stand down and avoid attacking any humans joining them and the demonic army obeyed.

Evil looked at the people that were now part of the demonic army and smiled.

"Despite seeing us in our true forms, they still support us," he said in underworld language. "I adore humans. Stupid and blind for life."

"Well brother, they're all clones after all," Devil added in underworld language and laughed. "Get one infected and countless others will be infected too."

Gabriel began walking towards Evil and they stood facing each other in the middle of the ground. Gabriel looked behind him at all the angels and people then looked back at Evil and nodded his head.

"You like what you see, Gabriel?" asked Evil, smiling. "I have an army far larger than you could ever have. The army behind me is larger than any from the past six wars and you know it. I'll spare your life and those who stand down now to wrap up this war quickly, but I'll enjoy terminating you and all who delay the process of us reaching heaven."

Evil pointed his index finger at the army behind him. The demons and Devil roared and growled.

Meanwhile, the one world new order's army soldiers divided separated from one another and joined either side, holding up flags and pointing their weapons at each other. People standing in the crowd on both sides occasionally booed each other but no one dared to attack, afraid of getting terminated by the supernatural beings among them.

Evil stepped forward to face Gabriel and smiled.

"Angels and demons face-off, isn't it, Gabriel?" said Evil. "You've won three wars in the past and so have we. This one is the last one but you know for sure that we'll win this war too."

"You are a child with a big mouth," said Gabriel, annoyed. "Let us confirm the time of the war because I have many important matters to attend to rather than wasting time with you."

"Oh, more important matters than this? Wow! So much for angels caring for humans' future," said Evil, nodding his head. "Well, we have seven years ahead of us to fight one another as you know, so why not we have a little fun first, just like old times. We let humans fight first and we collect their souls, just like before, and then we unleash our own war after humanity is wiped out by its own hands. At least we'll let them take care of themselves rather than having your creator or mine come and do it for them."

Gabriel looked at the crowd of humans around them then turned back to Evil.

"So be it but let them have their voice in it. Let them choose their own future," said Gabriel.

"I don't give a fuck what they choose or not but whatever, let's have a little fun," said Evil, floating up.

Gabriel joined him and together they began flying in the middle of the air, looking at the crowd below.

"Citizens of Earth," said Gabriel. "For thousands of years you have been in control of your future using the power of free will. Some used the power to join the bright side and some used it to join the dark side. This is the last time you can choose a side. Use your free will and join a side now please."

"Oh, shut the fuck up, Gabriel," said Evil. "Hey! You either choose my side or his side, now make up your fucking minds by just looking at the size of the armies. Who would you want to have on your side when everyone's fighting?"

People in the crowd whispered among themselves.

"We don't want you on Earth at all! Get the fuck out of our home! Fucking aliens!" shouted a general holding a flag bearing the universal army's logo. "We could deal with our own shit ourselves and without your fucking help! We neither want you and your army nor him and his army. All of you get the fuck away from Earth."

Many people from both sides left the crowd and joined the general.

"This is even better than the previous wars. We have now a new army to fight with," said Evil, laughing. "So cute!"

"Who said this was ever your home? Your land? Your Earth, little boy? You lived in our home, our lands, and our Earth," said Evil and the demons began growling. "Beneath this flat land is the kingdom of the underworld. You lived at the bottom of the underworld, you fools. No one's leaving Earth except you."

Demons began to growl and bark. Angels held their weapons more tightly and remained steady.

"Hey! You! Flying dude! Why don't you say anything? Didn't you say we were the citizens of Earth," said a young girl in the crowd, blowing a bubble gum.

"Being a citizen does not give the ownership of the land to you," said Gabriel. "You are citizens but not the owners of the land. Father almighty is the owner of all the lands on which you have dwelt and you were and are his tenants. It is time for you to go to your real homes, whether they are in the heavens or in hell below. The land you stand on will be destroyed completely after the war ends, as will your citizenships."

Many people in the crowd began moaning, falling on their knees or joining different sides, while some simply kept their heads down and prayed.

"Enough nonsense! You all have a fucking choice, to fight along with me or him or that little guy in that funny uniform. You guys really helped us get to where we are using your dark one new world order agenda. Without your efforts, my brother and I would probably not be able to be on the surface of the earth," said Evil, laughing.

It wasn't clear who started the war but someone threw rockets, killing countless people. Within seconds there was anarchy, as people attacked each other with whatever they could get their hands on.

Evil laughed as Gabriel quickly flew to the crowd supporting him and created a protective shield around them using his powers.

"They didn't even want to wait for us to start the war," said Evil, telepathically.

"I know this was one of your tricks, Evil. I'll kick you out of Earth, just like I kicked your father out of heaven," said Gabriel, telepathically.

"Hey! No cheating! I don't know who the fuck started the war but you should stop protecting them using the shield. It's their fight not ours to interfere with," said Evil, smiling.

Gabriel looked at the frightened adults and children in the protective shield.

"I am sorry, citizens. This is your war to fight. Remember this, regardless of the pain your deaths will not be in vain. You will be rewarded for what you fought for," he said, as the protective shield vanished.

"Good job, Gabriel," shouted Evil.

He then looked at the demons that were desperately waiting to attack humans and they put their heads down and growled, as they began to move back to the dungeon.

"I'll see you soon, Gabriel."

Evil looked at Devil, who was floating in the air above the demonic army.

"Any news from that fucking chosen one yet?" asked Evil telepathically, drifting close to Devil.

"We've lost his trace. He's fully turned into a wolf, the actual animal apparently. I don't think he can be of any use for father either. Do you think we still need to care about him?" asked Devil, telepathically.

"Chosen one or chosen dog?" asked Evil in underworld language, laughing. "EZ's still our guy. Father will probably have to use him to get to the heavens again. Let's go back to our temple and fuck some bitches, brother. We'll take care of John if he ever turns back into a human or whatever."

They moved back towards the dungeon.

The war was vicious, inhuman, and unbelievable. People began acting immorally, irrationally, and psychotically. It seemed as if people forgot about the existence of angels and demons around them. They only cared about killing the forces from the other side. Angels that were unable to help humans simply retreated to the Circle of Believers and remained there.

When the limited bullets and artillery ammunition ran out, humans began to fight with claws, knives, or anything that could take a life. One of God.SED's first actions had been to eliminate all weapons, and indeed access to all kinds of weapons, as far as humans were concerned, leaving them defenceless and unable to protect themselves in the time of need. He then introduced the one world army universal soldiers, among whom were Arms of Justice units and other ordinary human soldiers. God.SED's action prevented humanity from wiping itself out of existence by using weapons of mass destruction but also prevented them from protecting themselves during such dark days.

Chapter 47
True Love Waits

The war of humans had already begun when Sara and the massive wolf reached the area. Bullets were constantly hitting everything, people were dying, and no one seemed to be concerned. It was a very shocking scene to witness. While the massive wolf was running to find safety, an explosion happened nearby, throwing Sara in the air and slamming the massive wolf into the nearby burning vehicle. Sara was then smacked into the ground and remained there.

People that saw the massive supernatural wolf began shooting at him. The wolf quickly approached Sara while dodging bullets and covered her then poked her with his muzzle. Sara opened her eyes and after hearing gunshots immediately stood up, stunned at seeing many people approaching them holding weapons.

"They're going to kill us, John. I love you, just remember that," said Sara, terrified.

The massive wolf growled and turned around, looking at the approaching people before attacking them. After killing them all, he returned to Sara, blood still dripping from his mouth. Sara couldn't move because of what she'd witnessed but tried to hide her fear from the wolf by slowly raising her hand towards him. The wolf barked and growled at her.

"Easy, John. It's me Sara. I'm … I'm the woman you're in love with," said Sara, as she took a step backwards.

The wolf began growling more loudly and moved towards her. Suddenly, a bright light appeared in the air and Gabriel landed on the ground, standing between Sara and the massive bloody wolf. He then looked at the wolf and nodded his head.

"The blood is the reason he turned into an animal. He must have drunk a lot. His spirit is no longer pure at all," said Gabriel, his back facing Sara.

"Hi, hello!" said Sara, stepping forward. "Excuse me, but you're standing between me and my future husband, please move away, sir."

Gabriel turned around and looked at her.

"Stay back, child. I am the Commander of angels of the heavens above. Mind your language and tone, child."

The massive wolf began barking.

"I beg your pardon, sir, I respect and love angels but I'm the only one who can control John. He's not an animal but—"

Sara was interrupted as the massive wolf attacked Gabriel. He turned around, grabbed the wolf by its mouth and smacked him into the ground. The wolf remained there, whimpering.

"Hey! Stop that! Enough! You hurt him!" shouted Sara, walking towards the wolf.

Gabriel nodded. "Mannerless child. I do not have time for this."

He then wrapped his right arm around Sara's waist and with his right hand grabbed the massive wolf's neck and flew to the Circle of Believers at supersonic speed.

At the Circle of Believers, people were praying as quietly as possible, as angels with and without wings entered the community. They could all hear the sound of the chaos coming out of the wooden walls around the community but no one dared to leave her or his spot to go and look outside. Meanwhile, the angels with wings replaced the pray-ers and angels without wings, who were praying around the community. They then created a holy *Golden Halo*[60] around the area. People were relieved, as they'd no longer need to pray to be protected. They now had angels to protect them constantly.

Meanwhile, Gabriel flew to the community and landed in the middle of the community front yard, as everyone stepped back. Seeing him and his glory, everyone knelt. Gabriel threw the unconscious massive wolfman on the ground and placed the grumpy Sara on the ground. Joe and Shaina, who were in their angelical forms, arrived and knelt before Gabriel.

"Commander, it is good to see you again," said Joe in angelical language.

"It is good to see you too, brother and sister, and everyone in here. Please, rise," said Gabriel in angelical language.

---

[60] Golden Halo: A bright golden circle of energy made by angels that was used as a direct portal from heaven to Earth. This circle was made only when there was no opportunity for angels to enter the Earth using other methods of transportations.

"Sara, stay away from that wolf," said Shaina, approaching her.

"Enough!" shouted Sara. "I'm sick and tired of being told what to do. Your Commander smacked my love into the ground without blinking. Don't you angels have any feelings? Emotions?"

Shaina stopped moving towards her.

"Mind your language, child! You're in the presence of an archangel," said Luna, walking close to where Gabriel was standing.

The crowd once again knelt when they saw Luna.

"Great! A child's calling an adult a child. What the hell's going on in here?" Sara demanded.

"Silence!" shouted Lune and Sara was quiet. "Take the wolf and do what you must, Commander. We don't have much time before the real war begins."

"This wolf isn't going anywhere without me. I warn you, don't get close to us," said Sara firmly.

"Sara, dear, these angels are on our side," said Meagan, one of the nurses that lived in the community. "We all know about the vision of the chosen one. If John's truly the chosen one, the warrior that will defeat the Satanic army, then he must become angelical and transform out of his current form. Please, stay away and let the archangel Gabriel to do what he is here for."

"Please, Aunt Sara, let the bad wolf leave," said a few children in the crowd that were standing close to Sara.

She turned around and looked at the bloody massive wolf as her tears fell down her cheeks. She then patted and hugged him.

"I have no other choice, John. I must let you go now. I love you. Come back and fulfil your destiny. I will wait for you, my love," whispered Sara into the wolf's ear.

The wolfman slowly opened his eyes but before he moved, Gabriel grabbed him by the neck and lifted him up.

"Your community will remain safe," said Gabriel. "Brothers and sisters will maintain the Golden Halo protecting you from all the evil out there. However, should your faith diminish, you will bring chaos upon yourselves before the seventh year. Creator almighty, bless us all."

Gabriel flew towards the portal in the sky, while Sara remained crying on the ground.

"Sara, stop crying. Do you know who I am? I'm Luna, the oracle that sees the future. I have seen yours. You'll be reunited with John but you need to have patience. You need to be trained as well or you'll fail to save him in the future."

She nodded at other angels around her, who then began directing people inside the community building.

"Oh god, is he going to get into trouble again?" asked Sara. "I don't know how to wait, I'm so alone in here. Couldn't any of you do anything for him? For all us? Aren't you all aliens with powers?"

Luna wiped the tears from Sara's face and grabbed her arm to help her to stand up.

"We're here to help humans to choose the right path," said Luna, holding Sara's right hand. "We're not here to change their destinies. We've helped them for far too long and we've protected them for far too long. It's their time to help and protect each other by unifying against the dark side. Let's go inside, Sara. We have a lot to talk about and you have a lot to learn before John returns."

Luna and Sara began walking towards the entrance doors of the community building then entering it as others followed them.

A month later, around 3 am, Sara sat on the roof of the building looking at the Golden Halo and at the burning land around the community. The bitter cold landscape that had once been covered in snow now featured burning fire, lava and people engaged in war. Sara looked up at the portal in the sky.

"It's been a month, John. I miss you. I miss you a lot," said Sara as her tears fell.

She then took a deep breath, cleaning her face with the back of her hands.

"I'll wait as long as it takes to see you again, my love. True love waits."

Sara then stood up, patted the dust off her pants, walked towards the hatch and climbed down the stairs, closing the hatch behind her.

To be continued...

www.ingramcontent.com/pod-product-compliance
Lightning Source LLC
LaVergne TN
LVHW011417090225
803308LV00002B/127

ALLEY-OOP

To Judy

You are the strongest woman that I know. Cancer couldn't defeat you. Discouragement can't stop you. Life's disappointments don't harden you. You are a chosen champion. Because of you, I have been able to serve youth, families and churches for over 35 years. Now in our new season, let's continue to run ahead and build God's temple in His people.

WFH

Contents

Foreword

Bishop Walter Harvey is a nationally respected Pastor and Leader. He is widely known for his seasoned wisdom and experience in ministry. He has become a personal friend, mentor and advisor to me in my ministry.

As a Pastor in the NBA and Chaplain for the Milwaukee Bucks, I'm a basketball fanatic. There is something about a team being completely synchronized that shows a different level basketball IQ. The sport is most beautiful when the players learn to work together. The alley hoop is the essence of just that togetherness. It requires both players flow in complete harmony to ensure it's success. There could not be a better analogy for ministry succession.

This book has added extreme value to my life personally as a pastor who is the byproduct of ministry succession. This book helps highlight the areas in my journey that were extremely foggy due to lack of comprehensive understanding, as well as areas that I didn't know needed attention. It has given me greater clarity in ways to better structure our ministry and leadership team to plan for seamless succession in our church's future.

There are many reasons why succession plans need to be carefully thought out. This book fills the critical void in ministry succession planning. For many, ministry succession has been relegated to simply replacing a deceased pastor, which robs the ministry and the senior pastor of the joy of succession. For a church to grow and thrive beyond it's birthing generation, it has to have a successful plan for the transitioning of the predecessor and the positioning of the successor. The witty analogies and references to the game of basketball help paint a seamless vision to help pastors plan for those who will come after them.

Bishop Walter Harvey deals with the critical need to have "a new game plan" as you are transitioning ministry into a successor's hands. Succession can never truly be successful without the realization that the game plan for the predecessor will never be the game plan for the successor. New leaders should always mean new vision and plans. This requires the "Trust" factor between both players to be the strongest sentiment shared. The point guard has to know how to put the big man in the best position to catch the alley oop and trust that the big man will be there. The big man has to know exactly when to jump and trust that the point guard will pass the ball at the right time.

Kenneth Lock II, Pastor and NBA Chaplain

Introduction

Few things arouse a crowd of basketball fans like an alley-oop. An alley-oop play is when an offensive player passes the ball near the basket to a teammate who jumps, catches the ball in midair, and slam dunks it for a score before he touches the ground.

The artistry of the alley-oop has been painted on the canvas of basketball since dunking was allowed in the game. The artistic passes of Scottie Pippen to Michael Jordan, Kobe Bryant to Shaquille O'Neal, Jason Kidd to Vince Carter, Chris Paul to Blake Griffin, and John Stockton to Karl Malone are what thrills the crowd. The alley-oop is what defeats an opponent and fills the seats of stadiums.

Pastoral succession is the process of transferring the leadership, ownership, and authority from one directional leader to another. (Ruch, Nathaniel (2018), Preparing the receiver of the baton in the succession narrative, Pro Quest Dissertations Publishing, Minneapolis, Minnesota)

I wrote this book to help pastors, potential pastors, families, church leaders, and congregations through pastoral succession. An alley-oop is a perfect illustration of making a successful pass in pastoral leadership. It is my prayer that after reading this book, the predecessor and successor can both finish strong. Together they can score a slam dunk for the kingdom of God, causing those in the church leadership and congregation to give an ovation, standing to their feet, cheering and in awe after the slam dunk. Thus, the organization can continue its mission—scoring and winning.

In Alley-Oop, I share proven principles of the pastoral succession process. A church traveling down this road of pastoral transfer will often feel vulnerable and uncertain. That's understandable; it's risky. Prayerfully, this book becomes a place to turn for suggestions for a solid strategic plan. Within these pages are stories from all parties involved, practical guidance, biblical wisdom, and encouragement.

Please join me in praying for smooth pastoral transitions in our churches. May those who are in positions to pass the ball and those receiving it move together in harmony. May they and each congregation move with a keen sense of timing, unity, and honor. May it result in the body of Christ becoming healthier for generations to come. I know that it will if we prepare for succession.

"Then the LORD said to Moses, 'Behold, the days approach when you must die; call Joshua, and present yourselves in the tabernacle of meeting, that I may inaugurate him.' So, Moses and Joshua went and presented themselves in the tabernacle of meeting" (Deuteronomy 31:1).

I

The Decision

The greatest challenge in leadership is not attaining it but releasing it. The ultimate measure of your leadership success is what happens to the organization when you leave it. (Munroe, Myles, Succession: The greatest leadership failure, accessed October 3, 2021, #drmylesmunroe #mylesmunroe, March 15, 2020, Munroe Global)

LeBron haters remember "The Decision." In 2010, the Cleveland Cavaliers took his talents to South Beach and the Miami Heat. He won two championships with the Heat. He later returned to Cleveland and led the Cavaliers to an NBA championship in 2016. However, in 2018, LeBron decided to leave again, signing a free-agent contract with the Los Angeles Lakers.

In 2017, the year before LeBron's arrival, the Lakers drafted Lonzo Ball, a point guard from the UCLA Bruins. Lonzo had a stellar college basketball career. He was a dynamic point guard with remarkable passing ability, but at best, his outside jump shot was hit or miss.

Long story short, when LeBron James joined the Lakers, the team had a dilemma. The Lakers now had two-point guards. One of LeBron's decisions to shift to the Lakers was to move from a dominant scorer to a passer. The physical punishment upon his body over a long career weighed heavily. As a result, Lonzo Ball became expendable and tradable. LeBron knew that as the team's primary ball-handler, he needed additional offensively skilled and younger athletes. He needed someone to pass the ball to, finish successfully, and score. In 2019, the Los Angeles Lakers traded Lonzo and a bunch of other players to the New Orleans Pelicans for the young superstar Anthony Davis.

I can relate to LeBron James. In 1992 I joined the Parklawn Assembly of God church staff in Milwaukee, Wisconsin, as the Youth Pastor at age 32. I had seven years of prior ministry as a non-salaried youth pastor at Northside Church of God. In 2020, I transitioned out as the Lead pastor after 35 years of pastoral work. My skills increased over the years, but my stamina for the daily leadership requirements was decreasing. In other words, the grace to serve in that role was lifting, and a new passion was emerging within me.

I shifted my pastoral leadership role from the team's leading scorer to a passer. Like LeBron, I came to some conclusions and made a bold decision. At age 50, I said to myself, "A time is coming when I will need to pass the ball of leadership and shift from a producer to a reproducer." So, I began praying, "Lord, don't let me stay too long, and Lord, don't let me leave too early."

As a pastor, I care about my flock like a faithful shepherd. Leaving too early could mean leaving the sheep in harm's way. Jesus loved His sheep, too. He knew that one day it would be time to pass the church's leadership to His disciples. If He departed too early, the disciples might not have adequate preparation. On the other hand, if the shepherd stays too long, it can result in the sheep not getting the best care possible. I decided that if I remained in the lead pastor role after age 60, I would miss God's "kairos" moment—His specific moment in time for me.

That kairos moment to pass the leadership ball to my successor came at the beginning of the global COVID-19 pandemic in March 2020. COVID revealed the church's specific, opportune time for me to transition and to install my successor. That month I preached my last message as lead pastor. A few days after, the governor ordered a lockdown on public gatherings. The following Sunday, Pastor Marcus Arrington, my successor, had to conduct his first sermon as lead pastor on the Internet.

I prepared him in advance and knew for years prior that he could successfully lead the church, so I set him up for the alley-oop. He leaped into the air, caught it, and slammed dunked it into the basket. Our families, the church administrative board, the congregation, and the community applauded. Both of us are flourishing in our relationship and present roles.

God knows what He will do, if we are willing to trust Him and step out on faith.

In the last ten years of my pastorate, I kept my eyes open for a successor. I knew my position would not last forever. I desired a smooth transition. I wanted to pour my life experiences into another individual. I also prepared myself to step into another position in ministry. I knew what additional kingdom service I wanted to provide beyond the local church and lead pastor.

I began meeting with the church leaders, carving out a plan, and putting together a timeline. I didn't want the transition to occur abruptly. Pastoral succession brings various emotions to the surface. The leadership and the congregation need a sensitive shepherd who listens, responds clearly, and offers comfort throughout the process.

Unfortunately, too many leaders and church attendees have heard about or been involved in poor pastoral hand-offs. When the ball is dropped in basketball, it often ends up in the opposing team's hands. A dropped ball or turnover could mean the other team wins. For the Christian, our opposing team is Satan. We don't want him to be in control of the ball when pastoral succession takes place.

It is not only a good idea for a succession plan to be in place, but it is a biblical mandate.

The late Dr. Myles Munroe said in a YouTube message, "Many leaders die with the baton in their hands." ("Succession: The greatest leadership failure, accessed" October 3, 2021, #drmylesmunroe #mylesmunroe, March 15, 2020, Munroe Global.)

Unfortunately, then, the successor must pry the baton out of the dead man's hands. Imagine the children of Israel without a Joshua after Moses, no disciples after Jesus' ascension, and no Timothy after Paul's imprisonment. The picture is horrific and an inevitable defeat for the kingdom of God.

In my lifetime, I've witnessed very few positive examples of leadership transition. It seems to happen more often and more smoothly in White communities of Christendom, but seldom in Black and Brown churches. Some potential successors get weary of waiting. The lack of succession planning results in many independent churches starting. Too often, it happens where churches launch prematurely and without the blessing of the predecessor.

I've witnessed the misfortunes of congregations without a succession plan. Pastors leave in many different ways and circumstances.

*Pastors die in the pulpit. Their death leaves the church grieving and floundering.

* A new church plant or an existing church experiences sudden

growth, both a blessing and curse. The pastor of this growing congregation is overwhelmed and no longer wants to lead.

*The lead pastor or one of his family members becomes ill. His attention is now on getting well or tending to his family. The church suffers and declines.

* The pastor has declining mental and cognitive ability but refuses to heed the board's advice to retire.

*A missionary returning from the field, or a Christian social organization leader thinks he wants to pastor a church rather than continue his previous ministry. But then, after pastoring for a while, he sees his passions are elsewhere, and he decides to leave the church.

*A pastor is involved in moral indiscretion. The church must ask him to step down.

*The pastor announces retirement and identifies a successor but later changes his mind and stays in the lead role.

* The pastor's wife (or children) takes over the church in a power grab after the lead pastor dies or retires.

Most athletic teams have a deep bench. The first person called off the bench is the sixth man. They are usually a very proficient player. The coach and team realize that at any given time, a player can be injured. Someone else must be ready to step up and substitute into the game. From the first day, we start careers, be it sports, education, business, or religion (full time or as a volunteer), we should be thinking about the next generation of leaders.

Reproducing ourselves and preparing another leader to take our place is essential. The ideal time to look around for a potential replacement is day one, at the new Pastoral Installation ceremony! A wise church is well prepared with a written, detailed document—a strategy for emergencies and planned transitions. That document should be full of practical and biblical wisdom to ease the anxiety of all parties involved.

Perhaps you are asking these questions:

How do we do it?
Where are the successful examples?
What happens to me, the lead pastor, when I leave?
How will I make a living?
Will my legacy and contribution be forgotten?
Who is ready to receive the pass?
What will or should be my relationship with the former church and the new leader?
How will the transition affect my family?
What will my spouse's identity be in the new role?
How do I feel about letting go and moving on?
As a successor, am I ready? What else do I need?
Will the congregation accept me and new ideas?
Will the former pastor allow me to lead?

As a board, will this new leader be a good fit for our church?
How can we know for sure this is God's plan for our congregation?
What if we don't like or agree with the pastor's or board's choice of successor?

What is the situation that you are presently facing? What is causing you to think and pray about pastoral succession?

I understand the anxiety and uncertainty. Leadership transitions are sensitive. Pastoral successions can feel like you are out of control and in an in-between space. Circus acrobats yell, "Alley-oop!" just before they leap into the air. Alley-oop signals to their teammates, "Be aware and prepared to catch me!" In the same way, God wants the predecessor (passer), the successor (receiver), and the church (crowd) to step together into the future with confidence.

2

The Head Coach

A victorious basketball teams needs a wise head coach with a well-thought-out game plan.

Imagine a team without a coach. What players are going to start? It's time to start the game, and the players are arguing. After pushing, shoving, and threats—the loudest, strongest players get to play. The same chaos continues throughout the game as each player is doing their own thing. It's doubtful that any kind of championship will be won without a coach.

Once the players hit the floor, they need to be fully conscious of the plan laid out by the head coach, in tune with their teammates, and willing to pull together. The team has to be prepared to defend opponents and keep them from scoring. The ultimate goal is to score which takes determination and skill. All this makes for a winning combination.

I have witnessed several friends who were head coaches in basketball and football. These team leaders spend long hours preparing before and after the games developing a strategy for the subsequent victory. Coaches watch the film and get a vision even before the players arrive at the gym for practice. They have already mapped a pathway for the player's success.

Tragically, the wins or losses in churches are because the players on the court are disconnected from God. Like in basketball, players have to be connected to the Head Coach—the heavenly Father. If coach and the players are disconnected from one another, chaos in the church ensues, and a defeat is a result.

A lead pastor must know God personally and intimately. He must be committed to running the plays that God calls. If the game is not going as planned, the Lord has no problem calling for a timeout. And if you are incredibly disobedient to God's plans, He might sit you on the bench for a while! Also, a close relationship between the players and the coach will prevent them from running back to the coach after each play for the next step. They will know the coach's heart and run the team like it is on automatic pilot.

God was the Head Coach for Moses and Joshua. He set the two up for one of the greatest alley-oops in biblical history. Both leaders knew God, revered Him, and followed the Father's plan as well as His instructions. They adhered to the divine transition process as Moses turned over his responsibilities to Joshua. They successfully moved the congregation from Egypt, through the wilderness, and into the promised land.

Moses' initial contact with the Head Coach started as an infant. Moses' journey began, much like mine, with a praying mother. The book of Hebrews indicates Moses' parents, Amram and Jochebed, worshipped Jehovah with great faith (Hebrews 11:23). They knew about the Abrahamic covenant, the Hebrew children possessing their land (Genesis 12). Like the Jewish nation anticipated Messiah, at this time, the Hebrew children prayed for a deliverer to rescue them from the oppression of the Egyptians. When sons made their entrance into the world, parents wondered, is he the one? I can only imagine the conversation when the midwife placed Moses in Jochebed's arms.

"Amram, look at this baby!"

"Yes, Jochebed, he's a healthy boy."

"No, Amram, there is something else about this child."

"You are right. There is something unique about him. He could be the one, the deliverer. We've got to hide him from the Egyptian soldiers."

"The Egyptians will not kill him. Jehovah will help."

Moses started with a divine calling, a divine connection with Jehovah, his Head Coach. As an infant, he had no idea about the purposes of his life. But the Lord knew. Moses's held the clip board, listening to the Head Coach's instructions. God already worked out all the details. Eighty years later, in the presence of the burning bush was when the Father finally laid it all out. Only then did Moses realize the significant, unique plan the Lord had been preparing for him.

Moses was the ultimate pastor. What a diverse and deep resume. What a list of experiences and encounters with God. Moses started at the burning bush. He continued with the ten plagues and the Passover lamb. Next, he placed his staff down, and the Red Sea parted. Miracle after miracle. The list goes on and on. Imagine leading a congregation of millions of people for forty years, and most of the time, they are complaining. But through it all, Moses maintained a close relationship with God that anchored his soul and kept him in a place of humility.

Moses had his moments of doubts and uncertainty. But in the end, he realized God had a plan, and the Father was carrying it out. The congregations looked at Moses as the person leading them out of slavery. But Moses knew, God is my Head Coach, I'm executing His plan, I'm just a vessel or an instrument in my Father's hand.

When I played point guard in high school, I had to have a good relationship with my head coach. It didn't mean that I was brown-nosing to get favoritism. It meant being teachable, humble, and hungry to win. It was vital for me as the point guard to be an extension of the head coach on the court. To accomplish that, I had to have his heart and know what was in his mind. I had to run the plays that he called. But if the defensive team wasn't allowing that, it required me to be flexible and alter the play. Therefore, I had to pay attention in practice even before the actual game, and then when the whistle officially blew, I kept my eyes open to the coach's signals from the sidelines. I had to hear his voice over the noise of the court and even of the crowd. And when I could not see him, I knew that he trusted me to do what he wanted.

Wisdom from above. God, the Head Coach, set the events in motion for both Moses and Joshua. He is the sovereign God selecting leaders as He wills. The Lord chose these two men not because they were so good but because He is that good. He loves His people and chooses leaders to demonstrate His care. I often say, "He so loved the world that He gave His only Son, but He so loved the Church that He gave them pastors." God planned to take His people from slavery to emancipation to promised land so they could worship Him (Exodus 7:16).

Joshua, like Moses, stood on the plan of the Head Coach, not the naysaying crowd in the stands. Joshua believed in God's sovereignty in the entire process. When the spies came back and told the people, "The land is good, but we can't take it—too many giants," Joshua and Caleb were the only ones of the original generation who said, "No! God has promised us this land, and we can conquer it" (Numbers 13:30).

One of my desires and ongoing prayers concerning my successor was for someone who constantly had their ear to the Head Coach's heart—an individual with a serious personal prayer life.

Several times in our discussions, Pastor Marcus, my successor, mentioned his time in prayer, seeking the Lord, waiting for guidance and confirmation. When I asked what advice Pastor Marcus would give fellow successors, he pointed to Joshua's experiences in the tent with Moses. After Moses left the tent, Joshua stayed behind, no doubt, having his own personal time with the Father. Pastor Marcus believes, as I do, that private, intimate time with the Lord is a significant priority for a leader.

As a young man, Joshua learned one of the essential parts of his job—to refuse to leave the presence of the Lord. When seeking a protege, it's crucial to search for an individual who understands the importance of remaining in the presence of God.

Joshua, like Caleb, "had a different spirit" within him. This heroic, courageous, and bold spirit caused him to be selected above his brethren to lead the people of God into the Promised Land. I saw these same qualities within Marcus, and as a result, he too has entered new territory, God leading all the way.

We know from biblical history what happened after Moses' death when Joshua took the reins of leadership. During this time, I don't think either man fully understood the journey and the challenges ahead. But both men were committed to spending time in God's presence, worshiping, seeking His comfort, guidance, and instructions.

As a mentor, there is only so much you can impart from your experience. The new pastor is going to encounter new gameplays not listed on the past agenda. He's going to have to listen and learn from the Head Coach for himself. A man who listens to God is the kind of shepherd you want to leave to look over God's sheep.

Joshua witnessed Moses as he guarded the tent of meeting (Exodus 33:11). Moses mentored Joshua to have an intimate relationship with God. When Moses finished talking with God and left the tent of meeting, Joshua stayed behind in the tent. He developed his own pace, style, and conversation with God--unique and distinct from Moses. No doubt God began to give Joshua a new set of plays. Joshua had further instructions required to run when they reached the Promised Land. Moses's strategies and methods in forty wilderness years would not be effective where they were going.

"Thus, the Lord used to speak to Moses' face to face, just as a man speaks to his friend. When Moses returned to the camp, his servant Joshua, the son of Nun, a young man, would not depart from the tent." (Exodus 33:11)

Joshua's lingering behind in the tent of meetings raises some questions:

Why did Moses take Joshua?
Could Joshua hear Moses' conversations with God?
Why did Joshua want to stay behind?
Did Moses instruct him to stay?
Was it training time for his future leadership?
Was he getting familiar with the voice of God?
Was he simply captivated by God and desired to know Him, like Moses?
Had God captured His heart, and he couldn't get enough?

We have plenty of questions about Joshua's time alone in the tent. Many of these questions won't be addressed until we go to heaven. But I do believe some of them are answered when God identified Joshua. He called him "a man in whom is the spirit" (Numbers 27:18). The word spirit here means God's Spirit or the Holy Spirit, not merely a person with insight and wisdom. In those tent meetings with God, Joshua learned to listen to the voice of God and to be empowered and indwelt by God's Spirit. A leader attuned to the Head Coach will lead his team into victory. Phoenix Suns' head coach Monty Williams is this type of leader. After a two-win solid start in the best-of-seven 2021 NBA, the Phoenix Suns lost four straight games to the Milwaukee Bucks in the finals. But amidst the sting of defeat, Suns' head coach Monty Williams, an outspoken Christian, revealed his true character.

In a move that sports commentators said they'd never seen before, Williams entered his opponent's locker room to offer congrats to the champs.

"I just wanted to come and congratulate you guys as a man and a coach because you guys deserve it," said Williams, with an arm around Bucks standout and Finals MVP Giannis Antetokounmpo. "I'm thankful for the experience. You guys made me a better coach, and you made us a better team." Just before that visit, Williams fought back the tears during a postgame press conference. "I wanted it so bad," he admitted to reporters. "It's hard to process right now."

Through his words and actions, the coach solidified his reputation as a class act. "How can you not love Monty Williams," tweets Barstool Sports. On si.com, Jimmy Traina writes, "Let's hope Monty Williams gets that NBA title one day."

Williams, 49, was in the news five years ago after experiencing a family tragedy and remains vocal about the impact of faith on his life and career... "The essence of my coaching is to serve," he said at the postgame press conference. "As a believer in Christ, that's what I'm here for. And I tell [my players] all the time, if I get on you, I'm not calling you out; I'm calling you up. You have potential, and I have to work my tail off to help you reach that potential."

Williams was named coach of the year by the National Basketball Coaches Association, and he finished second in voting for NBA Coach of the Year. Amid the "ups and downs of the NBA," working for the Lord and seeking God first "have been a lighthouse for me."

In 2016, when Williams was an assistant coach for the Oklahoma City Thunder, Ingrid, his wife of more than 20 years, was killed in a head-on car crash. Three of the couple's five young children also were in the car but survived. The driver who caused the collision, who was under the influence of meth, also died. At his wife's funeral days later, Williams gave a moving eulogy that went viral. The coach acknowledged being in pain but quoted Romans 8:28, about God causing all things to work out for good. Williams also spoke about the importance of forgiveness and encouraged people to pray not only for his family but for the family of the other driver.

(For Suns' head coach Monty Williams, victory through faith in Christ was the ultimate prize. Stephanie Martin, a reporter for churchleaders.com (7/6/2021)

3

The Draft

Before I formed you in the womb, I knew you. Before you were born, I sanctified you. I ordained you a prophet to the nations (Jeremiah 1:5).

June is usually the time fans wait to see the NBA draft. However, because of COVID-19 in 2020, they had to wait until August. The draft historically started in 1947 and used to be quite complicated. In the '70s, the administrators simplified the selection. These days the draft process goes smoothly.

Each team selects one player in the first round and one in the second. The draft pick must be at least 19 years old and one year beyond their high school graduation. When a team chooses a player, it's called a "pick."

God's draft pick in 1993 for Parklawn? Bishop Walter Harvey. Like the prophet Jeremiah, my calling goes way back. Before I uttered my first words, let me introduce you to my dear late mother, Johnnie Harvey. She produced five children, of which I am the fourth and the youngest of four boys, with one younger sister.

As my mother pushed me in a stroller in our neighborhood, a Christian woman, Mother Pearl Brumfield, interrupted our walk. Mother Brumfield carried the reputation as an HRPPW (i.e., Holy Roller Pentecostal Prayer Warrior). She often knocked on doors in the neighborhood, asking people if they needed prayer. My mother had not made a commitment to Christ at this time. The woman asked, "May I look at the baby under the blanket?" My mother hesitated but then pulled the blanket away to reveal my beautiful face. (Okay, that's my addition to the story.) The woman began to prophesy about my future and told my mother, "This baby will one day be a pastor." My mother said nothing. She nervously pulled the blanket back over my head and moved on down the street.

Jeremiah, the prophet, wrote about his ordination service occurring within his mother's womb (Jeremiah 1:5). The Lord commissions His servants before conception, but extensive training needs to happen in most cases. So let me tell the truth. Before I became like a Jeremiah or a Moses, I was more like a Jonah. God selected me to be a pastor and minister, just like the prayer warrior told my mother. But my journey to the pulpit was not straight and narrow. God already knew what the details of my BC (Before Christ) days.

During that dark and confusing time, I felt the conviction of God's presence. I remember fearing God throughout grade school. The Catholic school I attended first through fifth grade probably instilled that fear within me. The male priests, especially the nuns, had a particular way of disciplining, making you fear God's wrath. They would hit your wrists with wooden rulers when you stepped out of line.

I also encountered the fear of God during grade school when I hung out with a few of my friends. We were looking to do something mischievous in the neighborhood. A Lutheran church held a paper recycling drive each year to raise funds. People brought their old papers and stacked them up in piles in the church parking lot. I tried to discourage them, but my friends decided to knock the stacks down. "Hey, ya'll, this is God's house, and He's watching." I had a fear of God but no knowledge of God. They ignored me and continued to scatter the papers before taking off running down the street. I heard them laughing with a devilish sense of joy.

I remained behind. I stacked up the piles of paper all by myself. I walked back home, still with the fear of God in my heart, even though I'd done the right thing. As I approached my neighborhood, my friends greeted me with chastisement and ridicule. "Hey, here comes the hero of the day, Mr. Goodie Two Shoes."

When I turned 15, my mother attended a revival one night and gave her life to the Lord. And guess who prayed with her at the altar and eventually discipled her? The HRPPW herself, Mother Pearl Brumfield, the same Christian who encountered my mother on the street when I was a child! Remember, she prophesied, "This child is going to be a pastor one day." She continued to mentor my mother, helping her understand holiness, the power of the Holy Spirit, and the power of the Word of God. My mother lived a victorious Christian life and became an intercessor, Bible teacher, and mentor to women through her guidance.

However, despite the spiritual changes in my household, between the ages of 15 to 19, I became a drug addict. Although I had regular access to marijuana and other drugs, I became a drug addict of a different sort because my mother also "drug" me to Church with her.

I sat on a church bench, in attendance to please my mother. I had no relationship with Christ. But even then, the fear of God continued to grow within me. The conviction of the Holy Spirit kept knocking at the door of my heart, wearing down my resistance. My mother was praying fervently for me.

During my teen years and young adult years, this fear of God and

His convicting presence continued. Throughout high school, I was known as "Walter, the walking Bible." This name came about because I knew a few scriptures and encouraged my friends to do right instead of wrong.

My athletic background is in basketball. Like many inner-city youths, basketball reigned as the number one sport in our neighborhood. I grew up watching black and white television broadcasts. I watched basketball players Wilt Chamberlain, Nate Thurmond, Cassie Russell, Dave Bing, Bob Love, Lew Alcindor (Kareem Abdul-Jabbar), Oscar Robertson, Wes Unseld, and Earl "The Pearl" Monroe. But my childhood idol and namesake were Walt "Clyde" Frazier. As a teen, I dressed like Walt Frazier. I even told people to call me Walt instead of Walter or my nickname "Frankie." I am a Junior named after my father, Walter Francis Harvey. My Dad's friends called him Frank, so I grew up as "Frankie." By the time I got to high school, my identity-seeking had gravitated towards "Cool Walt." Although a bit shy, I proved to be smooth on and off the court—with the ladies and basketball.

My high school, Milwaukee Lincoln, was a historic Wisconsin state powerhouse. I made the basketball team but rode the bench as the 8th or 9th man. However, in my neighborhood, I was the star. I lived near two basketball courts, and the closest was Holy Angels School playground--the Catholic school I attended as a kid. When I played basketball there, I was the man, a playground legend. If you walked down three blocks, you would come across the second court, a larger one called Atkinson Park. When I showed up, people respected me and considered me a good basketball player. However, some of the players outshined me--including the NBA all-star and coach, Terry Porter.

After my high school graduation, I decided to follow Walt Frazier. I attended Southern Illinois University and wanted to walk onto the basketball team. I tried to flee the city of Milwaukee, thinking I could outrun my mother's prayers. Long story short, I failed to make the basketball team at SIU. I didn't even try out. Drugs, sex, and a partying lifestyle prevented me from fulfilling my dreams.

I tried to go my own way, but God continued to pull me back, surprisingly sometimes speaking through unbelievers. While attempting to enjoy myself at drug-filled and drunken parties, non-believers called me out, "You look saved. You shouldn't be here."

I was a Jonah who also felt like Peter, one of Jesus' disciples, when the soldiers captured Jesus before His crucifixion. Peter warmed himself by a fire while the Savior stood just a few feet away. Peter heard the religious leaders falsely accusing Jesus, demanding His death. Peter continued to stand there watching, warming his hands, trying to act like he had nothing to do with Jesus. However, the people around recognized Peter as one of Jesus' followers, "Hey, this man, he was with Him." But Peter kept saying, "No, I don't even know the Man" (Mark 14:66-72).

My partying buddies kept busting me out with their "you look saved" comments like those accusing Peter. So, I smoked more marijuana, cursed a little louder, or did some other ungodly thing to try and convince them. "No, I belong. I'm a big sinner, just like the rest of you." All along, I knew the discontentment in my heart, but I tried my best to cover it up. During that first year in college, I failed and flunked academically. Relationally I damaged the hearts of women. I found myself in and out of unhealthy relationships.

At 19 years old, I surrendered my life to Christ. I no longer lived in my mother's house, but her prayers followed me. God chased me down; the conviction of the Holy Spirit hovered over me each day. Finally, I turned the tables and became a God chaser. Everything changed for me. I returned to my hometown, Milwaukee, for a fresh start.

One month after becoming a Christian, I met the woman of my dreams and prayers, Judy Martin. She has been my girlfriend for the last

42 years, 36 years as my wife as of this writing. We dated for six years during my remaining college years. Judy became one of God's instruments to set my feet on solid ground and establish me as a believer.

I began attending my mother's church, Northside Church of God. The church had a vibrant youth and young adult group. I soon became the youth minister. Judy and I loved the experience of mentoring young lives and minds for Christ. We happily served the youth there for seven years.

In 1992, God and the former lead pastor of Parklawn Assembly of God Church called me to take the youth pastoral position. I sacrificed to accept a non-salaried youth ministry role. I was working a marketplace job as a television host and producer. But I took the offer to become a full-time youth pastor. I had no clue that I'd be facing the decision to transition from youth pastor to senior pastor within a year.

I had been on the job as a youth pastor for less than a year at Parklawn when a leadership rift took place, and soon after, a church split. This incident is when I first personally experienced the devastation of a congregation without a leadership transition plan in place. There was no one to pass the leadership ball, and no one positioned to catch an alley-oop.

Church splits are messy, much like a marital divorce. The former pastor left Parklawn and decided to start a new church, leaving the members wounded. Some of them followed the former pastor, some remained. Still, others limped away, bruised, and disillusioned. I believe that Satan hoped for the death of Parklawn.

Let me clarify. The true Church is a living organism (a body, not a building). It never stops running, like the Energizer Bunny. The Holy Spirit is the battery inside the body of Christ. The gates of hell shall never win!!!

However, that local building sitting on the corner can die and close its doors. Churches fail for several reasons: no gospel witness in the community, no one has come to Christ in decades. The congregation is in denial and keeps claiming, "We are okay." Or a mindset among the people that "We don't need to change with the times."

So many churches have come to an end because of fights and splits. One of the most prominent church killers is the issue we are tackling in this book, a pastoral revolving door. The congregation has suffered by adjusting to several new pastors, with no leadership longevity or consistency. A congregation who must suffer through issues like these is sometimes wounded and never able to heal.

But Parklawn healed. We moved from that destructive, divisive place when I began as lead pastor to become a spiritually growing congregation. I led the congregation for almost 30 years and then turned the lead pastor position to Dr. Marcus Arrington, God's draft pick in 2020. This is his testimony.

God's pick in 2020--Dr. Marcus Arrington.

It's been a great journey that we are on right now, Bishop and me.

I'm originally from Philadelphia. When my family moved to Milwaukee, I eventually joined Bishop Harvey's youth group at Northside Church of Christ. Under his ministry, I accepted Christ. Neither of us knew what God had in store in our futures together.

I attended Grambling College for undergraduate school and got involved in the campus ministry. That's when God confirmed my calling into the ministry, but I was not thinking about becoming a pastor.

I spent a lot of my years trying to figure out, "God, what do you want me to do?" I ended up majoring in education and coming back to Milwaukee. I began to work for the Milwaukee Public School system and served in my previous church, doing what my hands found to do. I helped with the youth ministry and on the praise and worship team--trying to be as faithful as possible. I took more ministry involvement and more speaking engagements. I became more proficient in studying the Word, and I had more preaching opportunities. That gift of speaking was being honed and further cultivated—more confirmations about God's ministry calling. I had a greater sense of assurance in that area. But I didn't see myself as pastoring. After college, I became an assistant principal. While I was doing things in ministry, I was more focused on my career as an administrator.

I went back to school, got my master's degree, and went again for a doctorate. Before that, I'd gotten some theological degrees. So, I was in school a lot—acquiring and building.

The pivotal moment for me leading up to where I am now was in 2014. I got an opportunity to be a principal with Milwaukee Public Schools. I saw myself as, "Okay, this is going to be my place of ministry." I have another opportunity to minister to young people and colleagues." I started a Bible study for the students. I also partnered with a local pastor, and we began to pray two times a week before school started. So, I was engaged in ministry even in what most would consider a "secular" profession.

At one point, the Lord spoke to me and said, "You will not have a long career at the school." So, there would have to come a time when I had to decide about full-time ministry. It's one of those moments in your private time with God, where you think, "Ah, maybe I didn't hear you right, Lord." So, I kind of left that alone, literally. And I kept serving people, on my staff, in the community, trying hard to turn that school around and bring life there.

In the meantime, my family had transitioned to Parklawn. That's when Bishop and I reconnected. I was still a teenager in the youth group at Northside church when Bishop became youth pastor at Parklawn.

In 2011, my wife and I felt like God was changing our course, and we started visiting churches. Now, mind you, the only time I had ever been in Parklawn was when A. C. Green, the former basketball player, spoke at the church, maybe around '93. The church still had wooden chairs. So, my visit in 2011 was the first time since 1993. I wasn't sure if I would speak to the Bishop because it had been so long, But he recognized me, and we chatted briefly. I let him know what was going on with my family and me. He encouraged me: "Don't move too fast. Keep seeking God." We kept visiting. Eventually, my mom and my wife came with me for a few months. And then the Bishop set up a meeting with me and talked a little bit more.

The Lord gave me a dream, and the Bishop was in the dream. I can't remember all the details, but I knew through the dream, and God confirmed that Parklawn was where we were supposed to be next. I had peace about it. So, I told my wife, and we got into the new members' class.

I began to serve on the praise and worship team. At the time, I was in grad school, so I wasn't trying to do a whole lot. I also worked as an administrator, so I was busy. We had a toddler at home--a lot going on.

I shared with Bishop what we did at our previous ministry, but I didn't have any expectations. And then, in about 2013, the Lord dealt with me and said, "It's time for you to do what you were sent to Parklawn to do." I had gotten comfortable being on the praise team, but I knew there was more. I would nearly salivate whenever I saw the altar call and Bishop laying hands-on people. I always felt like, man, I need to be doing that, like I need to be in on that action.

So, I set up a meeting with the Bishop in 2013. I shared my heart. He shared his heart concerning young adult ministry. And from that moment, we began to kind of strategize around relaunching that ministry. I eventually became the young adult ministry coordinator of what was called Linked Generation (LG).

I also became a member of the Bishop's teaching team. Eventually, I spoke on a Sunday morning, which, you know, was a big deal. Finally, Bishop Harvey commissioned me as a minister in 2014, the same year God elevated him to become a Bishop.

Around 2018 or so, the Bishop first spoke to me about what God was doing in him. He was speaking to him about his next steps. The Bishop mentioned succession and the possibility of me becoming his successor. When he first said it, I was thinking, "What in the world?"

Again, I knew I was called. I knew I could share the Word and all those kinds of things, but I didn't see myself as a pastor. I didn't want to be a lead pastor. That was too much. So, I'll be the assistant pastor, help or support, lift arms, but I'm not the guy. I'm not the main go-to person. That was my attitude. When he first said it to me, I received it. I was honored. But pastoring is not something I wanted to do.

Then, as I was praying about what the Bishop said about succession, the Lord took me back to one of my journal entries. I wrote what I believed God had said. "There's going to come a time where you have to decide on full-time ministry." God also reminded me that He told me, "You're not going to be at your school long." And it hit me like a ton of bricks: this is it; this has got to be it.

Shortly after this, I went to the barbershop. There was a guy I didn't know. I had no idea he was a pastor. So, we talked about things, and as we left the shop, he began to give a word of knowledge. He said, "You know, you've been praying about some things. "You know, you're going to leave, and it's going to work." It was like additional confirmation. I spoke with my wife and had her assurance. So, I didn't know what would come or what to expect from that point on. But the next time the Bishop and I had a conversation about succession, I had peace. I knew this was the next step for me.

Bishop began to sit with me and layout a strategy for succession, a timeline. Then, we began to walk together even that much more intimately. He laid out the course. The process flowed to a tee. I really can't recall any point of the succession plan where we stalled. I mean, it was masterful how Bishop laid out the plan. The Bishop did not make a rash decision. Much thought, much prayer, much patience, and the plan were very methodical. My wife and I talked about it one day, we said, "it was surgical and precise. It was great."

On the other end, my last year as a principal ended up being one of my most challenging years. But in the middle of all the difficulties, the grace of God manifested. I knew He was in the midst of it all. I left the school better than when I found it. I was able to have a sense of peace—closure for me. I could now move on and fully embrace this new path that the Lord had opened for me.

So, I continued with the succession plan. I joined the Parklawn staff as Senior Associate Pastor in the summer of 2019. Once I joined the staff, it was a time of close mentorship with Bishop. He explained the lay of the land in terms of pastoral care and the nuances that came with it. I learned the elements, structure, and systematic things within the Assemblies of God denomination.

It was a year of new beginnings. I was preparing for the official passing of the baton. The Installation Service occurred in March of 2020.

What happened after that? COVID-19!

I said, "God really?" Bishop and I still joke about that. So, Bishop's last Sunday at Parklawn and my first Sunday as senior pastor turned out to be the first Sunday we had a virtual service.

Bishop continued to be and has been available. He continues to walk me through the process and makes himself accessible. He's been able to empathize; he too came into a challenging situation when he assumed the lead pastor role at Parklawn. I appreciate his sensitivity and guidance. It's wonderful.

Bishop and Judy are still members of Parklawn. We can continue to partner and go forward together. I think it would have been very scary if Bishop moved to another country or disconnected himself from the ministry, which usually happens in succession. The predecessor doesn't often have that level of engagement with the congregation.

I have a pastor friend in the city who took over a ministry. The former pastor, his predecessor, died. So, he can no longer connect and have those conversations like Bishop, and I do. If I'm curious about something, I send the Bishop an email or call him, and we can talk. I'm very fortunate in that regard.

I see my relationship with Bishop like Moses to Joshua. Moses was highly regarded and trusted by the people, firmly established in his legacy of leadership. Moses had led them out of Egypt, through the wilderness, and all these different monumental moments. It's similar to the Bishop's tenure of leadership. He's led Parklawn through various transitions, different stages, different milestones in the highlights, and times of difficulty. He has a level of trust with the congregation. Like Joshua, I have to earn that trust. I have to develop that relationship with the congregation.

But what is interesting—Joshua had his own battles. Moses had the Amalekites, but Joshua faced Jericho, the kings of the South, the eastern kings, and so forth. These foreign armies came against the Israelites as they attempted to occupy the land. So, Joshua also had his challenges with the Israelites, his own people.

I look at COVID as some of Parklawn's present challenges. Moses had his Red Sea. This pandemic is my Jordan.

4

The Contract

When an NBA draft pick is selected, the next big item on the agenda is the contract. The player's contract is their benefits package. When a team recruits a star player, they will sign a contract that provides base pay plus financial incentives and bonuses. The contract pays the player even more if the performance goals are met (such as the number of games played, free throw percentage, the team's record, or making the playoffs).

No professional player gets out on the court and begins a game without a contract in place. Unfortunately, all too often in the Christian community, we hesitate to talk about money. Instead, we quote verses about God's provision and make individuals feel bad as if they are not trusting the Father in the financial area of their lives. The scripture in Malachi about "robbing God" has beat up people, forcing guilt money out of pockets and purses into the offering plate. Hopefully, this type of practice has ended when discussing finances for an incoming and outgoing pastor and his family. Churches need to have a short-term and long-term financial plan.

Church leadership must possess both the will and the skill of financial literacy and stewardship of resources. If not, then they will mishandle the pass of succession. We are all on the same team, and each of us has an essential role in making an alley-oop. If we drop the ball, individual players, especially the corporate church, may miss the opportunity to advance in faith, maturity, and accomplishing the church's mission.

"Bread is made for laughter, and wine gladdens life, and money answers everything." (Ecclesiastes 10:19 ESV)

Money is often the reason many lead pastors refuse to let go of the pastoral reins of leadership. They may not have established a savings or retirement plan and therefore feel forced to stay in their current roles. Their big question is, how am I going to support my family? Church boards may be asking, how are we going to pay two pastors? Church members may be asking, what will happen to our beloved former pastor? How will we honor him and still care for our incoming leader?

Connection with a wise financial planner early in ministry or career can relieve this burden. In my case, I didn't start out making these wise financial decisions. In fact, for the first several years of full-time ministry, I was behind on IRS taxes, and penalties were accumulating. Wise financial consulting and self-discipline turned the corner for me. The church board also needs to understand its role. The church needs to care for the pastor and their family beyond a salary.

If you are a part of a church where the denomination works all this out on your behalf, great. Or if you happen to be in a church with a business-minded board who offered you a well-planned out package including tax information and retirement benefits, great. But if you are:

*In deep tax debt
*Without a financial nest egg
*About to retire
*About to plant a church

*Coming into a new situation and wondering how to proceed financially

Would you please allow me to share my experience and take the advice of my financial advisor Scott Larsen?

The IRS Don't Play. I love to play basketball, but I learned the hard way not to play games with the IRS. They don't play with taxes. They want it, all of it, and they want it on time.

Before joining the pastoral staff at Parklawn in 1992, I worked full-time in the printing and mailing industry marketplace. I had a second profession as a TV producer/host on Milwaukee Public Television. I had the opportunity to meet and interview national and local celebrities. My first day on the job assignment was to interview a Pulitzer Prize-winning Black journalist. I interviewed everyone from national politicians, mega-church preachers, billionaires, and athletes. Besides this being a high-profile, creative, and fun position, the part-time gig paid more than my full-time job. I was considered a 1099 contract employee. I didn't know what that meant. My focus was on the job and the pay. Did I mention that part-time income was more than my full-time salary? And the fun it offered me!

I was being paid as a contract employee during my television and early pastoral staff days. Neither employer was withholding State or Federal taxes from my salary. I was responsible for paying my taxes. I made the unwise choice of not paying them quarterly, hoping that I would be in a financial position and disciplined enough to pay them annually. I was ignorant of (not criminal in) paying taxes, poor stewardship on my part. As a result, I soon was in a financial hole of back due taxes, penalties, and interest of several thousands of dollars.

Some of the pastors at the church were using the tax preparation services of a Christian Certified Public Accountant. When I met Scott

Larsen in 1993, I was already thousands of dollars in debt to the IRS. Seeking counsel on financial matters, trusting bankers and financial advisors are not typical in the African American culture. One reason is we often do not know who to talk to, who to trust. Most pastors and church boards don't have the experts to advise them. As a result, they are left to assume that the tax information and practices they get from their pastor friends are correct.

Long story short, Scott helped me get on a road to financial recovery. He has proven to not only be a great financial counselor but a good friend and a coach to our church elder board during the recent succession planning process.

Suggestions from Scott.

When Pastor Harvey and I met, we began by assessing his situation. We looked at what he owed, how much he makes, his budget, how his compensation package was structured, and how he reported his income. We found that we could reduce his taxes by thousands of dollars every year by restructuring his compensation. We also increased his withholding taxes (the federal tax that comes out of an employee's paycheck) to equal what he should have been paying in during the year to avoid owing taxes. This deduction was a shock to his budget, but he survived. He had his IRS debt paid off and received tax refunds when he filed his taxes within three years.

Here are some of the practices that perhaps you and your church should consider also. You need to know how the income you are receiving is being taxed. Then you need to know the tax rules that affect you and how. When you are self-employed and are a sub-contractor and receive 1099 for the other income you have earned, you are on your own concerning your taxes. First off, you will owe social security tax (self-employment tax) on the money reported on your 1099. Not the 7.65% those regular employees pay deducted from their checks before they see it, but you owe 15.3%. As a self-employed person, you pay both the employees' half of Social Security and the employers. That stinks, but that is not the end of it!

In addition, you then get to pay income tax on the amount on your 1099 as well! If you have a business, the tax will be calculated net of all reasonable and deductible expenses. It all makes sense, but it stinks because you found out after the fact instead of while you were getting paid. For example, say you made $20,000 net and received 1099 for those earnings. If you are in the 12% tax bracket, your income tax would be $2,400. But that is not all. Now you need to add your self-employment tax (Social Security and Medicare tax) which is $3,060, to your income tax of $2,400. So out of nowhere, you owe $5,460 that you did not know that you would owe or even think about before doing your taxes. This scenario happens all too often.

The best advice I can give is always to understand how you are being paid. Then, understand how those earnings are being taxed. It is the same as in a basketball game: know and study your opponent! Learn all you can about your opponent! Use all available resources to beat your opponent!

Taxes are your opponent!

I heard a quote in a college communications class that describes this paradox perfectly when it comes to pastors, their taxes, and where they get their tax information, "It's not what you know that gets you in trouble. It is what you know that just isn't so!"

That quote explains why I became an expert in pastoral tax law. That is also why I developed, Ministryresourcecenter.com, a website that pastors can use free of charge to gain access to information they need to file their taxes with confidence and be a better steward of your tax situation. (See the resources page at the back of the book for information about "Fear in the Pulpit" and "Creating a Compensation Package.")

Pastors don't plan on failing when it comes to their tax situations. They, like most, just fail to plan! Many planning techniques can be used to help pastors save money on their taxes. Reviewing a pastor's retirement, housing allowance, health insurance, and ministerial expenses are essential when structuring a pastor's compensation. The church board's primary responsibility is to care well for their pastors and prepare a solid foundation for the church's future, including pastoral succession.

I also credit the Parklawn elder board, our governing body, for their consideration towards me as the outgoing leader and for installing some of Scott's recommendations. As a result, they structured a solid and generous compensation and retirement package for Marcus. Here are some of the perspectives they operated from, and I recommend them to you, the reader.

First, it is essential to see the big picture and not just focus on the immediate changes. I was already a legacy leader, meaning that I had served in one place for several decades. Any long-term leader's transition will affect the entire team (church board, pastoral staff, church members, and the community). Recognize the implications and opportunities that accompany the change. Prepare for some people to shift their membership both into and out of the church. Prepare for new sources of income and the opportunity to cultivate new relationships. See the big picture and embrace an abundance mindset instead of a deficit perspective.

Second, church boards need to understand their responsibility to care for both predecessor and successor. Boards should begin a discussion early on how to structure a pastoral compensation package for the incoming pastor. Not many church leaders even know who is considered a pastor in the eyes of the IRS. Understanding the unique tax treatment pastors receive under the tax code and reporting their income is also essential. Scott shared a resource, "Creating a Pastor's

Compensation Package." Remember that when structuring a pastor's compensation, every pastor's tax situation is unique and requires or allows different planning techniques. The first and most important thing to know about the pastor when structuring a pastor's compensation package is whether the pastor is "Exempt" from Social Security taxes. Another resource for you to read is "Should I Exempt Out of Social Security for my ministry income?" (See the Resource page)

When the board is structuring a pastor's compensation package, Scott encourages them to consider structuring a ministry position with specific components, not just a salary package. Maybe call it "Cost of the Ministry Position." This includes unreimbursed business or ministerial expenses, housing costs, and benefit costs that the pastor will incur. The pastor's compensation package should be structured to protect the church and the pastor by using the correct resolutions in elder meetings. There is a popular pastoral compensation structuring model called the "Dual Resolution" approach. The Dual Resolution approach signifies that the compensation plan for the pastor is not just a salary package resolution but may also have an accountable plan resolution, housing allowance resolution, and other benefit program resolutions. This approach can create significant tax savings for both the pastor and cost savings for the church.

Other critical financial and IRS conversations the church board must have include:

*The structure of the compensation package.
*That salary and wages are subject to income tax and self-employment taxes.
*That housing allowance is not subject to income taxes; however, it is subject to the self-employment tax.

In many situations, the pastoral benefits and expenses are taxed based on how the board structures or does not structure the compensation package. The church should work to maximize the non-taxable items inherent in the position of the pastor when structuring the compensation package. For example, health insurance premiums are sometimes included in the pastor's income, but they do not have to be if the pastor's package is structured correctly. Same with ministry expenses and contributions to the pastor's retirement. This is a tax savings of at least 27% to the pastor. Let's say, for example, that the pastor has $10,000 of ministry expenses and $10,000 in retirement contributions. If structured correctly, the pastor can save $5,400 or more in taxes—and that's every year!

Finally, after the board discussed Pastor Marcus's compensation package, they started to discuss my succession and retirement package and structure it. Key talk points were:

When would I retire?

Would I work part-time in transition?

Should I be exempt from Social Security? The IRS recognizes a change in life and ministry as one of the criteria for opting out. Not having to pay social security taxes would have a significant impact on my tax situation.

How much severance was the church going to pay me?

Who would receive the severance pay?

Should it be paid as a housing allowance?

I had matured in my stewardship of finances since 1992, when I started in full-time pastoral ministry. Since then, I still trust God's Word and claim those provision scriptures that my needs and my family's needs will be met. In addition, I add works to my faith. I rely on sound financial counsel and legal tax practices to secure my future and God's church. I am grateful to have a dream team around me of faithful church members, spiritual board members, a God-sent successor, and my loving family. We are all on the same team.

The church and church board have financially supported me in my next leadership season. My transition out as lead pastor was not retirement but a repositioning. I was sent out as an apostle to lead the National Black Fellowship as its president. Together, we fulfill a national mission as an extension of the Parklawn vision while staying connected to our local ministry.

The key to winning the game and advancing God's kingdom is a good game plan. The plan requires excellent and wise stewardship of the resources God puts in front of us. When we plan for retirement, pastoral compensation, and succession, we make it easier for all team members to shift out, up, and into their new roles.

5

A New Game Plan

Have you ever watched how professional athletes "retire"?

The one thing they never want to do is retire after a bad year.

They want to quit while they are ahead.

I can understand that.

It is better to go out with a shout of triumph than with a whimper of defeat.

(Robert L. Deffinbaugh, "Promise breakers and promise keepers (2 Samuel 21)," bible.org)

One of my friends, Pastor Derwin Gray, is a retired National Football League player. He jokes about the short career longevity of football players by saying that the NFL stands for "Not For Long." During this book's writing, several NBA Hall of Famers, Vince Carter, Dwyane Wade, and Dirk Nowitzki announced stepping away from the game.

The average career length for NBA players is 4.8 years, according to Business Insider. However, just because an NBA player is retiring does not mean their legacy won't continue. Some will have their numbers retired and lifted into the rafters as a memorial to their careers. Some will stay connected to the sport as announcers, owners, and coaches.

Brett Favre and Michael Jordan are two Hall of Famers. Each one also came back out of retirement to continue to play their respective sports. Famed country-western singer Kenny Rogers sang, "You've got to know when to hold 'em, know when to fold 'em, know when to walk away, and know when to run."

David's time to retire from active battle. During David's reign as king, the Philistines were constantly at war against him and Israel. David and his mighty men went down and fought against the Philistines. In the middle of the battle, David grew faint. Ishbi-Benob, a Philistine, a giant's son, whose bronze spear weighed 300 shekels, thought he'd take advantage of the king's weakened state. But Abishai came to David's aid, struck the Philistine, and killed him. Then the men of David swore to him, saying, "You shall go out no more with us to battle, lest you quench the lamp of Israel" (2 Samuel 21:15-17).

Let's face it; I am a man. Men have big egos. The name "Ishbi-Benob" means "pride." Pride can kill us in many ways. I have often resisted that inner voice telling me to hang it up, be it a relationship, a sports activity, fast food, or any multitude of things. When I obey the still small voice inside, it all goes well. When I disobeyed, I paid a heavy price.

I can only imagine David's private thoughts after his battle with Ishbi-Benob:

"Hey Lord, what happened out there today? I almost lost my head, literally. If it had not been for Abishai, I'd be rolling back into Jerusalem in a body bag. Father, I fought bears and lions when I was young and killed countless giants before. But today, I almost fainted in the middle of the battle. Lord, am I washed up? My men have already said this is my last battle. What now?"

David's men were also disturbed by this near-catastrophic loss of their leader. I imagine their locker room after-battle talk went something like this:

"Hey, we almost lost David out there."

"Yeah, he looked exhausted, and the Philistines saw it."

"Ab, thanks man, for stepping in."

"Our nation would have been in big trouble if David died today."

"We can't let it happen again."

"He can't go out with us anymore."

It's one thing to lose a soldier in a battle, but it's no joke when the king is killed. This incident indicated to David and his men that the king was no longer fit for man-to-man physical battle; he was not the foot soldier he used to be. However, this situation also displayed the wisdom and contributions of a team. David's men showed maturity and commitment by their decision to stop David's military career. And David modeled humility by not arguing but letting it go. Healthy pastoral transitions require the senior leader and the successor to humble themselves from pride and willingly shift roles and stay in their lanes. Pride and big egos kill so many leaders and hinder succession.

David had to deal with another succession issue down the road—this time with his son (2 Samuel 18). Absalom's pride told him that he should be the next king after David. He said to himself, "I don't even have to wait until my father dies. I can get the people to choose me now." He began to stand at the gate and do favors for the people to gain approval. At one point, he booted David out and took over. But Absalom could not overrule God's plan. Once again, David's loyal army defeated Absalom and placed David back on the throne.

This kind of conflict often happens in churches--a nasty power struggle and political battles over who will be our pastor. Sadly, many younger potential successors are too ambitious like Absalom. They are convinced: "I am ready to take over the church. Please put me in the game, coach. I am ready!!!!" They might be more committed to their success than have a heart for the team's success. Prideful, full of himself, Absalom almost killed his father trying to be the top dog. Ambition causes many younger impatient successors to abort their futures.

During my years in ministry, I have endeavored to raise mentees and empower young ministers. On several occasions, I thought, "I've found my successor." However, they were impatient for me to pass the ball. Our timing was off. Eventually, they left for another opportunity that seemed to fit their goals—no regrets on either of our parts. The kingdom is still advancing through all of our ministries. We are on Team Jesus, not building our empires. Sadly, a small number of the relationships did not end well. But I hold out hope that the gospel will continue to advance through each of us. I pray that we all will continue to grow, stay on our assigned missions, and maybe we'll be able to reconcile one day.

Senior leaders like King David and I have to trust our team to handle war without us. If we do, we will empower the team to win many more battles. More empowerment is what happened after Abishai killed Ishbi-Benob. Other giants came on the scene, and David's men wiped them out (2 Samuel 21:18-22). David's men killed the giants that David could not kill. Each new battle required new strategies and skills. One of these giants had six fingers and six toes on each hand and foot. This huge giant represented a new level of warfare. New levels expose us to new devils. After me, the generations are fighting the same battles and temptations, but the intensity is greater. Nevertheless, I am confident, with God, together, we will win.

For a smooth pastoral transition, just like a successful alley-oop, several key elements are needed:

Being willing to assist.

Awareness of the coaches' directions, your teammates, and the opposition.

Teamwork.

Agility, flexibility, and the ability to do more than one thing.

Trust and confidence in the receivers when you throw the ball.

Perfect timing.

Strength and stamina to keep going.

And finishing well, the ultimate goal is to add points to the score board.

Assist. Honestly, once Parklawn's transitional plan was in place and I identified the next lead pastor, I didn't struggle with passing the ball to my successor—several reasons why. When playing basketball, I loved setting others up for success. I loved to play the point guard in basketball. I loved to assist in helping others score.

An assist in basketball is the action of a pass to a teammate which enables them to score a goal and the passer is given the official credit for such an action.

I am what you might call "a playground legend" because I was an exceptional basketball player back in the day. However, now that I am older and wiser, I have resolved to stay in my lane and leave the game to younger, faster, and stronger players. As a result, my basketball skills have started to fade away—a little. I am by no means or stretch of the imagination the player nor athlete I was in my younger years, but I can still do some things on the court.

Parklawn Assembly of God, where I pastored for almost 30 years, historically held an "Old School versus New School" Basketball Game on New Year's Eve night. A traditional game between church members aged 25 and younger versus older guys and gals. In 2018, I got back on the court after a two-year retirement from playing basketball. I felt like Michael Jordan when he retired from basketball wearing number 23, then returned to the game wearing number 45.

On New Year's Eve night, I made my comeback at nearly 60 years old. The Old School team won and named me M.V.P. (Most Valuable Player). Did I get favored because of my Lead Pastor status? No way, I earned it. I recorded a triple-double for points, rebounds, and assists. However, I give a lot of credit to my teammates, especially two of my 30-something nephews, to set me up to succeed on the court. They gave me the alley-oop!

Basketball has always been an essential part of my life. My skills on the court have always been diverse. I am of average height at 6 feet but possess a 6' 6" wingspan, large hands, above-average dribbling ability, good shooting skills, and exceptional defensive ability. I prided myself on guarding and stopping or making it more difficult for the opposing teams' best players to score. However, my greatest joy in the game comes from making a great pass, scoring my teammates, and advancing our team. I love to make assists!

There are a couple more reasons I didn't struggle with passing the ball to my successor. Before coming to Parklawn, I was a television producer and host on Wisconsin Public Television. The program was an Emmy Award winner. Then, during my third year in this position, I received an invitation to be the youth pastor at Parklawn. It meant letting go of the television job and an excellent salary.

When I told some male friends about the offer, they thought I was crazy. Finally, one brother looked at me in disbelief and said, "Man, you are giving up a TV job! You have billboards of your face all over the city and the state. You mean that you are going to give all of that up?"

I looked at him with a smile of contentment and said, "Yep." And I did because I trusted that as I transitioned, God had prepared something else for me that I would only experience if I passed the ball. The same with retiring—I let the pastoral ministry position go because I was confident God has something in store in my future.

David retired from active battle but turned his attention to putting a plan for God's temple into effect. He designed the blueprint for the house of God that had never existed before. The king put together the worship services and wrote the music. His physical "slaying giant" sword was passed on to the younger soldiers, but his spiritual blade was sharpened. He put armor in place for the coming generations to fight the unseen enemy. Solomon, his son, the monarch who took the throne, walked into a well-oiled machine.

When I became a Christian at age 19, God blessed me with the good fortune to have mentors like Rev. Sandy Johnson, Ruth and Blanton Owens, and other adults at Northside Church of God. Mrs. Owens was both my youth and young adult Sunday School teacher and my Friday night fellowship leader; she taught me tough love by treating me like her son. She held standards of holiness and high character and modeled biblical femininity; she challenged me to honor young women as if they were my sisters. Ms. Owens encouraged us and poured God's word into us. These godly people lived life to the fullest for young people like me. She and Rev. Johnson, especially, passed a legacy ball to me to live a life devoted to lifting God's people.

My next chapter. It's been over 40 years since I began my journey with Jesus Christ. After leaving the role as lead pastor, Judy and I still want to help write the next chapter of the church's progress together. We will still attend the church when we are not on traveling assignments. It is my pleasure now to coach, cheer for, resource, and support my successor.

Like David, I don't see my role as retirement from pastoring but a repositioning to new positions. I consider myself like Paul and Barnabas, sent out by the New Testament church in Antioch (Acts 13). They worked together with the congregations to plant churches and ordained elders, teaching and strengthening the faith of believers. They broke ground and pioneered new unchartered territories. They raised, taught, and released ministry teams. Like the apostles, I'm trusting God to allow me to open new paths, activating, imparting, walking in great spiritual authority, and contending for the faith.

My new role focuses on church planting, especially in challenging places like America's inner cities, also international and national unreached people groups. I am also currently serving as the C.E.O. of the PRISM Economic Development Corporation (a Parklawn non-profit organization), president of the Assemblies of God National Black Fellowship of Churches, and an Executive Presbyter (Board of Directors) for the Assemblies of God. My new roles are congruent with the new season in the church. Several years ago, my congregation's leadership and members saw my ministry's fruit and effectiveness in these roles while I was still serving as lead pastor. I am grateful for a team that affirms the apostle's office and sees that there is life and ministry beyond the pulpit. As a result, together, we are still experiencing success and victories on and off the court.

I love to help release the potential inside of people. My satisfaction as a point guard was making an assist, not just in scoring points. The greatest basketball players make their team better. They don't just play to pad the statistics for themselves.

The other reason I didn't have a hard time letting go of my lead pastor position was a personal mission statement or life philosophy I had adapted over a decade ago: "LIVE FULL, LEAVE EMPTY!" One day I was praying and reading scripture in my study, and two powerful biblical stories solidified this new belief system within me.

The first passage is about Elisha attempting to extend his blessing to Gehazi. Elisha had already received an alley-oop of double portion blessing from his mentor Elijah to perform miracles and further his ministry. Elisha tried to do the same with his servant and probable successor, Gehazi. This passing to his servant might have resulted in quadruple blessings through Gehazi. Sadly, the servant aborted his ministry with desiring earthly material gain. Elisha healed a wealthy man named Naaman of his leprosy. Naaman tried to repay the prophet with silver and garments, but Elisha refused to accept the gifts. Greedy Gehazi ran after Naaman and lied, saying Elisha had changed his mind and now wanted the goods. When Gehazi got back in the presence of Elisha, God told him what Gehazi had done. Elisha said, "The leprosy that was on Naaman is now on you." Instead of catching the ball, Gehazi caught Naaman's leprosy (2 Kings 5:20-27).

God is a generational God. He wants the blessings to flow from one generation to the next. He is the God of Abraham, Isaac, and Jacob. He wants each generation to possess the same and even more power than the prior one. Jesus told His disciples in John 14:12, "Most assuredly, I say to you, he who believes in Me, the works that I do he will also do; and greater works than these he will do, because I go to My Father."

The second passage that developed my "live full, leave empty" philosophy is found in another passage about Elisha (2 Kings 2:9) After his death, those who buried him placed his body in a tomb, probably a cave. Several years later, a party of Israelites carried a dead man for burial. The Moabites, one of Israel's enemies, drew close. The burial party ran or hid, tossing the dead body into a cave. The tomb just so happened to be Elisha's. When the corpse touched the prophet's dead bones, the man miraculously came back to life. I can only imagine the shock when he caught up with those who'd placed him in that cave!

Scholars have interpreted this passage in several different ways, but this is what the story said to me. Elisha left this earth with a lot of God's power and virtue still wrapped up within. He wanted to give it to Gehazi, his servant, but Gehazi dropped the ball. I said to myself, "I don't want to die and still have stuff that God could have used inside me. I don't want to die with the ball still in my hands."

What happened with Elisha and the dead man reminded me of this quote: "The graveyard is the richest place on earth because it is here that you will find all the hopes and dreams that were never fulfilled, the books that were never written, the songs that were never sung, the inventions that were never shared, the cures that were never discovered, all because someone was too afraid to take that first step, keep with the problem, or determined to carry out their dream" (Les Brown, Facebook, 2/10/2019).

When I leave this earth, I don't want any unsung songs, unwritten books, unfulfilled dreams, or anything else going into the ground with me. The graveyard is full of people who keep saying, "Tomorrow I'll do it," but for many, they died with a life full of possibility before their "tomorrow" ever came.

Elisha died with power still in him. So, when the dead soldier was placed in the tomb and touched the bones of Elisha, he revived. The soldier stood on his feet. I don't want that to be my legacy. I want to live full and leave empty.

Big Shoes to Fill. Before the installation date, some said to Pastor Marcus, my successor, "You have some big shoes to fill." With humility and confidence, he would reply, "No, I don't really. I have my own shoes, and he is still going to need his." I applaud his recognition of the necessity to be himself and affirm that God would continue to use me. I am an old-school Walt Frazier fan, and he is an Allen Iverson, Philadelphia 76er, fan. I might prefer PUMA sneakers, and he might like Air Jordan's better, but we are on the same team and have different roles to play.

6

〰️

Awareness and Teamwork

The passer of on an alley-oop has his eye on everybody on the floor. He is fully aware of his team, the opponents, the time on the game clock, and the selected recipient of the ball.

Awareness. The ball-handler in a game is keenly aware of his teammates. He's always looking for the right opportunity to make a play, leading to a score. In practice, the team constantly repeats the alley-oop play. The passer has the coach's plans rolling around in his head. Combining that information with hours of preparation, the actual time on the floor, intuition about the game's flow, and knowledge of each player's strengths gives the lead passer a perfect setup for the alley-oop.

Joshua started his training camp early. The Scriptures first mention Joshua when Moses chose to lead the Israelite army into battle against the Amalekites (Ex. 17:8–16). From that point on, Moses begins to develop Joshua intentionally. They spent time together, getting to know one another. God was setting up the alley-oop.

Before he became a member at Parklawn, I knew Pastor Marcus had a rich spiritual legacy started by his parents. I knew he had demonstrated spiritual leadership in high school. Then he went on to college to become a Chi Alpha campus ministry student leader. I was friends with his former pastor and knew of his leadership before he joined me in ministry at Parklawn. Nevertheless, I allowed him a few years to learn and digest the culture and vision of the church. I also wanted Pastor Marcus to prioritize his family. I desired him to understand that his spiritual gifts and contributions were not being prioritized over their well-being.

After a few years, I invited him to occasionally join the teaching team at mid-week services and Bible studies. Next, I commissioned him as a minister in the church. A few years later, I invited him to audit elder's meetings, and then he was nominated and elected to serve on the governing board. The last step was nominating him as my successor and then hiring him as the senior Associate Pastor one year before the transition. More than any other activities, these appointments allowed us to spend time in the trenches of ministry together. We prayed together regularly and were able to see each other's strengths and weaknesses up close.

In times of church transition, it's essential to be mindful of everyone on the team and each person's position. The lead pastor, the potential new pastor, the board, and the congregation work together. Yes, important decisions are on the table. They have to be made. It's not merely a discussion about the leaders' credentials, the budget, church policies, and other concerns. It's vital to remember God is the Head Coach of the team. Be aware He is present on the bench, the floor, in the locker room, in times of victory and defeat. He is present as this group grapples with who, why, when, and what. Remember to acknowledge, God is in the room.

After Moses' death, the emphasis continued on God's presence with Joshua as the new leader. The Lord said to Joshua, "Just as I have been with Moses; I will be with you; I will not fail you or forsake you...the Lord is with you wherever you go" (Joshua 1:5; 9).

Pastoral transitions are vulnerable times for everyone on the team. The enemy looks to sow seeds of division, mistrust, impatience, and opportunities to steal the ball. During this transition, it's necessary to remind the congregation of God's presence and faithfulness in the past and present. And to also be assured of the same in the future. Transitions are excellent times to bring out the church's historical narrative, the memorabilia from the past, the old pictures. It's a time to be fully aware that God has brought us this far, and He will continue to lead us on.

As the day approached for my succession, I reminded our congregation of our history and destiny. Our past was glorious, but our future would be even brighter. We celebrated a rich legacy and anticipated an even better tomorrow.

Parklawn was founded in 1909 by a Pentecostal pioneer influenced by the Azusa Street revival. He started conducting healing tent meetings in Milwaukee, and people were getting saved and healed. Mostly Germans made up the early congregation.

As African Americans began migrating to the northern states in the early 1900s, many settled in industrial manufacturing towns like Milwaukee. But it was not until the late 1970's that our church received its first African American member and later its first staff pastor. The first African American lead pastor came on in 1989. He hired me in 1992 as Youth Pastor. Tragically, in 1993, he left the church, and a split occurred. Our church almost died because it did not have a plan of succession. There was no appointed leader, so more chaos emerged. During the confusion, I felt the call to become a candidate for the lead position. I was elected in 1993.

Since then, God has graced me with an internally secure mindset. I began to put a government and structure in place so the bylaws, congregation, and board would work cooperatively to ensure that the church would thrive and always have a godly leader. The Lord graced the church with a great young emerging leader to guide her in the future.

"Although the alley-oop is a fleeting moment in a game, those moments of exceptional playmaking create tight bonds between teams—euphoric highs relived long after the competition has ended, whether win or lose. They are the moments that, if slowed down enough, also contain lessons about the art of leadership" (Blake Atwood, "Leadership and the art of the alley-oop," churchleaders.com, 2/16/2012).

Everybody gets a ring. Jordan or Lebron? These two names are quickest off the lips of basketball fans debating the greatest of all time. In my opinion, Bill Russell is the GOAT (Greatest of All-Time). He played for the Boston Celtics from 1956 to 1969. Russell was the centerpiece of the Celtics dynasty, a five-time NBA MVP, and a twelve-time All-Star, winning eleven NBA championships during his thirteen-year career. He was the greatest defensive center the NBA has ever had seen. Even today, the NBA Championship Finals MVP trophy bears his name.

Have you ever heard of Mal Graham and Bud Olsen? No? Most people haven't. They were teammates with Russell on his last Celtics championship team. These two men primarily were bench players. They practiced and traveled with the team, wore the Celtic green, but rarely played. The combined minutes played for both players during the 1968-69 season equated to less than 150 minutes out of a potential 3,888 minutes. Together, they averaged 2 points that season. But guess what? Bill Russell, Mal Graham, and Bud Olsen all received championship rings.

Teamwork. Legendary Green Bay Packers football coach Vince Lombardi once said, "The achievements of an organization are the results of the combined effort of each individual. People who work together will win..." Leadership expert John Maxwell adds, "It takes teamwork to make the dream work, but a vision becomes a nightmare when the leader has a big vision and a bad team." (Fiona Adler, "Teamwork makes the dreamwork," www.actioned.com)

The popular acronym for TEAM is accurate: "Together Everyone Achieves More." If you are on the team and the team wins, it happens with teamwork. It doesn't matter whether you are a star performer or a bench warmer. You win together.

The term "team player" is often used in the corporate world and the world of sports. The implication is that an essential and sacrificial player makes the whole team better rather than a one-person show. The sweetest victories in sports and life are accomplished through teamwork.

Basketball requires a high level of teamwork. The head coach designs a play, and the team must work together to complete those plays on offense and defense. On defense, collaboration is critical as players must help teammates out and step in to cover an unguarded player if he is left open. It is common to hear "SWITCH" yelled during a game to help defend an available offensive player. There is probably more on-court talking between teammates in basketball than in any other sport.

In addition, the non-stop nature of basketball lends itself to a kind of ballet of teamwork complete with incredible body contact without pads and grace that is sometimes hard to believe. But there is no other play in any sport more beautiful than a well-timed and executed alley-oop!

In the body of Christ, Jesus is the head. The individual members of the body all work together in unity, although each person has a different gift or ability. No one is to be considered unimportant. Each member of the body depends on the other (1 Corinthians 12:12).

In pastoral succession, the church needs to function as a body. This relationship is not just something between the pastor and the successor. Nor should the full responsibility be placed on the board or a pastoral search committee. Individual church members, pastors, and board members make up the local body of Christ. Together they are on Team Jesus. It is teamwork that enables common people to do uncommon things.

The exodus from Egypt to the Promised Land took teamwork. God started with Jochebed and Amram seeing something in their baby Moses. Miriam, his sister, watched him float along the Nile River. The Pharaoh's daughter took him in and trained him in the ways of the Egyptians. Pharoah's wife challenged Moses to do what God was asking him to do. Aaron, his brother, was his mouthpiece and later the leader of his priestly team. Miriam became his worship leader. Jethro, Moses' father-in-law, gave wise advice. Joshua and Caleb brought back a good report after spying on the promised land. Aaron and Hur together held up Moses' arms while Joshua fought the Amalekites. These warriors made quite the team. The journey was not a solo act.

There are only five players on the court for each basketball team and only one basketball. Not everyone will get to score or play in the game. But it is a beautiful sight to witness when a team is united. Each person is aware of their gifts and talents, then uses them for the team's collective good.

Similarly, when a pastoral succession plan is started, the whole church must operate as a team in one accord. This process can be challenging if there are multiple potential young successors in the church and the lead pastor is close to retiring. The lead pastor may have a good relationship with all of them, but he knows that he can only select one of them to succeed him. The more significant question is, "Will those who are not chosen get bitter and jealous, or will they remain on the team, continue to contribute to its success, and sincerely support for the good of the church?

One thing is sure. A successful alley-oop pass can not only ignite the crowd of fans, but it can also unite a team. Even the team players sitting on the bench will stand, jump, and high-five the play.

7

Agility

Agility. In the late 1980s, Cross Trainer tennis shoes hit the market. These were shoes designed for athletes who loved to play numerous sports and mix up their exercise routines. I loved to wear these types of shoes when I played basketball because basketball requires so much agility—flexibility to turn on a dime. The shoes lacked the ankle support of regular basketball shoes, but they seemed to assist me with the sudden starts and stops during a game.

The game has changed over time. Today players are more focused on strength. But during my time, agility was king. I pride myself on being ambidextrous. I could shoot, pass, and dribble equally with either hand. Agility makes you more of a threat to the opposition.

I also had to be agile in my pastoral succession. I followed a lot of drama in the church. When the former lead pastor left, I had to find the baton, pick it up and determine which direction to run in the race.

In the same way, Marcus had to be agile in his new role as lead pastor though he did not follow drama and division inside the church as I initially did. It was a year of new beginnings and learning as he and I prepared for what would ultimately be the official passing of the baton crossover. On March 15, 2020, Dr. Marcus Arrington was installed as the next lead pastor at Parklawn Assembly of God. The following week, Wisconsin's governor declared all public assemblies to be closed due to COVID-19. The following Sunday, Marcus led his first service virtually. Talk about changing on a dime.

As I released the ball from my hand, Marcus caught it and had to do a 360 turn to get it to the basket and deliver the dunk. Marcus and I joke about that time of transition. Marcus shakes his head as if to say, "Really, God?" I thank God that I listened ten years in advance and mentally repositioned before the actual physical shift. For me, God couldn't have chosen a perfect time.

Joshua demonstrated his ability to be flexible as he led the new generation into the promised land and conquered the territory.

An initial example of Joshua's flexibility was when the spies returned from investigating the new land for Moses and the congregation. Ten men stood trembling in their boots, claiming, "We can't take it—too many giants. The opposition is too great." Joshua could have gone with the crowd, but he and Caleb stood on God's word and not popular opinion (13:25-33).

Another biblical example of agility is David and his mighty male warriors. The scripture described trained men, armed with bows, using both the right hand and the left in hurling stones and shooting arrows with the bow (1 Chronicles 12:1-2). Those mighty men knew how to use bow and arrow. And they also knew how to hurl stones in their battles with the enemy.

One of the most agile NBA players in the game today is Russell Westbrook, currently of the Los Angeles Lakers. He possesses speed, quickness, power, the ability to stop and start on a dime, and can change directions with ease, even while in midair. In 2020 he was traded to the Washington Wizards. Westbrook was traded to the Lakers at the end of the 2021 NBA season (by the way, the year of the Milwaukee Bucks second NBA championship, "fear the deer!"). The life of an NBA player requires personal and family agility, the ability to adjust from the uncertainty of the business and the sport.

God chose Joshua, not Aaron. God already planned for Aaron and his sons to head up the priestly responsibilities and Joshua to lead the military. Both men had to be agile, accepting God's calling and plan. When God appointed Aaron to take on the priestly duties, Joshua could have quit. He could have said, "Looks like this ministry thing is going to be a family favoritism arrangement. I don't have a chance—I'm out." But he didn't. He stuck around to continue to see what God had for him. His moment came years later when God appointed him to lead the new generation into the Promised Land. Selecting Aaron before Joshua's assignment could have been a big mishap. But the priestly responsibilities were not Joshua's calling nor what God had planned for him to do.

Here is a brief list of questions that can help the reader assess his agility and flexibility for pastoral succession. Honestly, answer these questions to test your agility.

How will you feel if you are (or are not) selected as the successor? How will your spouse feel?

Is there anyone in the church who desires to see you in the lead role more than you want it?

Can you remain on the team and still contribute with a sincere and content attitude if not selected?

Do you aspire to be a lead pastor?

Were you satisfied with the discussion and outcomes? If so, have you talked about this with your current lead pastor?

If not, why not?

Let's be honest. When one person gets chosen from several potential candidates for the lead position, emotions and reactions are not always positive. A hurt person can respond with confusion, anger, feel misunderstood, start gossiping, or engage in a campaign to split the church. They might leave the church and go somewhere else.

It takes a level of maturity to be able to swallow God's will when it stands contrary to what you thought was going to happen and what you thought was clearly God's will. Not being selected for the head pastor is hard. It is tough when the individual served faithfully and thought they had a good chance of becoming the lead pastor. That person may be ready to leave a job, bring their family up to a better financial place, or be prepared to move their ministry forward. When one person is chosen over another, that's death to a dream.

Then there is having to go home and report the news to the wife. Sometimes the spouse has her heart set on being the next first lady. The rejected candidate must deal with his feelings and then try to comfort his wife.

How will your spouse feel if you are not selected? Do they think you deserve the role more than the person who was chosen?

Let's face it, pastoring is a career, and it comes with ambition for the pastor and sometimes the spouse. Sometimes the spouse develops dreams for their pastor/spouse and an identity for themselves that makes it difficult to let go of the lead pastor/First Lady role and challenging to accept that their spouse was not selected for pastoral succession.

Rejection and disappointment are a constant fabric of life. Hopes unrealized, expectations unfulfilled, desires deflated and dreams coming to an end.

It is okay, even healthy, to recognize, "Hey, I'm disappointed. The pastoral search committee looked over me like I didn't even exist. They are planning to put another in place over me, and I've been the one here, serving all this time." Admitting one's disappointment is not a sin; it's a human reaction. But over time, what actions happen after that—that is where the sin could come in.

Be honest with yourself and others. Is God attempting to get you to move on to another ministry, another call? Be open to where this closed-door may lead you. Give up on unrealistic expectations. Ask God to give you knew dreams and visions.

Also, don't fake it. If you are hurt and disappointed, express your emotions to God and others. God is not upset when we bring our feelings into His throne room. Like Mary Magdalene, she had to learn the foot of the cross was the place for her shame, disappointment, anguish, or whatever else she might have felt. Surround yourself with people who will pray with you and encourage you.

If disappointment lingers in our spirit, it leads to discouragement, then depression, then defeat.
So how do we keep the ball from rolling?

My friend Pastor Ray Johnston, who leads one of the largest churches in America, has done extensive research on hope and discouragement. He writes,

When discouragement is present, storm clouds are on the horizon. Something is going to be attacked and potentially destroyed. Every marriage that has broken up, every person who has given up, every company that has gone belly-up, every venture that has failed, every church that I have ever seen a decline, every country that has gone downhill, and certainly every suicide ever committed, all shared one emotion--

discouragement. (The Hope Quotient: Measure it. Raise it. You'll never be the same, 2014)

The Bible is full of disappointed people. Sarah, Rebekah, Rachel, Hannah, and Elizabeth with barrenness issues. Job lost his family and possessions. Joseph grew up in a family that rejected him, even to the point of wanting him dead. Elijah expected accolades for his display on Mt. Carmel, only to have a queen threaten his life. Moses led thousands of complaining folks to the Promised Land, only to get there and hear them say, "We can't go in." Hello! Life does not go as we plan or anticipate.

However, the biblical character who gets the MVP award in this arena has got to be Jonathan, King Saul's son, and David's best friend. He was the king's son, the expected heir to the throne. But Jonathan saw and trusted the hand and plan of God. His father should have been training David instead of trying to kill him. Jonathan was a man who trusted God, not people. He embraced David despite his father's violence toward the next king.

David's own men at Ziklag rejected him as they talked about stoning him. His antidote was to encourage himself in the Lord (1 Samuel 30:6).

Jesus instructed His twelve disciples to shake off the reproach of rejection like dust from their feet and move on to the next town when people rejected their message for the kingdom of God.

Too many people of color in American don't do this well today. Instead, they bear the wounds of rejection, name-calling, and discrimination. Sometimes it is internalized oppression and manifests as anger, insecurity, and mistrust. Some divorced children also carry rejection.

If you are not selected to be the successor, shake off rejection. You could cause a church split or dishonor a once meaningful relationship with the leaving pastor or others in leadership. All too many inherit the spirit of rejection because of a decision made not in your favor. The spirit of rejection can be very contagious and spread to others.

Is your joy in the Lord tied to circumstances? If all is going well, I praise and give thanksgiving. If all is going wrong, I pout. When God brings multiple disappointments back-to-back, could He be teaching us how to respond in both good and bad times? When we experience disappointment, when we have been overlooked, rejected, told we came in second—it can generate doubt, hinder our spiritual growth, and develop into bitterness.

Start thanking God for what good you can see. A lead pastor who asks you to stay and continue supporting the next pastor might be a blessing in disguise. The leading pastor is responsible for the flock, having to answer to God on their behalf. The second man or other staff member is his support. Maybe God does not want you in the heat but one who encourages from the bench. Remember? When championship time comes—everybody gets a ring. But you warmed the bench to earn yours while the other players were out there sweating. God knows the best place for all of us.

Thanksgiving—the antidote to disappointment. Start right away. Maybe you won't spiral down into defeat, depression, and bitterness.

In Psalm 73, the writer starts by expressing his misunderstanding of the situation as he considered others. But then he went into God's house and thought about how God does things. Next thing you know, he had a new perspective.

He knew God, and God knew him.
"Yet, I am always with You.
You hold me by my right hand.
You guide me with Your counsel,

and afterward, You will take me into glory.
Whom have I in heaven but You?
And earth has nothing I desire besides You." (Psalm 73:23-26 NIV).

Is everything resolved? No, not yet. You still have a non-ministry job you don't like. You will have to figure another way to bring in more income into your household. Your wife is still fighting her disappointment and maybe blaming you. And then, there are those in the congregation who continually say, "it should have been you selected, not this other person."

"Though the fig tree does not bud and there are no grapes on the vines, though the olive crop fails and the fields produce no food, though there are no sheep in the pen and no cattle in the stalls, yet I will rejoice in the LORD. I will be joyful in God my Savior." (Habakkuk 3:17-18 NIV)

Things to remember about rejection: it's not a measure of your worth. It's a decision about a position, not a judgment call about you as a person. These things from Ephesians 1:3-14 are still true of you. Look how special we are to God! We are:

*Blessed
*Chosen
*Loved
*Predestined
*Adopted
*Redeemed
*Forgiven
*Lavished with grace
*Included in Christ
*Sealed with the Spirit
*Guaranteed an inheritance

8

Trust and Timing

"Whether a friendship, family relationship or business or personal partnership, any bond is built on trust. Without trust, you have nothing. With it, you can do great things" (Lolly Daskal, "30 quotes on trust that will make you think," inc.com, 2/5/2015).

Trust is essential. Trust is built, not stumbled upon.

Trust. The relationship between a point guard and the team's go-to scorer is built on trust. Championships and victories are within reach if a team has a dynamic duo. "Stockton to Malone" was a common phrase spoken by sports announcers whenever the Utah Jazz played a game. John Stockton was the point guard, and Karl Malone was the go-to scorer and power forward. It was common for Stockton to lead a fast break with the basketball in his capable hands and assist Malone as he cut to the basket.

Other dynamic basketball duos included Penny Hardaway to Shaquille O'Neal, Dwayne Wade to LeBron James, Scottie Pippen to Michael Jordan, and Jason Kidd to Vince Carter. These were dynamic duos because one was a great passer, and the other was a great finisher.

The finisher usually scored with a thunderous dunk. The finisher got most of the applause, but that would never have happened without the passer first releasing the ball and both teammates possessing great timing and trust.

Shaquille O'Neal broke several backboards with his ferocious style of dunking the basketball. LeBron James is soon to overtake Kareem Abdul Jabbar as the all-time leading scorer in the NBA. Jordan is, well, he is Jordan. Enough said! Vince Carter recently ended his career after playing 22 seasons. Carter was nicknamed "Insanity" because he possessed a 43-inch vertical jump. The kids call this "crazy hops." (Okay, they did back in my day, but that was quite a while ago.) His alley-oops and dunks are legendary.

Other dynamic duos were so successful that the fans not only stood to applaud but nicknamed their passes and dunks for the history books. Blake Griffin and Chris Paul were officially deemed "Lob City." Shawn Kemp and Gary Payton were known as "The Rain Man" and "The Glove," respectively. There is no Batman without a Robin. Stephen Curry and Clay Thompson of the Golden State Warriors are known as "The Splash Brothers" for their remarkable accuracy in shooting long three-pointers. Success comes with a successor, and that requires great trust.

Now imagine if these NBA passers could not trust their receivers for the alley-oop. If they hesitated when passing the ball or second-guessed. As Payton was about to pass to Kemp, he paused, lost confidence, and changed his mind, passing instead to another player. No, no, no! Teammates have got to trust each other, or the alley-oop will never make it to the basket for the dunk. There will be no score.

Go back to any of those names mentioned as the top alley-oops of all time. Ask, how was trust developed between the passer and the receiver? I'm convinced they would tell you about hours of practice and hanging together. They had to get to know one another, observe each other's playing styles, and be aware of their strengths and weaknesses. Then the confidence grows. Alley-oops look easy. Even coincidental. But that is not the case. They don't just happen.

Humans don't automatically trust one another. We need to talk, hang out, get to know one another, especially in a pastoral succession when the enemy can easily creep in and cause insecurities, jealousy, and divisions.

I am thankful that Pastor Marcus and I developed a relationship decades before we even started praying and dialoguing about succession. I was his former youth pastor. We reconnected almost ten years before he became the lead pastor. As I look back, I can see that the Lord helped us to build trust back then. The confidence built previously helped as I realized he was God's pick to take over the church. During the nearly two-year succession process, he and I worked hard to keep open communication lines. We shared fears and concerns both personally and for our families. I knew it was imperative to keep him close to me, so part of the succession plan included bringing him on staff full-time to co-lead with me and for up-close mentorship. This phase resisted any intimidation or apprehensiveness and gave assurance, stability, and trust to everyone on the team.

This assurance is crucial for everyone on the team to relax with the transition process. It is a matter of trust and knowing that God is in control. He is setting us all up for a smooth alley-oop. In the end, the church leaders, congregation, and community witnessing and watching the transaction will glorify God and stand up and cheer.

The lead pastor and the successor must have a mutually trusting and honoring relationship before, during, and after the handoff. Moses demonstrated no insecurities as he poured into Joshua without reservation. Moses was not the type of leader to withhold information that would help Joshua to succeed. Instead, he lived a generous and open-handed life.

Too many lead pastors remind me of a story one of my members told me. This member grew up in the deep, deep South of the United States. He spoke with a southern drawl as he described how union workers dealt with new employees. Instead of mentoring them and sharing information on working with the equipment, they pointed the new employee towards the unfamiliar piece and said, "Der it is." By this, they were saying, "There it is waiting for you to learn how to operate on your own. Good luck, but really, I hope that you fail and get fired. That way, the company will still need my services, and I will be secure."

The Apostle Paul carried no such attitude. Instead, he presented himself as a secure spiritual father and mentor. "Therefore, I testify to you this day that I [am] innocent of the blood of all men. For I have not shunned to declare to you the whole counsel of God." (Acts 20:27) Nor was insecurity the case for Moses. He poured love and the fear of God into the next upcoming generation so that when Moses died, Joshua stood equipped and ready to lead Israel.

Players earn one another's trust. Through their example, both on and off the court, a team member knows to look out for the leader's or passer's direction. They even can sense his intentions to pass the ball, sometimes without a conversation. That's how a teammate knows to get down the court even faster than the leader. The leader trusts his teammate to always perform his job to the best of his ability.

Both the passer and the receiver must be confident, competent, and have mutual trust. I trust you with the ball. I trust you to pass me the ball at the right time.

Moses and Joshua developed their sense of trust and timing by spending time with God and each other in the wilderness.

*Ecclesiastes 3:8 reminds us there is a time for everything, including a time for war. So, when it was time to go to war with the Amalekites, Moses chose Joshua. (Exodus 17:9)

*When it was time to receive the tablet of Commandments, Joshua was right at Moses' side. (Exodus 24:13)

*Joshua lingered at the Tent of Meeting long after Moses left when it was time to listen in God's presence. (Exodus 33:11)

*When it was time to send spies into the Promised Land, Moses selected Joshua as a representative. (Numbers 13:16)

*When it was time to speak up and kill the spirit of fear and rebellion after the spies' excursion, Joshua and Caleb spoke boldly. (Numbers 14:6)

*When it was time, God let Moses know the perfect time to pass the ball to Joshua. "So, the LORD said to Moses, 'Take Joshua, son of Nun, a man in whom is the spirit of leadership, and lay your hand on him. Have him stand before Eleazar, the priest, and the entire assembly and commission him in their presence. Give him some of your authority so the whole Israelite community will obey him.'" (Numbers 27:18-20 NIV)

Timing. After trust is built, there is still a matter of timing. Not every potential pastoral successor can handle the pass. In this case, the pass is set up with a conversation that begins with, "Would you like to be my successor one day?" Their immaturity may cause them to hear "today" instead of "one day." They might start dreaming and running ahead of the predecessor with ambition and poor timing and forget the call to serve until the ball is passed.

As it relates to successors, timing is crucial. Some potential successors came my way, but I did not pass the ball in their direction. Why? Impatience. A potential successor must have the ability to watch and wait.

In basketball, if a player is going for an alley-oop, timing is essential.

The receiver must be in the right place at the right time. If the receiver jumps too soon before the ball is passed, they will land without scoring. The ball will be turned over and go out of bounds.

Some successors are not ready or are not a good fit for the lead pastor role. This is not a bad thing, nor does it label the person as a bad person. It simply means this individual may not be ready or does not have the skills or character needed for the position, or God is not currently calling them to this position. The Lord might be trying to say, "You are in the wrong field; I want you to teach in a Bible school or be a chaplain."

In basketball and pastoral successions, timing can make or break an alley-oop pass.

At the right time, the passer has got to throw the perfect lob pass. Or, at the very least, a lob that's in the vicinity of a teammate at the right time. The receiver must time the jump to catch the ball, control it, and dunk it in a seamless motion. Sometimes the timing is right, but the pass is a little off target. The receiver must make timely and agile adjustments, again relying on a personal set of skills to help the team score.

I remember the first time I dunked a basketball. I was 18 and playing at my favorite playground court. Although it was exciting, I got more excitement out of making passes for others to score. That was how Earvin Johnson Jr. felt also.

I first met Earvin "Magic" Johnson on television. Magic was drafted into the NBA by the Los Angeles Lakers. He thrilled Michigan State Spartans' fans and triumphed over teams as he made spectacular passes to his teammates. But Earvin became "Magic" Johnson because of his ability to pass the ball, especially throwing the alley-oop lob to his teammate, Greg Kelser. In my opinion, Magic is the most outstanding passer the game has ever seen. But he had some tremendous teammates who could receive and finish also.

I've witnessed some amazing passers in my lifetime. LeBron James is the best in today's game, as I write in 2021. I've watched and admired John Stockton, Jason Kid, Chris Paul, Steve Nash, Mark Jackson, and Jason "White Chocolate" Williams. Williams got the nickname "White Chocolate" because of his flair in passing and ball handling. He was even famous for creating an elbow pass. But none were as gifted as Magic Johnson.

His 6' 9'" frame gave Magic tremendous court awareness and vision. He could see the court over his opponents. Magic perfected the alley-oop in college and the NBA.

The alley-oop is stunning to watch—if well-done. It is a thing of beauty. It requires skill and chemistry to pull it off--teamwork, precision passing, and impeccable timing.

Coach John Wooden of the UCLA Bruins was a champion and a Christian gentleman both on and off the court. His basketball team's style of play was old-school fundamental, yet he made room for each player's unique abilities. One of my favorite quotes by him summarizes this chapter as it relates to the patience required from the successor and the timing of the pass released by the predecessor. He said, "Be quick but don't hurry."

May the Lord grace both the current and the next lead pastor with a timed succession that is done God's way and in God's time.

9

Strength

Chris Broussard of FOX Sports wants sports fans to know that the best basketball player in the family of Reggie Miller, the Indiana Pacers' legend, and NBA Hall of Famer, was not Reggie but his sister, Cheryl Miller. On January 26, 1982, in California, Cheryl scored a record 105 points for Riverside Polytechnic High School; they beat Riverside Norte Vista 179-15. In that game, she became the first woman to dunk a basketball. Cheryl continued to break records and set milestones in college and the Olympics before a knee injury sidelined her basketball career. However, in 1996, Cheryl broke down barriers even after her playing days had ended by joining the TBS and TNT broadcasting family as the first female analyst to call a nationally televised NBA game.

There have been many door-busting female pioneers in basketball besides Miller.

The WNBA began in 1997 and has come a long way. But some things have not changed--namely, the respect and salary that women in professional basketball get compared to men.

The average salary for a female NBA player is $71,000 versus $6.4 million in the men's NBA, according to Christian Jope of wsn.com ("NBA vs. WNBA," 7/18/2019). Stephen Curry is one of the highest-earning NBA players, making an estimated $40 million per year. At the same time, Brittany Griner Briner is the highest-earning WNBA player at $113,000 per year.

There are plenty of messages out there about why women are called to pastoral ministry. I've listed several in the resource section of this book. Women in ministry is not my area of debate. However, I do want to acknowledge this fact: in several congregations after a history of male lead pastors, a woman now sits in that place.

Strength. If you are a woman in this role, I remind you of God's words to Joshua "Only be strong and very courageous." And if you are in a decision-making role in the church or part of the pastoral search committee and looking at the candidate, bank on it--a female resume will inevitably be submitted. I pray that you offer encouragement and strengthen the role of women in the church.

In our congregation, the successor selected was a male. I positioned him for success, lent my influence, voice, and credibility. I cheer for him and support his leadership and vision with the loyalty of Jonathan to David. If my alley-oop receiver had been a woman, I would have worked for her success in the same manner.

I understand this is a controversial issue. For some of you, your beliefs about women in ministry, particularly in the lead pastor role, won't let you even read this chapter. You are tempted to skip over these pages. Because you have already concluded that a woman in a ministry leadership position will not happen, there is no need for consideration. You have your biblical ground for dismissing it, or you are a part of a denomination that takes a stand against women pastors.

Others of you are open, incredibly open to the possibility. It's not a problem for you to pray about it and do some teaching from the pulpit to prepare your governing board and congregation's hearts.

In my own words, I am a recovering Christian chauvinist. I didn't always believe that a woman could serve in a lead pastor, elder, or church overseeing role. Before God repositioned me to succeed in my church's lead pastor role, he adjusted my beliefs and actions towards women in ministry.

My transformation started with scripture. I saw that women served in ministry in the early church alongside Peter, James, John, and Paul. In my opinion, Paul wrote to Timothy to correct the aggressive women who were dominating the Ephesians church in 1 Timothy 2:9-15, and he was not discriminating based upon gender. According to Galatians 3:28, God calls our Spirit into His family and the ministry. He is not as concerned about gender as we seem to be. We don't determine if a woman is called and which gifts or offices she is endowed by the Holy Spirit to receive. God does, and He did.

As we are prone to our opinions and interpretations of women in ministry, brotherly love and mutual respect must be centered on issues not critical to our salvation. This quote, "In essentials, unity; in non-essentials, liberty; in all things, charity," attributed to St. Augustine of Hippo (North Africa) and other theologians, should be a guiding principle. The Bible must be our final authority.

Only two passages in the entire New Testament seem to cancel the call to ministry for women (1 Corinthians 14:34-36 and 1 Timothy 2:12). I would propose that instead of prohibition, Paul is dealing with local problems in specific churches that needed correction.

There are various interpretations of what Paul was limiting when he said, "women should remain silent in the churches. They are not allowed to speak" (1 Corinthians 14:34). Paul used a word to limit the speech of women (sigato) that previously has been used to restrict the speech of those speaking in tongues if there is no interpretation (1 Corinthians 14:28) and of prophets if a prophecy is given to another person (v. 30). It is only under such specific circumstances that the speech of tongues speakers, prophets, and women are to be silenced in the church. (Assemblies of God, "The role of women in ministry," August 2011, ag.org)

Some women dressed immodestly (1 Timothy 2:9). 1 Timothy 5:13 Paul corrects younger widows. "And besides, they learn to be idle, wandering about from house to house, and not only idle but also gossips and busybodies, saying things which they ought not."

The above passages should be examined next to Paul's other statements, which do not prohibit women in ministry. The Apostle Paul was a strong advocate for women in ministry, and so am I. He consistently affirmed women ministers who labored to build
the Church of Jesus Christ, and so do I. As a Pentecostal, I believe we are in the days of grace promised by the Father where He will pour out His Spirit and men and women will prophesy, according to Acts 2:16-18.

When Jesus walked the earth, His main agenda was to bring God's salvation to the world and save man from sin. We know and acknowledge that. But if you observe Jesus' interactions, He also had other agendas He attended to while here. One was to elevate the status of women. Until that time, Jewish women were lower-class citizens. A man could divorce his wife for burning his supper or losing his socks in the wash. Society during that time considered women subservient to men, only needed to get pregnant to carry on a man's seed or legacy and care for the children.

Jesus talked with women and came to their defense. He let the world know that they may not be necessary to you, but they are essential to the Father and Him. Jesus gave women critical roles to execute for His kingdom. Women have tremendous influence and authority in scripture; God employed them to be His instrument.

Rev. Dr. Donna Childs is the pastor of Tabernacle Community Baptist Church in Milwaukee, WI. Her succession similarities to those of Dr. Marcus Arrington are amazing. Like Marcus, Pastor Donna had been a longtime member of her home church. She was born and raised in Tabernacle. Similarly, she too came out of the business and education arena. She was a teacher and then Principal of a Christian school. Before that, she was a basketball coach at a Milwaukee Public High School. Pastor Donna understands the art of making a successful pass both on the basketball court and in the professional realms of the educational arena and the church. Her educational background causes her to think with a growth, mentoring, and nurturing mindset. She says, "I think that leaders always should be thinking how to grow the next potential leader in their church."

Pastor Donna served her former lead pastor as a quasi-assistant pastor. No one knew that he would be called away. Or that Pastor Donna would become the next pastor. Upon the vacancy, the church started a nationwide search for a new pastor. Meanwhile, the congregation appointed Pastor Donna as Interim Pastor. The Search Committee narrowed applications down to three individuals they would bring before the church one by one for a vote. The committee recommended Pastor Donna to the church, and the church elected her during the pandemic in August 2020. "The things I learned as a principal and a director equipped and prepared me for this position as a shepherd. Some synonymous things take place as a principal and now as a pastor."

I asked Pastor Donna about the topic of women in ministry and those who oppose female pastors. She offers church leadership and female successors this advice. "The Lord is sovereign, and He can do what He wants to do, how He wants to do it when He wants to do it. God called me. Pastoring is not something that I would have chosen. It was not my career path. I have two brothers in pastoral ministry, and I still did not want to do what they did. I heard some of those things they went through. So that was not my goal to do that. God uses who He desires. The biggest thing I say to women in ministry is that your role is to prepare yourself. You do what you have been called to do, prepare yourself, study, be available, and then let God open the doors for you. My role is to rest and see what God does."

Rev. Dr. Joy L. Gallon ("Pastor Joy") pastors St. Mark AME Church in Milwaukee, WI. The AME church is the oldest African American denomination in the USA, established in 1787. The AME church bishops are elected for life and bound by bylaws to retire upon the General Conference nearest their 75th birthday. Presiding elders, appointed by the bishops, supervise pastors and churches in their respective districts and make recommendations to the bishop as to which pastors should be assigned to a church (the charge).

It was in this system that Pastor Joy was given the charge at St. Mark. She understands and has lived several unique successions. Before her current role, she held a high and prestigious position as a Christian education district director." I knew that season had come to an end, and people still can't grasp the fact that I gave that up willingly."

She sees the issue of sexism in the church much like the sin of racism. Both are rooted in power and control. Women are not being ordained and appointed to lead churches at the same rate as men. Some denominations don't give women the space to be what God has called them to be. Because she is a single female, the head of the household presents unique challenges and could have been used to ostracize her and keep her in a certain place. Fortunately, she had men who went to bat for her. It came at a great personal sacrifice to go against the status quo for some of the men.

Pastor Joy reminds me of US Vice-President Kamala Harris, the first female and first woman of color. Harris is inspiring young girls of color to dream that they can also become world leaders. Both women are blazing trails for future female leaders and successors. Pastor Joy says, "At the church where I am now, there are enough men with wives and daughters that want me to succeed, and they can buy in because they can see their wives and daughters in me."

She encourages male predecessors to have several important conversations regarding preparation for succession. These conversations will inform a lot of the ways one interacts with the congregation and successor. "First, have an internal conversation with yourself. Ask yourself what and when is the Lord telling me it's time to do something else?" This first conversation also prepares you for the next series of discussions with your family unit, then the church leadership, as well as the congregation to the fact that "I will not always be the woman who leads."

Rev. Dr. Beth Backes is a pastor/church planter of The Table in Seattle, Washington, and a denominational women's network leader that serves 380 pastors. As a network leader of women ministers, she understands, embraces, and normalizes the seasonal mindset and encourages potential predecessors to adopt it too. Her perspective is that she is the leader for this season but is not in a permanent placement. Therefore, she often intentionally drops in thoughts about "when the next leader is here" during women's meetings or conversations. In this way, succession becomes normalized.

Pastor Beth recognizes that Reformed theology has made it difficult for women to ascend to specific leadership roles, especially those seen as male-only roles. "Many teach," Pastor Beth says, "that a woman's place is in her home, submitting to her husband. She shouldn't even be in the workplace. This kind of teaching ignores both the biblical history and modern-day testimonies of women pioneering churches and ministries. Women have evangelized nations overseas and local people groups."

Pastor Beth says her District Superintendent, Rev. Don Ross, gave her an alley-oop to her current role. He is a male leader who normalizes succession through a visual on his desk. Don has a jar of marbles representing the number of weeks he still has left in his current tenure. He reminds visitors to his office that everything that we do is temporary. It has a beginning and an end date.

"You must normalize the fact that a leader will come after me," says Pastor Beth. "This kind of thinking helps people to hold leadership positions more loosely. We all have seen leaders who keep their roles with a death grip and refuse to let them go. Sadly, some still hold on, even when it becomes unhealthy and evident that they should let it go."

Unfortunately, too many male predecessors tend to look to their male college friends and counterparts to pass things off. Sticking with close male associates could be called the "good old boys' network." Women might receive the invitation to preach only on Mother's Day because some men fail to see they have qualifications that go far beyond women and family issues.

Pastor Beth offers some practical wisdom for both predecessors and potential successors.

1. Normalize succession. Why? It's a refreshing period. It takes the pressure off the people you lead, who will not make unhealthy attachments to you as the leader and expect you to always be in that role. Also, it takes the pressure off you, the leader, so that you might be free to pursue other initiatives in your lifetime.

2. Recognize when the vision spark is low. That could be a sign for succession. When things that used to give you energy now drain you, they are heavy and a burden. It might be time to pass the ball.

3. When you, the predecessor, begin to sense succession approaching, start looking for someone to pass an alley-oop. Pull them close to yourself and make them part of your team. Now you can both access personal readiness, competence, compatibility, chemistry, character, and calling as well as organizational DNA upfront. Lastly, you can then start having exploratory conversations about succession. Do it in the strictest confidence.

4. Don't name your successor without accessing their readiness. If you are premature with the announcement, it could manifest the successor's immaturity and cause them to start dreaming and planning too early. These dreams can become relational and organizational nightmares.

5. Bring the organization's decision leaders to your mindset and conversations to make whatever financial adjustments and portfolio changes are necessary.

6. Advice for potential female successors. You must take yourself seriously because no one else will take yourself seriously if you don't take yourself seriously. Language is essential, so refer to yourself as a pastor or a ministry leader in conversation. Talk about your education, talk about your experience, keep it focused on ministry-related topics, even when they want to sideline and go other directions.

7. Female successors should make friends with their male colleagues. Both male and female pastors tend to self-isolate. "At ministry-related social gatherings, we tend to self-segregate. Women talk to the women, and men talk to the men. Then we wonder, why aren't women being hired or being considered as a successor." When she walks into a mixed-gender room with ministry leadership, Beth has pointed out that she often sees women in the corner. So, she would make a beeline for the

men, ask them how their ministry was doing, what God was doing in their lives, and where they saw their church's future.

Pastor Beth also added, "I had to learn to redirect the conversation because as soon as I walked up to a cluster of men, they looked at me and started asking me about my children, about my husband, and my hair color. I had to bring the conversation back. No, I don't want to talk about those things. I want to talk about ministry. You know, those men ended up being the ones who started calling me, asking me to fill their pulpits when they were on vacation.

And as you know, of course, Mother's Day is the big one. Men always ask women to preach then. I always think, you know, 'I can preach other days of the year too.' You would think that would be my day off. I am a mother too."

As a male predecessor, I agree with Pastor Beth. Most men are not going to initiate friendships with women ministers for fear of the relationship appearing inappropriate. Therefore, healthy succession with female leaders will require maturity and security for both players. Neither party needs to be afraid nor deterred by the awkwardness. The kingdom is at stake. Let's make the pass. "Finally, my brethren, be strong in the Lord and in the power of His might" (Ephesians 6:10).

10

Finishing Well

An alley-oop is both a beautiful and risky play. The leader lobs the ball just barely out of reach so that his teammate is the only one who can catch it. The receiver must aggressively pursue the ball. In other words, "the leader does his best to set his team members up for success, but the results are up to the one catching the ball. It could end up as a rim-rattling dunk that reverses the tide of a game, or it can be a monumental failure worthy of ESPN's Not-the-Top-10 list. It doesn't take much for an alley-oop to turn into an alley-oops" (Ron Edmondson, "Leadership and the Art of the Alley-oop," 2/2012, ronedmondson.com).

I will never forget the 2021 NBA Championship Finals between the Phoenix Suns and "my" hometown Milwaukee Bucks. The Suns won the first two games of the series on their home court. Many people thought the championship was over because of the Suns' 2-0 lead. However, it is the best out of 7 games. It ain't over after a few games.

The Bucks returned home to Milwaukee and returned the favor to the Suns by defending their home court and winning the next two games. Series tied at 2-2. Now it was a best of 3 games series.

Game 5 was crucial back in Phoenix. The Suns were dominant in the first half of the game, leading by as many as 16 points. The Bucks showed resiliency and came back to take the lead. Late in the game, it seemed inevitable that the Suns had the momentum as they cut the Bucks lead down to one point with less than a minute left in the game.

Then Jrue Holiday and Giannis Antetekounmpo demonstrated the art of the alley-oop and the key of finishing strong.

Just as the Sun's leading scorer Devin Booker was making a turn to shoot and try to take the lead, he committed a turnover as Jrue came from behind and stripped him of the ball. To finish strong, you have to have strong and ready hands to receive the ball so that you don't drop it.

Jrue raced back up the court towards his team's basket and had an opportunity to pull the ball out and run out the clock. This strategy could have preserved the Bucks' one-point lead. Instead, he made a risky decision to throw an alley-oop pass to Giannis, who was also running down the court a few strides behind Jrue. Just as Giannis reached the free-throw line, he gave Jrue a quick hand signal to alley-oop the ball. Jrue had court awareness and lobbed a pass high in the air over the head of the Sun's defender to a place where only Giannis could catch it. One long stride later, he leaped in the air, caught, and dunked a perfectly timed pass.

The home-court crowd was shocked into silence while the hundreds of thousands of Milwaukee Bucks' fans watching at home erupted in cheers. The Bucks sealed a game five victory and went on to win game six back in Milwaukee. This win secured their second NBA championship. The first one was won in 1971.

When he was interviewed after the game, Jrue said, "I just threw it as high as I could and to a place where only Giannis could go get it." He wasn't worried that pass was too high for Giannis to catch either. That's why they call him the "Greek Freak." The players demonstrated excellent teamwork. Both had trust and confidence in each other to pass, receive, and finish strong. Their efforts resulted in a championship.

Finish well. Also, beautiful, and risky is pastoral succession. God has entrusted His Church and people into the hands of spiritual leaders. If a pastoral succession is botched at any point, the other team, Satan's team, could score for their kingdom. Yes, senior pastors get sick or die too soon. Yes, leaders might make mistakes and must redo plans. Or successors turn out to be not the one. All of that can happen and more. We that are passers and receivers must do all in our control to finish well.

The dream teams. Let's look, listen, and learn from four biblical dream teams who all finished well.

*Paul to Timothy. I have fought the good fight, finished the race, and kept the faith (2 Timothy 4:7 NIV). Paul was intentional about raising and releasing the next generation of leaders. In the Epistles, he lists dozens of men and women on his ministry team. Acts 16:1-3 describes how his number one draft pick, Timothy, joined the team. Timothy's natural father was an unnamed Greek man, but he and Paul possessed a spiritual connection like a father and son. Some of us may have the privilege of passing the ministry on to our sons or daughters. But most of the time, God must mastermind the spiritual DNA.

Why did Paul die with such assurance? I believe he knew he was talking to Timothy, his spiritual son, not just a servant. All humans are at least 98% the same in DNA or deoxyribonucleic acid. The 2% represents our differences. When praying about a person to step into your shoes as a shepherd over God's flock, you want to be sure you are getting a true son or daughter and not just a servant.

Spiritual sons and servants look alike and even act similarly but have some significant differences internally. These similarities explain why some "servants" can get away with making the team. They receive the leadership pass while secretly and inwardly, they can be focused upon their own agenda. It is because they share 98% of the organizational or predecessor traits while having 2% of a servant's heart and are still not a "son" or "daughter." Dr. Gordon E. Bradshaw notes that the true character of a servant surfaces when ministry circumstances get tough. For the servant, DNA stands for I "Do Not Agree" with my spiritual father. However, true spiritual sons are loyal to the mission and mandates of their pastor and their spiritual father. For them, DNA stands for "Do Not Abort"! (Bradshaw, Gordon E. (2011), Authority for assignment, Kingdom House Publishers, Lakebay, Washington.)

Pastoral succession will flourish when the ball is passed to a faithful son. Paul ended his life and letter to Timothy in complete confidence that Timothy would take the principles he'd taught him and pass them on to faithful men. Players would not merely pass the ball to team members for one game but would be passed through several generations.

We need faithful sons and daughters. But likewise, you want to be sure you have the genuine characteristics of a parent—not just an instructor or a teacher.

*Abraham and Isaac. Abraham answered, "God himself will provide the lamb for the burnt offering, my son." And the two of them went on together (Genesis 22:8 NIV).

Abraham was successful at passing on his faith to the generations after him. He is revered as the "father of the faith" of Christians, Muslims, and Jews. If you and I are looking for true sons, then we cannot be mere instructors as passers of the faith and the leadership ball. We must be fathers. The Apostle Paul reminded His spiritual children in the Corinthian church, "For though ye have ten thousand instructors in Christ, yet [have ye] not many fathers: for in Christ Jesus, I have begotten you through the gospel." (1 Corinthians 4:15 (KJV)

Paul used the word "pedagogues," meaning a boy leader or one who takes children to school, to describe an instructor. An instructor is essential but has limited contact and a fixed contract. They serve until it is quitting time or when school is out of session. Instructors also teach limited lessons or subjects and to limited ages or grades.

Instructors do not have physical contact with their students. However, parents live with their children and become their first and primary teachers. Being a spiritual father is much different. Being a father is a full-time job. He parents his children 24/7/365.

In Genesis 15:2-3, Abraham cried out to God to have heirs. He was not content to leave his inheritance to his servant Eliezer. Lord, turn the hearts of the fathers back to the children. And the hearts of the children go back to their fathers. Give us spiritual and natural children who will trust, follow, and obey the word and ways of God long after we are dead.

*Moses and Joshua. "And Joshua the son of Nun was full of the spirit of wisdom; for Moses had laid his hands upon him: and the children of Israel hearkened unto him and did as the LORD commanded Moses" (Deuteronomy 34:9). Moses had sons, but they are not mentioned. Even though Moses had natural sons, they were not God's choice to lead the Israelites out of Egypt and into the Promised land. Moses saw Joshua as a son.

Sometimes our "son" is a woman. Sometimes our successor will be a spiritual offspring rather than a natural one. Paul laid his hands upon Timothy, transferring leadership, power, and authority. Moses did so to Joshua as well. Sometimes in life and scripture, natural-born sons succeeded their fathers, as with Aaron the priest and his sons. In Caleb's case, his daughters succeeded him. (Numbers 11:16-17; 25-29)

Spiritual leadership is a heavy burden and serious responsibility. Spiritual sons lift the loads that the fathers carry. Joshua relieved Moses and received the delegated responsibility of fighting the Amalekites. Moses's hand still grew tired and his body weary as he prayed for victory for Joshua from the mountaintop. Aaron and Hur lifted his arms and set a rock underneath him to pray from a posture of rest. The result of their unity and mutual submission was a great victory for the entire team of Israelites.

If you desire to be a successor one day and are in a support role or position, ask yourself these questions. Are you lifting your leaders' hands? Are you refreshing them to carry the burden of vision? Or are you weight and drag that deters them from the big picture?

*Elijah and Elisha. "When they had crossed, Elijah said to Elisha, 'Tell me, what can I do for you before I am taken from you?' 'Let me inherit a double portion of your spirit,' Elisha replied." (2 Kings 2:9 NIV)

Greg Harper is one of my best friends and one of our church's elders. He has a motto he often uses, "Trust and obey--Just run the plays." A genuine spiritual father is like a coach who draws up plays for the whole team's success. Sons run the plays the father draws up. Ever since Elijah was commanded to commission Elisha as his successor, it meant that Elisha would have to run the plays of Elijah until he was ready to draw up his own plays. Those days came when the Lord sent heavenly chariots and horsemen to swoosh Elijah up to heaven. Then Elisha, the younger successor, picked up his spiritual father's cloak and began leading in the power of the Holy Spirit with a double portion.

Elisha also knew that his success as a leader depended on his having spiritual sons who would run the plays. You can only build and succeed with sons. Servants take away from the father's vision, but sons take the initiative to build it up. Servants serve inside the house, never initiate, simply do whatever they are told. We learn this lesson in 2 Kings 6:1-7. The sons of Elisha, the prophet, took the initiative to build newer and better living quarters. Sons often have more modern and better ideas than the previous leadership. They have a desire for expansion and upgrading. They feel that the place they currently live in is too small. Yet, Elisha's sons asked for their spiritual father's blessing. As a result, they worked together, miraculously, and in harmony.

As the sons built, they encountered challenges. One of them lost a borrowed ax-head in the Jordan River. They brought the problem to Elisha, and he provided a miracle, causing the ax-head to float (see 2 Kings 6:1-7).

The sons built, and Elisha blessed! When sons build and run the plays, the fathers bless the sons, allowing their new ideas in the building, and succeed.

Perhaps you are like me, in a season of life and age where you sense the time to shift from the lead role. Relax and rejoice over the spiritual son relationships. God has blessed you with these contacts. If you don't have those close relationships, start looking and listening for your successor. You will recognize them from their pursuit of you. They desire you, not what you have or can give them. You will know them from their hunger for spiritual truth.

They also don't just want head knowledge but to apply the truth they receive. You will distinguish them by their speech. Sons and fathers use the language of family. I often corrected church members for saying, "I wish your church had a food pantry," or "your choir didn't sound so good today." As a spiritual father, I would correct them and remind them that this is OUR church. Sons and fathers use "we, our, and us."

You will be able to identify them by their willingness to receive your correction and chastisement. True fathers correct without criticism and put-downs (Hebrews 12). Servants pass the blame on others, always making it someone else's fault, "they made me do it." Servants refuse to accept responsibility. They are still trying to explain or reason away their behavior.

When you find your successor, spend intentional time with them. Don't just do ministry work together but do life together. Enjoy each other's presence. Pass on to them the privilege and responsibility of carrying on God's truth and tradition.

"Too often we make the mistake of remembering what we should forget--our hurts, failures, and disappointments; and we forget what we should remember--our victories, accomplishments and the times we have made it through." (Joel Osteen, azquotes.com, "disappointment")

I I

Who Dropped the Ball?

Mistakes. The USA 4 x 100 men's relay teams have dominated the track and field world for decades. However, in the 2021 Olympics in Tokyo, the men did not even make the finals--hocking and considered unacceptable. Speed was not the issue; communication and teamwork were. Team USA included the world's fastest man Trayvon Bromell who led off as the first leg runner. But a bad baton pass on the second to the third leg cost them a spot in the finals.

A lousy baton hand-off is historically a nightmare for USA relay teams. Runners have been disqualified because the baton was dropped or not passed cleanly within the passing zone.

Pastoral succession is an exchange of the baton of leadership. The baton must be passed--not pried from the leader's hands. It must be passed smoothly and within the exchange zone. An efficient transfer of leadership requires timing, trust, and teamwork on the part of all involved. That USA track team will long remember the embarrassment and disappointment due to their mishandling the baton.

It is human nature for people to remember the bad things you did more than all the good you contributed. I am not immune to painful memories. My athletic prowess and basketball skills accelerated more and more after high school than during those early years. So, a real attraction was to have the opportunity to reunite with former classmates 30 plus years later and play in my high school alumni basketball game. It was an even sweeter thrill to play against our cross-town rivals.

During that game, I started strong offensively, and towards the middle of the game, the coach began trusting me with the ball as the point guard. The game was coming down to the wire, and we were down by just a few points. I had the ball at the top of the key. One of my teammates was posting up in the paint and demanding the ball. "Give me the ball, give me the ball!"

My mind suddenly clouded with who he was. Thirty years earlier, he had been our team's leading scorer, a city conference, and all-state star. He was highly recruited by colleges and even played semi-pro basketball.

I made a point guard mistake by listening to my teammates more than listening to the coach. I made a bad pass to him. It was hurried and weak, and we turned the ball over. The other team stole the ball, and we lost the game.

Okay, so that was not the end of the world. Life goes on after a loss in an alumni basketball game. If leaders drop the ball during pastoral succession, the stakes and the consequences are higher. A loose ball is not good news. The ball could end up in the hands of the opposite team--Satan and his cohorts. Dropped passes in succession now means that the whole team must hurry back down the court to play defense and hopefully take the ball back with a steal before Satan makes it to the basket.

During that alumni game defeat, I learned several important lessons and my nearly three decades of pastoral leadership that apply to succession. See if they apply to you. As the predecessor (point guard) passing the ball on, you must learn to silence the crowd's screams. People in the crowd (church and community) may seek to dictate your actions on the court. You must listen to the voice and instructions of God, your coach, even while your teammates are urgently demanding, "Give me the ball!" And at the same time, you are trying to control the fears associated with the risk of succession battling within yourself. If not controlled, it will likely lead to a bad pass and an unnecessary turnover.

Moses is my hero! Not only is he an excellent example of a leader who silenced the crowd so that he could focus on the voice of God as he made a successful pass to Joshua, but Moses also did this knowing that he was being replaced due to a foolish mistake.

Moses struck the rock out of anger one day, and he instantly disqualified himself from going into the promised land (Numbers 20:10-12). Nevertheless, Moses moved out of the way and prepared the people to go on without him. In addition, he prepared Joshua to be the best leader that he could be.

Sadly, some leaders are like King Saul--fired and forced to leave their leadership roles. The reason might be a foolish act like Moses', or it might be moral failure or ineffectiveness in the position.

In Saul's case, it's obvious. He messed up and disobeyed the Lord. God said, "Saul, you're out, and David is in; he will be Israel's next king. You are not following My instructions; your head has gotten too big." However, Saul didn't say, "Okay, God let me step down. I will train David and teach him everything I know. Especially how not to follow in my missteps." No. King Saul did not easily retire, nor did he willingly accept God's selection of David as his successor. As far as we know, Saul never repented of his disobedience that cost him the throne. And train David, yes, he did. He taught him alright, how to be a fugitive, running for his life. Saul got jealous of David, angry about this new arrangement.

He felt if anyone should take the throne, it should have been his son Jonathan.

Accept your new season and refuse to get bitter. Saul got caught up in a bitter spirit. Moses just said, "Okay, God, what are my next steps." Saul allowed that bitter spirit to control him. He thought he could reverse God's plan. All he had to do was to kill David.

Lead pastors beware of a jealous King Saul spirit. Test yourself if you are in the lead pastor role. When you are away on vacation, and the associate pastor or potential successor preaches and gets more accolades than you, what do you do? How do you feel? Do you rejoice with them or waddle in rejection?

What is your emotional health quotient? Can you prepare your successor with all that you have and all that is in your heart? Or do you hold back the wisdom and practical knowledge you have acquired? Can you prepare the congregation for the successor by celebrating them in advance of their arrival in the new role? Your successor needs you to be their champion, defeating the enemies and clearing the obstacles they will undoubtedly encounter. I have loved the new season of celebrating Pastor Marcus and supported him with my prayers, presence, participation, and promotion of his vision. Moses is my hero because he didn't take his ball and go home when he dropped the ball. He confessed, accepted his consequences, picked up the ball, and passed it onto the next God chosen leader.

Moses was not the only person in the Bible to drop the ball before transferring leadership. Joshua took the ball and made a successful crossover into the promised land. Just before his death, Joshua passed leadership responsibility to the Jewish fathers (see Joshua 24). He charged them with the famous words, "Choose for yourselves this day whom you will serve." A key lesson for successors, every person must make a personal choice accepting personal responsibility for their spiritual journey with God. No child, young adult, or generation can continue to rely on the strength of their parent's or predecessor's relationship with God. You must make it personal. Unfortunately, after Joshua died, the faith of the people also died.

The people pledged to serve the Lord, but unfortunately, backslid on their oath. "And Joshua the son of Nun, the servant of the LORD, died, being a hundred and ten years old. And also, all that generation were gathered unto their fathers: and there arose another generation after them, which knew not the LORD, nor yet the works which he had done for Israel." (Judges 2:8, 10)

How could this have occurred? How can it be prevented in your church and succession plan? Recognize that each successive generation is in danger of declining in pursuit and passion for God because the temptation is great to rest on the previous generations' accomplishments. Abraham passed on his blessings and wealth to Isaac. Then, this father did the same for Jacob. The most vulnerable generation was the third one, Jacob's. It is the one more likely to become cold, callous, or lukewarm towards God.

Fortunately, God was not surprised by this next generation after Joshua. He already knew they would drop the ball, so He put judges in place to help them along. The Judges' generation never saw God defeat a giant or get water from a rock or manna from heaven. Therefore, they asked the question that Gideon asked in Judges 6:13. "Gideon said to Him, 'O my Lord if the LORD is with us, why then has all this happened to us? And where are all His miracles which our fathers told us about, saying, "Did not the LORD bring us up from Egypt?" In Judges, significantly few Jewish people were old enough to remember Jericho walls falling or watch God give them the land they did not work for or deserve. So, it is very likely that they never read the history nor visited the monuments made by their grandparents to know the Lord or what he did for His people.

This story is a direct challenge to the upcoming generation of receivers and successors. Just like Joshua challenged his successors to choose who they would serve, I too say, "Hold on to the ball!"

Imagine a basketball team drafts a star rookie, joining a team of smart but aging veterans. The team had success in the past, but the rookie was selected to replace the leading scorer who just retired. The veterans rally around the rookie to teach him the new plays, reveal the tendencies and weaknesses of their opponents, explain each veteran's skill sets and specialties, and the things that will thrill the crowd and gain their continued loyalty. You would think that most young players would gladly receive this alley-oop of knowledge being passed down. Sadly, the rookie rejects the wisdom of the veterans and instead chooses to heed the advice of other rookie players. Their advice was to be selfish; a ball hog focused on padding their stats and scoring numbers. Forget about the crowd and the veterans. It is every man for himself.

This example is not hard to imagine because it happened in scripture. (See 1 Kings 12 and the story of Rehoboam). When Rehoboam became king, he rejected the counsel of the elders, which was to lighten the yoke of the people, take more of a fatherly approach, and be a servant to the people, and in return, the people would be devoted to the king's success. Instead, Rehoboam chose the young leaders' counsel to make the people's yoke heavier (vs. 10-11). In other words, to be harsh towards the people and display his strength. Rehoboam chose to lead by force and dictate by fear rather than servant-lead by love. The result was a divided kingdom. The whole team loses when the ball is dropped.

Successors must understand that authentic leadership is service and influence, not power and control. Insecure people fail to recognize this truth. They need people to follow them and feed their egos. Be careful of more devotion to your egos, logos, and bios. Be wary of being impatient and ill-prepared or out of position to receive the pass.

Potential leaders need to beware of personal resume building and personal goals and stats building versus kingdom building for the glory of God. Self-glory and honoring self are dangerous, especially for a person looking to be a pastor.

When an athlete draws attention to themselves, we call that showboating. All show but no scoring, no winning, that's not helpful to the team. These kinds of actions in a church are not aiding in the transferring process but can-do great harm.

Secure successors are fully aware that their predecessors and peers are walking books of knowledge, literally libraries in the flesh. Neither one wants those resources to die inside of them. They are determined to live full and leave empty.

African culture could teach Western successors a lesson in valuing fatherhood and elders. They acknowledge the older generation's wisdom and contributions versus a generation and culture that prioritizes independence. Embrace the principle of honor. It could be the difference-maker preventing you from losing out on the opportunity to move into the lead pastor position. Practicing genuine honor protects you from the danger of familiarity.

In the same way, a lead pastor can struggle with a "Saul Spirit," a potential pastor can show dishonor toward the sitting leader. It's possible to get too comfortable with one another. The younger or potential pastor starts seeing himself as an equal, a buddy rather than a disciple.

Yes, all of us are equal in God's sight, but we are different in roles and responsibilities. In the body of Christ, Jesus is recognized as the head of the body. But God has placed under-shepherds over the flock. This position of pastor, elder, or leader in the church needs to be respected. Titles do mean something.

Honor is important. The word honor means weighty, a heavy thing. Every human being has honor because we are made in the image of God (Genesis 1:26). Everyone is to be honored (1 Peter 2:17). The honor comes with a promise of blessing and good life (Exodus 20:12). This scriptural honor is often interpreted as a promised long life. My Daddy had his interpretation of this Bible verse, "I brought you in, and I can take you out." In other words, he threatened to shorten my lifespan if no honor and obedience were given!

Moral failure. Before closing this section, I want to address how moral failure will affect the church and succession. Succession should happen by the will and readiness of the entire team (church leaders, pastors, people, and successors). Ideally, a plan has been drafted; standard operating procedures are in place. A transition portfolio and file are ready for the next pastor (or department head or volunteer lead) to pick up and carry on. Preparation lessens the trauma of change everyone will experience in succession. Unfortunately, some successions happened abruptly and under forced circumstances due to a moral failure or firing a lead pastor.

First, know that God is not taken by surprise when a leader falls morally. The fall of man in the garden proves that God knows where man is and that the blood of the Lamb, Jesus covers a multitude of sins. As painful as this sin is, there is an atonement. Yet, the way to restoration will be difficult. It will require a commitment to honesty and transparency from the fallen leader. 1 John 1:9 advises us to confess when we sin. In other words, "If you mess up, fess up." God can and will restore you. James 5:16 also advises us to confess our sins to spiritually mature leaders. I call this principle "throwing up" as opposed to "throwing down" upon the people. A leader should be a follower. Having a spiritual covering and accountability helps prevent moral failure in the first place. If a leader does fall, then they should "throw up" and confess to their covering.

Leadership is not easy. Leadership is "bleeder-ship." You will bleed (not literally), but figuratively because it is hard work to lead people. Make sure that you are healed of emotional wounds so that you don't drip your own blood from human failings down upon the white wool of God's sheep. Therefore, it behooves spiritual leaders, predecessors, successors, and all God's people to live in community and accountability. We must submit and trust others to care for our souls, even when we fall.

May the Lord secure our hands to hold the ball and secure our feet to stand in a certain place. Psalm 18:36 NLT says, "You have made a wide path for my feet to keep them from slipping."

12

The Crowd

The basketball world's history books will never forget the year 2020. On March 11, Utah Jazz center, Rudy Gobert, tested positive for COVID-19. As a result, the NBA immediately suspended all games for several months. But in July of that year, the NBA Bubble was born! The NBA resumed play with the same players, officials, and rules but in a different venue and protocol. The Bubble was a protected and isolated space at Walt Disney World in Florida to protect players from the virus as the season resumed there. Particular medical protocols were used daily. However, the most significant difference was that no fans were allowed to attend the games. The crowd's absence provided some health safety measures but, at the same time, took away the psychological and emotional home-court advantage that teams enjoyed under normal circumstances.

The fans in the stands--cheering troops, dancers, and cheerleaders--play a significant role in athletics. Together they arouse and encourage the players to perform at the maximum level. In return, the team owners recognize their importance and provide incentives to keep the fans happy and return for more games. They even toss a cheap t-shirt into the stands, display a "kiss-cam" of loving couples, and might even ignite the "Wave" during a game. Every athlete appreciates the approval and cheers from the home crowd. Fans make a huge difference!

The fans in the arena are a lot like the congregants in a local church. Many preachers have more fans than Jesus does. Sad. The pastor's fan base in a church is more than oohs and aahs when things are going right or wrong. The congregates may not fully understand, but as pastors, we will have to stand before God and give an account for His sheep.

"Obey those who rule over you, and be submissive, for they watch out for your souls, as those who must give account. Let them do so with joy and not with grief, for that would be unprofitable for you." (Hebrews 13:17) "Shepherd, the flock of God, which is among you, serving as overseers, not by compulsion but willingly, not for dishonest gain but eagerly; nor as being lords over those entrusted to you, but being examples to the flock." (1 Peter 5:2-3)

In the end, God will want to know from us as overseers, "What happened here?"

A successful alley-oop thrills the crowd at a basketball game. They witness a great pass, secure catch, and thunderous dunk and finish with celebration and anticipation of many more scores. However, in the church world, there are so few successful alley-oop transitions carried out. Too often, we witness more pastoral leadership turnovers than assist. As a result, many of our pastors, church boards, and congregants live in doubt, skepticism, and often fear and anxiety regarding leadership succession.

No one likes to change except a wet baby. Human nature resists change, yet it is inevitable. Many would respond to this change with a desire to see a slow, long, traditional pass. Some pastors and church people would prefer no change at all. They would see the lead die with their boots on (or, in this analogy--with their sneakers) versus having a succession plan.

"Pistol" Pete Maravich had a non-traditional style of playing basketball. The late NBA Hall of Famer was a spectacular showman who helped liberate basketball in the 1970s. Maravich is remembered for dribbling behind his back, between his legs, and making accurate passes and creative circus shots.

But his moves were considered unnecessary during his era. Many coaches and fans were accustomed to a traditional style of playing the game. I'm sure many fans shouted to Pete from the stands, "Just play ball!" But then others cheered him on when he started his playground antics. They wanted entertainment. His showmanship made the price they spent on the ticket worth their money. Maravich finished his ten-year professional career as a five-time NBA All-Star. Unfortunately, at the age of 40, he died of an apparent heart attack while playing a pick-up half-court game with friends. In the end, "Pistol" Pete died with his sneakers on.

In the same way as with Maravich, there will be various responses to pastoral succession from those observing everything from the pew.

Avoidance. Some people cover their eyes, ears, and mouth; ultimately, they don't want to see, hear, or speak any evil or good. They don't want to know what's going on. When the pastor says, "There is a business meeting after church. You need to know about the changes in our church," the avoiders walk out before the session gets started.

Besides basketball, there are excellent sports movies that I like to watch, including the movie Remember the Titans. In this movie, there is a young white female who is the daughter of an assistant coach. This young girl knows more about the game of football than many coaches do. Yet when it comes to the most crucial game of the year, the championship game, she covers her eyes and says, "I don't want to see it. I don't want to see it." That's avoidance. Many in the church would cover up their eyes and live-in denial of the need for leadership succession.

Apathetic. Some congregants and fans are apathetic. Their eyes are not covered, but they're intentionally internally focused on themselves, period. They're distracted by their concerns. They live with a me-first attitude, period. When faced with the question and opportunity for leadership succession, their first question is, "What does this mean for me?" Sadly, many want to be more entertained by the players on the court and the preachers in the pulpit rather than see the organization healthy and strong.

Resistant. Some congregants and fans are resistant to leadership change, in total opposition to pastoral transition.

"Oh no, I'll never let my pastor go."

"Well, Auntie May, what if the pastor dies?"

"I'm going to crawl right in the casket with him. I don't want anyone over me but him."

They want to see the same team, the same players, the same coaches, the same results week after week, month after month, year after year. They're comfortable with consistency, no changing of the guard--especially the point guard.

Passivity. In most churches and most games, some fans don't care. They're willing to follow the crowd. If somebody in the stands starts the wave, they'll be glad to join in, but they won't initiate it. Most of them are happy to be at the game, just like many in the church congregation are merely happy to be a part of the church and have something to do.

Adapters. These are church members who, like sports fans, are anticipating and comfortable with change. Whenever the team owners make a player trade and send off a crowd favorite or bring in new players, they are ready to adapt and adopt. They knew long ago that nothing would remain the same. They understand the nature of ministry; the only thing constant is change. God is always up to something.

My older brother, Reggie, taught me many things about life. He and I grew up close. We shared bathrooms. This is embarrassing, but we even shared the toilet seat at times. When I turned 18, Reggie taught me how to drive. One of the greatest lessons he taught me applies to life and leadership today.

He taught me to look through "the turns." What he meant by that is when you come to a stop sign or an intersection, and you decide that you're going to turn to the right or the left, make sure you put on your signal, make sure you cover your brake, and slow down. Make sure you look both to your left and your right but don't just look at what's immediately in front of you. Look through the turns, look in the direction that you're headed. Look down the road to see what obstacles, what dangers, or what opportunities await you. By looking through the turns, you have foreknowledge, and you can anticipate and adapt beforehand.

The adaptors are the types of fans who are fully engaged in the basketball game. They are the ones who might purchase a statistics book. They know the score, the stats about the team. They might even be aware of the number of minutes that each player logs every week. These fans stay informed about the players' lives on and off the court. Their eyes are entuned to the floor and the bench. They're not so worried about what's happening in the stands, but they notice the expressions on the players' faces. These fans' have trained eyes. Their hearts are sensitive. They notice when a player is tired, injured, or needs something. The team's needs are more important than their selfish wants of avoidance, apathy, or resistance.

Be prayerful. In the same way, some churches (the crowd) and members of our leadership teams (teammates), and even potential successors attempt to intimidate and rush the pass. An unwise move most likely will create a turnover instead of a successful crossover. The relay pass can happen too soon or too late--outside of the exchange zone. As stated, timing is essential when a lead pastor departs, and the new pastor is put in his place. If the process goes too quickly, people may not have time to adjust to the changes. If the process drags on for several years, the congregation may lose sight of what's taking place, either insisting that the process hurry along or slow down.

Pastors and church people are human and therefore need grace. We are all subject to fickle emotions and foolish decisions. The word that I use for this is "sometimes." As a leader, Jesus experienced the "sometiminess" of the crowd. The same ones who cheered for Him and laid down palm branches on the road to Bethany also yelled to crucify him a few days later! Crowds are fickle, no matter if they are in an arena or a church sanctuary.

Here is a lesson for pastors. The lead pastor and the new pastor must understand past hurts that may be among the people. Some have attended churches where the transfer of leadership went badly. Some of them have gotten caught in the middle of a church split. Some have had to suffer through a crisis or lost a loved one without any pastoral care. Just like sheep who scatter when a poor shepherd is neglectful or absent, people in the pew suffer when no pastor is in place.

Jesus pulled from grace to lead and love fickle and foolish people. This grace came from a close relationship with His Father. In the book of John, Jesus says several times, "I only do what I see my Father doing." In John 5:19, "Then Jesus answered and said to them, 'Most assuredly, I say to you, the Son can do nothing of Himself, but what He sees the Father do; for whatever He does, the Son also does in like manner.'" Finishing well means not living for the crowd of fans. Jesus had an audience of One. We, too, should be living only for the "well done" of our heavenly Father. Watching where He tells us to go and following what He says we should do—period.

The crossover. The crossover is a basketball dribbling skill that draws the "oohs" and the "aahs" of fans. The crossover is when a dribbler fakes its defender out, causing them to trip, stumble, and fall, and go in another direction other than the direction the point guard or the ball handler is going with the ball. Basketball fans call this move "breaking ankles." Some of the best crossovers have been done historically by Chris Paul, Tim Hardaway, and Allen Iverson. If you want to be thrilled, I suggest you go back and watch Allen Iverson crossing over the great Michael Jordan.

Pastoral succession is a different kind of crossover. God is never caught up in the "oohs" and "aah" of the crowd. The same for the skillful point guard. It's vital that you secure the ball, that you eliminate turnovers, that you finish the field goal, passing the ball to your successor as Moses did to Joshua.

Holy Angels Catholic School was my favorite basketball court. The hoop and backboard were bolted to a brick wall. The wall allowed us to run and jump up and off the wall and dunk the ball.

I was 18 the first time I dunked a basketball at Holy Angels for real, without the wall. I was playing a friendly game of Hustle (21) with four of my friends. Another player who didn't live in our neighborhood and no one knew asked to join our game. He was talking big and bad and trying to intimidate us on our court. He was not even that good of a ballplayer. I got fed up with his trash talking. I rebounded a missed shot away from him while he and I were under the basketball and quickly exploded up and dunked the ball through the hoop with a burst of adrenaline. My friends whooped and hollered. The strange young man quickly and humbly left the court.

Although it felt exciting to get my first real dunk, I get more excitement out of making passes for others to score back then and even now. I want to see succession occur for the good of the team.

In the same way, my friends cheered for me after the dunk; they might have booed if I had missed the dunk. Friends can be "sometimes" fans too. In the matter of an alley-oop, the crowd is ecstatic when they see one taking place. The opposite is also true when one gets botched up. The crowd boos and are overly aggressive when the players mess up.

I close this section with advice for the reader who might be a church member sitting in the pew. Unlike fans at an athletic event, the congregants in a church have a responsibility: to God, to the outgoing and the incoming pastor, and their fellow church members.

To God: seek and put first His kingdom, not your own.

To the pastors: pray! Express gratitude for the outgoing pastor's service. Encourage the new pastor whenever possible. Pledge your presence and support to the new pastor.

To your church: help others who may not understand the need for a switch and want to maintain past operations. Remember the past and celebrate the future.

13

Post Game

We all must understand that our calling is permanent, but our position is not.

Romans 11:29 reminds me of this too, "For the gifts and the calling of God are irrevocable."

By now, as you read this last chapter, you see that succession is not just for corporations but also churches. It is rooted in scripture. The beginning book of the Bible lays the foundation for succession as God passes the ball to humankind. God gave Adam an alley-oop by creating the earth for Adam and Eve's dominion. The table was set.

Moses passed the ball to Joshua. Abraham to Isaac. Isaac to Jacob. Jacob to his offspring. Elijah to Elisha. David to Solomon. Jesus to His disciples when He says, "Most assuredly, I say to you, he who believes in Me, the works that I do he will also do, and greater [works] than these he will do because I go to My Father." (John 14:12)

So, it is biblical to have a succession plan.

If you are a senior leader, it is also wise to initiate the conversation rather than be forced to leave the organization. This final section offers more practical keys to prepare yourself, your family, your successor, board, and church.

Romans 12:18 says, "If it is possible, as much as lieth in you, live peaceably with all men."

The Scripture says, "if it is possible," letting us know lack of conflict will not always be the case. It is impossible to live in peace with all staff, church people, or board members in every situation. But neither are these causes not to execute a succession plan. Remember, the narrative and story of the church are more significant than any single person on the team. Besides, it is too vital for any person to hold the destiny of the church hostage. Therefore, have courageous, critical, and compassionate conversations. Communication is key!

It was important for the church to know that I was not leaving, nor had I received a better job offer, and there was certainly not a hint of a moral failure. I was not retiring but was repositioning for a lifetime of service and influence. A mantle of grace is upon our church. That mantle expands beyond Milwaukee--and beyond me. Together, we have been given a new wineskin from God to speak into cities and the nation.

Parklawn's best days and blessed days are not in the past. The best is yet to come. When we arrived at the basketball courts to play a pick-up game in my younger days, we claimed our spot in the rotation by declaring, "WE GOT NEXT!" Pastor Marcus and the members of Parklawn, embrace the next season! We believe and decree a fresh purpose, influence, vision, commission, and reformation.

Parklawn Assembly of God is an apostolic, prophetic, regional governing center to bring light to the world. Each day, members of the team decree that we are an apostolic, prophetic, regional, governing center that exists to bring light to the world through PRISM (Prayer,

Reconciliation, Investing, Strong Families, and Missions). By fulfilling the Great Commission, we give life, and by fulfilling the Great Commandment, we demonstrate love. We are a gateway church, anointed to teach, train, and release men, women, and children to do the works of Jesus Christ. We are a prophetic people and a community of worshippers who love the presence of God and seek to share His presence with others. By God's grace, we will faithfully steward the gifts given to us and contribute to the advancement of His kingdom in the Greater Milwaukee area and beyond.

Lead pastors, hear me when I say that there is much more life outside your current ministry position. If God is telling you to shift, then do it. Obey Him.

Passing the leadership ball in 2020 has freed my hands and heart to carry even more kingdom vision. I still have the privilege of serving the Parklawn family and Milwaukee community. I am a coach and advisor to Pastor Marcus for Parklawn as the apostolic leader of the house, focused on kingdom multiplication and discipleship. In the community, I serve as the CEO for our PRISM Economic Development Corporation, which is building kingdom ecosystems that allow community residents to flourish and thrive in just systems. For the Assemblies of God, I serve as an Executive Presbyter (Board of Director) representing 24 ethnic fellowships and as President of the National Black Fellowship (NBF). The NBF is sponsoring WI+H, a disciple-making movement inviting Christ-followers to be with people in community pain points (see www.with.city).

I am happier now than ever before. I loved and enjoyed my years as a lead pastor. I still love people and preaching. I grieve for the absence of these precious relationships and connections, sometimes grieve over a lost routine or role, but I have great peace and joy settled in my soul. What gives me the greatest joy is seeing God still bless and care for His church through Pastor Marcus' leadership.

I pray you and your church will be better because of the transition. Also, that your city and neighborhood will be transformed, and your church's influence will be even greater. Now let's go and score for team Jesus!!! I pray that your best days as a pastor, leader, or church member are not behind you but ahead of you.

14

Resources on Succession

"Set It Up - Planning a Healthy Pastoral Transition," by Dr. Parnell M. Lovelace, Jr., Church Smart Resources January 1, 2017

Clergy Financial Planning

"Fear in the Pulpit"
"Creating a Compensation Package"
"Should I Exempt Out of Social Security for my ministry income?"
All articles can be found at Ministryresourcecenter.com

Women in Ministry

"The Jesus-Hearted Woman: 10 Leadership Qualities for Enduring & Endearing Influence," Jodi Detrick, 2015, Salubrious Resources

"Emboldened: A Vision for Empowering Women in Ministry," Tara Beth Leach, 2017 Intervarsity Press

"Dare Mighty Things: Mapping the Challenges of Leadership for Christian Women," Hallee Gray Scott, 2014, Zondervan

"Man And Woman, One In Christ : An Exegetical And Theological Study Of Paul's Letters," Philip Payne

"Gods Women Then and Now," by Deborah Gill and Barbara Cavaness, Springfield, Mo., Grace, and Truth, 2004.

"Why Not Women : A Biblical Study of Women in Missions, Ministry, and Leadership." Loren Cunningham, David Joel Hamilton, and Janice Roger, YWAM Publishers 2000

"Not Without a Struggle: Leadership for African American Women in Ministry," Vashti M. McKenzie, Pilgrim Press, 2011

Walter F. Harvey was elected as the Ethnic Fellowship executive presbyter in August 2021, representing 24 ethnic fellowships within the Assemblies of God (General Board). He currently serves as the president of the National Black Fellowship of the Assemblies of God, which sponsors the WI+H movement and has vision to transform every urban pain point through a disciple making movement.

He has served as both an executive presbyter and ethnic/language group presbyter for the Wisconsin/Northern Michigan Ministry Network. He served as lead pastor of Parklawn Assembly of God in Milwaukee, WI for 28 years (1992-2020). Parklawn is an apostolic, prophetic, regional governing center noted for bringing light to the world. He continues to serve as the apostolic leader at Parklawn while also serving as CEO of PRISM Economic Development Corporation.

He holds a Bachelor of Science from Marquette University. He has served on various local and national boards. He is also a former sports chaplain, youth pastor, and an avid athlete. He is married to Judy Harvey and is the father of Nick and grandfather of Autumn.

For speaking engagements or teaching, leadership and coaching resources visit walterharveyministries.com